USA Today bestselling author **C**[...] girl who just wants to write and [...] novels and novellas. She loves ro[...] novels, superheroes, TV and cooking. For more information on Caridad and her dark, sexy romantic suspense and paranormal romances, please visit caridad.com

Addison Fox is a lifelong romance reader, addicted to happily-ever-afters. After discovering she found as much joy writing about romance as she did reading it, she's never looked back. Addison lives in New York with an apartment full of books, a laptop that's rarely out of sight and a wily beagle who keeps her running. You can find her at her home on the web at addisonfox.com or on Facebook at Facebook.com/addisonfoxauthor and X (formerly Twitter) @addisonfox

Also by Caridad Piñeiro

South Beach Security
Lost in Little Havana
Brickell Avenue Ambush
Biscayne Bay Breach

Cold Case Reopened
Trapping a Terrorist
Decoy Training

Also by Addison Fox

New York Harbor Patrol
Danger in the Depths

The Coltons of New York
Under Colton's Watch

Midnight Pass, Texas
The Cowboy's Deadly Mission
Special Ops Cowboy
Under the Rancher's Protection
Undercover K-9 Cowboy
Her Texas Lawman

SABOTAGE OPERATION

CARIDAD PIÑEIRO

GUARDING COLTON'S SECRETS

ADDISON FOX

MILLS & BOON

First Published in Great Britain 2024
by Mills & Boon, an imprint of HarperCollins*Publishers* Ltd
1 London Bridge Street, London, SE1 9GF

www.harpercollins.co.uk

HarperCollins*Publishers*
Macken House, 39/40 Mayor Street Upper,
Dublin 1, D01 C9W8, Ireland

Special thanks and acknowledgement are given to Addison Fox for her contribution to *The Coltons of Owl Creek* series.

ISBN: 978-0-263-32230-9

0524

This book contains FSC™ certified paper and other controlled sources to ensure responsible forest management.

For more information visit: www.harpercollins.co.uk/green

Printed and Bound in the UK using 100% Renewable Electricity at
CPI Group (UK) Ltd, Croydon, CR0 4YY

SABOTAGE OPERATION

CARIDAD PIÑEIRO

To my daughter Samantha Ann

So proud of you and all that you've accomplished with *Seoul Searching* and all your other books!

Chapter One

The frantic pounding on the thick wooden door echoed through the early morning silence of the ranch house, dragging Teresa Rodriguez from the bills that had forced her awake.

She rushed to the front door, her riding boots hammering against the wood floor, and jerked it open. Her stable hand Luis stood there wringing his hands, wide-eyed and pale as milk.

"You have to come. Frijoles is down," the young man said, turned and raced in the direction of the stables.

Teresa tore after him, fear chilling her gut. Frijoles was not only her best friend, he was also her top stallion. She had been counting on the stud fees from breeding him to pay off the last of her debts. Without him…

She sprinted across her driveway and the dew-damp grass next to the stables. Her feet skidded on the pavers surrounding the building as she rounded the corner to the stable entrance, raced to the stallion's stall and caught sight of her trainer kneeling in the straw by her horse. The large bay's body twitched and convulsed beneath his hands.

"What happened, Richard?" she asked, squatting beside him. She joined the trainer in running her hands across the horse's muscled flanks to try to calm him as he thrashed his legs, rousing the straw's grassy smell.

The older man shrugged and dipped his head in the direction of her stable hand. "Luis said that Frijoles started acting up right after he began his morning feeding. When he went to check on him, the horse collapsed. That's when Luis got me. I've already called the vet. She's nearby and should be here soon."

"What can we do in the meantime?" she asked, her gut twisting into a knot as the horse's muscles shuddered beneath her palm. It pained her to see her horse hurting.

Richard tightened his lips and settled his hazel-eyed gaze on her. "I could give him some activated charcoal, but it could upset his gut."

"Do we know what caused this?" she asked and stroked the horse's side. His skin was slightly damp, and his powerful muscles shook violently. Choppy and irregular breathing, as if he couldn't catch his breath after a long race, had her breath trapping in her chest with fear.

"Maybe something he ate," Richard said with a shrug. "Let's check his feed bucket."

She looked over at the young stable hand who stood a few feet away, nervously twisting his hands. Worry and guilt were evident in his eyes, and she rose and laid a hand on his arm to calm him.

"It's nothing that you did, Luis. Can you show me Frijoles's feed for this morning?"

Luis nodded, walked to the corner of the stall where a large plastic feed bucket hung and came back with it.

Frijoles had only eaten part of his breakfast, and as she examined it, she noticed something unusual. Mixed in with the alfalfa, oats and other nutrients were odd bits of green. She stuck her hand into the feed, sifted through it and discovered larger pieces of what looked like leaves.

Oval-shaped and dark green. Nothing she immediately recognized, but she knew one thing: they didn't belong in the stallion's feed.

She walked over with some of the leaves and held them out so the trainer could see them.

Richard's eyes widened in shock. "Where did you get those?"

"They were in Frijoles's feed bucket."

"Looks like belladonna leaves. They're poisonous and if I'm right, we can't wait for the vet. I'll go prep the charcoal." He leaped to his feet, raced out of the stall and toward the tack room, where they kept an assortment of supplies for tending to the horses.

The horse whinnied and tried to raise his head but failed and restlessly shifted his legs against the soft straw bedding on the floor again.

"*Tranquilo*, Frijoles. You'll be okay, *por favor*," she crooned, trying to calm the stallion so that he wouldn't injure himself.

The screech of tires heralded the arrival of the vet and barely a few minutes later, Dr. Miranda Ramirez raced into the stall carrying a large leather bag.

"How is he?" Miranda asked and knelt in the straw beside the horse.

"He ate belladonna," Teresa said and held out her hand to show the vet the leaves she had found in the feed. A second later, her trainer returned with a large bucket filled with the activated charcoal solution and long vinyl tubing.

"Definitely belladonna. Keep him calm," Miranda said while she took a blood sample.

"We'll confirm the poisoning with this and some stool samples," the vet said. She finished drawing the blood and reached for a vial of something in her bag. At Teresa's questioning look, she said, “Neostigmine. It’ll counteract the atropine toxin.”

Teresa kept her hands on the horse, stroking and crooning, trying to keep the horse still while Richard and Miranda worked together, feeding the tubing through the horse’s nostril until it reached his stomach. Once the tube was in place, Richard pumped the activated charcoal through the tubing with a large syringe while Miranda set up an IV with fluids.

“We may have to hospitalize Frijoles if he doesn’t respond to this,” she said as she inserted the catheter for the IV in the horse’s foreleg and wrapped a bandage around it to keep it in place. Then she prepped the fluid bag, connected the tubing into the catheter and laid the fluid bag on the horse’s flank. “I’ll get a drip stand in a second,” Miranda said.

“Whatever it takes,” Teresa replied. The bay was not only her top breeder, he was a combination best friend and therapist. Whenever she started wondering if opening the stables had made sense, Frijoles was there to listen or take her for a spin along the track to calm her doubts and worries.

Miranda laid a hand on her arm, her touch reassuring. “We’ll make him better. Don’t worry.”

Teresa nodded and attempted a smile, but it was as brittle as the thin layer of ice protecting orange trees against a freeze. She laid her hands on the bay and softly murmured to him, trying to comfort him.

Long minutes became an even longer hour. Her back ached from kneeling over the horse, but she kept at it, as did Richard and Miranda, tending to the horse until the trembling eased and his breathing became more regular. The bay was even relatively calm as Richard withdrew the nasogastric tube.

“He’s responding,” Miranda said happily and leaned back onto her haunches. “We’ll need to keep giving him the IV fluids and monitor for any signs of gut issues or laminitis.”

"*Gracias*, Miranda. Richard. You know Frijoles means the world to me," she said as they all came to their feet and wiped bits of straw from their pants legs.

"I have another call to make but will be back in about an hour to keep up the treatment," Miranda said, reaching for her medical bag. She shot another look at the horse and said, "Just keep him quiet and replace the IV bag when it's empty."

"I'll do that. Thanks again, Miranda," Richard said and held his hand out in the direction of the stall door. "I'll walk you to your car."

Teresa watched as Richard escorted the vet from the stall. She'd always thought her trainer had a thing for the beautiful vet. When Miranda offered him a shy smile, it seemed as if the feeling might be mutual. They made a good-looking couple.

Even at sixty, Richard was physically fit and imposing, with a thick thatch of salt-and-pepper hair, a strong jaw and sharp hazel eyes. Miranda was a decade younger, with coffee-brown hair just showing the first few strands of gray, chocolate brown eyes and an hourglass figure that would tempt most men.

Frijoles knickered as if complaining he didn't have her beside him, and Teresa kneeled next to him once more. "You're going to be fine," she murmured and stroked his flank.

The horse blew out a breath through his nostrils, almost in agreement, and closed his eyes, seemingly comfortable now that he had her attention.

Much like whoever had been playing the little tricks around the stables now had her complete attention. She'd tried to write off all the other things as forgetfulness or accidents, but they had stressed her out. The unlocked gate at the paddock that had let some of the other horses roam into a neighboring avocado grove. The small electrical fire in the corner of a shed that housed spare tack. The waterlogged packages holding the new silks that her jockeys would wear in a few months when the racing season began.

She couldn't keep on ignoring those incidents anymore and she suspected who was behind all the mayhem: Warner Esquivel, her former trainer who was being investigated by the racing commission. She'd fired him years earlier because she'd caught him drugging one of her mares. Now the racing commission wanted her to testify against Esquivel.

It was painfully obvious that she had underestimated what he would do to keep her quiet. Luckily, she knew what to do to protect herself, her people and her horses.

Pulling her cell phone from her jeans pocket, she dialed her friend Mia Gonzalez. Mia's family ran South Beach Security and she trusted that they could get to the bottom of whatever was happening.

Mia answered on the first ring. "*Hola, amiga*. It's so good to hear from you."

"I wish I could say this was a friendly call, but I need your help. Actually, I need SBS's help."

"Whatever you need," Mia said without hesitation.

Teresa breathed a sigh of relief, the first one since rushing to Frijoles's stall hours earlier. She hoped that with the Gonzalez family on her side, she could stop whoever was trying to hurt her and her business.

EVEN AFTER SIX months on the job it struck Matt Perez as odd to see his old friend Trey Gonzalez sitting behind a desk. Trey had always been an all-action guy from their time together in the Marines to their assignments on the Miami Beach police force.

But the desk job seemed to be working for Trey. Matt had never seen his friend looking happier, especially since his wedding a month earlier to Roni Lopez, who was still a detective with Miami Beach PD.

Although Trey's door was open, his head was buried in the papers on his desk, so Matt rapped his knuckles on the door to announce his arrival. Beside him his K-9 partner Butter bumped up against his leg and looked up at him, as if wondering what they were doing in the office. For the last six months they'd been spending time between an assortment of security jobs as well as training Butter on a variety of tasks. So far, the Belgian Malinois had been learning quickly and Matt hoped that in time, their working together would be as seamless as it had been with the K-9 partner he'd had while on the force.

"Come in, Matt," Trey called out and rose from the large glass-and-metal desk. He bro-hugged his old friend and bent toward Butter, but hesitated. "Is it okay to pet her?"

Normally he didn't permit people to treat his working K-9s as if they were domesticated companions, but Trey was the boss of his family's agency. As a K-9 officer for South Beach Security, Butter might have to one day interact with Trey, so it was good for her to be familiar with the other man.

"Sure. She should get to know you," Matt said and stood there holding the leash while Trey held his hand out for the dog to sniff.

Butter did that, but then hesitated and looked up at Matt, as if seeking his permission. With a smile, Matt said, "Good girl, Butter. This is Trey."

The dog finally sniffed Trey's hand, and sensing he was a friend and not a foe, the shepherd bumped her head against Trey's hand.

"You are a good girl," Trey said and knelt to rub the dog's head. Butter's tongue lolled out of her mouth with pleasure.

Looking up at Matt, his friend said, "I gather her training is going well?"

Matt nodded. "It is. She's got a great sense of smell and handles instructions well. We're still learning a few things, but she's going to be a great K-9 partner."

"That's good to hear, because we've got an important case for you," Trey said and straightened. As he did so, his gaze drifted over Matt's shoulder toward the door.

Matt turned to find Trey's baby sister, Mia, standing at the door, beautiful as ever. She looked well considering she'd almost died after being shot two months earlier during a case that had threatened her newlywed husband as well as the Gonzalez family.

She was dressed casually today in jeans and a loose, pale pink tunic top. It made her look younger, especially since he was used to seeing her all done up in the designer clothes and shoes she wore when doing one of her social media gigs with her cousin Carolina. The two women, affectionately called "the Twins," had been familiar fixtures when he'd patrolled the South Beach scene with his K-9 partner.

Trey walked over to hug her and said, "Good morning, *hermanita*. How are you feeling?"

"Stronger every day," Mia said and then sashayed to his side and embraced him. "Good to see you, Matt."

"You, too, Mia. How are you adjusting to married life and working with Trey?" he asked, aware that the family members had faced serious challenges in recent months.

"I'm doing well but Carolina is missing me. I'm sure she'd love some company," Mia said with a warm smile and a playful wink.

Even though Carolina was as smart and beautiful as Mia, Matt waved his hands in the air to dismiss any suggestion that he'd be interested in Carolina. "You rich girls are out of my league," he said and truly meant it. He'd been burned once by that kind of woman and had no desire to repeat the experience.

Trey clapped him on the back. "Let's get to it, then, although you may not like the assignment we're about to give you."

"Why's that?" Matt asked as he sat in front of Trey's desk and instructed Butter to lie down with a hand command. After, he rewarded his new partner with a "good girl" and the ear rubs she loved so well.

"Rich girl," Mia said with a laugh and sat in the chair next to him. "She's a very good friend who's working hard to get her business going and needs our help."

With a nod, Matt said, "Understood. What do you need me to do?"

Chapter Two

Teresa curled up close to Frijoles's flank, reassured by the regular breathing and restful muscles beneath her. She and Richard had tag-teamed throughout the night, changing out the IV fluid bags to keep the bay hydrated. The vet had returned several times as well to do another flush of the horse's stomach with the activated charcoal. Miranda and Richard had just left to get breakfast after the long night of worry and work.

The sound of footsteps on the pavement outside her horse's stall snared her attention. The shadowed figure of a tall man suddenly filled the doorway. Fear raced through her at the unfamiliar silhouette until a nice-sized dog came to sit beside the man and a smaller, more familiar, figure also joined him.

She stroked her horse's side with a reassuring caress and scrambled to her feet, brushing away any straw bits from her clothing.

"Is this a good time?" Mia Gonzalez asked and walked to the stall's entrance, but the man remained behind her, silent and still in shadow.

Frijoles had been resting quietly and blessedly improving, so it was as good a time as any. "Sure, but I need to stay close by," she said and gestured to the bay.

"Got it," Mia said.

Teresa walked out of Frijoles's stall but positioned herself where she could keep an eye on the horse. She hugged her friend and then faced the man who had finally moved into view and joined Mia in the space outside the stall.

She didn't know what hit her at the sight of him. He was tall. Well over six feet with broad shoulders that seemed as if they could carry the weight of the world. Dressed in pressed khakis and a polo branded with the SBS logo, he still had that kind of ramrod straight posture and precision dress that screamed military. But it was his blue-eyed gaze that captured her attention and held it. There was intelligence there, and determination. Also, that indefinable something that said not to mess with him. She was glad he was on her side. Or at least she hoped he was, since she sensed animosity in his glance as well.

Close to his leg a large shepherd waited, his long pointy ears straight up at attention and his tongue hanging out. It was a beautiful dog with light brown, almost golden fur with darker brown-black markings.

The man brought a strong hand to his mouth and faked a cough, making Teresa realize that Mia had said something she hadn't heard.

"I'm so sorry. It's been a long night," she said with a wave of her hand in the direction of the stall.

"That explains it," the man mumbled beneath his breath, earning a sharp elbow from her friend Mia.

She was confused until a light breeze wafted through the stable and she smelled herself much as he must have. Bright color flooded her cheeks, but she tamped it down and lifted her chin a challenging inch. "I had to take care of my horse."

"Admirable. I imagine…" He paused as he read the horse's name by the door of the stall. "Frijoles must be a big investment for you," he said, a slight drawl in his words. Texas, she guessed.

Frijoles was more than just an investment, not that this man needed to know. Holding out her hand, she realized it was smudged with dirt from the long night of caring for her horse. Determined not to let him faze her, she wiped her palm on her jeans and stuck out her hand again, daring him to refuse.

"Teresa Ramirez. I own Redland Ranch," she said, but thought, *Well, me and the bank.*

He took her hand. His palm was calloused. Slightly rough. The sign of a man who used his hands for a living. Strong, even as she knew he was tempering his strength for the handshake.

"Matthew Perez, SBS K-9 Division," he said, and his deep voice resonated inside, awakening chords that hadn't played in a long time.

Teresa glanced at Mia, unfamiliar with that part of her friend's family business. "Is this division something new?"

Mia smiled and nodded. "Trey has been taking over for my father and thinks it's time to offer more services to our clients. Matt is our first K-9 agent but not our last. We think having him here on the grounds directing our security detail is the best way to protect you."

Teresa looked between her friend and Perez. "Here? As in full-time on the premises?"

"We think that's best, if you have the space," he said, a hint of something in his tone that said he wasn't necessarily comfortable with the idea but was reluctantly going along with SBS's plans.

She didn't really have the space. She only had a small bunkhouse where her stable hand Luis lived. Richard and the rest of the staff lived off-site. As for her own home, there were three bedrooms, but having him there…

Glancing at him, it hit her that he'd be dangerous for her. There was something indefinable that called to her. Maybe it was the fact that she'd barely dated because she'd been too busy building the stables. No matter the reason, it would be hard having him around, but she'd put up with him to protect her horses.

Facing Mia, she reluctantly said, "I have a guest room at the ranch house."

IT DIDN'T TAKE a genius to see that Ms. Ramirez wasn't in love with the idea of sharing a space with him and he got it. There was a rich girl buried beneath the grungy jeans, dirt-stained T-shirt and disheveled hair. He'd pulled up pictures of her on his smartphone while Mia and he had done the short drive from the SBS offices in downtown Miami to the Redland area where the stables were located.

A woman like *her* wouldn't want a man like *him* in her space.

"I can bunk down in here. Maybe a cot in the tack room?" It would be uncomfortable, but better than him having to put on airs around her.

With a slash of an elegant dirt-stained hand, Teresa said, "There's no way you'd be comfortable and that wouldn't be fair, especially since I've asked for your help."

"Maybe we can bring in an RV and park it near the ranch house? Does that sound acceptable?" Mia said, obviously sensing the tension between the two.

In the time he'd been with SBS, Matt had seen how Mia managed to be the mediator and problem solver, which was maybe how she'd built her own fortune as a social media influencer before joining her family's agency. Clearly, she could read people well.

"That's a great idea. We even have a power station and water hookup to the side of the house that the RV can connect to. We sometimes use it for visitors who bring their own lodging," Teresa said, the earlier tightness of her body flowing away with Mia's solution.

"Wonderful. I'll call Trey. We can probably get one here by later today. In the meantime, would you mind taking Matt around to show him the property? That'll give him an idea of what other security measures we'll need," Mia said and then faced Matt. "I'll head back to the office to wait for your report."

"I'll get it to you as soon as I can," Matt said, and with that, Mia headed out of the stables, leaving him and Butter alone with their new client.

"Would you like to get cleaned up first?" he asked and eyeballed her. A mistake. It was impossible to miss the beautiful woman beneath the grime and horse smell. A heart-shaped face was framed by loose, sun-streaked light brown hair that just skimmed her fine-boned shoulders. Eyes as green and hard as emeralds met his gaze.

She tilted that dimpled chin upward and looked down her perfectly perky nose, appearing decidedly too royal as she did so. It was a good reminder that she was way out of his league. "I'm fine just the way I am."

"Great. Then let's get going, and while we're at it, you can tell me more about what's been happening on the property," he said and clapped his hands, impatient to get going.

"Let me get Luis to come and stay with Frijoles," she said. She stepped away for a moment to make the call and returned, gesturing toward the entrance to the stables. As they walked down the space, she explained the area to him. "These are the main stables. We have ten horses in here as well as a tack room where we keep saddles and other equipment."

One of the horses stuck its head out as they passed the stall, and Teresa stopped to stroke its nose. He paused as well, and Butter sniffed around the door to the stable before sitting at his side.

"This is Ay Caramba. She's one of my brood mares and expecting a foal any day now."

Matt nodded and watched as the horse knickered and tossed her head, as if wanting more of Teresa's attention. Teresa smiled and rubbed the horse's head. "No treats today, *chiquitica*."

"I guess no one messed with her feed?" Matt asked as Teresa moved away from the mare and headed toward the tack room in the stables.

"We checked all the other feed buckets. Only Frijoles's was poisoned," Teresa explained.

"Why Frijoles?" he asked, aware the horse was a winner from his brief research on the way over but needing to hear more from Teresa.

"He's my best stallion and…" She hesitated, clearly uncomfortable with revealing too much. When she failed to continue, he left it at that for the moment.

"Whoever did this knows he's important to the stable," Matt said to end the awkward silence caused by her reluctance.

Teresa nodded. "Yes, they know. They also seem to know how we work around here. They've done several things on the property without us seeing them."

"Like what?" He followed her into the tack room filled with an assortment of saddles and other equipment. At the far end of the room was another smaller room where he could see brightly colored uniforms hanging.

Teresa walked to the door of that room and gestured to the uniforms. "These are the new silks I ordered for this year's racing season."

"Silks?" he asked, confused by the reference.

"The uniforms. They're called silks because they used

to be made out of silk. They're not anymore, luckily for us, because the box that the delivery person left at the ranch house door got soaked. We thought it was the sprinkler system at first, but then realized it hadn't been on when the damage occurred."

If someone knew that the box had been placed there, they had to either be watching somehow or a regular on the ranch. "Could you get me a list of people who work for you?" he asked.

She jerked back as if struck and raised a hand to her chest, clearly surprised by the request. "You think one of *my people* might possibly be doing this?"

"Anything is possible," he said, aware of that after his many years in the military and on the police force. Sometimes the people you trusted most were the ones you shouldn't have trusted.

"You're barking up the wrong tree," she said, hurrying out of the tack room and stables.

"What would be the right tree?" he asked, chasing after her with Butter until they reached a utility ATV sitting just outside the stables.

As she climbed into the driver's seat, she said, "Warner Esquivel. He was a trainer who worked for me and who's being investigated by the racing commission. I'm supposed to testify against him in a little over a week."

Matt considered her statement and was unconvinced but remained silent. He commanded Butter up into the storage box behind the two seats of the ATV and rubbed her head to reward his K-9 partner. Slipping into the passenger seat, he asked, "Where to?"

Teresa waved her arm in the direction of the large open spaces beyond the stables. "The pastures and paddocks. That's where the first problems happened."

She whipped down the paved track that ran the length of

the stable building and onto a dirt path that wound through her property. The ATV bounced and rocked from side to side as Teresa steered along the edges of the fenced paddocks. She gestured with her hand to the area. "About a month ago, one of the paddock gates was left open and a few of our horses wandered into a neighboring avocado grove. At first, we thought there was a problem with the gate latch, but it was fine."

"Could someone have accidentally left it open?" he asked and grabbed hold of the door frame as the ATV rocked violently over some uneven ground.

She shrugged, and seemingly unfazed by the roughness of the ride, said, "That's what we thought. So we didn't worry, but then it happened again a few days later and that time one of the horses almost got hit by a truck in the grove."

The ATV slowed toward the end of the paddock and turned onto a narrow path that ran along a small stand of trees. She stopped the vehicle and pointed to one of the paddocks. "That's one of our better grazing areas. But about a week after the horses got free, a break in the irrigation system flooded the area."

"I assume the break wasn't an accident," he said with an arch of his brow.

"Not an accident. Someone used a shovel to make cuts along the irrigation line." Teresa drove the ATV down the edge of the property, which was quite large. She handled the ATV capably along the slightly rough path, the dirt on her hands incongruous against the very feminine pink polish on her nails.

"How much land do you have here?" Matt asked, taking in the large open spaces surrounded by the nearby avocado grove and the long strip of woods along one edge of the property.

"A little over twenty acres. We need about an acre per horse to have the right amount of land for grazing and exercise. To the other side of the stables, we have a track where we train and that takes a lot of space," she explained.

Matt let out a low whistle. "And I imagine it must take a lot of money for upkeep on that much property."

TERESA GOT THE sense that having money was a problem with him, so she decided to set the record straight.

"It takes a lot of hard *work*, Mr. Perez," she said, anger sharpening her tone as she drove away from the woods and back toward the stables.

"Matt, please. I'm not that formal," he said. It tempered her anger, but only slightly as he said, "No insult intended, but I imagine that with Frijoles winning as many races as he has—"

"The purses are not as large as you might think. Plus, horses are expensive to keep. It's not just the land," she said and gestured to the area around them as she parked the ATV on the path by the stables. She faced him. "There are expenses for the vets, farriers—"

"Farriers?" Matt asked, a puzzled look on his face.

"The person who shoes the horses and takes care of their hoofs. I thought a Texas boy like you might have ridden a horse in his day," she challenged.

A bright flush worked across his cheeks and with a wag of his head, he said, "A lot of hard work and money, but I imagine your parents are a big help."

Anger rose up again, making her wonder if it made sense to have this man around 24/7. "My family and their money have nothing to do with *my* business. I succeed or fail on my own," she said and hopped out of the ATV.

MATT SLIPPED FROM the ATV and motioned for Butter to join him. As the dog came to his side, a bright flash of light from the woods across from the stable warned him to act.

He grabbed Teresa around the waist and hauled her into the stables just as a bullet slammed into the wood of Ay Caramba's stall.

The brood mare nervously danced away, and Butter fought against her leash, aware of the danger, as another bullet nicked the door frame to the stable.

"Is there another way out?" he asked as the gunfire continued, spooking the horses as bullet after bullet peppered the brick building and the nearby stall.

She motioned to the far end of the stables. "We can open the other door."

He shoved a finger in her face and warned, "You stay here."

With a softly worded command to Butter, he and the shepherd raced to the far end of the stables. He carefully opened the large door made of wood and wrought iron, uncertain whether there was a second attacker who might fire from a different angle. The only gunfire was from the other end of the stable, so he rushed out, trying to keep out of sight of the shooter in the woods.

He worked his way to the edge of the building and once again caught sight of the flash of light, probably the sunlight reflecting off the rifle's scope.

If he'd had his old K-9 partner, he might have moved closer and sicced the dog on their assailant, but Butter was still a novice, and the attack command was relatively new to her. Plus, it was a long dash from the stables to any kind of cover.

But as another burst of gunfire slammed into the building, and the sounds of the frightened horses and Teresa trying to calm them registered, Matt had no choice but to risk it.

Chapter Three

Teresa's heart beat a staccato rhythm in her chest as the rain of bullets struck the brick of the building and the wood of Ay Caramba's stall. Her mare circled the stall, eyes wild with fear, while the horses in the nearby stalls responded, prancing and pacing in their stalls and voicing complaints in a chorus of nickers, huffs and whinnies.

She worried the mare might hurt herself and her baby but couldn't risk going in through the stall door as another bullet bit into the wood. She would be too exposed to the shooter if she went in that way.

But as another scared whinny came from inside Ay Caramba's stall, she had to do something.

She raced into Frijoles's stall, where an equally frightened Luis kneeled by the bay, trying to keep him calm.

"Give me a leg up," she said and motioned toward the wall between the stalls.

Luis was immediately at her side and offered his clasped hands as a way to boost her up. She grabbed the top of the wall and went up and over into the neighboring stall, where the mare was prancing nervously. Hurrying to the mare's side, she slipped an arm around her neck and stroked her hand down the horse's bulging belly, trying to calm her and move her out of sight of the shooter. Avoiding hooves that could crush a foot or worse if they landed on her.

As the sound of gunfire shifted away from the stables, the horse calmed but Teresa's fear remained with the thought of what Matt might be doing to draw the shooter away from them and to himself.

MATT MANAGED TO make it around the back of the stables and to the track area, where he found another ATV. He commanded Butter into the passenger seat beside him so he could protect her from the gunfire.

Speeding along a path toward the woods, he kept the paddock fencing as a barrier between him and the shooter. A bullet bit into the wooden fencing and ricocheted against the bumper of the ATV. A second one whizzed by his head, making him crouch lower to lessen the mass he presented to their assailant.

At the end of the path, he jerked the ATV to a stop and called out to Butter, "Come here, girl." Together they raced into the woods for cover.

Gunfire peppered the trees in front of them, sending bits of bark and leaves flying all around them, but Matt and Butter stayed low, avoiding the bullets. He reached into the holster tucked against the small of his back and withdrew the HK 9mm he kept there. Slowly he moved toward the shooter's position, keeping Butter close to his side. She hadn't had much attack training yet, but he hoped she would respond when commanded.

Not that hope was a plan.

He pressed forward and the shooter sprayed their area with gunfire again, but it was the kind of blind shooting that said their assailant didn't have their precise position. Reassured by that, he tried to move as silently as he could with his K-9 partner, almost crawling in the direction where he'd seen the flash of the rifle scope and heard the gunfire.

He guesstimated that he was no more than fifty yards from the shooter, but as he searched the area, there was no sign of anyone in the woods and the gunfire had stopped. The underbrush was thick, though, and provided good cover. He wasn't sure if the shooter had escaped.

Muttering a curse under his breath, he hurried forward until he noticed an area with trampled vegetation underfoot. He examined the ground and noticed a few brass casings from a rifle. A .224 caliber bullet for sure. Unfortunately, a common caliber for many popular rifles. That could be why the shooter had left the brass behind. Either that or he was an amateur who didn't know to police his brass.

"Come here, Butter. Find it," he said, motioning the dog into the flattened underbrush.

Butter sniffed around and began to paw the ground, letting him know she'd found a scent. At another "Find it" command, Butter took off and Matt followed, noticing the disturbances along the ground that had created a path through the woods. The shooter hadn't been careful to hide his tracks, maybe because of his haste to escape.

While Matt moved, he stayed alert to any threats, aware the perp might be waiting to take them out.

The far edge of the woods led to a grassy break between Teresa's property and the avocado grove. The shooter's footprints were visible along the ground, and he avoided them to preserve the crime scene. Barely yards ahead were clear tire tracks moving away from a spot where their assailant must have parked his vehicle.

Satisfied the attacker was gone and no longer a threat, he tucked his pistol back into its holster and whipped out the phone to call Trey. As his friend and boss answered, he said, "We're going to need more boots on the ground ASAP."

TERESA STOOD BY the entrance to the stables, arms across her chest as she tried to keep herself calm while an assortment of police officers and SBS personnel swarmed around her property.

In the stable area, one of the CSI members searched the area for remnants of the bullets while in the far woods another team worked the stand of trees.

Matt stood beside Mia and her tech guru cousins Sophie and Robbie. She had met the cousins more than once during visits to the Gonzalez family home and the recent dual wedding for Trey and Roni, and Mia and John Wilson, a multimillionaire tech genius who sometimes assisted the family with their investigations.

Matt looked in her direction and as their gazes met, she detected the worry in his expression but also compassion. With a wave of his hand, he invited her to join them, and she ambled over, stood between Mia and him as he explained what he wanted.

"I think we need to get some trail cams and security guards along the edges of the property as well as security cameras in and around the stables. Also, some cameras on the ranch house," he said, gesturing to the various areas with a sweep of his muscled arm.

"We can get some of that done today. I assume you want to be able to monitor the feeds?" Sophie said and Matt nodded.

Robbie looked back to where the SBS team had brought an RV and parked it beside the ranch house. "We'll have to make sure you have a clean internet connection in that RV to pick up the feeds."

"And enough power and room for all the monitors," Sophie said. It was impossible to miss the concern and doubt in her voice.

"You can have all that in the ranch house," Teresa said in a shaky voice, nervous about having Matt's presence in her safe space. But it was what made the most sense considering what had happened barely an hour earlier.

Mia picked up on her emotions immediately. “Are you sure? We can make the RV work.”

Teresa glanced from the RV to her house and appreciated the effort that Mia and SBS had already made, but the most important thing was putting an end to the danger.

“I’m sure. Whatever you need to do, only…” She hesitated as her mind raced with worry about not only how his presence would affect her, but also about how much this was all going to cost. She was barely making ends meet, and with this…

“We take care of our friends,” Mia said and laid a comforting hand on her arm, silently understanding Teresa’s concerns.

Teresa forced a smile. “*Gracias*, but I don’t expect you to do this for free.”

Mia nodded, as did Sophie and Robbie. “It won’t be free, but we won’t break the bank either. We know how hard you’re working to build this place.”

“I appreciate that. Whatever you need, just let me know,” she said, and they were about to resume their discussion when Luis ran up to them.

“*Señorita* Teresa. You have to come see,” he said, a broad smile on his young face.

They followed him to Frijoles’s stall, where the large bay was on his feet.

Teresa’s throat choked with emotion, making it almost impossible to breathe. Happy tears spilled down her face. Overwhelmed with relief, she turned, and Matt was there, his blue-eyed gaze understanding, drawing her in.

MATT COULD HANDLE a lot of things but not a woman’s tears. Especially as his eyes met Teresa’s and observed her immense love for the animal standing behind her in the stall. Love and relief. They pulled at his heart in a way that he hadn't experienced in far too long.

But she suddenly covered her face, stepped toward him and almost melted against his chest.

Surprised, he hesitated, unsure of what to do, but instinct took over and he awkwardly wrapped his arms around her to offer support as she cried out her emotions. He couldn't remember the last time he'd offered comfort, and it had been even longer since he'd received it.

"It's going to be okay," Matt said, and Teresa nodded against his chest.

"It is," she murmured and took a step back. She wiped the tears from her face, glanced up at him and said, *"Gracias."*

He didn't feel as if there was all that much for her to be thanking him for but nodded anyway. "We should get to work on securing this place."

"Yes, of course," Teresa said and turned to Mia, Sophie and Robbie. "I shouldn't keep you from doing your work."

Mia laid a reassuring hand on her arm again and gave her an understanding smile. "It's been a rough twenty-four hours. Why don't the two of us go back to the ranch house so you can get some rest while Matt, Sophie and Robbie deal with the police."

"That's a good idea. It'll give me a chance to get cleaned up as well," Teresa said. She ran a hand through her tangled hair and glanced at her dirty clothes.

The two women walked off in the direction of the ranch house, their heads tucked close as they chatted along the way.

Matt watched, drawn to Teresa's quiet strength and her beauty. It would be hard to ignore the beauty even as her strength threatened to pull him in. He'd always admired that in a woman, but he reminded himself that he was here to do a job and that Teresa was the kind of woman to avoid.

Facing Sophie and Robbie, he went over the areas in the stables where he thought they needed cameras. Then the trio walked outside, and he once again suggested possible locations for cameras and discussed the protection for the perimeter of the property.

"Teresa told me they've had incidents at various spots in the paddocks. Up until today, mostly nuisance kind of things. We need eyes on the ranch but it's over twenty acres and I can't imagine fencing all that in."

Sophie peered around the property. "You had a good idea about the trail cameras around the perimeter. It's such a large property that security guards alone can't keep it safe."

"I agree, but I plan on taking Butter around as well to keep an eye on the place," Matt clarified.

"A lot of ground to cover but we can put cameras on that paddock fencing as well to keep an eye on who's coming and going," Robbie said as he gazed over the property.

"Lights will help. Some motion sensor floods along the edges of the wooded area and by the stables and ranch house might be good," Matt suggested.

"Solar-powered will make them easier to install and we can get ones with wireless cameras built in," Sophie said.

Matt nodded. "That makes a lot of sense. Do you think you can get that done today? It's late already."

Sophie and Robbie shared a look. With a shrug, Robbie said, "It's a lot to do but if we bring in a few more of our techs, we can secure the house and stables today and finish up the perimeter by tomorrow."

"That's acceptable. We'll place a few guards along the perimeter. Butter and I will patrol the grounds tonight. Right,

Butter?" Matt rubbed the dog's head as she calmly sat beside him, patiently waiting for his instructions.

"We'll get to work, then," Sophie said, and she and Robbie walked away, but just as they did so one of the police officers who had been investigating the shooting approached him.

"Officer Perez," she said, recognizing him from his time on the police force. She was one of the younger officers and he remembered when she'd first come out of the academy. She'd been eager and easygoing, and from what he'd seen of her today, her time on the force hadn't yet dimmed her enthusiasm for the job.

He dipped his head in greeting. "Officer Ventura. It's just Matt now," he said with a broad smile.

"Matt," she acknowledged with a nod and opened her notepad. "Thanks for preserving the crime scene. The CSI officers have been able to collect several brass casings and bullets as well as casts of the footprints and tire tracks. Can you supply any details about the shooter?"

Matt shook his head. "When he first started shooting, I was too far away, and he was hidden in the woods. By the time I got closer, he'd escaped but Butter was able to pick up a scent."

"You keep on saying *he*," the young officer challenged.

"I only had a quick look at the footprints but based on the size and their depth in the softer ground, it was probably a man. Too big and heavy for a woman," he explained.

Officer Ventura nodded, pen poised over the notepad. "Anything else you can report?"

With another shake of his head, he said, "Nothing. SBS will be securing the property but anything you find out will be appreciated."

"We'll keep you advised of developments and hope you'll

do the same," the officer said, closed her notepad and tucked it into a holder on her duty belt.

"We will, Officer Ventura," he replied with an easy smile.

"Vanessa, please, Matt," she said with a sexy grin and walked away with a decidedly enticing sway despite the heavy leather belt cinched around her hips.

It took him a moment to realize she'd been flirting with him. He'd clearly been out of the game for way too long not to notice, but then again, he'd been focused on his career since joining the military at eighteen and the police force years later. His few relationships hadn't lasted long, and meaningless hookups had never been his thing.

For some reason, a vision of kissing Teresa Ramirez blasted into his brain. Driving away the unwanted temptation, he surveyed the area to find Sophie, Robbie and two of the SBS installers hard at work by the stables. He decided it was time to give Mia a report and see how Teresa was doing.

"Come, Butter," he commanded softly, and the shepherd padded beside him to the door of the ranch house.

Teresa's home was a simple but welcoming two-story farmhouse with a large, screened front porch that faced the circular driveway and a small pond. Fat cattails surrounded the pond at one end while colorful water lilies floated toward the front. A water feature in the center of the pond gently sprayed water that cascaded down to dance on the surface. A flash of gold and white hinted at the fish beneath the surface. He could picture sitting on the porch to watch the sunset and keep an eye on the nearby stables.

He paused at the door to the house, worried about what awaited him inside. Teresa had clearly experienced a roller coaster of emotions today, from worry at what had been happening to fear with the shooting and finally relief that her stallion was feeling better. He hoped that she'd be calmer and free of the tears that had tugged at his heart earlier.

Those tears had opened a crack in his heart that he had to seal right back up if he was going to do this job properly.

Sucking in a breath, he knocked and waited to enter.

Chapter Four

The shower had done her a world of good. Besides removing the stink and dirt from the night spent caring for Frijoles, it had helped wash away some of the fear. Especially now that SBS was here and taking steps to protect her and her business. It had also helped wash away the memories of what it felt like to be pressed against Matt's hard chest and the way his arms had wrapped around her. Hesitantly, almost clumsily at first, before he fully committed to comforting her.

He clearly wasn't used to such things, which made her wonder about him. Wonder what had shaped the man who had promised to keep her safe.

Shaking away those thoughts, she finished drawing a brush through her hair and headed out to the living room, skipping a blow-dry since she wanted to be able to take part in whatever SBS was planning.

As she stepped into the living room, Mia was just letting Matt into the house.

It was unnerving having him in her home. She didn't know why, but there was something about the K-9 agent that demanded her attention. When he walked in, he glanced in her direction and met her gaze.

Was there relief there and maybe something else? she wondered.

"You're feeling better," he said, and it wasn't a question.

She nodded. "I am."

Mia looked from her to Matt, her gaze questioning. "Everything okay?"

Matt nodded. "They're installing the cameras by the stables and should be able to do the ones in and around the ranch house by tonight. In the meantime, I'll do perimeter checks this evening as well as keep an eye on the camera feeds."

Mia asked Teresa, "Where would you like us to set up the monitors for the security cameras?"

Teresa gestured to the far side of the living room. "The formal dining room makes sense. I hardly ever use it."

"Great. Trey should be here any minute now. He's bringing the equipment, techs and dinner. Roni may be joining us as well to let us know what the police have been able to get so far in their investigations," Mia said, walked to the door of the dining room and nodded, confirming the space would be okay.

Dinner? Teresa took a quick look at her watch. It was just past six but with everything that had been happening she'd lost track of time.

"We can eat at the kitchen table. Can I get you anything while we wait for Trey?" Teresa said.

"I'm good. What about you, Matt?" Mia asked.

"Water would be good. Thanks," he said, and she was about to guide them into the kitchen when a knock came at the front door.

"Come in," Teresa called out and Trey hurried in, a large box in his hands. Behind him on the walk leading to the house were two women wearing SBS polo shirts and hauling a small cart loaded with equipment.

Trey slipped the box to one hand and came over to embrace her, one strong arm wrapping around her waist. "How are you doing?" he asked, his tone one of brotherly concern.

With a hesitant shrug, she said, "As well as can be expected."

"Where can I put dinner and the equipment?" he asked.

"Dinner is in the kitchen and everything else can go in the dining room. I think you know the way," she said because both Trey and Mia had been at her house several times over the years.

Trey walked back to Matt and handed him the box. "Do you mind helping Mia and Teresa get set up for dinner?"

"Whatever you need, Trey," he said and looked in her direction. "Lead the way."

She smiled, gestured toward a door at the back of the living room and walked there, Mia, Matt and Butter following her into a large, open-concept room that held the kitchen, informal living room and a big-sized, farmhouse-style table for eating.

Matt placed the box on a counter and with a flip of a hand in the direction of the sink, he said, "Mind if I clean up?"

"Make yourself at home," she said, especially since he would be making her home his home during his security detail.

He went to the sink, Butter at his side. While he washed up, soaping his hands and forearms, the dog waited at his side patiently.

"Can I get anything for your dog?" she asked.

"A bowl would be nice so she can get a drink. I have her food and other things in Mia's car and can get those later," he said, turned from the sink and whipped some paper towels off a holder to dry his muscled forearms.

While she went to get the bowl, Mia finished emptying the box onto the counter, and as she did so, the enticing aroma of citrus-marinated pork wafted into the air. Teresa's stomach growled, anticipating what she hoped would be Cuban sandwiches chock-full of roast pork, Swiss cheese and sweet ham. Grabbing a large mixing bowl, she filled it with water and set it on the floor by the end of the counter for Matt's dog.

Matt unleashed Butter and gave her a hand command. The shepherd headed to the bowl and lapped up some water before settling down on the floor, her large head nestled on her paws.

In an efficient ballet, Teresa took out plates, cutlery and napkins that Matt and Mia laid out on the table. It wasn't long before Trey walked in, Sophie and Robbie behind him. His phone dinged. He looked at it and said, "Roni says she'll be here in five minutes."

"I'm looking forward to hearing what she has to say," Mia said as she finished setting the table.

"Hopefully the police will have more info," Trey added and removed some other dishes from the box he had brought. "What can you tell us, Matt?"

Teresa walked over and took the takeout dishes to the table while Matt relayed what had happened earlier that day as well as the other incidents that had led to her calling Mia.

"Did you call him Frijoles because of his color?" Trey asked, brows furrowed as he puzzled about the name.

Teresa smiled and nodded. "I did. He's a black bay, so he's actually dark brown with a black tint to his skin and black points."

At Trey's slightly confused look, she explained, "His points—legs, ears and mane—are all black."

"He's a good-looking horse. Is it true you got him in a claiming race?" Matt said as he finished setting the table.

"He caught my eye in another race. Richard liked him as well. Thought he had untapped potential. Turns out Frijoles's father won over $2.3 million in purses, and we decided to put in a claim. He cost me $30,000 but he's been worth every penny," Teresa said, pride filling her voice.

A knock came at the door and Trey walked out to answer. He returned a second later with Roni. As he wrapped his arm around Roni's waist, Teresa noticed the baby belly bump that hadn't been visible at their wedding a month earlier.

Walking over, she hugged the other woman and said, "Welcome and congratulations. When are you due?"

"Another six months," Roni said with a grin and hugged her back.

"Will you keep working all that time?" Being an undercover Miami Beach detective wasn't the easiest of jobs.

Roni and Trey shared a look before Roni shrugged and said, "We've been talking about me joining SBS."

That prompted a big shout from Robbie and hugs from Mia and Sophie.

"That'll make it all of the family," Mia said with a joyful laugh.

"Well, except for Pepe, but you know how he is about SBS," Sophie said with a wry twist of her lips, reminding Teresa about the one Gonzalez cousin who wanted no part of the family business.

"I imagine Roni's tired, so why don't we get going on dinner," Mia said, ever the organizer and problem solver.

They settled around the large kitchen table, and she found herself sitting next to Matt whether by design or just plain bad luck. It was hard to ignore his presence between the size of him and his smell, something piney and clean despite the rough day they'd had.

A second later he handed her a plate with a Cuban sandwich, sweet *maduros*, rice and black beans, and she thanked him. Her appetite had been off since all the incidents had started but surrounded by the love and protection of the Gonzalez family and Matt, she was suddenly hungry.

She ate with gusto as the family started sharing the information they'd gathered so far, and it struck her how odd it was that they were mixing a family dinner and mayhem as if it was just any other day. But then again, maybe that was what made SBS so successful at what they did.

The bonds of family combined with brains and bravery made for an invincible mix.

MATT LISTENED INTENTLY as Roni ran down what the police had gathered so far.

"They have a partial on one of the casings, but it was smudged. They're not sure they'll be able to do anything with it," she said with a frown.

"What about the footprints and tire tracks?" he asked, impatient to hear more.

"Size ten sneaker. No ID yet on the brand. Off-road tires, a lug type typical of a four-by-four," Roni said.

"Common shoe size and tires," Matt said, worried that what the police had so far wouldn't help identify whoever wanted to hurt Teresa.

Trey nodded in agreement. "Too common and I assume there's no CCTV anywhere in the area," he said and took a bite of his sandwich.

"No CCTV. The area's too rural even though we're this close to Miami," Roni said and held her thumb and forefinger together to emphasize the small distance between the city and Redland.

"Poisoning Frijoles and the shooting are a big escalation of the other incidents," Matt cautioned and shot a look at Teresa. She had been eating heartily up until now, but with his words, she set down the sandwich and met his worried gaze.

Mia, who was sitting beside Teresa, laid a comforting

hand on her arm. "Don't worry. We'll get to the bottom of this. Right, Matt?"

He didn't fail to hear the warning in Mia's tone to be gentler with her friend. "That's right and now that we're here, the stables and Teresa will be safe."

Despite his reassuring words, Teresa said, "Esquivel wants to make sure I don't testify."

"What's the worst they could do to him if you testify?" Trey asked around a mouthful of sandwich.

With a shrug, Teresa said, "A lifetime ban isn't likely for just drugging a horse or using a banned substance. Maybe a few months or more."

"People kill for less," Robbie said, earning a sharp elbow from his younger sister, Sophie, and a hushed *"cállate"* urging him to shut up.

People do kill for less, Matt thought. But there was something about today's incidents that rankled him, and as he looked across the table to Trey it was obvious his friend felt the same way. That was confirmed when Trey said, "What if it isn't Esquivel behind today's attacks?"

Chapter Five

Teresa almost jumped beside him. "What do you mean? Who else could it be? He's been calling and texting me about the hearing, but I haven't responded."

Trey shot him another look and then glanced at Mia, who seemingly understood where Trey was going.

"Your parents—" Mia began, but Teresa immediately cut her off.

"My parents have nothing to do with the stable. Nothing," Teresa said with an angry slash of her hand.

Matt knew only a little about Teresa's background, basically what Mia had told him on the way over: that her parents ran one of the larger casinos in the Miami area. From what little he knew of casinos and gambling, there was always the risk of criminal activity.

Not wanting to upset her because of Mia's earlier silent warning, he said, "We know your parents aren't involved with the stables, but is it possible—"

"They're not involved with the mob. I know people think that about casinos, but my parents are clean and always have been," she said with another sharp and emphatic slash of her hand.

"But what if the mob wants them to be?" Mia said cautiously and comforted Teresa once again with a gentle hand.

Matt soothed her as well, stroking her back with a fleeting caress.

She shot him a half glance and he couldn't fail to see the sheen of tears in her eyes. His heart did that strange little constriction again before he pulled away to glance at the Gonzalez family members seated at the table.

"We'll have the stables fully secured by tomorrow night. That may keep whoever it is away," he said and silently added *for a little while.*

With a sharp dip of his head, Trey said, "It will. In the meantime, we'll investigate Esquivel from our end and reconvene here tomorrow night to share what we've been able to gather."

Roni picked up her sandwich again and motioned with it. "Eat up. We're going to need the energy, especially you, Matt. You're going to do patrols with Butter tonight?"

Matt nodded. "I am and I'll keep an eye on the monitors as well."

"If you want, Sophie and I can tap into the feed and take turns monitoring so you can concentrate on the patrols and get some rest," Robbie offered.

Sophie nodded her head in agreement. "I had planned on staying up late to work on some other things anyway."

"*Gracias.* I'll take any help I can get," Matt said. He plucked some of the meat and cheese from his sandwich and clicked his tongue to call over Butter. When she approached, he fed her the food as a treat.

"I APPRECIATE ALL you're doing but is there anything else I can do to help?" Teresa said, wishing there was more she could do to stop the menace to her stables. Especially now that it was threatening innocent people and animals. Matt, Luis and her horses could have been hurt today by the shooter. Richard and Miranda as well.

Trey hesitated and said, "Just keep an open mind about the investigation."

Teresa had no doubt what Trey wanted: for her to consider that something to do with her parents was causing the attacks. But she knew her parents and she knew they would never do anything illegal. Despite that, she said, "I'll try."

"That's all we ask," Mia said. Then they all turned their attention to finishing their meals with small talk about what they would each do and joking with Sophie and Robbie about how they would have to finally leave their computers to spend time in the countryside.

"You forget we've got our Whitaker family in Colorado. We're used to being out in the wild with them," Sophie said with a smile.

Teresa wasn't sure she'd call Redland the wilds of anything. Just over forty minutes from downtown Miami, it was a mostly agricultural area dotted with an assortment of fruit orchards, ornamental nurseries and some tourist attractions like Monkey Jungle and the Fruit and Spice Park.

"I've even been on a horse," Robbie said with a wry grin.

"It wasn't a pretty sight. I wasn't much better," Sophie added with a laugh.

"I have some saddle horses if you ever want to give it another try. Mia and I used to ride together when we were younger," Teresa offered and shot a quick look at her friend.

Mia chuckled and shook her head. "I managed to stay on, but you were amazing. You should show Matt your medals and trophies while he's here."

The heat of a blush erupted across her cheeks, especially as Matt turned that blue-eyed gaze in her direction. "You're a jockey? Aren't you too…tall for that?"

She shook her head. "I am too tall and heavy to be a jockey although I do train the horses. I did dressage."

"That's that fancy riding, isn't it?" he said with a low whistle.

"I figured him for a cowboy the first time we met and then he told me he was from Texas and confirmed it," Trey said, his tone that of a longtime friend.

"Not everyone from Texas is a cowboy. And I figured Trey for a spoiled rich boy what with his fancy clothes and haircut. I think he wanted to cry when they buzzed it all off," Matt teased back and mimicked someone running a razor across his head.

Trey dragged his fingers through the longer strands of his dark hair at the top of his fade cut. "Luckily it grows back."

Like it had for Matt, whose light brown hair was longer and with waves that emphasized his blue eyes, strong jaw and lips that… She wouldn't think about his lips. It was unwanted temptation to have thoughts about Matt she hadn't had in years thanks to the demands of building her racing stable.

"I guess you met in the Marines?" she asked, knowing that Trey had served before joining the police force and then his family's business.

Matt nodded. "We met in boot camp and then we were both stationed in Iraq. Trey was a grunt, and I was a dog handler."

Which explained to Teresa why Matt was now part of SBS's K-9 division. It also spoke to the loyalty between the two men that after their years of military and police service, they were working together again.

"And a good handler at that. Saved our butt from IEDs more than once. You can count on him, Teresa. Don't doubt that," Trey said with a jab of his finger in her direction to emphasize his words.

"I won't," she said and shot a half glance at Matt, who nodded to confirm his friend's statement.

"You *can* count on me," he echoed, reassuring her.

"Gracias," she said and smiled with gratitude.

With a loving look at his wife, Trey wrapped his arm around her shoulders and said, "I think it's time we got going. We've got a lot of work to do and I'm sure Roni's getting tired."

With a weary smile, Roni said, "I am a little beat, but I will reach out to the officers working this case."

Teresa suspected that as tired as Roni was, she'd be on the phone to her friends on the police force as soon as they left her property.

"We'll finish up what we can tonight and be back in the morning," Sophie said. Glancing at Robbie, she asked, "Do you want to do the last of the cameras or the monitors?"

"Monitors. The horses bring back too many painful memories," he said and chuckled.

"Once it's dark, I'll do my first patrol," Matt said, rising from the table. But as he did so, he grabbed his plate and said, "I'll help y'all clean up."

"Your mama raised you right," Teresa teased, appreciating that he hadn't assumed the womenfolk would do the cleaning.

He nodded, grinning. "My mama would be pleased by you saying that."

His drawl was decidedly more pronounced in this casual exchange, and she liked it maybe a little too much.

Mia also helped clean up while the rest of the crew finished installing the cameras and monitors. Matt went out to Mia's car to bring in his things as well as a dog bed, bowls and food for Butter, who had been patiently resting by the end of the counter. The dog quickly scarfed down the food, drank some water and then lay back down.

"She's such a good dog but who named her Butter?" Teresa asked as she looked at the Malinois.

Matt laughed. "Her breeder had a thing for the BTS K-pop band, so they named her for one of their biggest hits." Smiling, he knelt and rubbed Butter's long, pointy ears. "She is a good dog, and I should probably take her for a walk. Do you want to come with me?"

"Sure. Do you mind if I check in on the horses also?" she asked as she placed the last plate in the drying rack.

"Not at all," he said and together they strolled out of the ranch house and to the paved path to the stables, stopping to let Butter relieve herself. Matt cleaned up the mess into a poop bag that he left to pick up on the way back.

Once inside the stables, she went to Ay Caramba's stall and rubbed her hands along the mare's swollen flanks.

"You doing okay, *chiquitica*?" she crooned to the horse, who nickered and nipped at her shoulder. "Yes, I didn't forget," she teased and reached into her jeans pocket. She pulled out a sugar cube, placed it in the palm of her hand and the horse gently ate the treat.

"She likes her sweets," Matt said as he stood by the entrance to the stall and watched the exchange.

"She does, but they're not really good for her, so I keep them to a minimum." She walked out of the stall and secured the door.

When they reached Frijoles's stall, she was relieved to see the horse was standing and Luis was with him, holding up a feed bucket so Frijoles could eat. As she had done with Ay Caramba, she walked in and caressed the stallion's flanks, but he didn't budge from eating.

"I guess you're hungry, boy." She was happy to see he was feeling well enough to eat and so heartily also.

Matt stood at the stall door again, waiting, but Butter pawed at the ground near the entrance, impatient.

Matt spoke in easy tones to the dog. "Do you smell something, girl? Find it."

At his command the dog sniffed along the edges of the stall doors, moving to the far end of the building. Matt opened the large door to let the dog continue chasing the scent. Teresa followed behind them, wondering what scent the dog had found until Butter went directly to the shed where they had their spare tack room.

The dog pawed at the ground by the door and Matt glanced at her. "When was the last time you were in this shed?"

"Close to two weeks ago, when we emptied the tack after the small fire."

Matt nodded. "Please move back," he said with a pushing motion of his hand.

She did as he asked, shifting away from the door of the shed, and watched as he instructed Butter to sit. He dropped her leash and reached to the small of his back to withdraw his gun.

Her heart beat heavily in her chest as he grabbed the handle and released the latch to throw open the door, gun pointed into the shed.

After a sharp exhale, he said, "All clear."

Teresa released the breath she'd been holding and approached as he knelt by the door and gazed at the ground. "Someone's been in here."

Matt pointed to the ground, and she noticed half a dozen or so cigarette butts on the ground inside the shed.

"Did the fire start inside the shed? Maybe someone sneaking a smoke?" he asked.

Teresa shook her head. "No one on the ranch smokes and the fire was in that far corner by the electrical outlet. That's why we thought it was an accident, but then the other things happened, like the soaked silks."

"You didn't notice these butts?"

She shook her head again, more vehemently than before. "I'm sure they weren't there when we emptied the shed."

With a nod, Matt rose from his haunches and looked toward the house and stables. Raising his arm, he pointed in their direction. "From here he had a clear look at the house and stables. He'd know what was happening. When to do his attacks."

He reached into his jeans pocket and pulled out a plastic bag. Kneeling, he collected the butts, careful not to touch them. "I'll get these to the police so they can try to get some DNA off them. Maybe match it with a suspect in CODIS."

"CODIS?" she asked, unfamiliar with the term.

"Combined DNA Index System," he explained. "It's a database of DNA samples from criminal offenders. If whoever did this was arrested before, we'll get a hit."

"Will that take long?" she wondered aloud.

"Normally a few weeks but with Trey and Roni's pull, SBS might be able to get it done faster," he replied and held the bag up. "I need to call the PD to come and collect this."

"And what happens in the meantime?" she asked and followed him back toward the ranch house.

"We keep you safe."

Chapter Six

It was actually Trey and Roni who doubled back to pick up the evidence in order to drop it off with the detectives handling the case.

"Good job, Matt." Trey clapped him on the back.

"You mean 'good job, Butter.' She was the one who picked up the suspect's scent," Matt said, rubbing the shepherd's ears.

Trey smiled and patted the dog on the head. "Good job, Butter."

"We'll get this to the PD," Roni said as she took the evidence envelope from Matt.

"Thanks. It'll free me up to start the patrols now that it's dusk," he said and peered at the sky. By his guess, it would be dark within half an hour.

"We'll push them to do a rush on this," Roni said, and with that she and Trey left again.

Matt turned to Teresa. "You should go get some rest. It may take me a little while to patrol."

Teresa shot a hesitant look at the ranch house and then back at him. "I'm not really tired."

Despite what she said, he suspected it was more of an issue of her not wanting to be alone in the house with everything that was happening. He understood.

Jerking a thumb in the direction of the ATV by the stables, he said, "Want to come with me?"

"I'd like that," she said, her tone soft and grateful. It did something to his gut because he sensed she normally wasn't one to be indebted to anyone.

"You can tell me more about the stables while we patrol," he said as they slowly sauntered toward the ATV.

"I'm not sure there's much to tell," she said with a shrug.

Much as he had read her desire not to be alone earlier, he realized her reluctance to talk about the stables was more about humility than secrecy. Slipping into the ATV's driver's seat, he waited until she was settled on the passenger side and Butter was tucked into the storage box. He drove off in the direction of the track, an area he hadn't had a chance to explore before. Teresa had mentioned that it took up a great deal of the property and she hadn't been kidding. The track was a huge oval surrounded by the same kind of wooden split rail fencing that marked off the various paddocks on the other side of the property.

"What made you go from dressage to horse racing?" he said.

"I loved horses and couldn't imagine not being around them. I was boarding and training horses to pay for my dressage and realized that I loved the training part."

"And that led you to horse racing?" he asked and shot a quick look at her before he drove to the furthest part of the track, which was close to the street and visible to any passersby.

"An owner brought me a racehorse that was having a hard time getting into the starting gate. Someone recommended me since I'd trained one of their skittish animals. When I saw him race…it was magic. I got hooked on the idea of training my own racehorse."

He rounded the oval and caught sight of the guard whom

Trey had placed at the perimeter of the property, close to the avocado grove and near the road.

The guard waved at them as they came around the bend and Matt turned to ride along the edges of the property.

"Is that when you bought this place?" he asked, his gaze skipping across the ranch. As big as the property was, he was more impressed by how everything seemed to be in tip-top shape.

"I had a smaller ranch I had managed to buy with some of the money I earned with an endorsement deal. I sold that one and financed the purchase of this one."

Although he hated to ask, he had to know. "Did your parents help with that?"

"No," she shot back quickly and with a sharp slash of her hand. "Like I told you all earlier, my parents have nothing to do with my stables."

He decided not to press the issue. At least not until he'd done more research on her parents and their business.

"What was this property before?" he asked, peering all around the grounds.

"It used to belong to an orchid grower who went out of business."

She gestured to the strand of trees that separated the ranch from the nearby groves. "Some of the orchids are native and you might be able to see them in those trees during the daytime."

Matt had been scanning the area as they drove, and he thought he'd noticed some flowers. "I'll look for them in the morning."

"I can point them out to you if you'd like," she said and grabbed hold of the frame of the ATV as they hit a bump that had them both rocking in their seats. Butter let out a little bark in seeming complaint as well.

"I'd like that, but first and foremost I have to focus on

keeping you safe, Teresa." He shot her a look and said, "I plan on shadowing you around the ranch during the day if that's okay."

He waved at another guard situated at the deepest part of the property, near the spot where the shooter had hidden earlier that day.

"I'm okay with whatever you have to do," Teresa said but he could tell that she wasn't happy about the situation. He didn't blame her. Who could be happy about someone wanting to hurt you and your business?

They drove in silence until they reached the third guard positioned near the entrance to the ranch.

"Give me a second to check in with him," he said, stepped out of the ATV, and with a hand sign, commanded Butter to go with him.

TERESA WATCHED MATT as he ambled over to the armed guard. Matt had a long, lazy stride, but having seen him in action earlier that day, she wouldn't underestimate him. She also knew that he was not going to give up on finding out more about her as well as her parents.

She was absolutely certain that the attacks had nothing to do with them, but maybe it wouldn't hurt to let Matt and the rest of the SBS team confirm it for themselves.

In the meantime, she intended to do her best to convince them that it was her former trainer who was behind the incidents. But as sure as she was, it was troubling to think that Esquivel would resort to killing her to prevent her testifying. Especially since what he was being accused of normally only resulted in relatively minor suspensions of time.

"Penny for your thoughts, although I suspect they're worth much more than that," Matt said as he returned to the ATV and urged Butter back up into the storage box behind the two seats.

She had been so lost in those thoughts she hadn't noticed his return. "I was just thinking that Esquivel trying to shoot me is out of line with his possible punishment."

"What are they claiming he did?" Matt asked and hopped back into the driver's seat.

"I thought it was about his doping a horse. From what I've seen for similar incidents, I'm not sure they'd suspend him for more than six months or so," she explained again as they drove back to the ranch house.

"What if it's about more than that?" he asked, wheeling the ATV to a spot in the driveway in front of the house.

Teresa considered aloud what else it could be. "If it risked a horse's life or involved animal welfare claims, it could be years…but I never knew Esquivel to do anything along those lines."

Matt rocked his head back and forth, contemplating what she'd said. "Maybe we should dig a little into what he's accused of doing."

Teresa nodded. "I can look online or make some calls in the morning."

"Great. Let's get you inside. I'll make sure it's secure and then I'll take Butter for another walk around the stables."

"A walk" being a euphemism for making sure the area was safe, but she was okay with that. The constant worry about the attacks had been eating away at her. She had lost weight because her appetite was gone and hadn't really slept well in weeks.

The dinner with the SBS team was the first time in a long time that she'd been hungry and eaten anything of substance. She hoped that maybe tonight, with Matt in the house, she'd finally get some rest.

He walked her to the door, Butter at his side, and his large hand at the small of her back was surprisingly comforting.

When she unlocked the door, he urged her to stay on the porch and went in with Butter to make sure the inside was safe. Minutes later, he returned. "All good."

"I'll wait for you to get back before I turn in," she said and entered her home.

"I won't be long."

With a nod, he walked toward the stables, his easy stride taking him into the darkness. When she lost sight of him, she closed the door. Too nervous to just sit and wait, she went into her office and powered up her laptop, intending to read as much as she could about what the racing world was saying about Esquivel and his issues.

As soon as she popped in his name and did an internet search, article after article came up about her former trainer. Most of the stories speculated that the inquiries were about another of Esquivel's horses testing positive for a performance-enhancing drug. Nothing new, not that she'd known that when she'd first hired him.

Esquivel had been eager to work with her even though she didn't have an established track record. She had been grateful to have someone with his experience willing to work with a novice racehorse owner. When their first two horses had won a number of races, she'd been convinced that she'd made the right choice.

The money from the wins had helped her buy her current property as well as a foal with impressive lineage to train. She and Esquivel had trained the foal together for three years and had even more success until the horse had sliced a tendon during a race.

That was the first time that she and Esquivel had butted heads. Esquivel had wanted to have the horse euthanized for the insurance money, but she had insisted on saving the animal. It had cost her almost all her winnings from the foal to treat and rehabilitate him. Luckily, the stallion had been back on a racetrack in a little over a year and had won enough purses to make the stable profitable again.

Despite that, Esquivel had insisted that she'd made a mistake, and the continued tension between them had reached the boiling point when she walked into the stables one day and caught the trainer injecting one of her mares. Since they hadn't discussed any kind of treatment for the horse, she'd been skeptical about Esquivel's claims that it was only a vitamin injection.

She'd had Miranda take a blood sample, which had revealed the mare had been given a performance-enhancing drug. When she'd challenged Esquivel about the PED, he'd acted insulted that she would accuse him. His protestations had only worsened their relationship.

When barely a month later she'd caught him using a banned corticosteroid on another horse, she'd fired him and begun a search for a new trainer. Finding Richard was the best thing to happen to her. She loved working with him, and he had helped her build her stable into one with a solid reputation for winners.

The snick of the lock on the front door signaled that Matt and Butter were back. His footsteps and the jangle of Butter's collar grew louder as they approached her office.

"You still working?" he said, leaning an arm on the doorjamb.

She closed her laptop so she could give him her full attention. "Just trying to find out more about what's up with Esquivel."

He nodded. "Did you find out anything?"

"Surprisingly, no. I thought the articles would definitively say why the racing commission in New York would be going after him, but they didn't."

Teresa had an expressive face, and it was clear from her current look that she was puzzled by the lack of information in the articles.

"You think it has to do with the doping allegations, right?" Matt asked.

With a shrug of her fine-boned shoulders, she said, "I think that's why they want to talk to me. I can't imagine what else it could be about."

"Let me know if you find anything. In the meantime, are you okay with Butter being off her leash?"

"Of course. Anything you need for the two of you to be comfortable."

"Great," he said, reached down and unclipped the leash from Butter's collar. But the dog remained at his side, tongue hanging out of her mouth, which was why the breeder had sold her off for K-9 work. No one wanted a show dog with a tongue that wouldn't stay in its mouth.

"You should try to get some rest. I'm going to man the monitors," he said with a jerk of his thumb in the direction of the nearby dining room.

"I just have a few more things to do," she said, and he could tell she was determined to find out more about her former trainer. He understood. He'd gotten the sense she didn't like relying on others and he admired that. But it also made it a little harder to just think of her as another spoiled rich girl.

"Don't work too hard," he said and stepped away to get to work and put some distance between them. Teresa was way too intriguing, and he couldn't afford to be distracted on this assignment. Too much was at stake. With that thought paramount in his mind, he headed into the dining room to keep an eye on the Redland Ranch property.

Sophie, Robbie and the SBS techs had set up the nine monitors so that he could not only view them but also look out the windows of the dining room. The far windows faced the public road and entrance onto the property. A large SBS SUV and guard sat at the gate. The windows to his right faced the driveway, pond and the stables in the distance.

Leaning his hands on the desk pad protecting the mahogany of the dining room table, he peered from one monitor to the other, getting a sense of where Sophie and Robbie had installed the various security cameras. He had eyes on the stable areas and ranch house from one set of cameras. Another monitor displayed the track, and several other feeds came from the trail cameras they'd positioned along the perimeter.

The monitor dead center was free to check the status of the system, search the internet or do any other computer-related task. Just to be sure, he sat down and ran a system check that confirmed all was in order with the cameras.

"It's all looking good, Butter," he said as the shepherd sat by his side. He reached over, rubbed her ears and made a fist to instruct her to lie down. She immediately responded to the hand command. "Good girl," he praised her.

Since she had been so good that day, he took out a bag of biscuits from the bag he'd brought in earlier and offered her a peanut butter and bacon treat, one of her favorites. She gobbled it up happily, bringing a smile to his lips.

Satisfied all was well on the property, he texted Sophie to make sure he could reach her and got an almost immediate response.

"Don't you ever stop working?" he texted back.

"Do you?" she challenged, and he chuckled.

"Can you see the camera feeds?" he asked.

"I can. Let me know when you want to take a break."

In the military he'd sometimes had to go for a couple of days without any real sleep, but to stay sharp he needed at least a few hours of sleep.

"I'll catch some shut-eye in the morning if that's okay with you," he wrote back, and they agreed on a time where he could snag some rest.

He focused again on the monitors, but also felt the need to find out more about Teresa and her parents. Even though she was adamant there was no connection between what was happening and them, it just didn't make sense that the attacks were solely about Teresa testifying against her former trainer. Especially since the punishment was possibly only several months of suspension. But as Robbie had pointed out, people killed for less.

With that in mind, he did a quick search on the trainer. Several results mentioned his many suspensions over the years. That made him wonder if the racing commission hadn't decided on a much longer, even more permanent suspension in light of his history. Maybe that was what prompted the attacks and the escalation.

And yet there was still a nagging suspicion in his gut that it was about more and possibly not about the trainer.

He pulled up information on Teresa's parents and their casino, a small but exclusive property in Miami. There were a number of articles about the success of the business and a possible expansion into a second location at one of the old greyhound racetracks that had been shuttered when Florida banned dog racing.

It struck him as too coincidental that the recurring crimes on Redland Ranch and the boom in Teresa's parents' business were happening at the same time.

He kept on digging, reading up on the history of the business. The family had used to own a casino in Havana before Castro had come to power. After escaping the Communist regime like so many Cubans, the Rodriguezes had settled in Miami. After several years of struggle, they'd bought a run-down jai alai fronton and turned it around.

As popular as the ball sport had been in the sixties and seventies, it had started to see a decline in the eighties, according to the articles. There were assorted issues, including reports of murder and arson, and possible mob connections.

Teresa's family had apparently survived by doing a pivot to grow the casino side of the business while also keeping alive Miami's beloved jai alai by bringing in young athletes to play. Thanks to them and another casino, the sport was almost thriving in Miami again.

But did that mean the mob was also wanting to get in on the action again? Matt asked himself.

As much as Teresa might hate it, SBS had to investigate that possibility. He'd find a way to gently get Teresa to consider the likelihood that it was someone other than Esquivel who was trying to silence her.

While he'd been searching and reading, he'd also multitasked and kept an eye on the cameras. But so far there hadn't been any signs of activity except for Luis checking on Frijoles. Over an hour had gone by and he was getting stiff from sitting for so long. Much like Trey, he was used to being an all-action guy, so it was time for another patrol in and around the stables and the perimeter.

He shot up out of the chair and gave Butter a hand command to follow. As he walked out, he realized Teresa was still working at her laptop.

Her brow was furrowed, emerald gaze intense as she focused on the computer. The light cotton of her T-shirt clung to her delicate shoulders and stretched across generous breasts.

She really was beautiful, he thought, and battled a curl of unwanted desire as he stepped to the door of the room, needing to be close to her.

Chapter Seven

"You really should get some rest. You look worn out," Matt said as he rested a thickly muscled arm on the door jamb.

"Flatterer," Teresa teased, but hated that she hadn't been at her best in front of this man. Maybe hated even more that it mattered to her, because she wasn't interested in any kind of involvement with him.

"Just saying," he said in a laconic drawl that spoke words beyond those.

But he was right that she needed to get some rest. Shutting her laptop, she popped to her feet and said, "I just need to check on Frijoles one last time."

Matt nodded. "Butter and I will walk you over."

She found it funny he was including Butter, as if doing so made it more business than personal. But she got it—it had to stay business between them.

"Thanks. I'd like that," she said and meant it. His company—and Butter's—lessened the worry that had been dragging her down the last few weeks.

Together they strolled out of the house and over to the stables. Ay Caramba was in her stall, peacefully quiet, probably catching a nap before bedding down for a few hours.

Frijoles was up and Luis was keeping him company.

As the young man saw her, he said, *"Esta mejor. Gracias a Dios."*

"Muchissimas gracias," she echoed. *"Deberías ir a descansar. Es seguro ahora que SBS está aquí."*

Luis looked from her to Matt and back to her. He nodded and said, "I'll get some rest when Frijoles goes to sleep."

She knew better than to argue with her young stable hand. Since the time she'd hired him out of a program intended to help teens break from dangerous gangs, he had been determined to prove to her that she hadn't made a mistake. Besides being a hard worker, he'd also been doing well with his GED courses, and she hoped they'd be able to get him into college once he finished.

"*Hasta mañana*, Luis," she said, and Matt repeated the goodbye.

As they walked back toward the ranch house, Matt asked, "Is it true horses sleep standing up?"

She looked at him in surprise, wondering how he'd been brought up. "A Texas boy who doesn't know about horses?" she teased and instantly regretted it as his features tightened, almost painfully.

"I'm sorry. I didn't mean anything by it."

He raised his hands as if to stop her. "No need. Not all of us grow up on ranches."

Not wanting to press since it seemed to upset him, she said, "Most horses lie down for a few hours of deep sleep late at night. During the day they cat nap while standing."

"Survival instinct when they used to be in the wild, I guess," he said. As his gaze met hers, she realized he'd also had to find a way to survive and found herself wanting to know more about him.

They had reached her front door and she unlocked it, but as he had before, he gestured for her to wait while he and

Butter checked inside. When he returned, he dipped his head and said, "All clear. *Deberías ir a descansar.*"

"I will try to get some rest. *Gracias*, Matt. *Por todo*," she said and gently brushed a hand across his jaw in thanks.

THAT FLEETING CARESS almost undid him and he tore away from her and toward the ATV to do another round of patrol.

As he had before, he commanded Butter into the passenger seat, but she tilted her head at a questioning angle, as if asking him why he was leaving Teresa.

"Come on, girl. You know she's nothing but trouble," he said and quickly pulled away from the ranch house.

He circled around the stables to the track area, moving along a different route to see if there was anything new that might provide a clue as to who was behind the incidents. Nothing. He headed to the perimeter of the property, catching sight of the first guard at his post. The man waved at him in greeting and Matt pushed on to the farthest edge of the property by the stand of trees and the second guard. Another wave said all was well and he went to the front where the third guard was in place.

Pausing there for a second, he perused the residential road that ran in front of the property and the areas all around. Across the street from the stables was a private home with a low cement wall that ran across the front of that residence. The wall could easily provide cover for someone. He carefully pulled onto the street and slowly drove across the length of the wall, keeping a close eye for anything out of the ordinary. Nothing. But something about the property niggled at him and he made a note to go over and talk to the neighbors in the morning.

He circled back to the driveway and returned to the ranch house. Walking Butter one last time for the night, he headed in and found that Teresa was still up and waiting for him in the living room. She set aside the book she'd been reading—a romance novel, he could tell from the cover—and stood.

"I didn't get a chance to show you which room to use," she said and pointed a finger upward.

He nodded and, after grabbing the duffel he'd left there earlier that day, followed her up the stairs. As they walked down the hall on the upper level, she gestured to the first bedroom they passed and said, "You can use this room. The bathroom is right next door."

Stopping by the door, he said, "And your room is…" He needed to know the lay of the land in case of an emergency, he told himself.

She pointed down the hall. "Last door on the left."

With a nod, he said, "I should get back to work. *Buenas noches.*"

"Buenas noches," she said but he had already turned and raced down the steps, eager to be back to work and away from her.

As he made himself comfortable in front of the monitors and Butter settled down close to his feet, he forced himself to focus on the images on the screens and not on thoughts of Teresa getting ready for bed. It was an epic fail as his body tightened in reaction to those visions.

A text message popped across his screen. Sophie asking, "Everything okay?"

"Everything is okay," he replied even though things were far harder than he expected. And in more ways than one, he thought with a quick glance at the unwanted bulge in his khakis.

"Calling it a night. Will come online around five so you can get some shut-eye," she texted.

"Gracias. Get some rest."

"You, too," she said even though they both knew rest would be the farthest thing on his mind with all that was going on.

THE NIGHT PASSED without incident, and at five, as promised, Sophie had texted him that she would take over. He walked Butter so she could relieve herself and went upstairs for a few short hours of sleep. Butter lay on the floor next to the bed and he set an alarm for eight, and as he'd trained himself to do in the Marines, went fast to sleep.

He woke to the chime of the alarm and took a quick shower, dressed and headed downstairs to walk Butter and feed her. As he spilled food into the bowl, he thought about last night's meal and how eagerly Teresa had eaten. He wouldn't be surprised to know that she hadn't been eating well with all that had happened. He had noticed her clothes had been loose on her and she was a little too thin despite her very nice curves.

Since she still wasn't up, he decided to make them breakfast to hopefully remedy her lack of appetite. Rummaging through her cupboards and refrigerator, he found an assortment of things he could put together for breakfast. But first coffee.

He got a pot started and heated some milk for *café con leche*. After a satisfying sip, he got to work, cooking up some onion and garlic before adding bottled salsa. Then he threw in some oregano, cumin and a bay leaf, and set the mixture to simmer. Turning on a second gas burner, he charred some corn tortillas over the flames and placed them on plates. Last night's leftover black beans, not traditional but still tasty, got mashed, heated and spread over the tortillas.

Since he'd scrounged up a ripe avocado from the fridge, he sliced it and laid the slices next to the tortillas. Finished with her breakfast, Butter padded over to sit and watch him cook. He'd sometimes give her a treat while he cooked at home, and since she'd been so good, he went to the fridge, snared a small piece of cheese and tossed it to her.

She wolfed it down and resumed her spot beside him as he gave the salsa mixture another stir. The only thing left to do was to fry the eggs. And as he heated some oil and prepped the eggs, he heard signs of life on the floor above.

He had scooped the fried eggs onto the beans and was just spreading on some of the salsa when Teresa walked into the kitchen.

She had her hair up in a ponytail and looked refreshed, her green eyes bright and free of the worry that had filled them yesterday. The T-shirt and riding pants she wore were loose on her but couldn't hide the generous curves of her breasts and hips. Black riding boots completed her outfit.

"Buenos dias," she said, her voice sleep-husky.

Desire slammed into his gut as he imagined her saying that to him in bed, but he ripped his gaze away from her and concentrated on spooning the last of the salsa on the beans as he muttered, "You must have slept well. You don't look as tired as you did yesterday."

WELL, THAT WAS *a fine "good morning,"* Teresa thought as she prepped a cup of coffee for herself. A gentleman wouldn't have pointed out that she'd looked like death warmed over, but Matt was clearly no gentleman.

It stung, making her shoot back with, "At least I don't smell today."

His hands shook as he finished working at the stove and he turned, a chagrined smile on his face.

"I'm sorry. I just meant to say you look rested. Let's try this again. *Buenos dias*, Teresa," he said and held his hands out, as if in pleading.

Okay, maybe he wasn't a total ass. "*Buenos dias*, Matt. That smells delicious."

"Thank you. I hope you don't mind that I scrounged around to make us breakfast," he said, walked over with the plates and laid them on the kitchen table.

"I don't mind. This looks delicious. I love *huevos rancheros*." She grabbed napkins and cutlery, placed them next to the plates and took a spot at the table.

Matt sat kitty-corner to her, and she was once again struck by the size of him and his physicality. He wore an SBS T-shirt this time and it was tight across his shoulders and the hard muscles of his chest. A very nice chest, she remembered from her little crying jag of the day before.

Driving those thoughts away, she forked up some of the salsa, eggs, beans and tortilla. An explosion of flavor had her murmuring her approval. "*Dios mio*, this is so good," she said after she swallowed.

A slight trace of pink flared across his cheeks. "Thanks. *Mami* used to make me this for breakfast before I went to school and *Papi* went to work."

"She must be a good cook," she said and was unprepared for the sadness that darkened his blue eyes.

"She was. *Mami* passed when I was sixteen and then it was just me and *Papi* until I finished high school and enlisted."

"I'm sorry for your loss," she said, and he did a stilted shrug but didn't say anything. She didn't press because it was obvious that it hadn't been a good time for him and his father after his mother's death. That had likely been the reason for him joining the Marines.

The discussion cast a pall over the meal, and they finished it in silence. As he had the night before, Matt helped her clean up. His phone beeped just as they finished, and he shot a quick look at it.

"Sophie says a red Jeep is coming down the drive. Since the guard let it through, I assume—"

"That's Richard's four-by-four. He's my trainer. I'll introduce you to him," she said.

At the door she stopped to grab a riding helmet she'd left there, and Matt went to the dining room and returned with a radio. Together they walked out of the house and over to the driveway where Richard had parked his vehicle.

Richard eyed Matt warily, like a dad who had just caught an unwanted suitor sneaking out the door. Teresa understood. At times Richard had been like a second father to her. She gestured to Matt and Butter and explained, "Matt is part of the SBS team that's securing the stables. He'll be staying in one of the guest rooms until this is all over. That's his K-9 partner, Butter."

"SBS Agent Perez," Matt said and held his hand out to the older man.

Richard shook it and said, "Richard Wagner. I help Teresa train her racehorses."

After the introduction, Richard looked her way and said, "Were you still going to work Habanero today?"

She nodded. "I was. His owner is supposed to drop by later this week, and I was hoping we could show him how much he's improved."

"Is Habanero another of your racehorses?" Matt asked as they walked to the stables.

Teresa shook her head. "Just training him. He's a yearling and learning to be saddled. He's been a little skittish about having a rider on him and the owner asked me to help out."

"Teresa's a champ with the horses. She can literally make them dance," Richard said, fatherly pride in his voice.

The heat of a blush stole across her face, especially when Matt locked his gaze on her. "I'd love to see that," he said.

In the stable she first walked to check on Frijoles and Ay

Caramba. To her relief, both horses were doing well. Luis was in with Frijoles, giving him his morning feeding.

Comfortable with that, she walked to Habanero's stall and put on her helmet before going in gingerly to greet the horse. "Horses are herd animals and the herd protected them in the wild," she turned to him to explain. "When threatened, it's instinctual to flee, so they're always on alert, like now. His ears and tail are up, waiting to see what happens."

She approached the horse from the left, but slightly in front so he could see her. She also kept on talking so the horse would know she was nearing him. "*Buenos dias*, Habanero. How is my boy today?" She laid a gentle hand on the side of his face.

The horse bumped her with his head, and she laughed. "Yes, you will get a treat if you're good for me today."

"I'll go get the tack," Richard said and walked away to retrieve the saddle and other equipment she would need.

But when Richard returned just a minute later, his face was hard as stone. "Someone cut up all the bridles."

Chapter Eight

Matt walked over to examine the bridle that Teresa's trainer held up.

The straps that kept the bridle on the horse's head had been slashed, making it unusable. He allowed Butter to sniff the bridle, and she began to paw the ground as a signal that she recognized a scent.

Teresa left the horse's side to also take a look and pursed her lips after examining it. "We might be able to have them repaired, but that won't help me now." She glanced back toward the horse and said, "I can't afford to lose another day of training him."

"I might have a spare one in my Jeep," Richard said and hurried off to check.

"When was the last time you used them?" Matt asked as he fingered the ruined leather straps.

"We didn't train yesterday with all that happened, so it would have been the day before."

"Whoever poisoned the feed probably did this at the same time. Explains why Butter picked up on his scent in the stable area," Matt said and patted the shepherd on the head as a reward.

Richard returned with a bright red nylon bridle and a halter and handed them to Teresa. "I'll get the rest of the gear and meet you in the paddock."

Teresa nodded and approached the horse again, walking calmly and speaking slowly so as not to spook it.

Heart pounding, Matt imagined how quickly the horse could turn and send a thousand pounds smashing into Teresa. He gripped the stall door tightly, fighting the urge to go in and protect her, but without much of a battle she had the bridle over the horse's head and the bit in place. She snapped on the halter and led the horse out of the stall, but he instructed her to wait by the door to the stables.

He grabbed a radio he had clipped to his belt on the way out the door and checked with the guards that all was clear around the perimeter. Then he texted Sophie to check as well and when she answered in the affirmative, he said, "It's safe to go out."

Teresa nodded and walked the horse to the paddock directly behind the barn.

He kept a keen eye around the property and breathed a sigh of relief when he saw nothing out of the ordinary. With a hand command, he instructed Butter to sit down.

Matt's relief was short-lived as Richard came into the paddock with a saddle blanket and saddle. At the sight of them the horse's ears shot straight up, and he started prancing nervously. Butter sensed the tension, rose to her feet and did a little growl of warning.

"It's okay, Butter. Sit," Matt commanded, and the dog looked up at him in indecision. "Sit," he repeated, his tone slightly sharper, and Butter finally listened.

Inside the paddock, Teresa crooned, "Easy, boy," and kept a steady hand on the halter, forcing the horse to calm down.

Matt's gut twisted into a knot as Richard handed her the blanket and she arranged it on the horse, controlling the large animal with only the halter and her voice. But she did subdue Habanero, exerting her dominance over him as Richard slipped on the saddle and secured it into place.

As she had earlier, she went to the horse's left side and grabbed the reins while Richard took hold of the halter. In one smooth move, Richard locked his hands together to give her a leg up and she was suddenly up in the saddle.

The horse immediately backed away from Richard nervously and did a little buck and whinny. Butter responded to the action, rising to her feet again. Matt patted her head to reassure her and ordered, "Sit." This time she immediately responded.

Teresa didn't seem fazed as the horse did another little kick of its back legs. She softly urged the horse to quiet and kept a firm hand on the reins. The muscles of her legs tightened against Habanero's sides as the horse continued to fight her, but her control didn't waver.

It was a sight to behold, the beautiful woman taming the stallion. If she had any fear, she didn't show it. Little by little the animal quieted and then slowly responded to her commands. With a soft click of her tongue, she had the horse walking around the edge of the paddock. After a few turns around, she did another little click and lightly kicked the horse's sides, and the walk became a trot.

"Good boy, Habanero. That's it," she said as they went round and round the paddock.

"She's amazing, isn't she?" Richard asked from beside him.

He had been so intent on watching Teresa in case she needed help that he hadn't realized the man had sidled up to him by the split rail fence.

"She is," he murmured, appreciative of the skill and strength it had taken to control the horse.

"Contrary to what you might think, she hasn't had it

easy," the trainer said almost offhandedly, but Matt knew it was a warning.

"She's just an assignment," he said to make things clear to the older man.

Richard scoffed and nailed him with a sharp, hazel-eyed gaze. "You know what makes a good trainer?" he said but didn't wait for Matt's reply. "Intuition and being able to read an animal. Or a person. You're interested. You're just too dense to admit it to yourself."

Before he could protest the trainer's observations, Teresa trotted up and stopped the horse before them. "We made good progress today. If we can keep up his training in the next few days, I think the owner will be pleased when he comes by."

"I think so, too," Richard said. "I can try to repair some of the bridles if you want."

Teresa shook her head. "I'm worried that would be risky. We can't have one snap during training. The outfitter should be open soon and if Matt doesn't mind, we can run over there to buy some new ones."

"Whatever you need," he said, earning a rough laugh from the trainer.

Teresa glanced between them. "Something up?"

The trainer shot him a side-eye and said, "Just talking about animals and intuition."

TERESA'S INTUITION WAS screaming that there was something going on between the two men, but she didn't get a chance to challenge them as Richard said, "If you want, I'll get him watered and cooled down so you can get the replacement bridles."

She slipped off the horse and patted his flank. His skin was damp from both their exercise and his nervousness at being ridden. "That would be great. It shouldn't take us that long to get the new equipment so I can get back to work with some of the other horses."

"See you later," Richard said with a wave of his hand. He took hold of the halter to walk the horse around the paddock.

"My car's in the garage," she said.

As they walked back toward the house, he shot her a quick glance. "Do you mind if I drive? Just in case."

She didn't need to ask what the "just in case" was. He was clearly worried about an attack.

"I don't mind. I just need to get my car keys and purse."

When they reached the house, she unlocked the front door and quickly snagged her purse, pulled out her keys and handed them to Matt.

They locked up and left the house, and she keyed in a code to open the garage door.

She was about to walk to the passenger-side door when Matt swept an arm out to hold her back. "Let us check it out first."

He walked all around the SUV with Butter sniffing the ground and car. The dog took a long time by one of the tires, prompting Matt to do a thorough inspection of the wheel well and tires, but there was apparently nothing there.

After, he lay down on the ground close to the engine and looked beneath the car, Butter inching down beside him also. Luckily it was all clear. He jumped to his feet and he and Butter examined the gas tank area before finally opening the driver's-side door and popping the hood open.

She waited patiently as he looked all around the engine and then shut the hood.

Turning to her, he said, "All clear."

She wasn't about to question his judgment as to whether someone would try to blow her up. She had never thought someone would try to shoot her either, but they had.

Matt loaded Butter into the back and got comfortable in

the driver's seat. As he pulled out of the garage and down the driveway, she gave him directions on where to turn. The shop she used for her supplies wasn't all that far away, but it was in the most rural parts of Redland and literally sat on the edge of the Everglades.

"I'll never get used to all this being so close to civilization," Matt said with a laugh as he drove.

"To be honest, me neither, but I kind of like the quiet out here," she said as he drove down a long stretch of road surrounded by a mix of wetlands and mangroves.

"I get it. The city can be a challenge at times," he admitted, but didn't elaborate for long minutes.

"Is that because you're a country boy at heart?" she asked after his prolonged silence, wanting to know more about him and not just because he was protecting her.

He did a little shrug as he competently drove the SUV into the graveled parking lot for her supplier. The SUV rocked as a tire dipped into a pothole before he parked in front of the sprawling one-story building.

"We'll go in with you," he said, obviously avoiding their earlier conversation.

She hurried into the store, Matt and Butter following close behind, his head on a swivel as they entered. Butter likewise seemed to be taking everything in but remained calm.

An older man standing at the counter waved a hand in greeting, a broad smile on his tanned and lined face. "Morning, Teresa."

"Morning, Tiny," she replied with a little wiggle of her fingers and a smile.

TINY? MATT THOUGHT with a double take. "Tiny" was well over six feet, with shoulders almost as wide as that and a belly that bulged above a hefty silver buckle on his belt.

When he met Tiny's gaze, he realized the man was likewise giving him a once-over, obviously protective of Teresa.

Matt dipped his head to confirm he understood, and Tiny repeated the gesture.

Teresa had moved down a row in front of him and he chased after her, watching as she ran her hands over the bridles, selecting a variety of different ones.

"Aren't they all the same?" he asked.

With a little shrug of her shoulders, she held up one bridle. "This one's for Ay Caramba. She never liked having a bit in her mouth. The other ones are for training the horses for dressage, racing or just riding."

He recalled what she'd said earlier about getting back to work with the horses. "Do you race the horses? Don't you have a jockey for that?"

"We have one for the races. It would be great to have one training constantly with our horses, but usually they only come in for a day or so before a race to get used to the horse," she explained, then whirled and headed for the register.

With each thing that he learned about her, it was getting harder to think of her as a "little rich girl." Or at least as one like the woman who had ruined his life.

What kind of princess slept with her horse because it was sick or could control a powerful, thousand-pound animal through her force of will?

"Isn't that dangerous for you?" he said, imagining what might happen in a fall or if the animal bucked her off like today's horse seemed intent on doing.

She shrugged again and bobbed her head. "It can be, but I love working with the horses, and I can't afford to have a full-time jockey on the staff."

Much like she worried she couldn't afford the services

of SBS, he thought. Yet another reminder that maybe she wasn't what he had originally imagined.

At the register, Tiny raised a bushy eyebrow at the pile of bridles Teresa had placed on the counter for purchase. "Did that fire damage your tack?" Tiny asked.

He was surprised that Tiny knew about the incident. At Matt's questioning look, Teresa said, "It's a tight community."

Tiny laid a massive hand on hers as it rested on the counter. "It is and if you need me to do anything, just say the word." When he finished, Tiny looked in his direction with a warning glare.

"You don't need to worry about Teresa. She's in good hands," Matt said, provoking another glare and a lift of that hairy, very white eyebrow.

"Everything is okay, Tiny. And don't believe a word of what you hear," Teresa said, aware that news of the shooting the day before would also reach Tiny.

With a harrumph, Tiny rang up all the bridles, packed them into a large plastic bag and held it to Matt. Jabbing a finger in Matt's face, he said, "You take good care of her."

"You don't need to worry about her," Matt repeated and snagged the bag from Tiny's beefy hand.

Matt placed a protective hand at the small of Teresa's back and applied gentle pressure to guide her out of the store. With a click of the key fob, he opened the doors of her SUV, loaded Butter and the bag into the back seat, and got behind the wheel. Once Teresa was in and buckled up, he swiveled to face her.

"You have a lot of friends." The dedicated Gonzalez family, the overprotective Tiny, her loyal trainer Richard, stable hand Luis who adored her and who knew how many others.

A slight flush of color worked over her cheeks, and it had nothing to do with the sun-heated interior of the car.

"We should get going. I have a lot of work to do," she said and motioned with her index finger to the start button.

"Got it." He understood. He really wasn't into sharing about his past or his present, for that matter.

He started the car and cool air immediately blew out of the vents, chilling the heat and the awkward tension that had built between them.

Wheeling away from the store, he traveled back in the direction of the stables, but he had gone no more than a few miles when he caught sight of a white Jeep in the rearview mirror. It was moving very fast, making him keep a keen eye on it. As it neared, he caught sight of the laughing man and woman inside. Then the Jeep whipped around them and sped down the empty road in front of them.

He relaxed his grasp on the wheel, tension leaving him as the fear of danger passed.

But then he caught sight of an airboat skimming along the surface of the waterway beside the road.

It wasn't unusual to see one in the Everglades, but something about this one…

A heartbeat later the airboat surged onto the road behind them, the metal of the hull shrieking as it traveled across the pavement and clipped the back bumper. Butter reacted in the back seat, shooting to her feet and barking at the airboat.

The steering wheel jerked in his hands as he fought to keep the SUV on the road while the airboat shoved ever harder against the bumper, trying to drive them into the deadly waters beside them.

Chapter Nine

Teresa gripped her seat as the SUV fishtailed from side to side on the road, the groan of metal buckling as the airboat continued to push against their rear end.

Her heart jumped in her chest and fear tightened her throat until she could barely squeak out, “Matt?”

“Hold on. Just hold on,” Matt said, hands white-knuckled on the steering wheel as he fought for control.

Risking a quick glance behind her, she caught sight of Butter jumping from side to side on the back seat and barking as the masked man operating the airboat rammed against their bumper, working the controls to try to drive them into the water.

The SUV’s engine roared as Matt stomped on the accelerator, sending the car rocketing forward and away from the airboat. With that tiny bit of breathing space between them, Matt whipped the SUV to the right and away from the water’s edge. The vehicle tipped up precariously on two wheels before landing with a thud and crashing into the thick underbrush.

“Stay inside,” he shouted. Then he threw open his door, whipped out his gun and fired at the airboat rider as he whirled to attack them again.

The driver’s body jerked as a bullet apparently struck home.

Matt shot at him again, but the driver circled the airboat around, using the whirring blades to send a blinding cascade of air and debris in their direction.

Matt flinched as the barrage hit him, but Butter and Teresa were protected in the interior of the car. It let her catch a fleeting glimpse of the airboat as it bumped across the road, metal grating and sparking against the pavement until the airboat shot down the embankment and into the waters and grass of the Everglades. But her glance was enough to see that Matt *had* wounded the man. There had been a trail of blood down his left arm.

With the threat gone, Matt holstered his weapon and leaned into the car. "You okay?"

She tried to speak but couldn't. Her throat was still tight with fear, and she could barely hear past the pounding of her heartbeat reverberating in her ears. Nodding, she sucked in a shaky inhale before finally blowing out a rough breath.

"Okay. I'm okay."

With a slight incline of his head, he said, "I need to call this in to SBS and the police, so sit tight."

Sit tight? She didn't think she'd be able to take a step she was still so shaken. But she knew she had to do something to help out. She sat there, replaying everything that had happened. Trying to remember every little detail so she could provide that to the SBS agents and the police when they arrived.

The blaring sound of sirens approaching dragged her from the increasingly stuffy and hot interior of the SUV. She'd been so intent on remembering what had happened that she hadn't realized Matt had been all up and down the road with Butter, trying to find whatever evidence they could.

As the police pulled up just in front of the SUV, he walked over to the cruiser, and she hurried over to join them.

It was Officer Ventura and her partner again. While Ventura took their statements, her partner walked the roadway, arms akimbo, his head tucked down as he perused the asphalt and embankment.

"The airboat approached you from which direction?" Ventura asked.

Matt glanced at the Everglades and pointed at the waters. "From the southwest. From deeper in the Everglades."

That was met with a shrug from Ventura as if it was the only way it could have come. "Did you catch any part of the registration numbers?" the young officer asked.

Matt nodded. "FL and I think eight-two-two something." He shook his head and drove a hand through the wavy strands of his hair in frustration. "I was too busy trying to keep the car on the road."

"Three-two-two-five followed by an H and H, I think," Teresa said, remembering what she had seen as the airboat raced away from them.

"What about the driver? What can you tell me about him?" Ventura pressed.

"White male wearing a plain white T-shirt. Dark pants. Based on how he was sitting, I'd say he was over six feet. Muscular build. I think I shot him," Matt advised.

"You did. He was hurt. I could see blood on his left arm as he drove away," Teresa said and gestured to where she had seen the wound.

"We'll put in a call to local hospitals and doctors to see if anyone comes in for treatment. As for the airboat, if he didn't take any steps to conceal the numbers—"

"He probably stole it," Matt finished for the policewoman.

"Probably. Anything else you can think of, call me," Officer Ventura said and walked away to join her partner, not that Teresa thought they'd get anything useful from the scene.

Matt faced her and cupped her cheek. "You did good remembering the registration numbers."

His touch filled her with immediate comfort, and she reached up, tenderly stroked his face with her hand. "I had to do something while you were saving our butts," she said with a ghost of a smile and a sharp laugh.

A black Suburban pulled up behind the police cruiser and a second later Trey and Mia exited the vehicle. Trey stopped to chat with the two police officers while Mia hurried over to them.

"You're all okay?" Mia asked. Her glance darted from one to the other and down to where Butter patiently sat beside Matt.

Teresa nodded. "We're okay thanks to Matt."

Mia smiled and laid a hand on Matt's shoulder. "Maybe you should head back to the stables. I'm sure you have things to do, Teresa. Trey and I will finish up here."

With a quick dip of her head, she said, "I'd like that."

MIA HELD UP the keys to the Suburban. "Take our vehicle. CSI will be here soon to get whatever evidence they can from Teresa's SUV."

Matt nodded and slipped the keys from Mia's fingers. "Please keep us posted."

"We will," Mia said and together they all walked back in the direction of the police cruiser. As Mia peeled off to join Trey and the police officers, Teresa headed to the Suburban while Butter and Matt detoured to get the bag with the bridles.

Once they were settled in the larger vehicle, Matt drove the short distance to the stables and parked in the circular driveway in front of the ranch house. As he killed the engine, he looked at Teresa. "Are you really okay?"

Teresa sucked in a long breath, but then expelled it and nodded. "I am. Scared. Again."

He was about to say something when Teresa's phone rang. Her brow furrowed as she looked at the number but then didn't answer.

"Spam call?" he asked.

"Probably," she said, and they stepped out of the car. But as they walked toward the stables, her phone dinged to announce a voice mail.

Teresa paused and glanced at the phone, clearly puzzled. "They left a message."

Matt glanced down and noticed that the voice mail had lasted over a minute. Far longer than just a phone spammer might hang on. "Put it on speaker and play it," he said and tacked on, "Please."

She did as he asked, and a man's voice erupted from the phone. "Teresa, please. Please pick up. I need to talk to you. This is serious. You can't imagine how serious. Please call me back."

"Esquivel?" Matt asked as the voice mail ended.

"Esquivel," she confirmed, hands shaking.

He gripped her hands and stroked his thumbs across her skin, trying to calm her. "You can handle him."

She worried her lower lip with her teeth and did a few quick nods. "I can. Should I call him back?"

"Not yet. Let's wait for Trey and Mia to get here. You said you had some work to do." Keeping busy would help her not to think about Esquivel's call.

Offering him a weak smile, she said, "Work would be good. We normally train the horses in the morning, but with everything that's happening, our schedules are all off."

"Lead the way," he said and followed her to the stables. Richard was inside Ay Caramba's stall with Luis and attractive older woman he assumed was the vet. The vet was running her hands across the mare's swollen belly while gently talking to the horse.

"That's a good girl. You're going to be a mama real soon," the woman said, a soothing tone in her voice.

Teresa walked to the entrance of the stall and gestured toward the woman. "Matt, this is Dr. Miranda Ramirez. Our vet," Teresa said, and Matt dipped his head in greeting.

"How is Ay Caramba doing?"

Miranda smiled and kept on stroking the horse. "Any day now, Teresa. The foal is in the right place, and everything looks good."

"That's great to hear. Did you get a chance to check out Frijoles?" Teresa asked.

Miranda nodded. "I did and he's doing well. I'd give him another day of rest before taking him out for some light exercise. I've got to run, but I'll drop by again in the next few days to see how things are going."

"Thank you. You've made my day," Teresa replied and the relief in her voice was palpable as the vet walked away.

"I want to exercise Helado. Would you help me get him ready, Richard?" Teresa said, and at Richard's nod, she turned and walked toward another stall.

Matt walked beside her and said, "Helado? As in ice cream?"

Teresa grinned. "As in ice cream. He's almost all white and the first thought I had when I saw him was that he looked like vanilla ice cream."

Matt laughed. "I guess you were having a craving when he was born."

Teresa joined in his laughter. "I was. It had been a long night while we waited for him, and it was hot, and I was hungry for something cool."

She stopped by Frijoles's stall and the stallion came up

to the door to greet her. She stroked his face. “Good to see you’re feeling better, boy.”

The horse blew out a breath, almost as if in response. “I know you don’t like just lying around. I’ll take you out tomorrow morning,” she promised him as she stroked his head again.

Then they walked down a few stalls to where a beautiful white horse poked his head out of the stall.

“Helado,” Teresa greeted the horse, who tossed his head, sending the paler strands of his white mane into motion. She opened the stall door and stepped inside just as Richard came over with the tack for the horse. In no time Richard and Teresa had saddled the horse and Teresa walked him out of the stall.

“He is a handsome boy,” Matt said and stood beside Teresa. Butter sat at his feet but seemed restless.

Teresa glanced down at the shepherd and Matt stroked the dog’s head. “You okay, Butter?”

The dog did a sharp, short woof, worrying Matt. He rose and looked all around, searching for what might be upsetting the shepherd. Nothing seemed out of the ordinary in the stables. Just to be on the safe side, he said, “Let me clear the way to make sure everything’s fine.”

He walked ahead of them, Butter straining on the leash in front of him, decidedly anxious about something. As they paused at the door of the stables, a sudden motion on the ground to the right had him whipping his weapon out of his holster.

Just a cat, a black-and-white blur racing away from the stables.

Butter tugged at the leash, wanting to give chase, but Matt held her back. Then the shepherd quieted and sat at his feet patiently, tongue lolling out of her mouth while she waited for Matt’s command.

He shook his head. "Was that it? Just a cat?" he asked the dog, who looked up at him, totally peaceful. Almost smiling. "You and I are going to have to work on that," he said, thinking that his K-9 partner and he still had a lot to learn about each other.

With a wave at Teresa and Richard, he said, "Just a cat. I'm sorry."

Teresa smiled and walked up to him, holding Helado's halter. "Black-and-white?" she asked.

Matt nodded as they started walking toward the track.

"That's Big Ben. He's one of our mousers," she explained and drew open a gate to enter the track area.

MATT AND BUTTER stood by the open gate as Richard hurried past them and helped her up into the saddle.

With a slight kick to Helado's side, she walked him onto the track, and with another kick, she urged him into a trot around the track until she neared the spot where Richard stood with Matt and Butter.

The trainer raised his hand and gave her a signal to push the horse into a gallop. She shifted her weight forward, rose up in the saddle, and with the urging of her hands on the reins, she pushed him faster. Mentally she counted down a two-minute lick as the horse did the first mile around the track. With the eight furlongs completed, she was almost back to where Richard, Matt and Butter waited.

Richard flashed her another signal and she pushed the horse toward the rail and into his fastest speed, hugging the rail as they breezed around the track.

Sweat dripped down her face but she was instantly cooled by the air rushing past her as they raced through the afternoon. Life was a blur of greens and browns, and in that blur, she could forget for a moment all that was happening.

The shift of the horse's muscles beneath her was powerful, but she remained in control, riding higher in the stirrups and close to Helado's neck. His mane flew in the air, the soft strands whipping her face.

She pushed Helado, pushed herself, until she knew it was time to slow and cool him down.

Little by little she slackened his pace until they were at an easy walk around the track. Normally she'd hop off and let Luis or another of the stable hands walk the animals, but today she stayed on, relishing the time with the animal and the freedom from her current problems.

But as the sky darkened, warning that one of those typical tropical afternoon showers was on the way, she turned in and walked toward the trio waiting for her.

As she slipped off the horse, Richard said, "That was a good workout. Helado's times are improving quickly."

She smiled, pleased by that. "Sounds like we'll be able to race him this season."

Richard stroked the horse's shoulder and then moved lower past Helado's breast to his legs until he reached his fetlock. "All good. No sign of that earlier inflammation."

"That's good news," she said just as a rumble of thunder warned they should get inside.

They hurried into the stables and Richard said, "I'll take care of him. You should go get some rest."

"Thanks. I will," she said and as they headed back toward the house, Matt placed a hand at the sweat-damp small of her back. The touch was both possessive and protective and she didn't mind it.

"You were amazing out there," he said, obvious surprise and pride in his voice.

She tried to picture how he must have seen her but couldn't. To her today had been just another training session. With a hesitant shrug, she said, "*Gracias*, but it was just a regular day."

JUST A REGULAR day on an animal moving at least thirty miles an hour, if he had to guess. With nothing but a helmet on her head, which made him say, "I noticed you didn't have a whip."

"You mean a crop?" she asked, and at his nod, she explained, "I don't use one and I prefer that my jockeys don't either. It's a tough call because sometimes you need to possibly use it to prevent a collision, but I feel you can control the horse without it."

They had reached the end of the driveway and Butter pulled on the leash and began to paw the ground, clearly picking up a scent.

He stopped and laid a gentle hand on Teresa's arm to stop her. "Let Butter track this scent before the rain comes and we possibly lose it." Squatting, he rubbed the dog's ears and said, "Good girl. Find it, Butter."

He expected the shepherd to head toward the burned tack shed as it had the day before, but after sniffing around the area, Butter surprised him and headed up the driveway toward the entrance to the ranch. Head down, clearly on the scent, Butter moved to the road with Matt and Teresa following.

Pausing to make sure the road was clear of traffic, he let Butter cross over to the low wall marking the entrance to the neighbor's property and stopped there to make sure the area was clear. Before they moved forward, he said, "Do you think the neighbors will mind?"

Teresa shook her head. "They wouldn't but they're away. They're visiting their daughter and won't be home for another couple of weeks."

Matt bent and examined the tire tracks leading to the home. They looked similar to the tracks for the shooter's car that had been parked in the nearby avocado grove, but there was no car anywhere in sight.

Had the shooter made his escape across the neighbor's property or possibly even used it to hide?

Matt wasn't taking any chances. He pulled his weapon from the holster and glanced at Teresa. "Please stay here."

She shook her head vehemently, making the straps on her helmet swing with the movement. "No way. I'm going with you."

He was about to argue, but when his gaze locked with hers, the determination in her emerald eyes told him she would not relent.

Muttering a curse beneath his breath, he said, "Stay behind me."

Giving Butter another find command, he followed the shepherd as it ran the length of the wall in one direction and then doubled back to the driveway. There the dog went straight toward the house with Matt chasing after her and Teresa tucked safely behind him in case their attacker was in the house.

But as they approached safely, the heavens that had been threatening rain erupted, sending a deluge to soak them. The force of the storm was so powerful that it lashed them with rain as they stood by the door on the front porch, trying to shelter.

Shivering from the cold of the rain and teeth chattering, Teresa said, "There's a key under that flowerpot."

Matt lifted the pot with the wilted pink flowers but there was no key beneath it. Glancing at Teresa, he put his index finger to his mouth to urge her to silence and then pointed to the large window next to the door. If someone was inside, they would have seen them rush to the porch to avoid the storm, and he wanted her out of the line of fire.

Beside him, Butter was pawing at the door, alerting him that she had picked up the scent. He urged Butter back from the door so she would be out of harm's way as well and carefully turned the knob. With the nudge of his sneakered foot, he kicked the door open.

The door rebounded against the far wall with a soft thud.

Matt held his breath, waiting for an attack. Dead silence followed.

He carefully moved into the doorway, Butter tucked close to his side in case he needed to give the attack command. They breached the doorway where they'd be most vulnerable, but as he entered, it was clear that no one was in the home.

Stepping outside to where Teresa waited, arms wrapped around herself against the chill of the rain, he said, "It's all clear."

She hurried in as he examined the open-concept space that held a comfortable living room, kitchen and dining area. A plate with a few cigarette butts rested on the surface of the table beside a dirty, old-fashioned glass and bottle of rum. Beside him, Butter was pawing the ground, confirming that she had gotten the scent of their suspect.

"The Hendersons don't smoke," Teresa said.

Matt peered at the plate. The butts were from the same brand as they'd found in the shed. He observed the glass carefully. The fingerprints on its surface were obvious. "He left some nice evidence for us. If the police didn't get anything the first time, they will now."

"G-g-g-o-o-d-d," she said, teeth knocking together loudly, drawing his attention.

She was shivering, her body vibrating with cold as water dripped off her onto the terra cotta tile floor.

He muttered another curse and said, "We have to get you warm."

Leading her into the living room area, he grabbed a throw from the back of the couch and wrapped her in it. Since the storm continued to lash the house with wind and rain, he urged her onto the couch and flipped the switch by the fireplace to ignite the gas jets. Nothing happened.

"P-p-pilot-t-t is p-p-prob-b-bab-bly off," she said as she took off her riding helmet and laid it on the coffee table.

His phone started chirping and he yanked it from his wet jeans pocket. It was Mia calling. When he answered, she said, "We're at the house. Where are you?"

"Across the way at the neighbors'. Butter picked up the attacker's scent and it seems as if he's been here. Left cigarette butts and a dirty glass for us to analyze. Also, some tire tracks in front." He walked to shut the door against the rain that continued to pound the house.

"We'll call the police. Storm may take another half hour to clear, though. Are you dry and safe for now?" she asked.

He glanced at Teresa, who was still shaking from the wet and chill. "We're safe. Dry not so much. We'll stay here until the police arrive."

"We'll have some warm food waiting for you when you get here," Mia said and ended the call.

He issued a hand command for Butter to stay, and before she settled herself down, she shook the rain off her short fur.

Returning to Teresa, he sat beside her and scooped her up into his lap.

She came without protest and burrowed into his warmth.

He wrapped his arms around her and little by little her body stopped shaking. She peered up at him, and this close he could see the lighter green shards in the depths of those jewel-tone eyes. And that perfect nose and those full lips. Natural lips, not fake, model ones.

She can be a model, she is so beautiful, he thought, cupped her cheek and ran his thumb across those tempting lips.

TERESA HAD BEEN grateful for the heat his body had provided, but now there was a different kind of heat building between them.

The butterfly-light pass of his thumb on her lips was as intimate as any kiss, and her body responded to it, nipples tightening against her damp T-shirt. Heat and wet pooled at her center.

It had been too long since she'd been with a man, and it hadn't been a man like Matt. Big. Hard-bodied. Complex. She mimicked his action and cupped his jaw.

His skin was beard-rough beneath her palm. Hard much like the rest of him, but as she met his gaze, it was impossible to miss the need in his sapphire eyes.

Need that mirrored her own and she wasn't about to deny him or herself.

Bending, she covered his lips with hers, moaning at the feel of them and his muscled body against hers.

He returned the kiss, meeting her lips over and over until it wasn't enough, and he opened his mouth on hers with a soft groan.

His growing hardness registered against the softness of her hip and her insides pulsed with need as she imagined being with him.

The loud pounding of a fist on the front door and Butter issuing sharp, insistent barks had them jerking apart and shooting to their feet.

Her rough breathing sounded harsh and overly loud to her ears as Matt raced over and jerked the door open.

Chapter Ten

She inhaled sharply and ran shaky hands down her wet riding pants, trying to tamp down the desire racing through her body. Wrapping the throw around herself to hide any telltale signs of her need.

Idiot. You shouldn't have done that, she told herself as Matt let Officer Ventura and her partner into the house. With a short wave of his hand, he instructed Butter to come with them.

Matt led the officers over to the table and they stood there, water dripping off their hats and raincoats. Officer Ventura looked her way and said, "You say your neighbors aren't home?"

Teresa nodded. "They left over a week ago to visit their daughter."

Ventura said, "We'll bag this evidence and have the CSI lab analyze it. I have no doubt that they'll be able to get something from it. Once the rain lets up, we'll call them to take a look at the tire tracks as well, but they look like a pretty common pattern. At best they'll be able to confirm if they're the same as the shooter's in the avocado grove."

Her partner nodded and said, "Too bad they don't have a doorbell camera. We might have gotten a picture of the suspect."

"How do you think the suspect drove past you without you seeing him coming and going? This house is right across the way." Ventura gestured in the direction of the front door and the clear view all the way to Teresa's home.

Matt shrugged and dragged a hand through the waves of his hair in obvious frustration.

But it suddenly occurred to Teresa how that had happened. "This property was a farm that has another road in the back. It leads to a small barn on the outskirts of the old farm."

The male officer, whose name she didn't recall ever getting, faced her and said, "We'll have CSI check that area out as well."

She read the name tag on his dark blue shirt. "*Gracias*, Officer Smith."

He tipped his head and shot a look toward the door. "Rain's let up. If you don't have anything to add about what's happened here, you're free to go."

"Thanks, we'll let you get to work. We appreciate everything you're doing," she said with a smile.

MATT'S GUT TWISTED with jealousy as Teresa smiled at the officer, especially as the young man launched a too friendly grin back at her.

"Yes, let's go," Matt said and laid a possessive hand on her back. Applying gentle pressure, he guided her to the door, and they walked in silence to her house, Butter tucked close to his side. When he opened the door, the sounds of Trey and Mia filtered out along with the smell of something garlicky and earthy.

Inside, Mia was at the stove cooking while Trey stood at the counter, chopping lettuce. He looked up as they entered. "We were just making dinner. Roni, Sophie and Robbie should be here soon."

Mia half turned from the stove, wooden spoon dripping with tomato sauce poised over the pan. "You should get changed and comfortable. Dinner won't take long. Just some spaghetti and meatballs."

With a quick awkward glance in his direction, Teresa said, "It smells great. *Gracias*."

"Yes, thanks. We'll be back shortly," Matt said as Teresa wasted no time heading up the stairs, but at the door to her room, she paused, hesitant. Uncertain.

"About what just happened," she began in a low whisper and with a nervous glance down the stairs.

He held his hands up and waved them in a stop gesture. "It's okay, Teresa. It was just…we got carried away. It didn't mean anything," he said even though it had.

A flicker of pain drifted across her eyes before she shuttered her emotions. In a tight voice, she whispered, "Sure. Nothing. It meant nothing."

Before he could take it back, she whirled and almost slammed the door in his face.

Butter did a little bark, drawing his attention. The dog looked up at him and even there he detected annoyance with his behavior.

"Are you ladies all sticking together?" he said, and with a low whistle, asked Butter to go with him to the bathroom where he snagged a towel and rubbed the dog dry. Returning to the guest room, he took her off the leash and instructed her to lie down so she could get some rest after all that had happened that day.

Grabbing fresh clothes, he hurried to the bathroom, showered and changed.

Butter raised her head as he walked to the door of the guest room, instantly alert. "Come here, girl," he said, and when she did, he bent to rub her ears the way she liked. The dog smiled and he fixed his gaze with hers and whispered, "I promise not to be such an idiot."

Butter woofed out a short bark and wagged her head back and forth as if accepting that promise.

Together they went down the stairs and to the kitchen, where Matt gave Butter a fresh bowl of water and a serving of food. She immediately buried her head in the bowl, gobbling up the kibble.

"Is there anything I can do?" he asked since everyone was at work in the kitchen. Teresa was helping Mia with the pasta while Trey was still at the counter of the peninsula.

Trey half turned in his direction. "Why don't you set the table?"

"Sure," he said to his boss, only it was hard to think of Trey that way in a setting like this. Trey had turned his attention to chopping up some cucumbers and tomatoes for the salad, and again it struck Matt how odd it was that the family combined their work with everyday routines like this. But maybe that was how they managed to survive when work could consume so much of one's life.

It had certainly taken over Trey's life when he'd been a cop much as it had Matt's. Long days and sometimes even longer nights had eaten into his personal life, which was maybe why he hadn't had a relationship in what seemed like forever.

That's why I responded to Teresa the way I did, he told himself. Only the little voice in his head screamed, "Liar!"

As Teresa brushed past him to place a bowl on the table, her fresh scent teased his senses, sending his body into overdrive. He sucked in a breath to tamp his need down, but only managed to draw in even more of that potent aroma.

She stopped in front of him, her gaze puzzled. "Everything okay?"

He didn't trust himself to speak; his voice was so tight

with the emotion he was fighting. Nodding, he turned away from her to fiddle with the cutlery he had already set, and she walked to Trey's side.

Well, if he wants to avoid me, I can do the same, Teresa thought. She grabbed the salad bowl from Trey and took it to the table.

Matt stood there, hands clasped in front of him while he rocked back and forth on his heels, clearly uncomfortable.

She fought back making a comment. She didn't want Mia and Trey to think something was up, because it could affect Matt's employment and because she knew Mia would pick up on it.

Luckily the ringing of the video doorbell Sophie and Robbie had installed gave her an excuse and she headed to the front door. To her surprise, Butter, who had been lazing by her food bowl, hopped to her feet and hugged her side protectively as she went to the door.

While she walked, she checked who was at the door on her smartphone. It was the Gonzalez tech gurus, and she opened the door with a smile. "Works like a charm," she said and waved her phone in the air.

"Glad to hear," Sophie said and hugged her before she stepped inside.

Robbie likewise embraced her and said, "Heard you had an eventful day."

"You could say that," Teresa replied, as always surprised by Robbie's unrestrained candor, which could at times be off-putting.

He wrapped an arm around her shoulder and hugged her again. "It'll get better. Trust us."

His easy tone and the comforting weight of his hug alleviated some of her earlier upset at his offhand comment.

"I do trust you," she said and truly meant it. As crazy as

things had become in a matter of days, it would have been far worse without the presence of SBS and Matt. But even though Matt had saved her from physical danger repeatedly, he also presented a different kind of danger. One that could be as risky as the first.

They had barely reached the kitchen when the doorbell rang again, but Matt was already yanking out his smartphone to check. "It's Roni and John. I'll let them in." He rushed away, almost as if he was afraid to spend too much time in her presence.

She tried not to let it hurt and busied herself with adding another setting for John Wilson, Mia's newlywed husband, and helping Mia finish cooking the pasta so they could dole out heaping bowls of pasta and sauce to go with the meatballs and salad they had already placed on the table.

Welcoming Roni and John as they walked in, she was joined by Mia, who kissed her husband and said, "I wasn't expecting you tonight."

"I know how your family can be on an important case and figured this was the only way I'd get to see you for dinner," he said, wrapped an arm around her to draw her close and dropped a kiss on her forehead.

Teresa had met John a few times at other Gonzalez family events, but there was a relaxed air around him now that she hadn't sensed during their earlier meetings. His hazel eyes gleamed with joy when they settled on his wife just as Mia's azure eyes glittered happily with his presence.

As Trey joined Roni, he laid a possessive hand on the small bump of her belly and kissed her tenderly.

Teresa's heart constricted with a tumble of emotions at the sight of the two happy couples. Happiness. Sadness. Hope.

Dragging her gaze from them, she returned to the pot with the pasta just as the kitchen timer dinged to warn it was time to drain off the water. She shut off the gas and was about to grab pot holders to lift the heavy pot, but Matt was suddenly there to help.

"It's heavy," he said and moved the pot to the sink to empty the contents into a colander. When he finished, he transferred the pasta back to the pot and returned it to the stove.

Together they prepped bowls of pasta and served them as the family members set out sodas and water and then settled around the table, leaving two spots side by side for her and Matt.

Reluctant to be near him despite their teamwork on the meal, she had no choice but to sit and make the best of the situation. As it had the day before, her hunger awoke with the tasty smells of the food and the company of the Gonzalez family.

Their initial talk around the table revolved around John's new software program and Roni's visit to the obstetrician, but as the pasta bowls slowly emptied, the discussion turned to everything else that had happened that day.

"The police have confirmed that the airboat was stolen from a tourist company just a few miles away," Roni said as she twirled up a final forkful of the spaghetti.

"If he was watching us from the neighbor's property, he knew we were going somewhere, but not where," Teresa offered for consideration.

"Except he might have seen Richard go to his car for that bridle and assumed we'd be going to get new ones," Matt said.

"Or he may have a tracking device on your car," John said and glanced at Sophie and Robbie. "Do you have an RF detector with you?"

"I probably have one in the trunk," Robbie said. His fork clinked against his empty bowl. "Is there more?"

"In the pot," Teresa said, and Robbie hopped up to refill his dish.

"He's a bottomless pit," Sophie said with a shake of her head, prompting chuckles from the family members.

"I guess I am as well, especially since I'm eating for two," Roni said and rose to get more pasta, but Trey laid a gentle hand on her shoulder and said, "I'll get it for you."

That mix of emotions tugged at Teresa again at the warmth and easygoing nature of the family and the way they could mix their business with family as Sophie said, "We'll check Teresa's car after dinner."

MATT WAS GRATEFUL Sophie had shifted the discussion back to work. He didn't really know how to handle the family part since he hadn't had much of a family life once his mother had died. After that family dinners had usually been silent events, with his father sitting there slowly getting drunk while he shoveled in whatever simple meal Matt had managed to rummage together from the meager groceries in the house.

"What about the partial fingerprint? Any luck with that?" Matt asked, determined to move the investigation along so that Teresa could go back to her normal life and so could he. She was just too much of a temptation and he didn't know how much longer he could resist.

Roni said, "It was only a partial and smudged, but they think they have a suspect." She paused and gazed at Teresa in a way that had him worrying about what she would say next, and he wasn't wrong to worry.

"The suspect is Finn Walker, a low-level criminal with mob connections. This is his mug shot." Roni swiped open her smartphone and handed it to Teresa, who narrowed her gaze to peer at the photo.

Teresa shook her head and passed the phone back to Roni. "He doesn't look familiar."

"Walker has served time for bookmaking, money laundering, assault and loan sharking. He works for Tony Hollywood," Roni said, which earned a low whistle from Trey.

"Tony Hollywood is trouble. He's a big deal in the mob world and that makes me wonder what he wants with Teresa," Trey said.

Teresa's tension at the mention of the mob registered as her body stiffened beside him. As much as he didn't want to take the discussion there, he had to, because it was the only thing that made sense.

"What if what he wants has more to do with Teresa's parents," he said.

Teresa reacted in anger as she had the night before. "My parents have nothing to do with the mob," she said with a sharp slash of her hand.

Matt took hold of that hand and applied gentle pressure to reassure her as he said, "And maybe that's the problem. Maybe the mob is using you to get to your parents."

"That's a possible scenario, but if they were threatening harm to Teresa, wouldn't her parents have warned her?" Mia glanced at those sitting around the table, clearly inviting their thoughts.

"Have you told your parents about what's happening?" Sophie asked.

Teresa shook her head. "I didn't want to worry them."

Mia jumped in with, "Which means if they did get a threat and thought that nothing was happening—"

"They wouldn't believe there was really a threat," Trey finished for her.

"And they probably wouldn't say anything to Teresa so she wouldn't worry," Matt said and squeezed Teresa's hand again to offer support, since she was clearly troubled by where the investigation was going.

He was therefore surprised when she said, "I think it's time we talked to my parents."

Chapter Eleven

Teresa sat silently in the passenger seat as Matt pulled up to her parents' casino in the West Miami area.

"Are you ready?" he asked, obviously aware of how difficult a conversation this would be.

The pressure in her chest nearly cut off her breath, but she managed to say, "I am."

They exited her SUV, which had been checked for a tracking device the night before by Sophie, Robbie and John. They had found a small device buried in a hard-to-see area in the wheel well that Butter had hesitated over. To make sure the car wouldn't be tracked again, the trio had fashioned a wireless detector that would warn them if the car was compromised.

Beside her, Matt's head was a on a swivel, constantly on alert to look for any danger, Butter at his side. She wondered if he'd ever been to the casino and if not, what he'd make of it and her parents.

"Have you ever been here before?" she asked as they walked up the steps to the front doors. Palm trees and lush foliage lined the edges of the sidewalks and steps, giving the area a very tropical vibe.

"No, I haven't. I'm not much of a gambler."

"I'm not either. My parents built this to look just like the family casino in Cuba," she said. The front facade of the neoclassic structure had several doorways on both floors with semicircular windows above each door and a balcony that ran the length of the second floor. In the center of the building was an ornate triangular pediment featuring her family's coat of arms.

"It has that vibe. I've seen pictures of buildings like this in Cuba," he said, holding the door open for her.

"Gracias," she said. They entered the casino and were immediately assaulted by the cacophony of noise from the slot machines and gaming tables. A security guard approached them as he took note of Butter, but then backed away when he realized the dog was with Teresa.

They pushed to the back of the building, which held a large jai alai fronton.

She paused at the glass wall that separated the fronton from the rest of the casino. A wide swath of stadium-style seating held many spectators watching the players in the glass-enclosed court whip the ball around using handheld wicker *cestas*.

"They're very fast," Matt said as he also viewed the action on the fronton.

Teresa nodded. "Some say it's the fastest ball sport in the world."

MATT COULD BELIEVE it as the men with the long baskets on their hands caught the ball in those baskets and sent it speeding across the walls of the court. They watched for a few minutes more until Teresa said, "My parents' office is right off the fronton area."

She gestured with a hand to the side of the building where a guard stood by a door, hands clasped before him while his keen eyes kept vigilant for anything out of the ordinary. The stern look on his face faded as he caught sight of Teresa.

"*Señorita* Teresa. So good to see you again," he said with a broad smile and held the door open for them. Past the doors there was a reception area where a young Latina manned the desk. She also smiled as she saw Teresa and said, "Your parents are waiting for you."

"*Gracias*, Yolanda," she said, but paused at the door to her parents' office. Glancing at him over her shoulder, she said, "Are you ready?"

Ready as I'll ever be, he thought and nodded.

They walked into a very modern, luxurious and unusual office. Two large desks sat at either side of the room, facing each other. Behind each desk were bookcases filled with an assortment of books, photos and other mementos.

Along the wall, perpendicular to the two desks, was a seating area with a leather couch, two chairs and a coffee table. An older couple sat on the couch and rose as they entered.

The woman sauntered over, hugged Teresa and kissed each cheek. *"Mi'ja, tan bueno verte,"* she said.

"It's good to see you, too, *Mami*," Teresa said as her mother came to stand before him. She was slightly shorter than Teresa, even with the three-inch heels she wore, and her dark brown hair was in a short bob that framed a perfectly made-up face, which had barely a wrinkle. She perused him and Butter at length before extending a bejeweled hand with gold bracelets that dangled at her wrist. "Raquel Rodriguez. I'm Teresa's *madre*."

He hadn't needed her to tell him, since the two women bore a strong resemblance. They had the same nose and chin, but Teresa's mother had dark brown eyes and not Teresa's amazing emerald color. *"Señora* Rodriguez. *Encantado de conocerte,"* he said even though he suspected her parents weren't happy to meet him.

While he'd been greeting her mother, Teresa's father had

come over to heartily hug his daughter and now shifted to greet him.

He was an imposing man, almost as tall as Matt, with broad shoulders and a muscular abdomen beginning to thicken with age. The first brush of gray silvered the light brown hair at his temples, and when he offered Matt a handshake along with a smile, it lit up his forest green eyes.

"It's good to meet you, Matt, is it? Please call me Jorge," her father said with none of the formality he'd sensed from her mother.

"*Sí*, Matt Perez. I'm with SBS," he said as Jorge swept a thickly muscled arm in the direction of the chairs in front of the couch.

"We know SBS well. They handle some of the security for the casino," Raquel said as she returned to the couch, perched herself on the edge of it and smoothed the skirt of her red dress over her knees.

He took a seat and glanced at Teresa, waiting for her to begin. She fidgeted in her seat for a second before she said, "*Mami. Papi.* There's something we need to discuss."

"Is it about your horses?" her mother said with a wrinkle of her nose, disdain dripping from her words.

Jorge reached out and laid a hand over his wife's tightly clasped hands. "Raquel, *por favor.* Let Teresa finish."

Teresa sucked in a rough breath and held it, as if trying to control herself. Clearly mother and daughter had butted heads more than once about the stables.

After releasing a long exhale, Teresa said, "We've had a number of incidents at the stables. That's why Matt and SBS are involved."

She gestured to him with a shaky hand, and he thought it was as good a time as any to jump in and explain. "We've determined that our possible suspect has connections to Tony Hollywood. I assume you're familiar with Hollywood."

Her father blew out a snort. “Familiar? You might say that. We went to the same private school before going our separate ways.”

Matt glanced at Teresa, whose hands were gripping the arms of the chair so forcefully her knuckles were white from the pressure. Aware of how difficult this was for her, he couched his words carefully. “When you say you went your separate ways, I assume that means you haven’t heard from him in some time.”

“We don’t work with people like Tony Hollywood,” her mother said, face as chilly as the tone of her words.

Matt nodded. “I understand, but does Hollywood want to work with you? Have you had any issues with either him or—”

“Any of his friends?” Jorge said with an arch of a salt-and-pepper eyebrow.

At Matt’s nod, her father continued, “You know the mob had quite a lot of influence in many of the casinos in Cuba.”

Matt nodded once again and said, “I know the history.”

“*Bueno*. What you may not know is our family’s history. Both my family and Raquel’s owned one of Havana’s most well-known casinos. Rumor has it the mob tried to work their way into the business, but our great-grandfathers made it clear—” he raised his fists in emphasis “—that the mob has no place in our casino. We think that message has been well understood over the years.”

Matt got his meaning loud and clear but had to press since Teresa’s life was at stake. “No recent push—”

“Nothing,” Raquel immediately shot back and then glanced at her daughter. “I may not approve of what you do, but we would never ever do anything that could hurt you or your business.”

Message received. Again. Pushing to his feet, he peered

at the two matching desks and said, "I imagine you both have a lot of work to do."

"We are never too busy for you, *mi'ja*." Jorge slowly rose and held his hand out in the direction of his daughter, who stood, slipped her hand into his and hugged him.

"Gracias, Papi," Teresa said and as she stepped away from him, the bright sheen of tears glimmered in her emerald gaze.

With a sniffle and a brief, stilted hug of her mother, she whirled and hurried to the door.

Matt offered his thanks to her parents and chased after Teresa. As he and Butter caught up to her, he said, "That went…well."

An indifferent shrug was her only answer while they sped through the casino, out through the glass doors and down the steps to the sidewalk, where Teresa finally stopped, bent and sucked in a few rough breaths.

He stroked her back tenderly, gentling the upset that had been caused by the meeting.

When she straightened, she said, "I'm sorry. It's just that… *Mami* and me…she will never forgive my not coming to work for the casino."

Even in just that short meeting he recognized Raquel could be a formidable force and dealing with her could be difficult. "You're following your dream. She should be proud of that."

With a rough breath, she said, "I guess she is. When I won my first race, she and *Papi* were there, but I got the feeling she had wished we'd lost."

"Her loss," he said and laid a possessive hand at the small of her back. "We should head to the SBS offices and make that call to Esquivel like we decided last night."

"Do you think Sophie and Robbie will be able to trace the call?" she asked as they walked to her car in the nearby parking lot. Although there was a space reserved for her closer to the entrance—probably part of her parents' desire that she come work for them—he had made her park in the general area to avoid attracting attention.

"If he's smart, he's using a burner phone, but we should still be able to check the call detail records to find out where he may be located."

He hopped into the driver's seat and once she was buckled up, he pulled out of the parking lot and drove to Brickell Avenue in downtown Miami, fighting midday traffic. Forty minutes later they had parked and gone up to the upper floors of the building and the SBS offices.

Trey and Mia met them at the front desk.

"Please let Sophie and Robbie know that we need them in the conference room," Trey said to the receptionist, and they all walked into the nearby conference room to wait for them. While they did so, Mia pressed a button by the front door that made the glass wall of the conference room opaque for privacy.

As soon as the Gonzalez cousins had arrived, the meeting began.

"You went to see your parents this morning?" Mia asked. Compassion was evident in her voice and gaze.

"Just now. I had to work one of the horses this morning," Teresa replied and quickly added, "They said they had no connections with Tony Hollywood or anyone else in the mob."

Trey laser focused on Matt. "What was your read?"

With a dip of his head, he said, "I believe them. I don't think they're involved with Hollywood or anyone else. I also think they wouldn't do anything that might hurt Teresa or her business."

"Glad to hear that. If we consider that thread closed, let's move to Finn Walker. Roni's contacts say they're still waiting for the DNA analysis on the cigarette butts, but the fingerprints on the glass confirm he was in your neighbor's house," Trey said.

"Are the fingerprints enough to arrest him?" Teresa asked. She nervously tapped a pen on the notepad in front of her.

"No, not yet, but the noose is tightening." Trey reached out to cover her hand and offer a reassuring squeeze.

"They have an address for Walker, but when they went to question him, the place was vacant," Mia said.

"Do you think we could have the address? I could take Butter to see if she can pick up a scent there," Matt tossed out for consideration.

"We can try to get it. In the meantime, let's reach out to Esquivel. See what he has to say." Trey peered at Sophie and Robbie. "Are you ready to record the conversation?"

Sophie nodded. "We're ready. If he's using the same phone number, we'll have Roni ask the PD to request the call detail records for us to review."

Mia glanced at Teresa. "Are you ready?"

Chapter Twelve

Am I ready? she asked herself. It had taken her the better part of the morning to work up the courage to speak to her parents. She was still shaken by that meeting, but then again that wasn't anything new. Dealing with her mother's disapproval always bothered her.

But she wasn't some wilting wallflower. She could do this and gave a decided nod. "I'm ready."

She pulled out her smartphone and swiped to the voice mail Esquivel had left. Displaying the number, she glanced at the two techies who nodded as one to say they were set. She hit the button for the speakerphone and dialed, holding her breath while it rang and rang.

Over and over the tone sounded, almost echoing in the conference room. She was about to hang up when a breathy voice answered. "Hello?"

"Warner? It's Teresa."

"Teresa, *dios mio*. I've been hoping you'd call," he said, still slightly out of breath as if he was running somewhere.

Trying to stay neutral, she said, "I'm calling. You said this was serious."

"It is, Teresita. *Por favor*. You can't talk to the racing commission. *Por favor*," he pleaded, and the sounds of traffic drifted across the line. Esquivel was clearly on the move.

"Why shouldn't I? We both know I fired you for using a banned substance on my horse."

"It's about more and it could be dangerous for you," he said, breath choppier.

"Dangerous?" she said, voice rising in anger. "More dangerous than poisoning my horse, shooting at me or trying to run me off the road with an airboat?"

"Deadly…dangerous…believe…me," he said, barely able to talk between his huffing breaths and the noise in the background.

"Why, Warner? Why is it dangerous?" she pressed but Esquivel didn't answer.

A short curse filtered across the line before it went dead.

"Did you get all that?" Trey asked his cousins.

"We did. We'll have Roni get the call detail records for that phone number."

"Can you analyze the sound? Maybe make out where he might be?" Matt asked.

Robbie nodded. "We can try. There was a good deal of background noise. Maybe too much."

"And he was on the run. That was obvious," Trey said, a glower on his handsome face.

"He sounded scared," Teresa added, almost starting to feel a little bit of pity for her former trainer.

"Last time my informant sounded like that he ended up dead," Trey said, and it was obvious that he blamed himself for that.

"Hopefully we can find him before that happens," Matt replied and then faced her. "Can you think of anything besides the doping and banned substances that would warrant having the racing commission involved?"

She sorted through her assorted memories of working with Esquivel, but nothing popped free. "I can't."

"But Esquivel thinks you might have other information. That was clear to me," Mia offered.

Teresa shook her head, unable to disagree but also unable to nail down what Esquivel thought she had on him. "He does, but I can't think of anything."

"And there's Walker in the mix as well. Is he working for Esquivel or Hollywood?" Trey said and doodled something on the pad in front of him where he had written the names of the three suspects.

"Or working alone. What if he's working on his own? What if there's something Teresa has seen that involves only him?" Matt suggested and then glanced at her. "Are you sure you haven't seen Walker before?"

"Could I see a picture of him again?" Teresa asked.

Mia opened a folder sitting in front of her and pulled out Walker's mug shot. She passed it to Trey, who sent it around the table until it reached Teresa.

She laid the photo on the table and scrutinized it. "There's something here, around the eyes," she said and circled an index finger around that area but then shook her head again. "But I just don't remember him. Do you mind if I keep this?"

With a wave of her hand, Mia said, "Go ahead. I can print out another one for the file."

"Gracias," she said and folded the photo in half, intending to look at it again in the hopes of remembering something useful.

TERESA TOOK THE folded photo and fingered it over and over, almost as if that might provide a clue as to what connection she might have to the mobster. When she lifted her gaze and met Matt's, it was clear she was upset with today's developments, and he knew just the thing to make her feel better.

"If there's nothing else, Teresa, Butter and I should get back to the stables," he said.

Trey eyeballed him and then shifted his gaze to Teresa. "Nothing else until we're able to get the call detail records and Sophie and Robbie can analyze the recording."

"Great," he said, and Teresa hopped to her feet beside him, obviously relieved that it was time to go.

"I appreciate all you're doing," she said, ever polite and correct.

The Gonzalez family members all rose from the table and as they walked out, Trey laid a hand on his shoulder and urged him away for a second. Head bent close to his, he said, "Everything okay with you two?"

Matt peered in Teresa's direction as she stood by Mia at the elevator bank, waiting for him. Because he couldn't lie to his friend, he said, "Tense at times. Confusing."

Trey tracked Matt's gaze as he remained focused on the intriguing stables owner. With a nod, his friend said, "I get it, Matt. Just be careful. There's a lot at stake."

"I know," he said and hurried away from Trey to the women, who had been speaking softly while they waited. As he approached, a slight flush of color painted Teresa's cheeks, making him wish he could have been a fly on the wall to hear what they'd been discussing.

"Everything okay?" he asked and clasped his hands in front of him to keep from touching Teresa, afraid that Mia would read way too much from that action.

"We're good," Teresa said and then hugged Mia. "Please keep us posted."

"We will and don't worry. Progress may be slow, but there is progress," Mia said and walked over to call the elevator to the floor.

The door opened barely seconds later and Teresa, Butter and Matt hurried in for the ride down to the lobby. Uneasy silence filled the space until they reached the ground floor and he asked, "Do you mind if I walk Butter for a bit?"

"Not at all. She's been such a good girl," Teresa said and went to pet the dog, but then pulled back, recalling that she was a working K-9.

He wanted to say it was okay, but he had to keep that separation between work and anything personal for Butter. Especially since he'd failed spectacularly at maintaining that separation himself.

"She is a good girl," he said and rewarded Butter with an ear rub and a treat he had tucked into the pocket of his khakis earlier that morning.

On the sidewalk outside the building, he gave Butter a longer leash so she could explore and relieve herself while Teresa and he slowly strolled a few feet away.

As they walked, Teresa said, "Have you had her for long?"

"Six months give or take, so we're still learning to work together," Matt said with a slight lift of his shoulders and a quick glance all around to make sure it was safe.

With a side-glance at him, she said, "Is that how long you've been with SBS?"

He nodded. "It is. Before that I was with Miami Beach PD's K-9 unit."

From his peripheral vision, he noticed Butter squatting by a nearby streetlight pole and stopped to let her relieve herself. As he did so, he swept his gaze all across the plaza in front of the building. Satisfied all was secure, he focused on Teresa.

A mistake. Big mistake.

She'd dressed up more today, probably in deference to the visit to her parents. A pale yellow sundress bared her shoulders and arms that had a slight T-shirt tan thanks to her work with the horses. The lemony color accented that tan and the deep jewel-like color of her eyes.

A soft bark jerked his attention to Butter. The shepherd

had taken a spot right next to Teresa and was gazing up at him as if to ask, *What's up?*

He coughed to release the pressure that had built in his gut at the sight of Teresa and blurted out, "We should head back. I know you have work to do."

"I do. I need to see if Frijoles is up for some exercise," she said, and they quickly walked to her car. When they slipped inside and he started the short drive back to stables, he said, "Frijoles is important to you."

HIS STATEMENT WAS more of a question, wanting an answer she wasn't sure she was ready to give. But he'd shared a little bit about himself just minutes earlier and so she shared as well.

"He's my best stallion. His stud fees will help immensely and I'm hoping that when his foal is born, it will be a winner as well."

"His foal? Is that the one Ay Caramba is carrying?" Matt asked with a quick glance in her direction.

"It is. He'll be a dad any day now," she said, joy filling her at the thought of the foal's birth and training it for the future.

"And we'll make sure he and his horse family will be okay," Matt assured her.

"Horse family?" She laughed, prompting a chuckle from Matt.

"Yes, horse family. Just like your family," he said.

He surprised her with the sudden shift to something not necessarily as happy as the coming birth of the foal. He cast a quick, uneasy look in her direction and said, "I'm sorry. I know I've hit a nerve."

"You could say that," she said with a harsh laugh.

"Your mom—"

"My *mami* and me is…complicated." She shook her head

before plowing on. "I know she loves me and wants the best for me."

"Sounds like you're trying to convince yourself of that," Matt said, ever observant. While the first meeting had been awkward, in the days since then she'd come to realize there was a lot more to him than just his handsome face and all that tempting muscle.

"I know she loves me, but ever since I took a bad fall a few years ago, she's been determined to have me join the family business," she admitted, surprised at herself for confiding in him.

He must've realized she'd said more than she'd intended to, so he apparently decided to share a memory that was more personal than anything he'd revealed before.

"I get it. When I started playing football, I think my mom wanted to package me in bubble wrap to keep me safe when I took a hit," he said with a laugh.

She smiled and joined in his laughter. "I guess moms just want to keep us safe."

With a grin as he pulled off the road that led to the stables, he said, "Just like you want to keep Frijoles and his horse family safe."

His infectious grin and the laughter in his voice yanked another chuckle from her. "Just like that," she said and added in a slightly more thoughtful tone, "Just like you want to keep us safe."

"It's my…job," he said, but his hesitation made it obvious that it was about more than that for him. A burst of warmth flared to life inside her chest, bringing comfort and unexpected hope. She didn't want to think about what she was hoping for.

Unsure of what to say, she opted for, "I appreciate all that you're doing."

His answer was a short grunt, and luckily, he was already turning into the driveaway for the stables. When he parked the car in front of the house, he said, "I'm going to patrol the grounds. See if the guards have anything to say."

With a quick bop of her head, she said, "I'll go work Frijoles."

TERESA DASHED FROM the car and as she did so, Butter gave a little bark, clearly disquieted by her departure.

Matt half turned in the seat and rubbed Butter's ears. "She'll be okay, girl. Frijoles wouldn't hurt her," he said, recalling the friskier horse she'd tamed days before. Not that an accident couldn't happen while she was training. Even though he didn't normally follow horse racing, he'd seen news reports about the death of a horse or jockey during a race.

But Teresa could take care of herself on a horse, he thought, although he planned on doing some research to find out more about the fall that had freaked out her mother.

Exiting the car, he freed Butter from the harness securing her in the back seat and walked her to the ATV for their patrol. Not wanting to disturb Teresa's workout on the track, he patrolled the driveway first, checking in with the guard at the gate who had been instructed to keep an eye out for any activity at the neighbor's house.

Nothing, so he pressed on, moving slowly along the perimeter of the grounds, vigilant for signs of any activity or changes that would say someone had been there. He stopped at the second guard who had nothing to report, and then finally moved toward the track and the last guard on duty. But as he neared the track there was no sign of Teresa, Richard or Frijoles.

His chest tightened with pressure and the sudden pounding of his heartbeat in his ears almost deafened him. Finishing the route, he rushed back to park by the stables. When he did so, Butter grew agitated and began pawing the seat beside him.

"What's wrong, Butter? Find it," he said, and the shepherd took off in the direction of the stables entrance.

Chapter Thirteen

Gun drawn, Matt raced after his dog, who had gone to the open door of Ay Caramba's stall. Teresa's trainer, Richard, stood there, hands on his hips as he watched what was happening inside. Butter was at his feet, pacing back and forth across the opening, obviously agitated.

Matt joined them. Teresa was inside the stall at Ay Caramba's head, calming the horse while Dr. Ramirez had her hands inside the mare. Luis stood by with a handful of towels.

"The foal's position is a little off. Miranda has to shift his legs," Richard whispered, and Matt holstered his weapon.

"Got it!" Miranda called out. When she pulled her hands out, she was holding two spindly legs covered by a thin white sack.

Miranda leaned back. The horse's sides heaved, and more of the legs and sack became visible as well as…

Was that a nose? Matt thought and suddenly there was a head.

The sack split open and dangled downward, revealing the foal.

Miranda pulled on the legs as the mare pushed, and Teresa tried to calm the horse, who had begun to prance.

"Easy, girl. You're going to be a mom soon," Teresa crooned.

Another push and the foal's body emerged. Miranda cradled the horse and Richard rushed forward to stand by Teresa. "You should help Miranda," he said.

Teresa kneeled by Miranda to assist, and with another push, the rest of the foal and sack spilled from the mare.

Miranda and Teresa cradled the foal and moved it away from Ay Caramba's hooves, the remnants of the sack trailing from the foal to its mother. Teresa cleared away the sack from the foal's face and body and then the vet and Teresa gently laid the foal on the ground. For long seconds the foal was motionless.

Matt sucked in a breath and held it, waiting for any motion that said the foal was alive, but nothing happened immediately.

Miranda grabbed a handful of straw and whisked it across the foal's nose and the baby abruptly reared its head and sat up.

"That's it. That's a good boy," Teresa said and tenderly ran a hand across the foal's side, pulling away the remnants of the amniotic sack. Matt realized that the foal was still connected to the mother with the umbilical cord.

Recalling how EMTs had dealt with pregnant mothers, he gestured to the cord. "Don't you have to cut that?"

Teresa grabbed a towel from Luis and wiped her hands clean as she walked to Matt and Butter's side. Butter had calmed down and sat by his side, intensely watching the foal.

Shaking her head, Teresa said, "Not in horses. There's still blood flowing from the mother to the foal that's essential. If it doesn't come off naturally, we'll cut it off once the flow stops."

Ay Caramba walked closer to the foal, dipped her head and nudged her baby, who shifted his head to look up at his mother.

"It may take the foal several minutes to try to get to its

feet," Miranda said as she rose from beside the foal and slipped off the long surgical gloves she was wearing. Turning them inside out, she tossed them into her medical bag and grabbed the bag.

Richard and Miranda walked to the entrance to the stall and waved at Luis to join them.

"We should give them a little alone time so we don't stress them out," Miranda explained. "It could be a couple of hours for the foal to start to nurse and also for the afterbirth." She ran a hand across Richard's arm. "Unless something seems out of the ordinary, I'll be back tomorrow to check on them."

"Thank you for everything, Miranda. I know you must be exhausted," Teresa said and went to hug the older woman but paused since they were both wet and dirty from the birth.

"A little tired but so happy to see them both healthy," the veterinarian said with a full-lipped smile.

"I'll walk you to your car," Richard said, laying a hand at the small of her back, and the two strolled out, heads bent toward each other, chatting.

"Is there anything else we need to do?" Matt asked, unfamiliar with what happened during the entire foaling process.

"We should leave them alone for a little bit. You have eyes on this area, right?" she asked.

Matt nodded. "I do."

"Great. Luis, it's okay for you to go home and get some rest. Matt and I can keep an eye on them."

"Hasta mañana," Luis said with a wave and walked to the far end of the stables and the nearby bunkhouse.

"Hasta mañana," Matt and Teresa replied in unison.

"If you don't mind, I'd like to get cleaned up," Teresa said. She snagged a towel from the pile Luis had brought out of the stall and wiped her hands again, leaving dirty streaks on the cloth.

"Not at all. I need to do some things before dinner," he said, ignoring the fact that even covered in who knew what had come out of the horse, she was still the most beautiful woman he'd ever seen.

They hurried to the house, where Teresa went upstairs and he raced to the monitors, intent on checking things out, but also to research something that had been bouncing around in his head since their drive back to the stables.

With Butter settling in beside him, he took a quick look at the screens. Nothing seemed out of order. If anything, it tugged at his heart to see the foal awkwardly find its footing and approach its mother. Ay Caramba bent her head and nuzzled her baby, almost protectively.

Matt understood that protectiveness. His mom had been fierce and always in his corner.

Much like Teresa's mom seemed to be, despite her misguided, passive-aggressive behavior.

Sitting down at the computer, he typed in Teresa's name and pulled up a few articles about her fall. It hit him then why her mother had such fear about what Teresa was doing. Teresa had taken a freak spill during a dressage event when her horse spooked and threw her. She'd broken her back so badly the doctors had feared she might be paralyzed. Her miraculous recovery had surprised them, but it had taken over a year for her to return to riding.

He sat back in his chair, a whirlpool of emotions swirling through him. Shock. Worry. Pride. Respect.

"She's quite a woman," he said to Butter, who sat up, a puzzled look on her face. Bending to massage her neck and rub her ears, he said, "It's okay, girl."

Only it really wasn't, he thought. With everything he learned about Teresa, it was harder and harder to ignore what an amazing woman she was. Harder to deny that she intrigued him. Made him want her in ways he hadn't wanted a woman in way too long.

Sucking in a breath to fight back that need, he took a last look at the monitors. Satisfied that all was well, he texted Sophie and Robbie to set up a schedule for them to take over the surveillance. When they sent back a time, he thanked them and headed to the kitchen, where Teresa was pulling things out of the fridge to make dinner.

"How can I help?" he asked.

"I'm just going to make some picadillo. Is that okay?" she said as she laid a package of ground beef on the counter. There was already a pot on the stove, probably rice cooking.

"I love picadillo. My mom used to make it for me a lot." The simple dish of seasoned ground beef was comfort food at its best and inexpensive. Plus, leftovers could be used to fill empanadas or tacos.

"What was she like, your mom?" Teresa asked as she cut up some peppers, onions and garlic.

"My *mami* was…amazing," he said and since Teresa had the meal under control, he set the table and then joined her by the stove, where she had tossed the vegetables into a skillet with olive oil. It took only a few seconds for the aroma of the frying vegetables to spice the air.

Teresa stirred them and then looked up at him as she said, "You miss her."

Since there was no denying it, he said, "I do. She always believed in me."

TERESA HEARD WHAT was there beneath the words: his mother had believed in him when no one else had.

"Moms…it can be complicated," she said and placed the ground beef in with the vegetables, using her wooden spoon to break up the pieces as the meat browned. She turned down the heat on the pot of rice as the water started to boil.

"It's hard to sit back when someone you love could be hurt."

The tone in his voice yanked her gaze from the skillet up to meet his blue-eyed gaze. There was worry there and she tried to dispel it.

"I know what I'm doing," she said, returning her attention to the meat in the pan.

"Accidents happen when we least expect them, don't they?"

The words hung in the air, and she tried to ignore them, plucking capers and olives from their bottles to add to the skillet. She opened a can and poured tomato sauce into the skillet before adding a few raisins and seasoning the mix with cumin, oregano, salt and black pepper.

"Teresa?" he pressed at her prolonged silence.

"It was a freak accident," she said, realizing that he had done some homework since their morning meeting with her parents.

"But you get why she worries. You were almost paralyzed," he said and reached for the cover on the rice, but she playfully swatted his hand back.

"You have to let it steam so it's fluffy," she explained.

"Got it," he said and laid his arms across his chest, drawing her attention there. Reminding her of what it felt like to be held in those arms. Of that hard chest beneath her cheek, heart beating loudly for her. So tempting, but before she gave in to that temptation—again—she wanted to know more about what had shaped him. Especially since he'd obviously delved into her past.

"You hardly mention your dad," she said, giving the picadillo a stir.

He shrugged his broad shoulders. "Not much to mention."

"You had a good relationship with him?"

Another shrug was his reply, but that wasn't going to cut

it with her. "Come on, Matt. You obviously know my deepest, darkest—"

"He wasn't there for me," he blurted out and shook his head, the motion so strong it sent the unruly waves of his hair shifting back and forth. In a softer voice, he said, "When I needed him the most, he didn't have my back."

Sensing his upset, she laid a hand on his shoulder and stroked it gently. "I'm sorry."

"Don't be. I learned my mistake," he said, words curt and filled with pain.

Pressing him might bring more pain, but it was like pulling off a bandage. It hurt when you did it but then felt way better.

"What was the mistake?" She shifted her hand up to cradle his jaw.

His muscles jumped beneath her palm as he said, "I dared to fly too close to the sun."

IT SHOCKED HIM to admit that, but he knew she wouldn't be satisfied unless she knew the whole story.

"I played football in high school. Good enough that I got a scholarship to a division one college, only… I dared to get involved with girl who was way out of my league." The memories came so fast and furious he had to stop and take a long breath to hold back the emotions they aroused.

"She was the sun," Teresa said and stroked a thumb across his cheek, the simple gesture comforting.

"Her daddy didn't like that she was involved with someone who was literally from the wrong side of the tracks. He went to the cops and said I'd forced myself on her and that's all it took. When word spread, I became an outcast in town and the college pulled my scholarship."

"But you didn't do it. Didn't the police investigate? Didn't your father stand up for you?"

He was grateful she trusted him enough to know it had all been a lie. What he wouldn't have given for more people like her when he'd been eighteen and fighting the system alone.

"My dad was either too afraid or too drunk to back me up. As for the police, they cleared me, but the damage was done. I tried to get my scholarship back, but the coach said they couldn't risk the bad publicity."

He laid his hand on hers and gently turned it to take her hand into his. "*Gracias* for believing in me."

"I have no reason to doubt you. You've always been truthful. You did call me smelly the first time we met," she said with a cute wrinkle of her nose.

"I'm sorry I did that. I was in rich girl denial mode because you were…" he began, but then stopped and muttered a curse. Shaking his head, he locked his gaze on hers and finally admitted what he'd been fighting since first laying eyes on her. "You were—you are—the sun."

DIOS, BUT THAT was way more than what she'd expected him to say. Worse, she liked it way too much. Liked him way too much.

She leaned into him and went up on tiptoes until her lips were barely an inch from his and his warm rough breath spilled against hers. "My parents are rich. I'm just a girl with some horses," she whispered and closed that final distance to kiss him.

He groaned at that first contact and stiffened, but as she kept on kissing him, her mouth mobile against his, he finally wrapped an arm around her waist and hauled her close. Over and over they kissed until the slight crackle from the stove and slightly toasty smell had them pulling apart.

Teresa shut the gas on the pot with the rice and whipped off the cover. "It's overcooked."

Matt leaned closer to the pot and peered inside. "I like the *raspas*. Those hard bits at the bottom are tasty."

He was being overly kind, although her *papi* had always teased her *mami* that he liked the toasty rice as well on the rare occasions when her mother cooked and messed up.

"We should eat. I have to check on Ay Caramba and her foal," she said and quickly served up the picadillo and rice.

As she laid the plates on the table, Matt held up his smartphone to show her the camera feed in the stables. Mama and baby seemed to be doing fine, but she was still itching to see them.

They finished their meal quickly. While she was loading the dishwasher, Matt gave Butter a fresh bowl of water and food. The dog gobbled up the kibble quickly, almost as if she was as eager as Teresa to go see the new baby.

Back in the stables, they headed straight to Ay Caramba's stall where the foal was nursing, and the mare had apparently passed the afterbirth without any issues. Teresa carefully scooped it up in case the vet wanted to see it, mindful that new mothers could be overprotective and possibly dangerous.

"They're both doing fine." She closed the door to the stall, nudging Butter out of the way since the dog was intently watching.

"I'm always surprised at how animals seem to know there's a baby around," she said as Matt demanded Butter's attention with a hand signal.

They strolled to Frijoles's stall and the bay walked up to the door and stuck his head over the edge. There was something almost excited about the way he tossed his head and did a little prance. She smiled, stroked his nose and said, "Yes, you did good. Your baby is beautiful."

The horse huffed out a breath as if to say, *I sure did.*

Matt hesitantly reached out to likewise rub the horse's

nose, and after he did so, he held his hand out to Teresa and she slipped her hand into his.

Together, they finished a look around the stables and then headed outside to the ATV. Matt didn't need to ask if she wanted to go with him. She eased into the passenger seat while he loaded Butter into the storage box.

He started up the ATV and they did a run around the perimeter of the property, checking in with the various guards stationed there. Luckily there was nothing to report.

Matt detoured to go around the track and the rear of the stables and she enjoyed the quiet of the coming night. In what seemed like too short a ride, they were back at the house. After taking Butter for a walk so she could relieve herself, they headed inside, but at the door they hesitated, awkwardness creeping in.

Matt jerked a thumb in the direction of the dining room. "I should get to work."

Not that he hadn't been working during the drive, but she got what he meant. Being together on the drive and during their dinner had felt like anything but work. But she was reluctant for their night together to end.

"I can make some coffee if you'd like."

A broad smile lit up his face and turned his blue eyes to a jewel-like sapphire. "I'd like that."

He dropped a quick kiss on her cheek, whirled and rushed to the dining room.

Chapter Fourteen

Matt braced his hands on the tabletop and peered intently at the various monitors.

All was peaceful, especially in the stables where Ay Caramba and her foal had lain down, the baby tucked tight to her mother.

The whir of the grinder in the coffee machine rang through the house, distracting him for a second. But then he returned to perusing the monitors, wanting to make sure that the area was secure. That Teresa and her horses were safe.

Satisfied, he sat down at the computer and checked his email for updates from his colleagues at SBS. An email had just come in from Sophie and Robbie. He opened the analysis of the call detail records for Esquivel and the report on the tape recording.

He had barely opened the attachments with the analysis when his phone rang. Trey was calling.

"Hola, jefe," he teased since Trey wasn't a fan of anyone calling him "Chief."

A bark of a laugh burst across the line before Trey said, "Very funny. How's it going?"

"All is good here."

"I didn't want to push with Teresa there, but what was

your read of her parents?" Trey asked just as Teresa came in with two mugs of steaming coffee.

Matt shot her an uneasy look, but then forged ahead. "The Rodriguezes insist that Walker or Hollywood have no connection to their casino."

"Do you believe them?" Trey pressed.

Teresa sat beside him and placed the mug before him with a shaky hand, obviously aware of what they were discussing.

Matt met her gaze as he said, "I believe them. I don't think there's any connection to the casino."

He was therefore surprised when Trey said, "The analysis of the cell phone data and recording says the contrary. Why don't you look at the reports, talk to Teresa and call me back."

The line went dead, and he put the phone down on the table and faced Teresa, who had overheard bits and pieces of the conversation.

"It has nothing to do with my parents."

He laid his hand on hers as she cupped the mug, as if she needed the heat to chase away an inner chill.

"I believe you and them, but we have data that says otherwise." He released her hands, returned to the keyboard and brought up Sophie and Robbie's analysis.

He hadn't done much work with call detail records, but his SBS team had made it easy to see what had led Trey to his conclusion. With a finger, Matt explained the first page of data to Teresa.

"These are the numbers Esquivel has called as well as the switches and cell sites that picked up the call," he said and then flipped to the next page of the report. "Sophie and Robbie plotted that information on a map."

Teresa's sharp, surprised exhale cut through the air. "Those locations are all near the casino."

Matt nodded and pulled up the SBS report on the voice

recording. Sophie and Robbie had peeled away Esquivel's voice to isolate key noises in the background and identify what they were. They had embedded those noises in the report and Matt clicked on one to play it.

What sounded like a whir was followed by a few electronic tones, another louder whir and then coins dropping into a bucket.

"That sounds like a slot machine," Teresa said, defeat clear in her voice.

Matt wasn't about to accept the results so quickly. As a cop, he'd more than once come across cases that seemed clear-cut but weren't.

"Is there another reason why Esquivel would be in this area? Family maybe?"

With a slow shake of her head, she said, "As far as I know, most of his family is in the Little Havana area."

Matt nodded and pressed on. "Any other gambling locations in the area?"

Teresa tipped her head from side to side and then said, "There are a few places in and around the casino that try to glom business."

"Would they have slot machines?"

"Probably. They're cheaper than gaming tables with dealers."

"I'll head there—"

"*We'll* head there," she immediately corrected.

Matt smiled, nodded and cupped her cheek. "We'll head there as soon as you've finished your morning chores."

"*Gracias*. You don't know what it means to me that you're willing to trust me that it has nothing to do with my parents," she said, and a small smile slipped onto her features.

The pat response would have been to say that he was only doing his job, but in just a few short days Teresa had become much more than that.

"I do know. I know your parents are important to you and I believe them, and you, when you say it has nothing to do with the casino. But if it doesn't—"

"Why are Walker and Hollywood involved with Esquivel?" she finished for him. "I get it."

With a few quick taps on the keyboard, Matt pulled up Walker's mug shot. "You say he doesn't seem familiar."

TERESA LEANED FORWARD and focused on the photo, looking at every aspect of his face. A weasel-like face, narrow with a pointy nose and long chin. Unfamiliar except for the eyes. Crystal-blue eyes, cold as ice.

"His eyes," she said and circled a finger in their general direction. "They seem familiar but the rest of his face… It's too…skinny," she said and motioned to her own face to better explain what she meant.

"If his face was fuller?" He grabbed a drawing tablet and pen from the tabletop and manipulated the image to make Walker's cheeks and jaw broader.

As he did so, something clicked in her brain. "Can you put a full beard on him? Make his hair darker? Longer?"

With the pen, Matt drew in a beard in a darker brown, colored in his hair and lengthened it. When he did so, Teresa gasped. "I think I've seen him. With Esquivel and more than once."

"Where?" Matt asked and saved the photo.

Teresa peered at the image and then screwed her eyes shut, trying to recall. With a shake of her head, she said, "Three or four times at different racetracks. He was working in the stable areas."

"Is it possible he was involved with the doping?" Matt asked.

She nodded. "It's possible. If what I'm remembering is right, he had access to administer the drugs."

"That's probably another reason the racing commission wants to speak to you," Matt said and closed the photo.

"Maybe it's time we spoke to the representative for the commission. Find out what it really is that they want from me," she said and finally took a sip of her coffee.

"I agree. If the racing commission has put Esquivel and Walker together, we'll know it has nothing to do with the casino," Matt said, and she didn't miss the worry in his voice.

"But we won't know what Hollywood has to do with this," she said, aware of the reasons for his concern.

"We won't, but if Hollywood is involved, we will figure out how to protect you," he said, cradling her cheek. He stroked it with his thumb and then dropped it down to lovingly trace the edges of her lips.

That touch, gentle and full of tenderness, reached deep inside, igniting the need for his touch, but also for him. For the man he was, strong and caring.

Leaning forward, she brushed her lips across his and invited him to join her.

A rough breath exploded from him as he said, "This is crazy." But even though he said it, he met her lips with his, accepting her invitation. Driving his hand into her hair to hold her close as they kissed, breaths melding. The kiss deepening as she opened her mouth and tasted him.

Her moan split the air, stunning her with the need in that simple sound.

HER BODY JUMPED beside his and he sensed the surprise there and tempered his kiss.

Shifting away from her, he met her emerald gaze, nearly black with desire, and ran his thumb across her lips, moist from his kisses.

"We need to take this slow."

A sexy and yet also innocent smile slipped onto her lips. “Slow is always better.”

Already hard with passion, he almost forgot his responsibilities, tempted to take her upstairs and show her just how slow and good it could be. But he was a man who recognized duty and honor, and that made him temper his hunger.

“I want you, Teresa. I can’t deny that, but not until I know you’re safe.”

Her smile dimmed but didn’t harden with his words. “I knew you’d say that, and it only proves to me why you’re a special kind of man.”

Special. It had been way too long since he’d felt that way. Not since he was a teen and his mother had been alive. Not since the debacle that had cost him his future as a college football player and had driven him onto an unknown path that had led him here. To her.

“I’ll walk you to your room so I can get back to work,” he said, needing space from her to focus on what was happening on the monitors and also to advise Trey that Teresa had been able to identify Walker.

He rose and held his hand out to her, and she slipped her hand into his. With his free hand he commanded Butter to follow them up to the door of Teresa’s room. At her door, he dropped a quick kiss on her cheek, not trusting himself to do more.

“Get some sleep. We’re going to have a busy day tomorrow.”

“I’ll try. You get some rest also,” she said, brushed a fleeting kiss across his lips and closed her door.

Matt waited there for a heartbeat before hurrying back to the dining room with Butter at his side. He shut the door, needing privacy, and dialed Trey as Butter sat at his feet.

“You finished reviewing the reports?” Trey immediately

asked. The sounds of a television filtered across the line until Roni apparently muted it.

"We did and yes, the locations from the calls are near the casino, but not at it." Matt sat down and pulled up the information again.

"What about the background noises that Sophie and Robbie isolated? It sounded like a slot machine to me," Trey countered, clearly convinced that the attacks on Teresa had more to do with the casino than whatever the racing commission was investigating.

Matt was determined to convince him otherwise. "I agree, but Teresa says there are locations in and around the casino that also have gaming. Plus, after we played around with the mug shot and gave Walker a beard, something clicked with Teresa."

"Meaning?" Trey pressed.

"She thought she saw Finn Walker at a couple of different racetracks. It's possible he was working with Esquivel to dope the horses," Matt explained and then pushed on. "I think we need to talk to the racing commission as soon as possible to see what they want with Teresa."

He heard the muffled sounds of Trey and Roni chatting but couldn't make out what they were saying. A minute later, Trey said, "We can arrange that. Anything else?"

"Once Teresa finishes working the horses in the morning, we're going to check out those locations around the casino," he said.

Muffled voices came again before Trey said, "Roni said to be careful. If Hollywood is involved, it could be very dangerous. We've already reached out to our contacts over at the Organized Crime division to see if they've heard anything."

"Keep me posted."

"Will do. Try to get some rest," Trey said and ended the call.

Matt laid his phone down on the table and focused his attention on the report that had the locations of Esquivel's calls, pinpointing the addresses. Satisfied with the list he compiled, he perused the monitors again. There was no activity, so he rose and called for Butter to follow him with a low whistle.

The shepherd padded beside him as he walked out of the house and toward the stables. Teresa's horses were more than just her business. They were a piece of her heart and he wanted to make sure they were all safe and sound.

In Ay Caramba's stall, the spindly-legged foal was still next to his mother but awake and nursing. The sight brought unexpected joy and peace through him. He pressed on to Frijoles, who was asleep in his stall as were many of the other horses as he made a round of the stables.

Satisfied all was in order, he did a quick stroll around the perimeter of the building, and after, circled the house and walked to the pond. From there the guard at the entrance to the property was visible, doing his own rounds along the road.

Matt watched, waiting until the guard had returned to his vehicle before walking Butter along the edges of the driveway so she could relieve herself for the night.

At the front door, he rubbed her ears and gave her a treat. "You're a good girl."

She jumped up on his shoulders and licked his face before settling down at his feet as he stood on the porch, surveying the property for one last time before going back into the house.

Locking the front door, he unleashed Butter and said, "Stay, girl. Stay. No one comes in without you barking. Got it?"

The dog licked his face again before circling around

and around and lying down across the floor before the front door.

"Good girl," he said once more, left a treat by her nose and then headed to the dining room.

All was peaceful for the moment, but if Hollywood was involved in whatever was going on, that peace wasn't going to last for long.

Because of that, he pulled up all the reports again to review them. Then he searched the internet for anything he could find about the ruthless mobster. Article after article came up about his various crimes, including the possible murder of a casino owner nearly a decade earlier. Despite all the allegations, the police and FBI hadn't been able to secure enough evidence to charge Tony Hollywood with any of the crimes.

Which only made him even more determined to keep Teresa from becoming another of Hollywood's victims. Armed with that determination, he worked through the night to prepare for the next day. Promptly at five as agreed, Sophie came on board so he could get a few hours of sleep.

Softly he tiptoed out of the room and toward the front door.

It was dark in the room, as the sun had yet to come up. Butter was still on guard. As he approached, she rose to her feet and turned in his direction, ready for action.

"Easy, girl," he whispered, and at that, the shepherd dropped to the ground once more.

He tiptoed up the stairs, careful to bypass the third step since he'd noticed that it creaked, and he didn't want to wake Teresa.

At her door he paused. Listened. Nothing.

He was about to keep on going when the door to her room suddenly flew open and Teresa stood there, wearing nothing but an oversize cotton T-shirt.

Chapter Fifteen

She shouldn't have opened the door, but she hadn't really been sleeping. The soft tread of his footsteps had drawn her and now there she was. Now there *he* was.

His hair was rumpled, as if he'd run his hand one too many times through the thick waves. A barely-there smudge beneath his eyes, like charcoal on a drawing, highlighted their intense blue. Lines of tension bracketed his mouth until he saw her, and a soft smile inched across his lips.

"Buenos dias," he said and leaned a forearm on the door-jamb, pulling his polo shirt tight against the hard muscles of his chest.

"*Buenos dias,* although the sun isn't up yet." She flicked a hand in the direction of her window and the darkness outside.

"More reason both of us should get in bed and get some sleep," he said, shifting away from the door.

"Matt," she said and laid a hand on his arm to stop him. "Please don't leave me. I don't want to be alone."

He blew out a tortured breath and drove a hand through his hair. "If I stay, neither of us is going to get much sleep."

She held her hands up in a surrender gesture. "I promise I'll keep my hands to myself."

A wry twist of his lips advised that he either didn't believe her or if he did, he wanted it to be different. But neither kept him from stepping through her door, taking her hand and walking to her bed.

She climbed back in as he toed off his shoes and lay down on her bed as close to the edge as he could.

As she inched next to him, it was impossible to miss the stiffness in his body. She smoothed a hand across his chest. "Relax. You'll never get any sleep if you don't relax."

LIKE HE COULD relax with her luscious curves pressed into his side and the tease of her silky hair along the underside of his jaw. As she shifted to settle even closer to him, the movement roused a flowery scent from the strands. *Jasmine, maybe?*

"You smell good," he murmured.

A carefree laugh burst from her, and she leaned her head on her elbow to gaze at him. "Not horse smell, huh? You never did apologize for that."

"Can't handle the truth?" he teased and urged her head back down against his chest because otherwise he would be too tempted to kiss those smiling lips.

"Mmm," she hummed and soothed her hand across his chest again. "Truth is, I'm not happy about what's happening in my life, but I'm glad it brought us together."

Together. That word ricocheted in his head over and over as he lay there, fighting the urge to kiss her. Fighting the desire to turn and cover her body with his. Slip that thin layer of cotton off her and explore all that smooth, lush skin.

"Relax," she said again, sensing the tension that had escalated with his thoughts.

He inhaled deeply, counted to ten and slowly released his breath, willing his body to soften. Forcing any thoughts of what he wanted to do with her from his brain. Repeating that long inhale in, exhale out, until he finally found some peacefulness.

When a soft snore spilled from her lips, he smiled and finally let slumber claim him.

THE DIM SOUND of Matt's phone alarm warned that he'd be up and about soon.

She heard her door open, and minutes later the whoosh of water through the pipes as he showered.

While some bacon was frying, she slipped bread into the toaster oven and turned it on. Melting butter in a skillet, she beat a few eggs and spilled them into the skillet.

She had just finished scrambling the eggs when Matt came into the kitchen, Butter trailing behind him.

"Buenos dias. Otra vez," she teased, reminding him that they'd already wished each other a good morning.

He sauntered over, laid a hand on her waist and whispered against her lips, "You're a woman of your word."

He kissed her, leaving her no doubt that he wished she'd broken her promise to keep her hands to herself.

She opened her mouth on his, returning his kiss, and letting him know that she wished she'd broken her promise as well.

They drifted apart, breathing heavily. The smell of toast and bacon, and the shrill sound of Matt's phone ringing reminded them that their lives were not their own and passion would have to wait.

Matt whirled from her and answered his phone. After a second, he said, "Let me put you on speaker."

He walked back to her side and held the phone up between them while Butter took a position at his feet, head cocked as if ready to listen as well. "Go ahead, Mia."

"Trey and I called the representative for the racing commission and after explaining what was happening, we convinced them to reschedule the interview. There's just one thing," Mia said.

"What is it?" Teresa asked, wondering what was putting such uncertainty in her friend's voice.

"He's insisting on having the interview in person," Mia explained.

"When will he be able to get here?" Matt asked, clearly worried about any delay.

"Tomorrow. We arranged for him to come to the SBS offices. Is two o'clock good?" Mia asked.

It would interfere with the training she'd had planned for her client's skittish horse, but finding out what the racing commission was investigating could help put an end to the threats to her life and the stables.

"Whatever you need. I'll be there," she said.

"Great. Also, Roni thinks we may have the DNA results today. We'll keep you posted when they come in," Mia said.

Matt and Teresa shared a look and Matt said, "Teresa and I are going to check out those locations around the casino later. We'll let you know what we find out."

"*Gracias*. Be careful out there," Mia said and ended the call.

Matt was about to put away his phone when she laid a wobbly hand on his to stop him. "Do you think the DNA will prove it's Walker?"

"I think so," he said with no hesitation.

Fear tightened her gut and made her hand even shakier against his. She looked down, avoiding Matt's gaze. He dipped his head and put himself in her line of sight, making it impossible for her to avoid his gaze.

"You're worried that it'll be him because of your parents?"

She pursed her lips, afraid to admit it. Afraid that if it was Walker, it meant Hollywood might be involved.

Matt cupped her jaw and gently urged her head upward to meet his gaze directly. "Whatever the DNA says, we will deal with it."

With a curt bob of her head, she said, "Let's eat before it gets cold."

It didn't take a genius to see Teresa was upset, so he didn't press. He followed her into the kitchen, and she spooned out eggs and forked bacon onto the plates. He gingerly plucked the toast from the toaster oven, fingers burning as he placed them on a dish.

He laid the dish on the table between the place settings and returned to the counter to pour himself some coffee and freshen her cup. Grabbing both coffees, he placed them on the table. Then he refilled Butter's water bowl and scooped out food for her.

Butter gobbled down the kibble quickly and looked up at him as if waiting for more. "Are you hungry, girl?" he said and affectionately rubbed her ears. Feeling guilty since she'd spent the night guarding the front door instead of with him as she usually did, he fed her a treat as well.

She followed him to the table and lay down beside him as they sat to eat.

Breakfast was relatively silent, with the barest exchange of words about how good the eggs were and how he liked his bacon crispy. He didn't press, aware of her fears and knowing that talking about it right now would do little to alleviate them.

But he was sure her horses and work would help and the sooner she got to the stables, the quicker she'd feel better. Because of that, he made short work of his meal, and she did as well. Together they cleaned off the table, got everything in the dishwasher and were off to the stables in barely minutes.

When they arrived, Richard and Miranda were with Ay Caramba and her foal.

"How are they doing?" Teresa asked and leaned by the entrance to the stall. He stood just behind her, and Butter slipped to the open area in the doorway, intently watching the two horses, her quirky tongue hanging out of her mouth.

Miranda's broad smile answered them even before she spoke. "Mama and baby are doing great."

Teresa's body visibly shook as relief swept through her. "That's good to hear."

Richard stroked his hand across the foal's flank and grinned. "He's strong like his papa. I feel it in my bones that he's going to be a winner."

Teresa's full-lipped smile was free of worry and her emerald eyes glittered with joy as she said, "I can't wait to see him run."

"What are you going to name him?" Miranda said and strolled over to where they stood.

Teresa's shoulders dipped up and down and then she looked at Matt. "What was your mom's name?"

Brows furrowed, he asked, "Alejandra. Why?"

That full joyous smile came again. "Let's call him Alejandro after Matt's *mami*."

He was touched and cupped her cheek. "You don't have to."

She caressed her hand with his. "I want to. She was very special to you and this foal is very special to me."

Just as Teresa was very special to him. "*Gracias*. I hope Alejandro will make Papa proud."

"Speaking of Papa, he's doing very well all things considered," Miranda said, walking toward Frijoles's stall.

"Is he up for a workout? An easy one?" Teresa asked.

Miranda nodded and rubbed the horse's nose as Frijoles ambled over to the stall door.

"He is, but a very easy workout. *Verdad*, Frijoles?" Miranda crooned and stroked the horse again.

Frijoles tossed his head excitedly, as if understanding her. With a smile, Miranda said, "My work here is done. I will be back tomorrow to check on Ay Caramba and Alejandro."

"Sounds good and thank you for everything," Teresa said and hugged the other woman hard, holding the embrace for a long moment.

"*De nada*, Teresita. I know how important they are to you," the older woman said and shot him a look over Teresa's shoulder, as if to say, *"She's important to me."*

"*Gracias*, Miranda," he said with a slow dip of his head to let the older woman know he understood her concern.

The vet nodded, stepped away from Teresa and walked to where Richard waited by Ay Caramba's stall. Together, Miranda and Richard strolled to the car.

"Can you help me saddle him up?" Teresa asked Matt but didn't wait for his answer to hand him Frijoles's halter.

She opened the stall door and hurried away to the tack room, and he led Frijoles from the stall and into the passageway in the stables.

Teresa returned in no time with a saddle blanket and saddle. She laid the saddle on a nearby bench and placed the blanket high up on the horse's withers. "Let me get the saddle for you," he said.

He handed her the halter and walked over for the saddle, but Richard was already there, lifting it and placing it on the stallion. Once the saddle was firmly cinched, they walked out to the track area, where Teresa saddled up and urged Frijoles into a slow walk.

"They look good," he said, and Richard smiled, but it was a tight, almost brittle smile.

"They do. How are things with the investigation?" the trainer asked and laid his arms across his chest.

Something about the man was suddenly rubbing him wrong. "Moving along. You worried?"

Richard jerked his head toward Matt in surprise. "Me?" he said and tapped a finger on his chest.

Matt nodded slowly. "You. Is there anything you need to tell us?"

Richard blew out a harsh breath and shook his head. "Cops. Always nosing around."

"I'm not a cop. At least not anymore," Matt clarified and narrowed his gaze to examine Richard's face, worried he had misread the man.

Richard looked away and shook his head. When he finally met Matt's gaze again the sadness was evident.

"I had issues. Before Teresa signed me on, I was drinking. Heavily. Lots of rumors about me making mistakes with the horses," the other man said, unshed tears sheening his eyes.

"She trusted you," Matt said, knowing that Teresa's kind heart would have been willing to give Richard a second chance.

"She did, which is why I'd do anything to keep her safe. Get it," Richard said and poked his index finger into Matt's chest. At once, Butter shot to her feet and growled at the man protectively.

"Easy, Butter." Matt signaled the dog to sit with a hand gesture.

Butter whined and held her ground, teeth bared at Richard. "Sit, girl. Sit," Matt commanded, and the dog finally listened.

"I get it and I'll do the same," Matt confirmed with a determined dip of his head.

"Good. If you don't mind—"

"You want to watch the workout," Matt said, and the trainer turned his attention to Teresa as she kicked Frijoles into a slow trot around the track, completing the oval.

As she neared their spot by the rail, Richard gave her a signal and Teresa moved Frijoles into a measured canter, taking him around a few times before pulling up next to them at the rail.

"He feels strong," she said and bent to rub her hand down the horse's shoulders to his chest.

Richard took hold of the reins and stroked the side of the stallion's face. "He does, but let's not push it today. I'll cool him down since I imagine you have things to do," he said and risked a quick look in Matt's direction.

"We do. *Gracias*," she said. She slipped from the horse's back and handed the reins to Richard.

Richard walked Frijoles back to the stables and Matt watched him go, wondering how to raise the issue of the older man's past with Teresa.

"I saw the two of you talking," Teresa said as she took off her riding helmet and let it dangle from her fingertips.

"We were. Richard said you gave him a second chance," he said while they strolled toward the house.

"I did and I wasn't wrong to do it. Richard has been sober for years and has really made a difference around here," she said without hesitation.

"Good to hear." Matt studied her face intently. She had a smudge of dirt on her cheek, and he wiped it away with a finger.

She smiled at the gesture. "*Gracias*. I can get dirty, which is why I'm going to take a quick shower before we head out."

"While you do, I'm going to patrol just to be on the safe side," he said. He had no doubt Sophie and Robbie would have alerted him if they were worried about anything, but he wanted to have his eyes on the property.

She brushed a quick kiss on his lips and rushed away to the house while he headed to the ATV, loaded Butter into the passenger seat and took off to inspect the property.

He wheeled the ATV onto the dirt track that ran between the paddocks, where a number of horses were peacefully grazing. Swinging around to detour around the track, he found everything was quiet as Richard walked Frijoles around the area and then turned him in the direction of the stables.

At the end of the track, he whipped around to run the ATV along the perimeter. But as it had been for the last few days, there was no sign of any activity. A good thing? he wondered. Or were Esquivel and Walker planning something big? Could they even know that the date for the racing commission interview had been moved up?

Because of that, he slowed the ATV for a more thorough examination of the area. Once he reached the front of the house, he detoured to take Butter for a walk around the neighbor's property. There was no new evidence that anyone had been there, maybe because Walker had realized that they'd caught on to his hideout.

Satisfied that nothing was happening at that adjacent property, he loaded Butter back into the ATV and returned to Teresa's home. He walked the shepherd all around the area to make sure everything was secure. He also instructed Butter to find a scent just in case Walker had been in and around the house, but the shepherd didn't get a hit.

A mixture of relief and worry swept through him as it had before, because sometimes the quiet times could be the most dangerous.

He checked the sliders by the back porch. Locked. Walked back to the front door. Also locked.

Good job, Teresa, he thought, and pulled out the key to let himself and Butter inside.

Teresa was just bounding down the stairs, freshly showered and dressed casually in a teal cap-sleeved shirt that hung freely over faded, curve-hugging jeans. Her hair was loose, the shoulder-length strands swinging around her heart-shaped face and stunning eyes. The color of the shirt brought out flecks of a lighter blue-green in those emerald depths.

"You look…amazing," he said and drank in the sight of her.

A faint splash of pink colored her cheeks and a coy smile swept across her lips. *"Gracias."*

He gestured toward the front door. "Ready to go?"

"Ready as I'll ever be," she said, rushing toward the door and out to her car.

At the car, she held the keys up in the air and jingled them almost in his face. "You should probably drive and keep an eye out for more airboats."

He understood why she was making light of the incident. It made it easier to handle the fact that someone was trying to silence her. He swiped the keys from her hand and said, "I sent you the casino sound Sophie and Robbie isolated. I was hoping it would ring a bell with you. No pun intended."

"Not intended, but still a good pun," she said and hopped into her SUV.

He harnessed Butter into the back seat and climbed into her car.

Teresa was fiddling with her phone as he whipped down the driveway. At the entrance, he waved at the guard positioned there and pulled onto the road for the drive to her parents' casino.

Barely a minute later, the sound of a fake spin was followed by a few electronic tones, another louder whir and then coins dropping into a bucket.

"Totally a slot machine," Teresa said and tapped her phone again to repeat the sound.

He couldn't disagree. "We'll head to the first location we

identified with the call detail records and see if there are any slot machines with that same sound."

"What if…what if we can't find it?" Teresa said and nervously shifted the phone back and forth in her hands.

He reached out with one hand and laid it over hers, calming that restless motion. "Let's take this one step at a time."

She forced a smile, but then worried her lower lip with her teeth in a telling gesture. He tightened his hold on her hand, offering a reassuring squeeze while he continued to drive.

Shaking off his hand, she tapped her phone to play the casino sound again and again, as if trying to memorize it. He didn't interfere, using her actions to also store the sound in his mind in the hopes they could identify where Esquivel had been when he'd made the call. Hoping that if they could, maybe someone at the casino would remember seeing Teresa's old trainer and help them track him down.

Thirty minutes later, he pulled into the parking lot at her parents' casino, avoiding Teresa's reserved spot again in favor of one close to the exit so they could easily walk across to the locations pinpointed by the SBS cell phone data analysis. While they walked across together, Butter close to his side, he kept vigilant for anything out of the ordinary.

Nothing. Again. He blew out a relieved sigh and hoped it wouldn't be short-lived.

TERESA GLANCED AT Matt from the corner of her eye. "Everything okay?"

He wrapped an arm around her shoulders and drew her closer. "Everything is okay. Just trying make sure you'll be safe here."

Teresa nodded and they crossed the street and pushed through the door of the small arcade that housed a number of slot machines and electronic gambling games.

Ambling through the space, Teresa focused on the noises

bursting from the various machines. Besides the fake spinning sounds, a variety of musical tones and beeps signaled wins, but after at least half an hour of strolling around and stopping at a few machines, they hadn't gotten a solid hit.

"Time to head next door," Matt said, and with a nod, Teresa followed him to a slightly larger gaming arcade beside a small hotel that seemed to catch Matt's eye since he stopped to look at it.

"What is it?" she asked.

Matt dipped his chin in the direction of the hotel. "We don't have any hits from there, but...it's the kind of place you'd use for a 'quick stay,'" he said, emphasizing his words with air quotes.

"Do you think we should check it out?" she asked, and he nodded.

"Maybe later. Let's take a look around this place first since we got a hit here." He gestured with his hand toward the gaming arcade.

As they entered the building, Teresa wrinkled her nose from the stale smell of old cigarette smoke that lingered in the space. Much like at the earlier location, there was an assortment of electronic gambling machines spewing out a cacophony of noises into the air.

They circled around, listening carefully, working the perimeter first. As they neared a side exit door into a common space between the arcade and the hotel, a sound caught her attention.

She laid a hand on Matt's arm to slow him and Butter. "I think I heard something."

Closing her eyes, she focused on the sound, and it came again from the left. She opened her eyes and pointed in the direction of a row of slot machines. "I think it's coming from there," she said and took off toward those slots.

An older man sat on a stool before one, pushing buttons to make the bet. With another push, lights flashed and the reels in the machine went around and around. Lemons, bars, cherries and assorted fruits spun until they came to an abrupt halt. The man did an excited little jump as the machine started playing music and the electronic sound of coins falling resonated in the space.

"That's it. That's the sound," Teresa said excitedly.

The gambler turned to face them, clapped his hands and with a broad smile said, "That's the sound of money, honey."

"It sure is. Do you mind if we watch while you gamble some more?" she asked, well aware from visits to her parents' casinos how superstitious gamblers could be.

"You're my lucky charm. Stay as long as you like," he said. After a few more spins, the sound came again, announcing that he'd won.

This time Matt had his phone ready and recorded the sound. When he was done, he said, "I'm going to send this to Sophie and Robbie to confirm it's the same sound."

While Teresa understood, she had no doubt this was the same sound from the background of Esquivel's call. Looking around the space, she said, "He was here when he called. And this machine is right near the side exit to the hotel."

"Which means he could have been making a quick escape to that hotel," Matt said and started walking toward the exit, but as he neared it, Butter pawed the ground in a motion that was now familiar to Teresa.

Butter had found Walker's scent.

Chapter Sixteen

"This is so not good. Stay close," Matt said, sweeping his arm around to tuck Teresa behind him.

"Find it, Butter," he said and let the leash have some slack for the shepherd to nose around and stay on the scent.

Head down, sniffing, Butter tracked the smell through the small courtyard separating the two buildings. Near the entrance to the hotel, Butter detoured to a side stairway. After pausing there for a few seconds, she bounded up the stairs, Matt and Teresa almost running to keep pace with her. Two flights later, the dog went up half a flight, but then doubled back, nearly knocking over Matt and Teresa in her haste to return to the floor below.

They rounded the corner and Butter started barking, nearly ripping the leash from Matt's hands.

Matt looked down the balcony connecting the rooms and caught sight of a man moving quickly away from the open doorway of one of the rooms. He wore a Dolphins ball cap and had his head tucked down into the collar of a dark blue windbreaker. His hands were also jammed into the pockets. As Butter continued barking, the man shot a quick look in their direction.

It was Walker.

"Stay here," Matt said to Teresa and raced after the man,

giving chase along the balconies. Butter kept pace with him, straining at the leash and barking.

At the end of the one balcony, Walker flew down the stairs, taking the steps two or three at a time until he reached the ground floor and turned the corner of the staircase.

Matt did the same, Butter jumping down the steps with him, but he lost sight of Walker after he made the turn. But Butter still had his scent and tracked him across the street and into a nearby supermarket.

"Mister, no dogs. Only service dogs," said a burly security guard and blocked Matt's way as he entered.

Matt pulled out an ID. "I'm with SBS. We're tracking a suspect."

The man flashed a quick look at the ID and stepped aside, hands raised in apology. "Sorry, dude."

"Find it," Matt said, and Butter was immediately on the scent again, rushing down the produce aisle and toward the back of the store. At the end of the row, someone had overturned a cart with produce and a clerk kneeled nearby, trying to clean up the mess.

Butter hurtled over the mess and Matt followed. No sign of Walker anywhere but Butter, still in pursuit of him, almost dragged Matt to the far end of the store.

When they reached a door marked Employees Only, Butter pulled away and began pacing back and forth nervously.

"Sit, Butter," he commanded. As he neared the door, he realized why Butter had hesitated. Someone had spilled bleach all along the entrance to the area.

He shoved the door open, and the smell was even stronger in the short hallway. A wet trail of bleach shimmered beneath the overhead lights down the length of the hall.

It was a risk to let Butter walk in the bleach and possibly burn her paws and he worried she'd be unable to pick up the scent again after the smell of the chemicals.

Muttering a curse, he walked back to his shepherd, bent and rubbed her ears, breathing heavily from the run. "You did good, girl. You did good."

Rising, he walked back toward the front door, intending to ask the guard for any security tapes, but as he reached the man, Matt's cell phone started ringing.

Teresa. He answered immediately.

"You've got to get back here, Matt. It's Esquivel. He's been stabbed."

TERESA HUGGED HER arms around herself as the EMTs raised the gurney and rolled it out of the hotel room. The police officer beside her—an Officer Lazlo—said, "Can you tell us again why you were here, Ms. Rodriguez?"

She told herself not to worry that he was looking at her like a suspect, and again repeated what she had told them earlier. "As I said, SBS Agent Matt Perez and I were trying to find Esquivel's location. Agent Perez's K-9 partner picked up a scent—"

"For Esquivel?" the officer said, pen poised over his notebook.

Teresa shook her head vehemently, sending strands of hair shifting against her face. "No, for Finn Walker. SBS and the police think he's responsible for a number of attacks against me and my stables. When Agent Perez and I got to this floor, Walker was running away from this room."

The officer looked away from her and down the hall, drawing her attention in that direction.

Matt was hurrying back with Butter.

"I assume this is Agent Perez and his K-9," Officer Lazlo said with a sharp arch of a brow.

"It is," she said just as Matt joined them.

"SBS Agent Matt Perez." Matt held out his hand to the officer.

The officer shifted pen and pad to one hand and shook Matt's before resuming his questioning. "This young lady…" The officer paused to glance at his pad for the information. "Teresa Rodriguez. Any relation to the casino—"

"Yes, they're my parents but that has nothing to do with this," she said, wishing that the subject of her family and their business wouldn't come up as often as it did.

The officer held his hands up as if in apology and continued, "She says you were here investigating?"

"We were. Our suspect is Finn Walker and we saw him leaving this room a short time ago. I gave chase, but he got away."

"Can you positively identify him?" the officer asked.

"I can. I've also asked the security guard at the supermarket to provide us with the video feeds from their security cameras. They should show Walker running into and out of the supermarket," Matt explained.

"We'll ask for a copy of that security footage as well. Wouldn't want any chain of evidence issues. Officer Perez, wasn't it?" Officer Lazlo said and narrowed his gaze as he examined Matt's face.

"Formerly Officer Perez with the K-9 division. You can also call Trey Gonzalez at SBS for any additional information you may need," Matt said.

At the mention of Trey, the officer's eyes widened. "Detective Gonzalez from Miami Beach PD?"

Matt dipped his head to confirm it. "Retired from the PD now, but one and the same."

The officer closed his pad and tucked the pen into his breast pocket. "I will reach out, Agent Perez. In the meantime, my partner went with the victim to try to get more information from him in case…"

Teresa didn't need him to finish to understand. *In case Esquivel didn't make it.*

"We should get to the hospital as well to find out what we can," Matt said and laid a possessive arm at the small of her back.

Bending his head close, he said, "Are you ready to go?"

She nodded and as they walked away, Matt said, "What happened?"

Teresa sucked in a breath, fighting back the fear that hit her again as she remembered the scene she had walked into just a short time earlier.

Sensing her upset, he stroked a comforting hand up and down her back, giving her the strength to speak.

"When I got to the door of the hotel room, I heard a groan. The door was ajar, and I pushed it open. Esquivel was lying there in a pool of blood. I ran to the bathroom to get some towels and applied pressure to the wounds while I called 911."

"Was Esquivel conscious? Did he say anything?" Matt asked as they crossed the street and returned to her SUV.

"He said Walker's name and that he was sorry. Not much else." She shivered as the memories assailed her. "There was so much blood, Matt. So much."

Matt slipped his hand to her waist, grasped it and turned her into his embrace. "I'm sorry you had to see that."

Battling back tears, she said, "What if he dies? No one deserves that, not even Esquivel."

"Let's pray that he doesn't and can answer some questions for us, including why Walker is willing to kill to keep him silent."

A ROUGH SHUDDER wracked Teresa's body at his words, making him sorry he'd uttered them and reminded her that Walker was out to kill her as well.

"I'm sorry, Teresa. That was thoughtless," he said and

continued to hold her until the tension fled her body and she stepped back, wiping away the trails of tears from her face.

"I'm okay. I can handle this," she said and nodded decidedly, as if trying to convince herself of that.

"You already did. If you hadn't acted as fast as you did, Esquivel would have probably died in that hotel room." He walked her over to the passenger side of her SUV.

She hopped up into the SUV and he hurried around to the driver's side, loaded in Butter, got in and quickly maneuvered out of the spot and out of the parking garage.

A tense silence filled the vehicle. As Matt peered at Teresa, he noticed that she was rubbing her hands across her thighs and rocking back and forth slightly in her seat. He reached out and slipped his hand over hers. Twined his fingers with hers and offered her a tender smile.

She smiled back, but it was strained, and tightened her fingers on his. "I'm okay."

"You are," he said, certainty in his tone as he deftly drove one-handed through the streets of Miami and to the medical center where Esquivel had been taken. It took a few spins around the parking lot before he found an empty spot, and barely minutes later, they were in the emergency room.

Together they strode to the desk and Matt pulled out his SBS ID. "Here to see Warner Esquivel. He was just brought in by Miami PD."

The nurse pursed her lips and eyed him but must have decided he wouldn't go away without an answer. She faced her computer, tapped a few keys and then ran her finger across the monitor.

"They've stabilized him, and he should be on his way to surgery shortly. You can wait here. If you need any additional information…" She paused and pointed in the direction of the Miami PD officer who had exited the ER exam room. "You can ask her and unless that's a service dog—"

"It's my K-9 partner," he said and pivoted in the direction of the officer who walked their way as she noticed them by the desk.

"Agent Perez," she said with a respectful dip of her head.

Matt smiled and copied her gesture, offering a friendly nod in greeting. "Officer Vega. Ms. Rodriguez and I are here for Mr. Esquivel."

Vega looked from him to Teresa. "Multiple stab wounds to the abdomen area including a knife wound to his liver and gall bladder. They've taken him to surgery to repair the damage."

Matt handed her his business card. "Teresa and I are going to wait here and would appreciate you keeping us apprised of any developments."

"There's no need for you to be here," the officer said, and her gaze skittered from him to Teresa once again.

"I'd feel better if… I were here in case he… I need to know he's going to be fine," Teresa said, her words broken and stilted.

He laid a hand on her back. "Esquivel used to work for Teresa," he explained.

The officer's eyes narrowed, keenly assessing Teresa. Seemingly satisfied with his explanation, she tapped his card against her notepad and said, "I'll need to check with my superiors about giving you updates."

"I understand, Officer Vega. Any information would be of assistance," he said, and the young officer walked away.

But as she headed to the entrance to the ER where the police car with her partner had just pulled up, Trey marched through the door and joined them in the waiting room.

Trey stroked a hand down Teresa's arm. "Are you okay?"

AM I OKAY? she wondered and looked away toward the exam rooms. With a shrug, she said, "As well as can be expected."

Trey offered her a sympathetic smile and skimmed his hand down her arm again. "Esquivel owes you his life. Hopefully once he's conscious he'll realize that and help us with this investigation."

She tilted her chin up a determined inch. "And if he doesn't survive?"

"Let's hope that's not the outcome," Trey said.

Matt blew out a disgusted sigh. "Not much of a plan."

Trey nailed him with his gaze. "You're right. It's not. But I've got Sophie and Robbie working on the security feeds from the supermarket. Hopefully they will help identify Walker and once we get the DNA results later, it'll be enough for the district attorney to get a judge to issue an arrest warrant."

Trey gripped Matt's shoulder and squeezed as if to reassure him. "This has been a rough few days. Why don't you take the rest of the day off and go get some rest."

Matt glanced at her from the corner of his eye, and she shook her head.

"We'll just stay a little longer if you don't mind," Matt said, understanding that Teresa needed to be here more than she needed rest.

With a toss of his hands, Trey said, "I guess we wait."

"No need for you to stay," Matt said, but Trey was insistent.

"I want to talk to Esquivel as much as you and the police do. Let's head to the surgical waiting room," Trey suggested, and they walked out of the ER and made their way to the waiting area.

Trey plopped into one of the cushioned chairs and the fake plastic leather groaned with his weight.

Matt slipped an arm around her waist and guided her to a small sofa next to Trey's chair.

She gingerly eased onto the sofa. Matt took the spot beside her and laid his arm across her shoulders.

The movement didn't go unnoticed by Trey, but he said nothing. She was grateful for that. What she was unexpectedly feeling for Matt was all caught up in the maelstrom of emotions surrounding the attacks and what had happened barely an hour earlier.

In her mind's eye she could still picture Esquivel lying there in a pool of blood. Him begging her as he'd seen her and realized the woman he was trying to kill might be his only salvation.

For a hot second she had been tempted to do nothing. To just let him die in the hope that the threat would die with him. But she couldn't and not just because she wanted to know why Esquivel wanted her dead.

She just couldn't let another human being die.

Matt must have sensed her upset since he rubbed her shoulder and drew her closer. "You've got to stop thinking about it."

Maybe in his world that was how you learned to deal with things. You acted when needed and then you stopped thinking about it. But as she met Matt's caring blue gaze, it was clear he was thinking about it. About her and all that had happened.

She offered him a tender smile and cupped his jaw. *"Gracias."*

His brow furrowed and his gaze narrowed in puzzlement. "For what?"

"For understanding. For having my back."

"Always. I'll always have your back," Matt said. Relief swamped her and when he pulled her closer, she nestled into his side.

Trey eyeballed the gesture once again and his lips thinned

with worry. Because she didn't want to cause any problems for Matt at work, she straightened slightly and created a little space from him.

MATT GAZED AT Teresa as she put some distance between them. Puzzled, he looked upward, and realizing Trey's interest, he moved his arm away, clasped his hands and hung them between his legs. Needing to dispel the nervous energy in his system, he bounced his legs up and down, mentally counting down the long minutes until a doctor walked out of the staff area.

The doctor wore pale blue scrubs and appeared to be in his early thirties, with short-cropped, black hair. Handsome if those preppy-looking types were your thing.

They rose and the doctor approached, his hazel-eyed gaze guarded beneath a furrowed brow. "I'm Dr. Halston. I'm the surgeon who operated on Mr. Esquivel. Are you here for him?"

"We are. South Beach Security Agents Gonzalez and Perez," Matt said and then gestured to Teresa. "Ms. Rodriguez was a former employer."

The doctor's eyebrows flew upward. "No family?"

Matt glanced at Trey, who said, "Police are trying to track down his daughter. For now, we're here since Mr. Esquivel is involved in a case we're investigating. How is he?"

The doctor hesitated, clearly worried about the breach in normal protocols, but then, with a slow tilt of his head he said, "Mr. Esquivel came through the surgery but there was substantial damage to several internal organs. He's unconscious right now and should survive, although his recovery will be slow."

Matt nodded. "When can we speak to him?"

A weary shrug lifted the doctor's shoulders before he

said, “He may be unconscious for hours, but unless you’re family, hospital policy won’t permit you to visit.”

Frustrated, Matt ran a hand through his hair and said, “Esquivel is involved in several attacks against Ms. Rodriguez. We need to speak to him about those attacks.”

The doctor tossed his hands up in the air. “And I need to follow hospital policy. I’ve already told you too much as it is. If you need anything else, contact the hospital administrator or better yet, have Miami PD interview Mr. Esquivel.”

“We had planned to do just that. In the interim, you should know that the man who stabbed Mr. Esquivel is armed and dangerous and may try to finish the job. You should arrange for extra protection for your patient,” Trey said and jerked his head in the direction of the elevators.

Matt took the hint and laid his hand against Teresa’s back to urge her there, and Trey followed them. At the elevator, Trey pushed the button and said, “We’ll ask the PD to work with us to interview Esquivel and put a uniform at his door but that may take some time.”

As they boarded the elevator, Trey’s phone rang, and he answered. He listened quietly, a grim look on his face that slowly relaxed as his lips tipped up in a smile. “That’s good news, Roni. I’ll let them know.”

He ended the call and faced them. “The PD’s DNA results are in and confirm Walker was the one who shot at you. Sophie and Robbie have been able to do screen grabs from the video that show a man who looks like Walker in the supermarket.”

“That should be enough to secure an arrest warrant,” Matt said as the elevator stopped, and they walked out into the hospital lobby.

“Combined with your testimony it should be. The detectives on the case have finished processing the scene and have asked that you meet them at headquarters so they can interview you," Trey said.

Against his hand, Teresa's body was shaking badly despite the brave face she had put on so far. It hurt his heart to know she was hurting so badly and that he could do so little right now to make her feel better. So he did the only thing he could think to do.

Chapter Seventeen

"I think it's time Teresa went home and got some rest," Matt said, ignoring his boss's request.

Teresa's body trembled with fatigue and nervousness despite Trey's good news about the DNA and video evidence. With a bob of her head, she said, "No, that's okay. I'll go. Anything that will help end this nightmare."

"Detectives Mattson and Cross will be waiting for you. I think you know them, Matt," Trey said with a sharp look in Matt's direction.

"I do. They're good guys, Teresa." He took hold of her hand and twined his fingers with hers.

"I guess we should go," she said, and after bidding goodbye to Trey, they walked out to their car and made the half-hour drive along Miami streets to police headquarters.

Matt parked and they hurried across the brick-and-cement paths in the plaza in front of the building, a low-rise modern structure with dark red columns and mirrored tile. A multistory, rounded tower with more mirrored tile sat like a guard to the left of the entrance with its floor-to-ceiling glass. They pushed through the entrance and to the receptionist desk where Matt asked for the two detectives.

"I'll let them know you're here. Have a seat," the receptionist said but Teresa was too anxious to sit. Instead, they walked to one side of the waiting area and stood by the windows.

"Relax," Matt said as she wrapped her arms around herself and looked away from the waiting room filled with people and out to the plaza area. A white police car emblazoned with green and gold stripes and the police department emblem in gold pulled up in front of the building and parked. Two uniformed officers exited the car, and she recognized them as the officers who had interviewed them earlier.

It was Officer Vega who saw them standing by the windows and walked over as soon as she entered the headquarters.

"I assume you're here to see the detectives?" she asked and when Teresa nodded, she added, "We're headed there as well and can take you."

She and Matt followed the officers, clearing security and riding up to the floor where two detectives were waiting for them. The first detective, an older gentleman, introduced himself. "Detective Dante Mattson. This is my partner, Detective Alicia Cross." He gestured to the younger blonde woman next to him.

"Good to see you again, Perez. Private life seems to agree with you," Detective Cross said with a too friendly smile.

Jealously flared through Teresa and she thrust her hand out. "Nice to meet you. Teresa Rodriguez."

Cross's upturned smile dimmed a bit, and she shook Teresa's hand, not that she had much choice since she'd almost stuck it in the detective's face.

"If you don't mind, we'd like to get your statements on today's incident," Mattson said, a kindly look on the warm brown skin of his face. He motioned them toward a nearby interview room with a sweep of his arm.

Teresa hurried to that room, Matt and the two detectives

close behind her. When she sat, Matt took a spot beside her while the detectives positioned themselves across the way.

She told herself it wasn't "us" against "them" since there was no doubt that she and Matt had nothing to do with Esquivel's stabbing, but somehow it felt that way to her. As Matt twined his fingers with hers and tenderly squeezed, it was almost as if he was reading her mind and trying to quiet her unease.

Detective Mattson spoke first, his voice deep and soothing as if he, too, sensed her anxiety. "We understand there have been a series of incidents directed at you and your business."

"It's why I reached out to SBS," she admitted and glanced at Matt from the corner of her eye.

"And you believe Mr. Esquivel is behind these attacks?" Cross said, her probing gaze drifting between her and Matt.

"Mr. Esquivel and a Finn Walker. I believe you have DNA evidence and a partial print that connects him to the case," Matt clarified.

Mattson and Cross shared a quick, almost disbelieving, look before Cross said, "And this Walker is the individual you saw leaving Esquivel's hotel room?"

Teresa quickly nodded. "Butter—Matt's dog—picked up Walker's scent in the courtyard between the casino and the hotel. We followed Butter and as we reached the second floor, we saw a man walking out of the room. It looked like Walker."

Matt jumped in with, "Butter signaled he was the source of the scent. Butter and I gave chase."

An uneasy silence followed, and Mattson skewered her with his gaze before flipping through his notepad. When he stopped on a page, he paused as if to read it and then said, "When Mr. Perez was chasing the unsub—"

"Unsub?" Teresa asked, not understanding the term.

Matt gently squeezed her hand and said, "Unknown subject, only we know who he is." Matt glared at Mattson and said, "It's Finn Walker. I'm certain you'll be able to pull fingerprints and DNA from whatever was used to stab Esquivel."

"No weapon was found at the location. Where was Esquivel when you entered the room, Ms. Rodriguez?" Mattson said and scrutinized her again, his voice now direct and almost accusing.

Her heart stopped beating for a long second before it started hammering furiously and so loudly she almost didn't hear the detective as he pressed her for an answer. "Ms. Rodriguez?"

"You can't possibly be suggesting that Teresa—"

Cross jumped to her feet and jabbed her finger in the direction of the door. "Mr. Perez. Maybe it's better that you step outside while we speak to Ms. Rodriguez."

Her tone made it clear that it wasn't a suggestion.

Matt slowly rose, but then leaned close and whispered in her ear, "You can do this."

Teresa met his gaze, offered him a strained smile and nodded. "I'll be okay."

With that, Matt left the room and the questioning continued.

"Where was Esquivel when you entered the room?" Mattson repeated.

Teresa splayed her hands on the table, inhaled slowly and then answered. "He was on the floor and there was a lot of blood. I got some towels and tried to do what I could to stop the bleeding. Then I called 911."

Cross leaned forward, closing the distance between them, and challenged, "You helped Esquivel even though you thought he was behind the attacks against you?"

Teresa held her hands up in a "you're kidding" gesture

and parried with, "If you found an…unsub…who was injured, wouldn't you help them even though you thought they'd committed a crime?"

That seemed to set Cross back, since the other woman sank into her chair and said, "Are you willing to provide us with a DNA swab and fingerprints?"

"I have nothing to hide. I did not stab Warner Esquivel," she said with total conviction.

"Great. I'll go get the swab kit and fingerprint scanner." Cross shot to her feet and left the room.

MATT WAS PACING outside the interview room when Detective Cross came storming out and nearly tripped over Butter, who was sitting by the door to the room.

He reached for her arm and stopped her. "You can't possibly think that Teresa had anything to do with Esquivel's stabbing."

Cross glared at his hand, and he shifted away and held his hands up in apology. "Sorry, Alicia."

The apology softened her attitude, but only slightly. "As a former officer, you of all people should know we have to investigate every lead," Cross said.

"Teresa is the victim here. Esquivel is involved in the attacks against her," Matt urged, hands held out in pleading.

"Which gives her a motive to hurt him. She had the opportunity as well since you were off chasing Walker," Cross pointed out and continued, "You might remember that from when you were a cop. We have to investigate every possibility."

She didn't wait for Matt's reply, hurrying down the hall and leaving Matt to pace back and forth again until she returned with a swab kit and fingerprint scanner. With an angry glare in his direction, Cross swept past him and, avoiding Butter who stood by the door, pushed into the room.

It seemed like hours before Teresa exited the room, pale and shaken, followed by the detectives.

He wrapped an arm around her waist and pulled her close to him. Her body trembled against his and he tried to soothe her. "They just have to investigate every angle."

"I know," she said but her voice lacked conviction.

"Let's head home. Check on Alejandro and his mama," he said and her body visibly relaxed.

"That sounds like heaven." She smiled, only this time the smile reached up into her eyes, turning them a deep green.

"I'm glad it does. Come, Butter," he said, and the dog rushed to Teresa's side as if aware she needed the support.

"Good girl," Teresa said and rubbed the top of her head.

Normally Matt wouldn't want someone petting his K-9 partner, but he suspected Teresa might be a more permanent part of his life in the future. If she was, bonding with Butter would be a good thing.

With that thought, he hurried them out of police headquarters and to Teresa's SUV. As a precaution, he had Butter check the area around the vehicle, but she didn't pick up on any scent. He hadn't thought Walker would be so bold as to come near police headquarters what with all the CCTVs in the area, but he wasn't willing to take any chances.

Once they were in the car and driving to the stables, Teresa said, "Why do you think Walker tried to kill Esquivel?"

That question had been bouncing around in Matt's head since he'd lost Walker in the supermarket and returned to find that Esquivel had been attacked. But all the answers were troubling and would only worry Teresa.

"I really don't know," he said with a reluctant shrug.

Teresa hesitated for a long second. "You do know but you won't say. I can handle it, Matt."

He blew out a harsh breath and shook his head. "I'm sorry. I just don't want to worry you," he admitted.

"Because you think Hollywood sent Walker to tie up loose ends?" she said, voicing his worst fears.

With a nod, he said, "If Hollywood is behind this—"

"It's the worst possible scenario. No one crosses a mobster like Hollywood," she said and inhaled shakily.

"That's true, only… Walker has been careless. Once Mattson and Cross look at all the evidence, there's no doubt Walker is their prime suspect in all of these attacks but that would lead them straight to Hollywood," he mused out loud.

"And Hollywood wouldn't like that kind of attention."

Matt smiled at how quickly she got it. "No, he wouldn't since it might affect his business to have the cops poking around."

"Will the cops poke around?" she asked and peered at him intently.

He did a quick lift of his shoulders. "They should. Maybe once they've exhausted all other leads."

"Which could take a while." She sighed in disapproval.

"Unless we get to it first. I'll call Trey later and see what Roni and he think about talking to Hollywood," Matt said and pulled off the highway to drive the last few miles to the stables.

Brow furrowed, Teresa said, "Do you really think SBS would do that? Do an end run around the police?"

Matt vigorously shook his head. "Not an end run, but the Gonzalez name carries a lot of weight with the PD and Roni is a respected detective. If anyone can get them to move faster, it's the two of them."

TERESA DIDN'T DOUBT the influence of the Gonzalez family. Besides her friendship with Mia, it was one of the reasons she had reached out to them.

"I can't say enough how much I appreciate all that you're doing for me," she said, grateful for SBS and for Matt.

He took hold of her hand. "It's what we do, and as bad as this all is—" he looked away from the road to gaze at her, adoration in his eyes "—I'm glad it's brought us together."

She offered him a shy smile. "I'm glad as well."

He ripped his gaze from her, and they finished the remainder of the drive in silence. As Matt pulled into the driveway, he paused to check with the guard at the front gate. The SBS agent hopped out of his SUV and walked over to the driver's side.

"All good?" Matt asked.

"All's quiet. Nothing unusual. Night-time guard should be here in about an hour to take over," the man said, tapped his hand on the edge of Matt's window and walked back to his SUV to resume his duties.

"Sounds good. Keep us posted," Matt said and drove down to park in front of her house.

He turned in the driver's seat to face her. "It's almost dinnertime, but I assume you want to check in on your horses."

She grinned, feeling much better now that she was home, and he was with her. "I would."

"Let me just text Sophie and Robbie to arrange for them to monitor." He quickly texted and then said, "Let's go."

They hurried to the stables entrance and went straight to Ay Caramba's stall. Joy filled her heart at the sight of the foal nursing from his mother.

"Alejandro looks good," Matt said and sidled up to stand beside her, his hand at her back, stroking tenderly.

"He does. It's such a relief," she admitted. If Alejandro was as strong a stallion as Frijoles, it would help build her stable's reputation for breeding winners.

"Let's see how Frijoles is doing," she said and they ambled over to the next stall, where Frijoles stood sedately until he noticed them and pranced over to the stall.

"*Hola*, Frijoles. How is *Papi* doing?" she murmured and stroked his face.

The horse snorted and tossed his head, almost as if he were answering. "Yes, you're a good daddy."

"And looking well," Matt said from beside her.

"Looking great. Maybe I'll be able to do a full workout with him tomorrow." She strolled away from him to inspect the rest of the stalls and horses.

Everything was in order until they turned the corner and Luis was suddenly there, pitchfork in hand. He lowered the weapon as he realized who it was.

"*Perdóname*. I heard someone in the stables and wanted to make sure the horses were safe," he said in Spanish.

"*Está bien*, Luis. Everything is okay here," she said, and with a nod, Luis walked back toward the nearby bunkhouse, pitchfork still in hand.

"He's very loyal and responsible," Matt said, and she detected the question in his tone.

"I helped him get a visa so he would be able to stay in the country. We're working on getting him a green card next," she explained. They walked toward the house, stopping halfway to allow Butter to relieve herself.

"That's very caring of you, what you're doing for Luis," he said and paused by the door to the house, searching out her features in the growing dark of dusk.

She gestured to herself. "I know how fortunate my family is to be in America. The kind of freedom we wouldn't have in Cuba. Neither would Luis in his country."

MATT UNDERSTOOD. It was why his grandparents had left Mexico. "I get it, Teresa. My family's story isn't much different."

She smiled, only there was sadness there as she said,

"Except I'm sure you've been back to Mexico. It's not the same for Cubans."

"I know that. Trey and I have talked about how hard it is with all the travel issues with both governments."

Teresa blew out a rough breath and unlocked her door. "You can't even imagine. Besides, as hard as it was for my grandparents and parents to leave Cuba, why would they want to go back to a country that isn't free?"

"It wouldn't make sense," he agreed as they walked into the kitchen together. Teresa went to the fridge while he took care of feeding Butter and giving her fresh water.

When he finished, he headed to the counter to stand by Teresa, who had hauled out some hamburger meat from the fridge and was forming it into nice-sized patties.

"Can I help?"

She jerked her head in the direction of the refrigerator. "I've got some potato and macaroni salads in there if you like."

"I like," he said and went to the fridge to take out the salads. He also snagged a string cheese to give as a treat to Butter after the exceptional day she'd put in.

He peeled off the wrapper and fed it to the dog, then placed the salads on the table and then set it.

The smell of beef panbroiling in a skillet soon filled the kitchen, making his stomach growl.

Teresa, spatula in hand, looked over her shoulder at him and smiled. "Hungry?"

Walking over to her, he wrapped an arm around her waist and jostled her playfully. "Starving. I like my burger medium if that's okay. Cheese, please."

"Me, too. Rolls are in that bread box at the end of the counter. I've got sliced cheddar in the fridge."

He dropped a kiss on her temple, grabbed the bag with the rolls from the bread box and got the cheese to hand it to her. He also pulled out mayo, ketchup and mustard and laid them on the table along with the rolls.

Barely a minute later, Teresa came over with the skillet and he scrambled to put the rolls on their plates so she could dish out the burgers.

"Looks delicious. *Gracias*," he said, hugged her and kissed her cheek.

They sat and the meal was silent as hunger drove them to make short work of the burgers and salads.

Matt's stomach was pleasantly full, and he leaned back in his chair to rub it playfully. "That was so good."

Teresa mimicked his actions, grinned and patted her belly. "Very good. How about some coffee and flan for dessert?"

"I won't say no." But as he grabbed his plate and stood, his cell phone chirped.

Sophie calling, which worried him.

As he answered, she said, "A white Jeep is barreling down the drive and it's not ours. Our guard isn't giving chase."

Matt pointed an index finger at Teresa and said, "Please stay here."

"What's wrong?"

Matt signaled to Butter, who immediately came to his side. But Teresa ignored his request and rushed to him.

"What's wrong?" she asked again.

"Trespasser in an SUV. Please listen and stay inside," he said and raced out the door.

Chapter Eighteen

Matt bolted out of the house, Butter loping alongside him, and despite his instructions, Teresa wasn't going to just stand there, especially as a bottle crashed against the corner of the house and a wall of flames erupted across the vinyl siding.

She grabbed a hose, but Matt shouted, "Not water. Get an extinguisher."

A second later he was firing at the Jeep, but the 4x4 did a sharp turn, dipping up onto two wheels for a moment before racing back in the direction of the entrance. As Matt and Butter chased after it, she ran to the kitchen and grabbed a fire extinguisher from beneath the sink. She sprinted outside to tackle the flames licking against the house.

Directing the nozzle at the fire, she squeezed the handle and powder spewed out of the extinguisher. It knocked down the flames closest to the house, but the spray barely lasted a minute. As it ended, she threw the empty canister aside and started kicking up the dirt from the landscaping to tame the last of the fire.

Matt and Luis joined her a minute later and between the three of them they were able to tamp down the last of the flames.

"You okay?" Matt asked and took hold of her hands while Butter sidled up to her side, in protective mode again.

She nodded and rubbed Butter's head. "I am. What happened?"

"I don't know. Let me go check with the guard. Stay, Butter," he said and ran up the driveway to the SUV positioned at the entrance.

Teresa hung back, kicking dirt and stomping the ground where the fire had been to make sure it was well and truly out while Butter sniffed around the edges of the landscaping. Luis nudged loose soil all around the corner of the house where the vinyl siding had melted slightly from the intense flames.

"The fire is out," Luis said and jammed his hands on his hips as he examined the area and bent to check the siding.

"We're good. *Gracias*, Luis," she said and stepped back to examine the damage to the house and landscaping, Butter protectively at her side once again.

Matt came running back. "Guard had just come on duty and got surprised. He was Tasered, probably by Walker."

"Is the guard okay?" she asked and glanced toward the SUV at the gate where a man stood by the vehicle, hand to his head as he shook it as if to clear it.

Matt nodded. "He's okay but shaken. Trey is sending backup guards to secure the property as well as someone to take the guard to the hospital to make sure he's fine."

He stooped down to examine the ground and the house. Standing, he motioned to the remnants of a bottle near the side of the house. "Molotov cocktail. Let me get a bag from the house so I can preserve that evidence."

The sudden shrill sound of sirens blared into the night and a second later, flashing blue and red lights lit the road. A police car turned into the driveway. It slowed by the SUV and the guard stepped over to chat with them and then gestured in the direction of the house. A second later, the police car hurried down and parked in the driveway.

Officers Ventura and Randall stepped from the car and walked over, a blend of concern and suspicion etched on their faces. Teresa crossed her arms around herself, worried about both the incident and the earlier questioning from the detectives.

"Good evening," Officer Ventura said and whipped a pad and pen from her breast pocket. "We got a call that someone had tried to torch your house?"

Waving his hand in the direction of the entrance to the property, Matt said, "I'm pretty sure that it was Walker who Tasered the guard, drove down the driveway and tossed a Molotov cocktail at the house. I fired at him and gave chase, but he got away."

Ventura eyed Matt, the damage to the house and then peered at Teresa pointedly. "Do you have anything to add to that, Ms. Rodriguez?"

Determined to guard her words and her emotions, she said, "Nothing else."

The two officers shared a look. Randall returned his attention to her and rocked back on his heels. He was about to say something when the sound of a car coming down the drive snared their attention.

A black SUV hurried down while a second vehicle stopped by the guard at the gate. The black SUV stopped just behind the police cruiser and a second later, Mia and Trey hurried out of the car and came to them.

"As soon as Sophie said something was wrong, we came," Mia said and embraced Teresa.

"Officers. Thank you for getting here so quickly. I'm sure you understand this has been traumatic for Ms. Rodriguez, so if you don't mind—"

"Detective Gonzalez—" Randall began, but Trey held up a hand in a stop gesture.

"Just a civilian now, Officer Randall. If you don't mind, Ms. Rodriguez has an important meeting tomorrow and needs to get some rest," Trey said and signaled Matt with a jerk of his head.

"Let's go, Teresa," Matt said, wrapped an arm around her waist and led her back into the house, Butter at his side.

After they'd entered and closed the door, she shook her head and pointed at her chest. "I don't get it. They were looking at me like I had done something," she said, tears threatening.

"THEY WERE JUST doing their job," Matt said and slipped his hand down her arm to twine his fingers with hers.

"Then why is Walker still on the loose? Why are they looking at *me* as a suspect?" Teresa lashed out and flung an arm in the direction of the officers outside.

The thud of car doors in the distance made Teresa whirl to face the door and Butter barked at the sound. Barely a heartbeat later, Mia and Trey entered, heads bent together.

"Everything okay?" Matt asked, picking up on their vibes and quieting Butter, who had been nudging his leg, apparently sensing the unease.

Trey nodded. "I've set the officers straight about what's been happening here."

"And the detectives?" Matt asked, ruffling the fur on the dog's head and urging her with a hand gesture to lie down.

"They called me to confirm why SBS was involved, and the discussion went well. I don't think they'll be looking at Teresa any longer." Trey fixed his gaze on her. "Mia and I think it would be best if you went to the SBS penthouse tonight. It'll be more secure, and since the racing commission representative is coming to our offices anyway, you'll be right there."

"What about my horses? The training?" Teresa said, the tone of her voice rising with each syllable.

"We took the liberty of calling your trainer. Richard will come over early in the morning and I'll stay here tonight to make sure nothing else happens," Trey said, jamming his hands in his pockets.

Mia reached out and laid a hand on Teresa's arm. "This makes the most sense, Teresa. You need to keep your head straight for the meeting tomorrow."

Even though Teresa nodded, the tension in her body and tightness of her fingers laced with his warned she was less than thrilled with the possibility. Still, it made sense, so she said, "I just need to pack a few things."

She yanked her hand from Matt's and raced out of the room. Matt was about to give chase, but Trey swept his arm out to stop her.

"Give her a little time to get her head together. Plus, you need to get your things packed. Whatever you need for Butter," he said, then bent and rubbed the dog's head.

"You want me to go with Teresa?" he asked, surprised by the possibility.

"Don't you want to go?" Mia asked, brows wrinkled over her assessing blue-eyed gaze.

Matt tightened his lips and looked away, before shaking his head and blowing out a harsh laugh. "I do. This is more than just a job now. It's personal."

Mia gave a little chuckle and grinned. "I knew it was about more than that before you did, Matt. Why don't you get ready, and I'll drive you, Butter and Teresa back to the SBS building."

He nodded, handed Trey Butter's leash and hurried off. He tossed his toiletry bag into a duffel he hadn't really unpacked. Down in the kitchen he packed Butter's food and bowls into a reusable shopping bag from a stash that Teresa kept in one of the lower cabinets.

When he returned to the front door, Teresa was already there, clutching an overnight bag with a designer label that said it probably cost more than what he made in a month. Barely days earlier, that would have been a big red stop sign. But now he knew better. Knew her better.

He grabbed hold of Butter's leash from Trey and held out his hand to Teresa. She slipped her hand into his. Her palm was slightly rough, the hand of a woman who wasn't afraid to work hard or get dirty. The hand of the kind of woman who could stand at the side of someone like him.

"Are you ready?" he asked and held his breath as he waited for her answer.

SHE'D LET FEAR dominate her life for the last few days and she was yearning for something different than that tonight. Smiling, she squeezed his hand.

"I'm ready."

"Great," Mia said and clapped her hands. "Let's go before it gets too late. You need to be sharp for your meeting tomorrow."

"I will be," she said, and they bid goodbye to Trey and followed Mia out the door and to the SUV.

"Make yourselves comfortable in the back," Mia said, and they tossed their bags in the trunk area and hopped into the back seat. Butter jumped in, sat between them and laid her head in Teresa's lap. Surprisingly, the dog tried to give an affectionate lick to Teresa's face and she laughed. "Sorry, no doggy kisses."

As Mia drove down the drive, Teresa turned to gaze lovingly at her home, wincing at the sight of the ruined siding. She was nevertheless grateful that they'd been able to put out the fire before any major damage had occurred. But as she'd packed her bag, dozens of questions had bounced around her brain, including why Walker would firebomb her house.

"Do you think Walker knows I'm speaking to the racing commission tomorrow?" she mused out loud while she stroked Butter's head as it lay in her lap, and the dog emitted a satisfied sigh.

Mia met her gaze in the rearview mirror and said, "If he does, he probably got the information from Esquivel."

"Right before Walker stabbed him. But how did Esquivel know? We only just arranged to move up that meeting," Matt said and reached across the width of the seat to hold her hand.

"A leak at the racing commission?" Mia offered.

Teresa tapped the air, connecting the dots between all three. "Which would explain why Walker was trying to scare me off in the first place. Someone tipped off Esquivel and Esquivel warned Walker."

"But if Esquivel and Walker were partners, why would he try to kill him?" Mia asked as she navigated the dark rural roads in Redland.

"To shut him up so he wouldn't talk to the cops?" Teresa said.

Matt shook his head. "Cops don't scare people like Walker, but Hollywood is a whole different kind of scary."

"Are you saying that Walker *and* Hollywood aren't involved in this? That it's just Walker?" Mia said and turned onto Route 1 for the last part of the drive to downtown Miami.

"Hollywood would be pissed either because it could threaten his business or because they cut him out of the deal," Matt said, still worried that Hollywood had a part in the attacks.

Teresa had worries as well about everything that had happened that day, including why the police would suddenly be looking at her as a suspect. Even though Trey had said that he'd talked to the detectives, it bothered her that they had even considered she could stab Esquivel.

That question and what seemed like dozens of others kept circling around in her brain as she sat in silence, watching the various towns along Route 1 flash by. Comforted by Butter's head in her lap and Matt sitting beside her.

The activity along those smaller towns faded as they reached downtown Miami's business area, quieter now that the skyscrapers were devoid of office workers and rush hour traffic.

In no time Mia was turning into the underground lot for the South Beach Security building and parked in one of the spaces reserved for the Gonzalez family members. She noticed there were a couple of other cars still parked in those spots. *For Sophie and Robbie?* Teresa wondered and didn't realize she'd said it out loud until Mia said, "My cousins are still hard at work. They're trying to see if they could pick up Walker's white Jeep in any of the CCTVs on the main roads."

"There are probably a lot of white Jeeps on the road," she said, sorry that the tech gurus were spending yet another late night on her behalf.

"It's their job and they love solving puzzles like this," Mia said, catching the apology in her voice.

"I appreciate that and everything that you're doing, Mia. I don't know how I could ever repay that," she said as worry of a different kind took hold, namely what the bill from SBS would look like when it came.

Mia swiveled to face her and said, "Like we said when this started, don't worry about that. We take care of our friends."

"Gracias," she said, but as they exited the car and walked toward the elevator, Matt stopped.

"I need to walk Butter before we call it a night," he said.

"We'll meet you in the penthouse. We've coded your badge to give you access to that floor. We'll take your things up," Mia said, making it clear that Teresa should go with her and not Matt.

"I won't be long," he said and walked Butter up the narrow ramp that led to the street.

She watched him disappear out of sight as he turned the corner onto the sidewalk and sighed, missing him already.

"You've got it bad," Mia said and passed a hand down her back to urge her in the direction of the elevator.

She couldn't deny it. "*Sí*, I do and it's a little…scary."

"I get it. I was terrified about what I was feeling for John at first, but Matt is a good man," Mia said and pushed the button for the elevator.

At this time of day, the elevator came down immediately and they boarded to head to the lobby where they cleared security and went to a different set of elevators. Mia tapped her badge against a pad in the elevator and cleared their access to the penthouse.

Teresa had heard rumors about the existence of the exclusive and luxurious space, but nothing could have prepared her for what greeted her as the elevator door opened.

Chapter Nineteen

Matt ambled with Butter along the sidewalk in front of the South Beach Security building. As the shepherd stopped to relieve herself, he gazed at the tall Art Deco–style building that housed SBS. Looking upward at floors with the offices and the penthouse above them, he saw that there were still a number of lights on, because work was a twenty-four-hour responsibility at SBS. But then a light snapped on in the penthouse.

Mia and Teresa.

Beside him Butter barked, as if to remind him to clean up, which he did, and then they hurried into the building. The guards in the lobby nodded as he approached the security desk and he waved and badged himself through the turnstile. Inside the elevator he tapped his badge against the keypad and cleared access to the penthouse.

He'd never been there, since the space was reserved for Gonzalez family members who were working late, important visiting guests or clients who needed extra security.

When the elevator opened on the topmost floor, he walked right into the penthouse apartment and had to stop for a moment to take in the views from the floor-to-ceiling windows that made up the far wall of the open-concept room. Beyond the buildings in downtown Miami, the waters of Biscayne Bay glittered beneath a full moon. To the left, lights sparkled on the MacArthur Causeway and in nearby South Beach. A gleaming white, multistory ocean liner sat in port while beyond that stood the towers on Fisher Island and South Pointe.

The open-concept space of the penthouse was appointed with a mix of modern, lacquer-and-steel furniture and Spanish colonial antiques. A large and comfy-looking leather sectional sat in front of a fireplace and to the right was a high-end kitchen that any top chef would be delighted to use. Just to the side, and close to the floor-to-ceiling windows, was a large glass-and-steel dining table that could easily hold a dozen people. Considering how hardworking the Gonzalez family was, he could imagine that it had been used often by some or all of them during a late night of work.

Matt bent to ruffle the shepherd's fur. "Wow, Butter. This is just…wow."

A sound from beyond the kitchen had them both turning to see Mia and Teresa walking into the kitchen area.

Mia held a key card in her hand and waved it in the direction they had just come from. "The two bedrooms are that way. Teresa's already gotten settled in her room," she said and handed Teresa the key card. "This will give you access to the building, SBS offices and the penthouse."

She walked over to Matt and had to gaze up at his greater height despite the three-inch heels on her Louboutins. "Make yourself at home. Only your two cards will open the penthouse elevator between the hours of 9:00 p.m. and 9:00 a.m. You can buzz us in with this," she said and sashayed to the elevator to point at a button near the doors.

"We'll see you tomorrow. Since the meeting is at two, why don't you come down at twelve for lunch and to get a report on the investigation?" Mia said and hit the button to open the elevator door. She stepped on without waiting for a reply from them, leaving them alone in the silence of the almost cavernous space.

They walked toward each other, stopping in the gap between a coffee table and the fireplace. Staring at each other, uncertain, until Matt took hold of her hand and smiled.

"I'm going to get Butter settled for the night. Why don't you get comfy? Maybe see what's on the television," he said and lightheartedly swung her hand.

AS IF SHE could ever get comfortable with the way she was feeling inside, all achy and fluttering from even the simple touch of his hand and the knowledge that they were totally alone in this over-the-top penthouse that rivaled the Presidential Suite in her parents' casino.

"I'm in the bedroom to the right. I loved the views of South Beach." She slipped her hand from his and kissed his cheek.

He smiled again, a tender and understanding tilt of his lips, and strolled toward the kitchen and the bedrooms beyond.

She walked to a wet bar she'd noticed when she'd first come in and poured two fingers of an aged rum into the glasses. Returning to the large sectional, she set out coasters and laid down the glasses as Matt set out Butter's bowls and filled them. He unleashed the shepherd and at his stay command, the dog settled down next to the kitchen island.

Matt sauntered over to the sectional and took a spot next to her. Grabbing a glass, she nestled against him, her back tucked into his side. Her bare feet sank into the butter-soft charcoal gray leather.

Leaning forward, he picked up a glass and wrapped an arm around her waist, pulling her even tighter against him, her head pillowed on his shoulder.

They sat there for long minutes, sipping their rum, enjoying a peace and quiet they hadn't had in days. The weight of his hand across her midsection was comforting, but it was too easy to imagine him moving it upward to…

She nearly choked on the rum she'd been sipping and set the glass down with a trembling hand. Turning, she kneeled, and splayed her hand across the middle of his chest. His heartbeat pounded strong and erratic beneath her palm.

"Matt… This is… I've never felt this way about anyone." She stroked her hand across his chest and then upward, past the hard line of his collarbone. Pausing by the sensitive skin at the side of his neck, she traced the pulse beating there with her index finger before cupping his jaw and running her thumb across the hard edges of his lips.

They parted beneath her finger as he said, "I never thought a woman like you—"

"A rich girl?" she teased with an arch of a brow.

"You're nothing like any rich girl I've ever known. Like I said before, you're the sun and…" He shook his head and looked away, but she applied gentle pressure to urge him to face her.

Leaning forward until her lips were a butterfly-light brush against his, she said, "I'm just a girl who more than anything wants you to kiss her right now."

DIOS, MATT THOUGHT, but he couldn't resist her any longer because he was just a boy who wanted to kiss her more than he wanted to breathe.

He closed his mouth over hers, savoring the warmth of her lips and the sweet taste of fine rum and Teresa. Kissing her and holding her close until it wasn't enough for either of them.

She shifted to straddle his hips, her center nestled against his hardness. She moaned as she pressed herself to him and kept on kissing him, her hands cradling his face to urge him on.

"Matt, please," she said, and he reached between them and cupped her breast. Her nipple was hard beneath his fingers, and he tweaked it with his fingers.

Her breath exploded against his lips, and she leaned her forehead on his and watched as he caressed her.

The pressure built in his jeans until he knew he couldn't hold off much longer.

"Teresa, tell me now that you want to stop, otherwise—"

"I don't want to stop."

WITH A GROAN that reverberated through her body, Matt surged to his feet with her in his arms, marched through the living room and to the bedroom past the kitchen. He hurried in but stopped dead at the sight of the large king-size bed positioned in the center of the large room across from a wall of floor-to-ceiling windows.

"Mia made sure to tell me all the glass has a privacy film on it," Teresa said and trailed a kiss along the hard length of his jaw.

"Mia never fails to surprise me," he said and rushed to the side of the bed where he let her slip to the floor, her body flush to his. Not an inch of his body wasn't in contact with hers and it was all lean, rock-hard muscle. She ran her hands across the broad slope of his shoulders and down his arms to link her fingers with his.

"She sees things others don't," Teresa said and urged his hands to her waist as she rubbed her hips back and forth across his hard length.

Matt slipped his hands to her buttocks and stopped the motion but urged her ever tighter to him.

"She does but I don't want to talk about Mia." He eased his hands to her waist to grab hold of her T-shirt and inch his hands beneath to her bare skin. Inch by agonizing inch he slipped his hands up until he was cupping her breasts.

Teresa sucked in a shaky breath and glanced at him as he caressed her, running his thumbs across the hard tips until she moaned and said, "What do you want to talk about?"

A wry grin crept onto his lips, and he chuckled. "I don't want to talk about anything at all," he said and urged her down onto the bed.

His weight pressed her into the mattress for barely a second and then he was standing and jerking off his clothes. His polo shirt flew off, exposing the hard planes of his chest with their smattering of dark brown hair that trailed down his middle to…

She licked her lips as his khakis and briefs hit the floor, exposing him to her. He kicked away the pants and she reached for the hem of her T-shirt, but he stayed her hands.

"Let me," he said, grasped the hem of the shirt and slowly lifted it over her head as she sat on the edge of the bed.

Tenderly he eased the T-shirt over her head, revealing her breasts in her serviceable cotton bra and making her wish she'd worn something sexier.

Maybe next time, she thought as he undid the clasp to bare her breasts to his gaze.

"You're so beautiful," he said and cradled their weight in his hands, teasing the tips with his fingers before kneeling to kiss the tips and then trail a line of kisses down her center until he reached her jeans.

He paused there and glanced at her, asking permission to proceed.

She licked suddenly dry lips and nodded.

He undid the clasp and slowly tugged the denim down until he could snag her panties as well. But as the dark curls at her center became visible, all restraint fled him, and he hurried to yank the jeans off her body.

Dios, but she is beautiful. I could kiss her until I don't have breath, Matt thought as he slipped his hands beneath her buttocks to pull her into the center of the bed, where he covered her body with his and kissed her.

He shifted his kisses to her breasts while he slipped his hand down to part her center.

"Matt." She gripped his hand, as if she was afraid of falling.

"It's okay, Teresa. It's okay," he said, and she came apart beneath the first gentle caresses of his fingers.

"I'm sorry. It's been so long," she said as she grasped his wrist to keep him from moving his hand.

He was probably a Neanderthal for being pleased at that confession, but in truth, it had been a long time for him as well.

"Me, too. Give me a second," he said as she released his wrist and stroked her hand up and down along his hard length.

With a low moan, he surged to his feet and left her only long enough to remove protection from his wallet. He tore open the packet and removed the condom, but she took it from his hands and urged him to his back.

Straddling him, she slowly rolled the condom over his length, and he gritted his teeth because her touch nearly undid him.

"Matt?" she asked, hesitating, and he cradled her waist and urged her over him.

"I love you, Teresa."

"*Te quiero*, Matt," she said and sank down onto him, riding him until they were both shaking, breaths rough in between kisses until Teresa's body stilled as another release tore through her.

He murmured soft words of encouragement as her climax ebbed and then he shifted her beneath him, seeking his own release. Driving into her, drawing her ever higher until they both shattered together.

HER HEART GALLOPED in her chest as he lay on his back and nestled her into his side beneath the covers. Under her ear his heart beat a rough rhythm as well and she lazily stroked her hand across his chest until their heartbeats slowed and the first hint of tension crept into his body.

She propped an arm on his chest and leaned her head on her hand to gaze down at him.

"Having second thoughts?"

He pursed his lips and met her gaze directly. "No and… yes. I don't normally mix business with pleasure. I wish we could have met in some other way."

"Only you don't do rich girls," she teased, tugging playfully on his chest hair.

"Only you're not a rich girl, remember?" He mimicked her actions, wrapping a lock of her hair around a finger and pulling on it gently to bring her in for another kiss.

She kissed him and then settled back into his side. "I'm truly not. We were barely breaking even and now with all the costs of the security…"

Her voice trailed off uneasily at the thought of what she would have to pay SBS.

Matt ran a hand down her back and said, "When Mia and Trey said not to worry, they meant it. I don't know how they do it—"

"They're rich," Teresa said, well aware of the Gonzalez family wealth.

With a shrug, he said, "They worked hard for it and don't really shout out about it. Except maybe for Mia, but that's all her money from the social influencing gigs."

"And her husband, John Wilson, I imagine. What's he worth now?" Teresa asked.

"Billions," Matt said in a voice that mimicked Dr. Evil.

She laughed as he intended and soothed a hand across his chest again. "I'll try not to worry about that since there's so much else to worry about," she said as the pleasure from the earlier lovemaking slowly faded and the reality of her situation crept in.

Matt flipped onto his side to face her. Cradling her cheek, he urged her to meet his gaze. "We're almost at the end of the race, Teresa. Tomorrow we'll know why the racing commission wants to talk to you and hopefully that will tell us why Walker and Esquivel don't want that to happen."

More than most, Teresa knew there were no guarantees at the end of any race. The upsets when a dark horse beat the odds. She wanted to think of herself as that dark horse that came out a winner.

I'm already in the winner's circle with Matt, she thought and inched upward to kiss him, wanting to restore the earlier happiness she'd experienced in his arms.

As he pressed her into the mattress and pinned her there with his body, she lost herself in the joy of his loving and the possibility of a future with him.

Chapter Twenty

For the rest of the night and through the morning, Matt did his best in a variety of ways to keep Teresa from thinking about what she would have to do later that day.

They'd made leisurely love while watching the sun come up over Biscayne Bay. After a short nap, they'd made love again while they showered together. Together they'd cooked breakfast and eaten it at the dining room table, tossing bits of bacon to Butter who eagerly ate the treats.

He'd left Teresa only long enough to take Butter for a morning walk.

When he'd come back up to the penthouse, Teresa was standing by the wall of windows, arms wrapped around herself. Back ramrod straight in a gesture he recognized well. She had dressed in a sedate black dress, her hair up in some fancy kind of topknot, probably to look more formal for the interview.

She was preparing herself for what would happen in a couple of hours.

She turned as he walked in and managed a smile, but deep brackets beside her lips warned of her strain. "Richard called. He said the workout went well today. He also said everything was calm at the stables. No more incidents."

He unclipped Butter's leash and the shepherd lay down

by the edge of the sectional at his hand command. Walking over to Teresa, he stroked his hand down her arm to twine his fingers with hers. "That's good to hear. It's almost time for lunch. Do you want to head down to the SBS offices?"

She slowly inhaled, held her breath, exhaled and then nodded. "It's as good a time as any."

With a quick dip of his head, he led her to the elevator, stopping only to leash Butter again. They stood shoulder to shoulder in the elevator, Butter sidling up to Teresa, who smiled and patted the dog's head.

As they entered the reception area, the young Latina at the desk smiled and quickly seated them in the conference room just behind the desk. When they sat side by side at the table, the receptionist hit the button to make the windows opaque and give them privacy.

"They've thought of everything," Teresa said as she peered at the now milky white wall.

In the six months that Matt had been working for SBS, he'd realized the same thing. "They're very thorough. It's why their business is growing, like the new K-9 division Trey added." He patted Butter's head as the dog sat beside him in the gap he'd made by moving one of the conference table chairs.

A knock on the door came before Trey walked in, followed by Mia, Sophie and Robbie. "Good afternoon," Trey said and laid a leather portfolio on the conference room table. "We have lunch coming up in about ten minutes. After that we'll call Roni to get an update on the police investigations."

"Sophie and Robbie are also going to share anything new with Roni so she can report back to the detectives working the case," Mia said as she took a spot next to her brother, while Sophie and Robbie sat across from them and next to Matt and her.

"*Gracias.* Your quick thinking saved my house last night," Teresa said, glancing at the tech gurus who had been so helpful.

They smiled, looking so much alike it was as if they were almost twins despite the nearly two-year age difference between Robbie and his younger sister.

"Anything for a family friend," Sophie said and laid a hand on Teresa's to reassure her.

The conference room phone chirped, and Trey answered. "What is it, Julia?"

"The food is here. May we bring it in?" the receptionist said.

"Of course. Come on in," he said and a second later, Julia opened the door and directed the delivery people on where to set up the sandwiches, salads and sodas on the large credenza at one side of the conference room.

Once they'd left, Mia said, "*Por favor*, help yourselves."

Robbie nearly bolted from his chair, leaving Sophie to roll her eyes and chuckle. "He's always hungry."

She rose and walked over at a more sedate pace, as did Mia and Trey.

When Teresa didn't move right away, Matt leaned close to her. "Aren't you hungry?"

IT WASN'T JUST that they'd had a healthy breakfast earlier that morning. A weird combination of knots and butterflies alternated in her stomach, almost painful in intensity.

Teresa ran a hand across her midsection and said, "More like nerves. I'm not sure I can keep anything down."

He nodded, understanding. "I'll get you something and maybe you'll feel more like eating after we hear what Roni, Sophie and Robbie have to say."

She wasn't sure she would feel like eating but didn't argue with him as he rose and returned a few minutes later with two plates piled with food. He left her again to retrieve two sodas and placed one in front of her. Thanking him as he set the plate in front of her, she sat there in silence for several minutes, sipping her soda, while others satisfied their hunger before Trey made the call to Roni.

Trey peered around the room and focused on her still uneaten meal. "Are we good to call Roni? Teresa, are you okay?"

She nodded, and to ease Trey's worry, she poked at the potato salad on the plate before forking some up to eat.

Seemingly satisfied with that, he dialed Roni, who immediately answered. "*Hola, mi amor.* I have some good news for you," she said.

"That's good to hear," Trey said and glanced her way again.

Teresa ate another forkful, and in all honesty, maybe they'd had the right idea since the food traveled down easily and seemed to be calming the battle raging in her belly.

"Police recovered a bloody knife from under the bed in the hotel room. Walker's prints were all over it. Teresa is no longer a suspect in Esquivel's attempted murder," Roni reported.

Relief swamped her and the fork slipped from her nerveless fingers and clattered on the table.

Matt stroked his hand across her shoulders and leaned close to whisper, "You okay?"

With a shaky breath, she said, "I'm better now."

She picked up the fork and some more salad, as if to prove she was truly okay, and Trey continued with the call.

"Anything else to report?" Trey pressed his wife.

"The DA is asking for an arrest warrant for Walker and—" Roni paused and the muffled sound of her voice speaking with someone else drifted across the speaker before she returned to the conversation.

"We just got word that Esquivel is conscious. Mattson and Cross are on their way to interview him. Hopefully he can provide additional information on Walker and his whereabouts," Roni said.

"Maybe we can help with that. Mia's John gave us access to his software, and we were able to predict possible routes that Walker would use to leave Teresa's place," Sophie said, and Robbie jumped in with, "Using those predicted routes, we picked up Walker's white Jeep in some CCTV footage after his last attack."

"Tell me it's good news," Roni said.

Robbie grinned, his light blue eyes alive with excitement. "We were able to trace the Jeep onto Southwest 248th Street. We worried we'd lose him if he got on the highway, but he just kept on going straight until he turned off. We think he went to Black Point Park."

"There's a marina and restaurant there, right?" Mia asked, forehead wrinkled over her blue gaze.

"There are. We're trying to tap into the CCTVs at the marina and restaurant to see if we can confirm that Walker is in that area," Sophie explained.

"Great work, *primos*. I'll let the detectives know so they can get some uniforms to canvass the park," Roni said, thanking Trey's cousins for their excellent work.

In the background another voice came across the line, prompting Roni to say, "I've got to go. We have a lead on another case."

"Cuidaté, mi amor," Trey said, his gaze warm and full of adoration as he asked her to take care.

Like the kind of adoration in Matt's eyes as he once again stroked her back and glanced at her.

Smiling, and finally feeling as if they were close to the end of her nightmare, she grabbed her sandwich and ate.

MATT WAS GLAD to see that Teresa's anxiety had dimmed enough for her to eat. He worried her calm wouldn't last once the racing commission rep arrived to do his interview or until Walker was in custody.

"I know having the uniforms canvass Black Point makes sense, but I'd rather go with Butter and check it out myself," he said.

Butter sat up at the mention of her name and gave him her attention. He snagged a bit of ham and cheese from the last piece of his sandwich and fed it to the shepherd as a treat.

"I agree and I'd like to go with you as soon as the racing commission rep arrives," Trey said.

Teresa's body jumped beside him, probably at the thought of tackling the interview without him at her side. He hesitated, unsure that leaving Teresa alone for the talk was a good idea.

"Matt?" Trey said and flipped a pen from tip to top over and over on the surface of his portfolio.

Mia reached out a hand to stop her brother's nervous gesture. "If Teresa would prefer not to be alone, I can stay with her."

Matt peered at Teresa. Deep slashes framed the edges of her tight lips and her pupils seemed huge in her emerald gaze.

"I can stay—"

"No, it makes sense for you and Butter to track down Walker," she said and vehemently shook her head, shaking loose strands of hair from her fancy topknot.

Teresa looked at Mia and her smile relaxed the tiniest bit. "*Gracias*, for volunteering to stay with me. I really appreciate that."

"*Bueno*, so we're set. Let's finish lunch so we can all get to work," Trey said, hopped up from his chair and returned to the credenza to grab another piece of sandwich.

Mia chuckled and leaned closer across the broad width of the conference room table. "He thinks that if Roni is eating for two, he should also," she teased her older brother.

Trey shook his head, laid the plate on the table and flexed his arms. "Not an ounce of flab, *hermanita*," he shot back.

Matt laughed at the siblings' interaction and from the corner of his eye caught Teresa's action as she picked up her own sandwich and ate.

A good thing, he thought and sat back to take in the discussions as Trey and Mia spoke to their tech guru cousins on what their next steps would be. Sophie flipped on a large monitor on the far side of the conference room and pulled up a satellite image of Black Point Park. Using a laser pointer, she highlighted where they'd lost sight of Walker's Jeep on the nearby road and also the location of the restaurant and other buildings in the park.

"My money is on him being in one of those vacant boats," Matt tossed out for consideration, thinking about how Walker had used the absent neighbor's home as a hideout.

"I agree," Trey said, rose and approached the monitor. "There's a walkway that skirts the marina. Walker could use it to access the docks there." He pointed out the path in the satellite view.

"If he's been there, Butter should be able to pick up a scent," Matt said and reached down to pat his shepherd's head.

"Good. So it's agreed that Matt and I will check out Black Point, Sophie and Robbie will continue to try to get eyes on Walker, and Mia and Teresa will deal with the racing commission rep," Trey said, returned to the table and sat.

"It is," Teresa said, although still clearly hesitant.

“It’s what makes sense. If Walker is at the marina and Butter can track him down—”

“It’ll end this nightmare,” she finished for him. Offering him a smile filled with resignation, she said, “I understand, and I’ll be fine with Mia at my side.”

“You will be, *amiga*,” Mia chimed in from across the table.

Not wanting to waste another moment, Matt said, “If we’re done with lunch, I’d like to go to Black Point Park.”

Trey nodded and pushed to his feet. “I’m with you. If you don’t mind, we’ll be on our way.”

Matt unfolded his length from the seat and, uncaring of how unprofessional it might look, brushed a quick kiss across Teresa’s temple. “Don’t worry. Walker’s days of freedom are numbered.”

Chapter Twenty-One

Teresa didn't think she could be quite as sure as Matt about finally apprehending her attacker. But as the Gonzalez cousins exited the room, leaving her alone with Mia, she stared across the table at her friend and said, "How can Matt be so sure? Walker's been one step ahead of us the whole time."

"He has managed to surprise us more than any of us would like, but Sophie and Robbie's lead seems solid. If they're right, Walker has boxed himself into a corner."

"Unless he escapes by sailing away," Teresa said and waved a hand to mimic his gliding free.

"Not this time. I just feel it in here," Mia said and tapped a finger to the middle of her chest.

"I hope you're right," Teresa said but couldn't stop worrying not only about Walker escaping, but about Trey's and Matt's safety.

Ever observant, Mia said, "They'll be fine. They're both licensed to carry, and Butter is a weapon as well when needed."

It was hard to picture the protective shepherd with her goofy tongue and melty chocolate eyes as dangerous, although K-9s were often trained to attack.

Not wanting to continue the conversation, Teresa shot a quick look at her cell phone. "It's almost time."

Mia peered at her pricey, gold-and-diamond Pasha de Cartier watch, just like the one Teresa had sold to pay some of her stable's expenses. "It is. We'll be meeting in another of our conference rooms. Do you need to take a break before we go there?"

That morning's coffee and lunch were warning her not to delay, especially if the meeting with the racing commission representative went longer than she expected.

"I do need a break. It'll be good to stretch as well," she said, unused to spending so much time sitting or idle. Although she could really get used to spending time with Matt in bed once this was all done.

She met Mia by the door to the conference room and they strolled down the hall together, chatting about the new foal as well as an upcoming party at a local country club to which they'd both been invited. Once they were finished in the women's room, Mia escorted her to a smaller but well-appointed conference room next to the larger one they'd just vacated.

Mia was just pouring her a glass of ice water when the conference room phone chirped. She answered and then said, "Please show them in."

Them? Teresa wondered. She'd expected only one representative from the racing commission.

Two men came to the door of the conference room and Mia invited them to enter.

Teresa recognized one of the men from the New York races in which her horses had run. The man with him screamed "cop" with his black suit, starched white shirt and black-and-red striped tie. Her guess was confirmed as he reached into his jacket pocket and pulled out a badge.

"Ms. Rodriguez. Special Agent Rick Santoro," he said and offered her his hand.

She shook it and glanced at the familiar man. "Mr. Babcock, if I remember correctly."

"You did, Teresa. May I call you Teresa?" he said and shook her hand effusively, dimming by the barest amount the anxiety she was feeling from the presence of the FBI agent.

"You may. This is Mia Gonzalez. She and her family run South Beach Security and I've hired them for protection, but I'm sure you're aware of that already," she said as Mia shook both men's hands and then urged everyone to take a seat.

"We are and I'm sorry if our investigation is somehow responsible for placing you in jeopardy," Babcock said. He set his briefcase on the tabletop, opened it and extracted a large file.

"A heads-up about the danger might have been nice, Mr. Babcock," Mia said, her tone so frosty they probably didn't need air conditioning in the room.

"I'm afraid I'm to blame," FBI Agent Santoro said and laid a large hand across the front of his chest.

"Care to explain?" Mia said, clearly ready to fight on Teresa's behalf. Teresa was grateful for that. Mia probably had way more experience with FBI types like Santoro than Teresa ever could.

"First, we'd like to ask Ms. Rodriguez some questions," Santoro said and glanced in Babcock's direction.

Babcock opened the file and nervously flipped through papers, scattering a few on the tabletop before he yanked out a photo and slid it across the table to Teresa.

"Do you know this man?" Babcock asked.

It was a grainy black-and-white photo of Walker with a racehorse. He had the beard and longer hair that had made her not recognize him at first, but she now had no doubt about who he was.

"It's Finn Walker, only he's clean-shaven and has a buzz

cut now." She was passing the photo back to Babcock when she noticed something familiar. "This photo's from one of the Saratoga races, right?"

"It is. You're very observant," Babcock confirmed, retrieved the photo and then passed over a list of about ten or so races that had occurred the year before.

Teresa scrutinized the list but was puzzled by it since it contained races in which she hadn't participated. "I don't understand."

"You raced a number of horses last year. Can you identify at which of these races?" Santoro asked.

She was starting to get the feeling she'd had yesterday with the two detectives and was about to speak when Mia stretched her arm in front of Teresa to stop her.

"Unless you can give us some rationale for this line of questioning, Teresa may wish to ask for the presence of a lawyer," she said.

Santoro glared at Mia. "Ms. Rodriguez is not in custody, so there is no need for a lawyer."

The FBI agent was clearly underestimating Mia's tenacity. A pit bull would give up more easily than Mia.

"Nevertheless, we'd like to hear your rationale before continuing."

Santoro gritted his teeth and the muscles in his jaw clenched from the force of it. A too long and very hostile glare focused on them before he said, "Go ahead, Babcock."

Almost timidly, Babcock gestured to the list. "That is a list of races that we suspect were fixed."

"Fixed, as in—"

"Walker paid off the owners or jockeys to change the results and was aided by Esquivel, who doped the horses if they didn't agree," Santoro clarified.

Teresa held her hands up and waved in a hold on gesture.

"And you think I took part in that? I run a clean business and I didn't even have entries in quite a few of these races."

Babcock coughed uncomfortably and looked at the agent again, as if seeking permission. When the agent nodded, he said, "We don't think you have anything to do with the fixes. But we believe you may have seen Walker with the horses in question. Do you think you can identify when you saw him in the stable areas?"

Teresa shared a look with Mia and at her friend's go-ahead lift of her chin, she picked up the list and reviewed it carefully, trying to recall when she might have seen Walker. When she examined it, she realized she had seen him in at least four or five of the races on the list.

Placing the list in the middle of the table so that Babcock could see it, she pointed to the entries. "I think I saw him at these races."

"Are you sure, Ms. Rodriguez?" the FBI agent pressed.

She nodded emphatically. "I'm sure. Is that why Walker wanted to stop me from talking to you?"

"It is. As a witness, we'll need you to testify—"

Mia raised a petite hand in the air to stop him. "Who else is involved in this fixing scheme? Tony Hollywood?"

The red flush creeping up the FBI agent's face warned he wasn't a fan of Mia interfering. Despite that, he reluctantly answered, "We have no evidence that Hollywood was involved, although he is a target of another investigation we're running. Walker appears to have been acting only with Esquivel."

Mia was about to push the agent again until Teresa laid a hand on her friend's arm. It was a surprisingly calm hand, maybe because it was reassuring to know that the danger might end with Walker's apprehension since Hollywood wasn't a part of this scheme.

"We can discuss my testifying once Walker is in custody," she said.

Sensing they were done for the day, Babcock jumped to his feet, hastily stuffed everything back into the briefcase and slammed it closed. "We appreciate that, Teresa. Again, we're so very sorry for all the trouble you've had."

"And I'm sure you'll make it up to me by bearing the costs of all the damages that occurred to my home and business because of your failure to act," Teresa said and rose from her chair.

Babcock stuttered and stumbled, and Santoro jumped in to save him. "I'm sure Mr. Babcock can discuss that with his superiors."

Santoro held out his hand to Mia. "I wish I could say it was a pleasure," he said, but with a hint of humor offsetting the dig.

"The same, Special Agent Santoro," Mia said, shook his hand, and then did the same with Babcock.

Teresa waited and then offered her goodbyes to the two men, but as they were walking out the door she said, "By the way, you may want to check for a leak in your office. After last night's attack, I'm sure Walker knew we were meeting today."

Santoro dipped his head. "We'll take that under advisement," he said, and Mia escorted the two men from the room.

When her friend returned, she sat in the chair, and they faced each other. Mia took Teresa's hands in hers and said, "It's good news that Hollywood isn't part of this."

"It is and let me say, I'm glad I had you in my corner. How did you learn to handle people like Santoro? He was kind of intimidating."

Mia threw her head back and laughed, an almost musical sound that had Teresa smiling.

"You forget Trey is my older brother. Even before he was a marine or a cop, he'd grill me if I came home even one minute late," Mia said but there was no doubting the love and affection for her overprotective sibling.

"You handled them pretty well yourself," Mia added and chuckled.

Teresa likewise laughed, imagining what it must have been like to have an alpha like Trey as a brother. But with that came the niggle of fear once more at what Trey, Matt and Butter would encounter at the marina.

"Tell me again they're going to be all right," she said.

Mia squeezed her hands and drew her in for a long hug. "They're going to be all right," her friend said, but the slight shiver in her body and waver in her voice indicated she was also worried about the two men.

When they separated, Mia said, "How about we go up to the penthouse and you can tell me more about your new foal while we wait to hear from them?"

Teresa slowly pushed to her feet and held out a hand to her friend. "I think that sounds like heaven."

Chapter Twenty-Two

Matt sat silently beside Trey, who hadn't said much either since they'd left the SBS offices, but Matt was sure Trey was processing the kiss he'd witnessed earlier in the conference room. When his friend tossed a quick glance in his direction, Matt braced himself for the question he was sure would follow.

"You and Teresa. I'm not normally in favor of our agents becoming involved with clients, but…tell me it's not just a fling," Trey said, knuckles white on the wheel from the pressure of his grip.

"It's not a fling. I'm in love with her," Matt admitted.

"Teresa is an amazing woman, but…" Trey's voice trailed off and his worried glance said it all for Matt.

"You don't want me to get burned by another rich girl," Matt said with a laugh and shake of his head. "I get it, Trey, only like you said, Teresa is an amazing woman. She's nothing like the girl who ruined my life."

"No, she's not. Remember that and don't break her heart," Trey warned.

Matt shook his head again and teased, "Or I'll have to deal with you."

A sharp bark of a laugh and wry grin escaped Trey's lips. "*Hell*, no. You'll have to deal with Mia."

Matt held his hands up in surrender. "*Dios mio*, anything but that."

"Good," Trey said and pulled into the parking lot for the restaurant in Black Point Park. He stopped the car, faced Matt and said, "Let's go."

Matt hopped out of the car and opened the back seat to free Butter from her harness and clip on the leash. Rubbing the shepherd's head, he said, "You're a good girl. You're going to find him, aren't you?"

Butter gave a little woof and licked his face. "That's it. A good girl."

He eased the dog from the back seat and walked toward the rear where Trey had popped open the back hatch of the SUV. Trey handed Matt bulletproof vests for both him and Butter.

At Matt's raised eyebrows, Trey slipped on his vest, and said, "No sense taking any chances. Walker is way too dangerous."

He couldn't disagree. Bending, he slipped the vest on Butter and then tugged on his own vest, making sure that he could easily reach the gun tucked into the holster at the small of his back.

Once they were suited up, they hurried to the restaurant perched at the tip of land next to the water. Metal-roofed, hut-like buildings were open to the fresh air and surrounded by tables and brightly colored shades to protect patrons from the sun.

They approached the hostess stand and the young woman's perfectly manicured eyebrows flew up at the sight of them in their SBS-branded vests. "H-h-ow m-may I h-h-elp you?" she stammered.

Trey handed her a photo of Walker. "Have you seen this man around?"

With a shaky hand, she took the photo and peered at it.

Shrugging, she said, "Maybe. He's got a scruffy blond beard and wears a beanie a lot."

Matt glanced around the restaurant, which had both open-air and indoor seating, but didn't see anyone matching that description. "Has he been in today?" he asked.

The hostess shook her head and handed the photo back to Trey. "No. Not yet."

"Did you see where he came from?" Trey asked and likewise did a quick sweep of the area to look for Walker.

"No. It can get busy at night. People are coming off their boats and want drinks and a meal," she explained.

"If you see him, be careful and call 911. Ask for Detectives Mattson or Cross or you can call us," Trey said and handed the young woman his business card.

"Got it." She laid the card on the hostess podium with a nervous look at them.

As they sauntered away from the hostess, Trey tracked his gaze all across the park property. "Left or right?"

"Let's let Butter make the choice. Find it, girl," Matt said, and Butter immediately went to work, sniffing around the thick grass along the edges of the path leading from the restaurant and toward the larger set of docks to the left of the dining areas.

Matt and Trey followed the shepherd as she searched for the scent and as they did so, they caught sight of Mattson and Cross speaking to a couple at the end of a dock. It was the farthest one from the restaurant and judging from the headshakes of the couple, they hadn't seen Walker around.

Matt took a long look around the grounds to decide where to go next since the docks searched by the officers seemed to be a bust. Next to the docks was a path that fed into the Black Creek Trail, which ran on both sides of the water. The trail also wrapped around the restaurant toward a smaller set of docks. It worried him that if Walker had access to a boat there, he could easily use Black Creek to escape into Biscayne Bay.

"There's nothing for him in that direction," Matt said, pointed to the path and looked toward the restaurant. "Let's head back that way."

"You're the boss," Trey quipped, but followed Matt's lead as he commanded Butter to find the scent again.

Nose down, the shepherd searched the ground, but didn't hit on anything until they reached the steps for the restaurant's waterside dining area. At the steps, Butter hesitated and sniffed back and forth across the steps. A second later, she pawed the ground and Matt said, "Good girl. Find him, Butter. Find him."

The shepherd took off at a faster pace, head bent low as she followed the scent, weaving in and out through the tables where patrons sat enjoying meals and drinks. People seemed shocked at the sight of them with their vests as they hurried past, led by the dog who had zeroed in on Walker's scent.

They reached the end of the dining area and Butter rushed along a cement path that led back to a circular parking lot. The shepherd nosed around the trees and grass there, and tugging on her leash, cut through the landscaping and to the smaller group of docks. Unlike the other marina area, where dozens of boats were moored, there were only six or so boats secured in this area.

Butter urged them on, straining at the leash, but as they neared the first dock, a man with a beanie emerged from the cabin of a small boat. As he noticed them, he stopped short, whipped out a gun and opened fire.

The first shot caught Matt in the ribs, driving the breath from his body and freezing him in place from the shock of the blow.

Trey grabbed the back of his vest and hauled him behind the cover of a car parked nearby. Butter quickly came to his side and at his command, stopped straining at her leash and sat beside him.

Matt muttered a curse as the pain of the impact finally registered. Bullets pinged against the metal as Walker kept on firing at the car.

As the shots ended and the empty click of a revolver registered, Matt risked a glance around the edge of the bumper. Walker was undoing the ropes from the cleats on the dock to make his escape in the boat.

"Not going to happen," Matt said and pushed to his feet, gun trained on Walker.

Trey followed him, weapon also drawn, and shouted, "Stop right there, Walker."

But Walker kept trying to undo the ropes and Matt knew there was only one way to stop him in time. He released Butter's leash and gave the attack command. *"Útok."*

Butter galloped down the dock and threw herself at Walker, driving him down onto the wooden planks. She bit his arm to keep him in place while Walker thrashed and kicked, trying to free himself.

As Matt reached them, he trained his pistol on Walker and called off Butter. The dog released Walker and sat at Matt's side, but leaning forward, ready to attack again.

Trey flipped Walker onto his stomach and pinned him down with a knee in the middle of his back. He was reaching for his zip ties when Mattson and Cross came rushing down the path toward the dock, apparently having heard the shots.

"I think you can take it from here," Trey said, but waited for Cross to take out her restraints and secure Walker.

Once the restraints were in place, Trey slipped off Walker and the detective hauled him to his feet. "Finn Walker. You're under arrest for the attempted murder of Warner Esquivel and Teresa Rodriguez," Cross said and then started a recitation of the Miranda rights.

Since the situation was under control, Matt and Trey walked back to their SUV for the return trip to the SBS offices. But as they reached the SUV and Matt slipped off the vest, he groaned at the pain in his side and rubbed the tender area.

"We should have someone take a look at that," Trey said.

Matt shook his head. "Nothing broken. I'll be okay."

"I'll feel better when a doctor tells me that," Trey said, and as eager as Matt was to get back to Teresa and let her know her ordeal was over, he knew better than to argue with his boss and friend.

TERESA HAD WANTED to rush to the ER as soon as they'd finished the call from Trey and Matt, worried that Matt's injury was worse than what they were admitting. But Mia had calmed her down, reassuring her that Trey wouldn't let Matt take any chances and that they should wait for them in the penthouse.

The hour seemed more like twenty-four as she paced back and forth in front of the windows, waiting for Matt's, Butter's and Trey's return.

When the whooshing of the elevator doors announced their arrival, she rushed there and nearly launched herself at Matt as he stepped off.

His rough groan and indrawn breath worried her, but he wrapped his arms around her and held her tight. "I'm okay," he said and Butter gave a little bark from his side, as if to confirm it.

Realizing that her exuberant welcome might have caused pain, she said, "I'm sorry. I didn't mean to hurt you."

With a tender smile, he cradled her jaw and said, "Just bruised. Nothing to worry about."

He wrapped an arm around her waist and walked with her deeper into the penthouse as Trey walked over to Mia and hugged his sister. With a hand command, Butter sat at their feet, patiently waiting.

"It's over. Walker's in custody and Esquivel will survive. DA is already speaking to Esquivel to try to get him to flip on Walker," Trey said and peered in her direction. "Roni will keep us posted on whether Walker makes bail. In the meantime, we'll keep our guards in place at your location."

"I'll go home with you if you want, Teresa," Matt said and tightened his grasp on her waist.

"I want, Matt," she said, prompting Mia to grab her brother's hand and tug him toward the elevator.

"I think it's time we go, *hermanito*," she said and pushed the button to open the elevator door.

"We'll keep you posted," Trey said as they boarded and the door closed, almost in his face.

ONCE THEY WERE ALONE, Matt faced her. "Are you sure you want me to go with you?"

She offered him a lopsided grin and stroked her fingers across his cheek before cupping his jaw. "I want that more than anything, Matt. I want *you* more than anything. I hope you want the same thing."

"I do. I never thought I would say that about someone like you—"

"Because of what happened before?" she said, brow furrowed over those amazing emerald eyes.

He nodded. "Because of that, only there you were sleeping with your horse and then standing there dripping in I don't know what after birthing that foal. And when you ride, it's like seeing the wind."

She did that lopsided grin again and ran a hand through his hair. "I thought I was the sun?" she teased, reminding him of what he'd said days earlier.

He chuckled and shook his head. "You're that, too, Teresa. I love you and I want to spend the rest of my life finding out everything about you."

She rested her forehead on his and locked her jewel-like gaze on him. "And I want the same, Matt. I want to spend the rest of my life learning everything about you."

Matt kissed her and hugged her tight and at their feet, Butter gave a little bark, jerking them apart.

Laughing, Teresa kneeled and rubbed the dog's ears playfully. "And spending time with you, too."

Butter licked her face, earning a wrinkled nose from Teresa as she stood again. "I'm not a big fan of doggy kisses, but I guess I'll have to get used to them."

"What if I make them up to you with Matt kisses?" he said with a wry grin.

She laid her hands on his shoulders and urged him close. "I think that's a deal I can live with."

"Glad to hear that," he said and sealed the deal with his kiss.

* * * * *

GUARDING COLTON'S SECRETS

ADDISON FOX

For our wonderful Colton readers. Thank you for going on these adventures with us!

Chapter One

Chase Colton stared at the men and women assembled around his boardroom table bright and early Monday morning and braced himself for the inevitable. "As I shared in my email when I called this meeting, my focus as the new CEO of Colton Properties is transparency. No questions are off-limits."

He saw a few eyebrows raised at that last bit, but resolved it would be the truth.

His legal counsel was already leaning in, the man's voice low, his lips barely moving. "Sir, I'm not sure that's the best course of action."

Ignoring Tim's concerned visage, Chase addressed the table even more determined than when everyone had filed into the room. "Transparency. Accountability. Honesty. It's how I'm running Colton Properties moving forward. So, please—" he extended his hands "—feel free to ask me what's on your mind."

"I'm sorry about your father, Chase." As first comments went, it was something of a softball, but he appreciated the warm smile that creased Sonja Rodriguez's face. His head of marketing was a gem on any day, but the clear support from such a senior member of the team was encouraging.

"I'm sure I speak for us all when I say you have our sympathies on Robert's passing."

It had been a little over three months and Chase was still getting used to the idea that his father was dead. Robert Colton had been a force in life, both as a parent and as a real-estate maven in their growing corner of Idaho, Owl Creek. Both aspects of his father's life affected Chase equally, as his son and as the recognized heir apparent to the leadership and management of Colton Properties.

"Thank you, Sonja. It's been a difficult few months. My father cast a very long shadow in life."

"Would that long shadow have anything to do with the siblings you didn't know about?" The question seemed to hold the deliberate air of a challenge. Clint Roebuck, their lead property scout, liked to play big man whenever he could—but it also made him the perfect person to ask the question. Everyone else in the room was dying to know the same, but Clint's pugnacious tone would hopefully make the rest of the crowd sympathize with Chase.

"It's true that since my father's death my brothers and sisters and I have discovered a half brother and half sister. We're dealing with that as a family."

"And we're dealing with it as a business," Clint pressed. "You can't tell me that if someone wakes up one day and finds out they're related to a bigwig like Robert Colton they don't want a piece of his empire?"

Chase had walked into this aware it wouldn't be easy, but Clint's taunting tone was like sandpaper over the raw feelings he hadn't yet dealt with.

Feelings he wasn't sure he ever would.

Keep cool, Colton.

"While my family is working through equitable division of assets for my additional siblings, the succession plans for Colton Properties have been in place for a long time. I've worked at the company since getting out of college and am the best Colton for the job."

"But your newly discovered siblings could make things difficult. Here. For us."

"Clint," Sonja hissed. "I think Chase has been pretty clear on next steps for the business."

Clint looked about to argue when their office manager, Althea, wheeled in replacements for their coffee service. A table full of eyes stared longingly at the refreshed carafes and Chase figured it was as good a time as any to take a break. There'd be more questions—it was inevitable—but the break for coffee and another round of pastries off the sideboard would give people more time to loosen up and figure out how to frame those questions that might be difficult.

"Why don't we get fresh cups of coffee and a bit more breakfast and we can pick back up in fifteen?"

The dismissal provided the bell for round one and people quickly stood, their quiet murmurs filling the room as they moved toward the refreshed coffee. Although he was itching to go to his office to mentally regroup, Chase stayed in the conference room, talking to various folks and deftly ignoring Tim's efforts to catch his eye, no doubt to quietly tell him all the reasons why this meeting was a bad idea.

He leaned in when Sonja walked over to him, her dark brown gaze warm as she laid a hand on his arm. "Days like this show us what we're made of." She tilted her head toward the rest of the room. "It shows others, too. People do understand this is a difficult time for you and your family, and that you're doing your best."

"People who aren't Clint, you mean." He kept his tone even and his smile easy, but the resentment spiked hard in Chase's gut all the same.

"Even he'd admit in the moments when he wasn't trying to be the biggest jerk in the room that you're dealing with a lot."

"I can handle it."

Sonja assessed him, her fathomless dark eyes seeming to see far more than Chase was comfortable sharing. "I recognize I'm a woman of a certain age," she began. Before he could dismiss her reference, she waved a hand. "Both my kids are now married and having children of their own. It's a good place to be, Chase. Welcoming the next generation. It makes the decisions of the prior generation seem less dire."

"Decisions?" Chase asked. "Isn't that just a nice word for sins?"

"I'll stick with decisions. But you have to know I'm right. Finding someone and settling down would go a long way toward making this—" she gestured to the room at large "—feel less all-consuming."

"I'm my own man, Sonja. My father's behavior isn't about me. And the romance dance isn't for me, either. It never has been."

It was a fact his family knew—hell, the whole office knew—and, Chase admitted, it was the excuse he gave every woman he dated. He wasn't the marrying kind. Not anymore, after surviving a divorce in his late twenties that had decimated him. He just wasn't cut out for forever with someone else. Colton Properties was his life and he liked it that way.

Besides, having a partner wouldn't have made any of the fallout from his father's secret life any easier.

Sonja looked about to argue when Chase glanced pointedly at the sideboard. They'd held back a few paces from the line to keep their conversation private, but as a spot opened up, he gestured her toward it. "Please, go ahead and refuel."

She did as he asked, obviously recognizing the space wasn't conducive to their conversation, and Chase took another moment to refocus and consider his next move. He dated and enjoyed the company of women, and that was as far as it went. His focus—his *full* focus—needed to be on business.

This staff meeting was scheduled for an hour and then he'd planned a few one-on-ones with key members of his leadership team later that afternoon to go through even more specifics. While the succession plans for him to become CEO had been in place for some time, there were still the realities of his father's will. Luckily, the early feedback from Nathan and Sarah, his half siblings, was that they had no interest in being involved in Colton Properties.

But a secret family was a big deal, and so was the passing of a company's owner, no matter how well prepared or codified the man's wishes had been. Chase had spent his life training for the day when he'd take over as CEO and he couldn't afford to lose focus or let his personal shock and grief cloud what was best for the company.

He had a room full of people depending on him.

A room that suddenly seemed to shrink as a woman rushed in, her hair flying behind her as she ran smack into him.

His first thought as he suddenly held an armful of woman was how glad he was that his coffee cup was still empty.

His second thought barely qualified as one, as sheer instinct and a shocking swell of desire hit him with the force of a wrecking ball. Full, rounded breasts pressed against his chest, the delicious scents of vanilla and almond filled his senses and the softest skin he'd ever felt filled his palms.

It was only as the woman lifted her head, her deep brown eyes going wide, that Chase felt the first stirrings of real concern.

He could have unhanded her.

Should have stepped back and let her go.

So why was he still standing here, his arms wrapped tight around her, even though her slight frame seemed steady?

SLOAN PRESLEY REVELED in the strong, muscled arms that still held her and briefly considered faking a faint to ensure he didn't let go.

Which was ridiculous in the extreme.

Ridiculous, yet deeply tempting.

A temptation she nearly succumbed to when she realized she and the tall, sexy man still wrapped around her had the full focus of a room full of interested gazes.

How had she gotten herself into this?

She mentally tallied her mess of a morning. An overnight power outage had kicked her bedside alarm out of commission so that she'd only had the clanging of her mobile from across the room. Then she'd had to clean up after her sick cat just as she was about to race out the door, already late. And then, the oddly impossible parking situation when she'd pulled up to the building in downtown Owl Creek.

She eyed the man who held her. "You don't look like Arthur Ryan, the owner of Ryan Partners Marketing."

"Who do I look like?" His green eyes crinkled at the corners and Sloan couldn't deny the man's appeal. Mischief lit up that gaze, only adding to the temptation factor, along with full lips that even now twitched with humor.

"Not the man I met on an introductory video call."

"That might be because Arthur Ryan has office space in the building next door. We share the parking lot out back. I helped him find that space myself when his firm grew large enough to upsize."

Sloan finally found the will to extricate herself, both because those arms had grown far too comfortable and, well, *hello*. Room full of interested people watching them with collectively bated breath.

"This isn't Ryan Partners Marketing?"

Those eyes did more of that sexy crinkling. "No, ma'am, it's not."

"Which means I'm not only now monumentally late for a prospective client meeting, but I've managed to be late and directionally challenged, all with an audience."

Mr. Sexy Smile glanced at the rest of the people assembled in the room before he shrugged his broad shoulders. "Afraid so."

"This isn't happening." Sloan barely avoided the small, squeaky moan that threatened to spill out.

"Again, I'm afraid to have to tell you that it is."

"May I use a private area to make a call? I need to reach out to Arthur and make my apologies. Hopefully, he'll still agree to see me."

"Chase, why don't you let this woman use your office and give her some privacy for what will likely be a difficult call? Arthur Ryan's a tough cookie." Sloan glanced at the kind face peeping out from behind the man, a broad smile on her face. "In fact, why don't you take her there yourself."

Mr. Sexy shot a strange glance, clearly fraught with *something*, at the woman before turning his attention back to her.

"Chase, is it?"

"Chase Colton," he said and extended his hand. "And you're at my family's company. Colton Properties."

"Sloan Presley." Sloan took it, his large palm engulfing her. Warmth ran up and down her arm as their gazes met once more, that vivid, vibrant green drawing her in. "I can see you're in the middle of something. I really am so sorry to disturb."

"Nonsense," the kind woman behind Chase chimed in once more. "We were taking a quick breakfast break. Another five minutes won't hurt anyone. Go on and make your call in Chase's office."

"Yes. My call." Sloan nodded, dropping his hand as she willed herself back into the moment. A moment where she was not just late for a client meeting, but now the object of attention for nearly two dozen people. "I need to make that."

"I'll walk you to my office."

Chase Colton gestured her back into the hallway she'd not even looked at as she'd rushed in. If she had, Sloan now realized, she'd have seen the large sign dominating the wall behind the front desk declaring that this was the office of Colton Properties.

Her hand still tingled—hell, *all* of her still tingled—as she followed him down the hallway, his long strides eating up the distance. Her initial impression of a big man was accurate, but as she took in the lines of his body, she could see that he had the firm, lean strength of a swimmer, with wide shoulders tapering down to slim hips.

And a high, firm butt that was impossible not to admire as his black slacks pulled taut against his body as he walked.

Get. It. Together.

The refrain in her head kept time with her footsteps as the two of them wove toward the back of the office. Since his last name was on that sign she'd ignored in the lobby, it would stand to reason his office was something big and cushy, overlooking Owl Creek from some wide-windowed corner of the building.

"I am sorry to interrupt your meeting."

For the first time she saw a flicker of stress underneath that warm smile. "It can keep for a few minutes. Especially since our office manager just refilled the coffee."

"Those pastries did smell good. Even in my dazed haste I could smell the gloriously distinct scents of yeast and sugar."

"We'll see that you get one on your way out."

"I didn't mean—" Sloan broke off. Did it matter? "Thank you. That's very kind."

"Of course."

He gestured toward the phone. "Feel free to make your call."

She stood there, inside the wide, cavernous office that carried all the trappings of power, yet felt strangely empty. As if the man who worked there—the man she watched even now, while also trying not to gape at just how attractive he was—was somehow absent from the place.

Like no matter how much time he spent here, it wasn't quite his.

Which, Sloan supposed, was why she was here, wasn't it?

"Mind if I close the door?"

He nodded. "Be my guest."

She was closer to the exit, so she crossed the few feet to close the thick wood door, scanning the hallway to confirm it was empty. When she heard the firm snick of the latch catching, Sloan turned back to Mr. Sexy, her gaze direct.

"Okay, Colton. I think we convinced them."

CHASE WATCHED AS the slim woman standing inside his now-closed office transformed before his very eyes. The haphazard, rushed form who'd collided with him inside the office conference room, running on adrenaline and the fear she'd missed a meeting, had vanished.

In its place was a force of nature. That slim frame that looked willowy and soft grew, somehow, steel straightening her frame.

"You think so?"

"I know so. The entire room watched what was going on. You did a good job with the moony eyes, too."

For reasons he couldn't name, that stung a bit. "You did a decent job yourself."

"Just like we planned."

And they had planned it, hadn't they? In a series of calls

he'd taken from his home office, on his own personal communications devices, unwilling to bring this anywhere near Colton Properties.

The calls had left him frustrated at his next move, even as he knew it was inevitable. Which was why he'd hired one Sloan Presley, founder, owner and chief hacker at SecuritKey, who'd come highly recommended by his cousin Max. Max's FBI work had put him in contact with Sloan on several different projects and she fit the bill for what Chase needed: an independent party who could do some discreet hacking into the Colton Properties network and servers to ensure no one else was doing anything nefarious.

They'd hatched the meet-cute ruse because his bachelor status was widely known around Colton Properties and, even more widely, throughout Owl Creek. He'd never been great at relationships—a fact he'd proved spectacularly with his first wife—and after divorcing he'd sworn off ever attempting marriage again. But he'd also spent his adult life being told he only needed to find the right woman to fall head over heels.

Hadn't Sonja hinted at that very point in the conference room?

Which made this the best approach to keep his questions about threats to Colton Properties under the radar. People would be so focused on the idea he'd found a girlfriend they'd have no reason to question her presence or the time she spent with him. Subterfuge, yes, but they'd never have pulled it off if he'd simply hired her as an employee.

So when Sloan had questioned him about the job and whom he was trying to avoid—and the answer to that question was basically *everyone*, family included—they'd hatched the girlfriend plot. He hated lying to his loved ones, but since the news of his father's double life, he'd come to realize there wasn't anyone he could really trust.

"So much for transparency, accountability and honesty," Chase muttered. He thought he'd said it low enough, which made Sloan's raised eyebrows that much more pointed.

"You're battling a hidden force, Chase. One who can destroy your business and all you've built. Root out that dishonesty and you can go back to running the business however you'd like."

She was right. He knew that and he knew what he had to do to preserve his company. But when had life gotten so complicated? And how, in a matter of months, had his father's betrayals changed the way he thought about his family?

Even as he recognized they had in every possible way.

He was the oldest, damn it. It was his job to look out for his siblings. To protect his mother. And now, he was staring at a life of lies, churning through every conversation he could ever remember with his father, trying to find a shred of truth.

All while the answers remained elusive.

His mother's sister, Jessie, had run off, leaving her husband and four children, vanishing as if she'd never been. His Uncle Buck and his cousins had been devastated, trying to rebuild their lives after that horrific betrayal. They'd done a decent job of it, only to find since Robert's death that Jessie was not only very much alive, but also had been living a secret life with his father and the two children they'd had.

It was mind-boggling, Chase acknowledged, with the additional layers of grief, anger and deep-seated betrayal fighting for top of the heap of the emotional damage at any given moment.

It was that fact that continued to resonate deep within him, forcing his hand with the decision to reach out to SecuritKey's owner. Sloan Presley was just what he needed. A neutral third party under a signed confidentiality agreement.

He looked at her now, still positioned on the opposite side of his office. That spine of steel hadn't wavered, but it was the rest of the woman that really drew him in. Long hair settled around her face in soft, curly waves, those compelling, deep brown eyes alert and sharp. Her skin was a pretty shade of light brown that his fingers itched to trace, her long arms drawing his gaze in the short-sleeved, conservative blouse.

There was something about the woman that was captivating.

Which was the very last thing he needed to worry about right now.

So he'd ignore those sparks of attraction and force himself to forget the feel of her when she'd been wrapped tight in his arms.

They had work to do.

"We fooled them, Chase."

"No doubt about it." He nodded. "That was an award-winning performance."

"Then let's get to work."

Chapter Two

Let's get to work.

The words still rang in his head an hour later, his staff meeting wrapped after he gave one more excuse to *help* the woman in his office, as he and Sloan mapped out a plan for the week.

He had to give the woman credit—she came prepared.

Their entire contact up to now had consisted of those calls, mostly on the phone and then the final one on video. He'd thought her competent before, but seeing her in action only ratcheted that feeling even higher.

And then there was his reaction to her beauty.

He was a man who appreciated an attractive woman, but he wasn't normally this distracted. But Sloan was…

Well, she was the whole package.

Beautiful, yes, in a way that hit a man over the head. And then there were her computer skills.

SecuritKey had come highly recommended, and he could see why. Its founder was a whiz with a computer.

He would never have called himself a digital expert, but he knew how to navigate a laptop to do his work, program basic commands in their database and navigate through spreadsheets, all in service of running a successful business.

Next to Sloan, though, he felt like a kindergartner with his first computer.

The woman had some serious skills.

"I recognize this is a difficult subject, but would you walk me through the financial implications of your father's other family?"

Chase had struggled with that himself—and based on the questions this morning, his staff were worried about the same—yet something about it coming from Sloan felt different.

Up to now, he'd felt varying levels of shame, embarrassment and the sheer lingering fury of betrayal.

But with her, it was…

Well, it was okay, somehow. And he hadn't felt that way since the discovery of his father's secret life and the half brother and half sister he hadn't known he had.

Was it because he'd hired her to do a job?

Or was it her?

In the end, Chase realized it didn't matter. What did matter was working with her to uncover the problems he suspected with the books and figure out where he had a snake in the garden of Colton Properties.

"*Financial implications* is the polite term we're using now for lying to your family for decades?"

He'd meant the comment as a joke but didn't miss how flat the words felt to his own ears.

"I'm sure this is difficult. Monumentally so. But maybe we can take a slightly different tack. One that focuses on the finances and the records instead of the more scandalous aspects."

It was funny. If anyone else had framed it quite that way, Chase wasn't so sure he wouldn't have been offended.

Scandalous aspects.

The Colton family had become the hottest scandal in Owl Creek in decades.

Yet even with that public embarrassment, Chase had to admit Sloan had a point. Because separating what was happening at Colton Properties from his personal upheaval was essential if he wanted to get underneath his very real problem.

Something improper on the books was a fact.

Records that didn't add up were facts.

Rooting out a problem that had everything to do with swindling Colton Properties and nothing to do with his father's secret life was a fact.

And facts were something he'd had precious little of for far too long.

That first horrible blow of losing a parent had been crushing. But to then realize the man he'd loved and damn near revered for thirty-six years wasn't whom he'd believed he was had been killing him these past months.

On a hard exhale, he nodded. "Okay. Focus on the financials. What can I give you to move this along?"

"Access to the books is a place to start. I can do a proper digital forensics audit on the work while also searching for irregularities."

"You can do that on spreadsheets."

Her grin was broad and the words behind it held a confidence that bordered on cocky. It was…endearing. In a way he'd never have expected.

Here was a woman who knew her worth and didn't question it.

It was impressive. And deeply fascinating.

"We're also going to need to come up with excuses for me to be here. Reasons I have to log on to the network or something I need to do for my own job."

"Lie to my staff, you mean."

"Chase." He saw real compassion in her gaze, even as her voice remained strong. Soft, but still steel-edged all the same. "We've been over that part. It's lying if you do it indefinitely. I'm one person, here in a consultant capacity, to help you ferret out a highly confidential problem. When we find the problem, you can move on to running Colton Properties exactly as you want to."

"It still feels wrong. Especially with the realities of my father's lifetime of lies."

"I wish there was another way."

Once again, Sloan was the competent voice of reason. Chase realized that if he continued hemming and hawing, he would be as much a problem and an impediment to her investigation as the person attempting to swindle the company.

He sighed and looked up at her. "I'm usually far more decisive than this."

"You're grieving. I'd be a bit surprised and—" She broke off, seeming to pull herself up short.

"You'd be surprised at what?"

She shook her head, her mouth a grim line. "I'm sorry. I speak my mind far too quickly."

"I'd like to hear it."

Once again, her gaze was direct when she spoke, even if the words came a bit slowly. "To be honest, I'd be disappointed if you weren't struggling a bit. I'm deeply sorry you're going through this, but you're human. You're entitled to a range of emotions and feelings that don't all line up like numbers on a balance sheet."

"I thought the numbers on my balance sheet were the problem."

This joke hit far better than his earlier one and Chase felt a small moment of triumph when that thin line of her mouth turned up into a wide smile.

"Touché."

"But thank you. I've spent my life being the decisive one, especially as the oldest child. My job here at Colton Properties has only reinforced that."

"Then that means your faith has been shaken the hardest by your father's actions."

For someone who spent her life staring at a computer screen, Sloan Presley was pretty damn perceptive.

And once again, Chase was right back to that list of attributes in his mind he seemed unable to stop thinking about for long.

Yes, she was beautiful. But that beauty was matched by an inner calm and serenity, and a level of *understanding*, he'd really never seen before. Or certainly not in someone so young. He didn't know her exact age, but at thirty-six himself, he figured he had at least six years on her, if not more.

Was she even thirty yet?

And did it really matter?

He wasn't dating her. And the fact that his mind kept veering back to attraction had no place in this discussion at all. The only reason they'd even hatched the dating angle was to have a reason for her to come and go in the office without anyone being the wiser.

And yet…

He kept circling around that simmering level of attraction, anyway.

On his part at least.

Since he had far bigger issues, he'd better start focusing on the task at hand and off the very beautiful Sloan Presley.

The future of Colton Properties depended on it.

WHAT WAS SHE THINKING?

Chase's calm attitude and his even tone as they spoke of his business seemed to have seen them through that awkward moment, but Sloan couldn't help but wonder what had possibly gotten into her.

She *never* told a client what she actually thought.

Hell, she never told *anyone* what she actually thought of their behavior.

People claimed they wanted honesty, but no one truly did. They wanted a sanitized version of their behavior that was fed back to them, reinforcing all the things they wanted to hear.

Not what they actually needed to be told.

Wasn't that why she had a job?

Human beings were capable of any number of things and her ability to ferret out those things—especially the bad things—was why she had a successful business.

They'd moved past those difficult moments when she'd analyzed the impact of his father's death and moved right on to the files she'd ultimately need to review on the business. Chase Colton was the height of professionalism and accountability as they worked through a quick list of needs and how they'd go about setting her up to review the files.

"I pulled down a few files just to give you a sense of the business. We're privately held but still create the equivalent of an annual report for our records and to share with any potential investors on projects. I've also downloaded the monthly spreadsheets I work off with Finance. We do a soft close each month and then a formal close at the end of the quarter."

It was impressive, Sloan thought, as he walked her through the various aspects of the business. Although privately held, as CEO he ran Colton Properties like a publicly held business. The files were designed to show proper reporting on the work, their investments and overall cash flow in and out of the company.

She was anxious to dig in to those monthly reports. No

matter how well someone thought they had hidden their activity in the books, the month-by-month review would give her a strong sense of where to look.

"That's a really good start. I'll begin there and then let you know what else I might need."

"Of course. I've got the files already downloaded for you." He got up and crossed to his desk, then pulled a small drive out of his desk drawer. When he returned to her, he didn't sit down again, even as he handed over the drive. "So we should probably work out the fake dating part of this, too. We'll need to be seen around town a few times."

Sloan took the thumb drive, tucking it away into a small pouch she kept in her bag for work. It gave her the small moment of normalcy she needed as she considered how to play this.

Yes, the idea of posing as a couple had made sense when they'd hatched it in their planning meetings.

But now?

Seeing Chase Colton in person and realizing the man was far more attractive than even their brief video call suggested—it was a bit like having her brains scrambled.

She'd done her research, as she would for any other job, but nothing had fully prepared her for the impact of Chase Colton in the flesh.

The man had a lethal sort of intelligence that, coupled with those amazing green eyes and that broad-shouldered swimmer's build, was…well, it was sort of devastating.

Which was a serious problem seeing as how they were going to be playacting a romantic relationship for the next few weeks.

It was a new business strategy for her—she'd never even considered it before—and now that she'd committed to it, she had to be all in.

But ever since she'd barreled into the Colton Properties

conference room, Sloan had been wondering what, exactly, she'd gotten herself into.

Or why a fake dating ruse had seemed like a good idea when they'd come up with it on their last call.

"Where do you normally take your dates?"

It was a casual question, and it matched his prompt perfectly. Yet even as she asked it, Sloan felt the heat creeping up her neck.

"I have a few favorite restaurants. But there is another problem. I should have given it more thought but the talk today in the conference room made me realize I might have made a bit of an oversight."

She'd spent precious little time getting to know Chase, between their calls and now this morning's face-to-face, but she hadn't gotten the sense this was a man who didn't think through every situation in fine detail.

So his admission was something of a surprise.

"What type of oversight?"

"If we're seen for any length of time, and, based on your estimates this is going to take a few weeks, my family is going to want to meet you."

"Oh."

The Colton *family*? As in all of them?

She already knew he was one of six children who were the biological offspring of Robert and Jenny Colton. Then there were the two additional children from his father's secret life.

Whatever she'd been bracing for, the revelation that she would need to meet his family wasn't it.

"Isn't that a lot of people?"

"More and more every day." Chase grinned and she couldn't help but respond in kind.

"I thought your half siblings were sensitive ground."

His smile softened, a clear ability to add a bit of self-deprecating humor going a long way to make those godlike features seem a bit more human.

"Yeah, it is sensitive. But a few laughs can't make it any worse."

"No, I suppose not."

"But to your question, we *are* sort of a lot when we get together. There are my five siblings, and three of them have new significant others in their lives. And then, there are my four cousins. And now, there's Nathan and Sarah, who have sort of kept their distance but who are part of all this, too. And since we're getting to know them, leaving them out seems wrong, somehow."

"Of course, it is."

"They're half siblings to all of us."

"You gave me a sense of the situation on the phone, and I also know your cousin Max, but when you say 'all of us,' what do you mean?"

"My Uncle Buck and Aunt Jessie had four kids."

"But your Aunt Jessie is the mother of Nathan and Sarah?"

"Yep. She's also my mother's sister."

Sloan's head spun with the implications of it all. Two families that then crossed and created even more family.

She didn't want to judge.

Not only wasn't it her place, but she'd also learned a long time ago that people had precious little control of three things in life: what others thought of them, what others expected of them and what their family members did of their own accord.

And still, the emotional implications of all Chase and his siblings and cousins had learned in the past few months was staggering.

"Did your cousins know their mother was alive?"

Of all the various aspects of Chase and his family's situation, that aspect somehow seemed the most cruel.

"They knew she was alive but when she left my Uncle Buck it was like she divorced her children, too. She never came back or showed support for them in any way. She sent flowers for her mother and father's funerals when each passed, but that was all anyone heard from her."

"How terrible."

Sloan knew Chase's cousin, Max Colton, from the work she'd done over the years for the FBI. He'd recommended her to Chase for this job and she now thought about the man she'd worked with off and on through the years. Stoic and singularly focused on his work, he wasn't one to let his emotions show.

Had that been because he felt abandoned by his mother all those years ago?

And if that built a person's frame of reference for life, how much worse would it be to discover they'd not only abandoned you, but also gone on to make a new family?

Her own upbringing had been quiet at times, but good. She was an only child, so life was about the three of them, just her and her parents. Her Portuguese mother had come to Chicago on a nanny assignment and met her father a few months after coming to the US. They'd courted and fallen in love and her mother had never gone back to Portugal.

But she and her family had visited Europe through the years and many summers her relatives had come to them. Add on the large family her father came from and Sloan had always felt she'd been given the best of both worlds. A solid, warm, supportive upbringing and deep roots in her extended family that ensured she was never alone.

She'd always been something of an outlier in her Chicago neighborhood growing up, with her Portuguese mother and

Black father, but when she was with her large families on both sides, she was always welcomed.

Always loved.

And she'd always known who she was.

How awful would it be to have that all taken from you? Upended in a way that those roots you'd believed so strong and firm were revealed to be resting in very shallow ground.

SLOAN WAS A difficult woman to read, but Chase could only imagine what was going through her mind at the complexities of his messed-up family. Even as those musings lingered, he also sensed she was professional enough to find a way forward.

It was his nature to believe things would work out.

Hadn't he done that after his divorce?

He'd married Leanne because he'd believed they were in love. And it had turned his life upside down to find out that he'd been the only one in the relationship who felt that way. His wife had been far more enamored with his standing in Owl Creek and his last name than actually building a life and a family together.

In the end, he'd seen her for what she was. Too late to have avoided a wedding and an expensive divorce payout, but soon enough that they hadn't brought children into the world.

For that small benefit, he counted himself lucky.

The children they'd never created even luckier.

"The files you gave me should keep me busy."

Sloan's words interrupted his maudlin thoughts and Chase pulled himself back to the here and now. He still had that lunch to get to and needed to get her out of his office so they didn't arouse so much interest that their burgeoning fake romance wouldn't be believable.

"That's good. And, um—" He broke off, not sure why the

sudden attack of nerves. "Let me walk you out and when we're in the lobby I'll make an offer for dinner."

"That's a good plan. I'll get my dazzled face on."

He thought she was pretty dazzling just the way she was but held off saying anything. He wasn't a man who did relationships—Leanne had ensured that—and he wasn't about to start now.

So it was time to compartmentalize how attractive he found Sloan Presley and concentrate on her real reason for being here: the rat inside Colton Properties who was stealing from his business.

"There is something I've been meaning to ask you."

Sloan had already stood and was settling her laptop into an oversize shoulder bag. "Of course."

"You did a really good job of coming off as frazzled and late this morning."

"That's because that part wasn't an act."

They had given each other minimal prompts on how they'd set up their meeting, both deciding it would be better to let it play out, but even he hadn't been able to dismiss how real their faked meeting had felt in the conference room.

"What was it?"

"A result of a sick cat and impossible-to-find parking in your lot downstairs."

"It was damned convincing."

"I'll remember that next time I'm cleaning up cat vomit."

"My sister Ruby is a vet. If you need anything, I can hook you up."

"Thanks. I think Waffles was just letting me know he wasn't crazy about our new digs, but if he doesn't settle I'll be sure to get her number."

It was one more layer of involvement between Sloan and his family but he hated to think of any animal sick. And if his sister found out there was a distressed animal in a hundred-mile radius of her, she'd hunt it down until she found it and nursed it back to health.

Since Sloan's bag was packed and already on her shoulder, Chase had to admit he'd stalled long enough. "Let me walk you out then."

The hallway looked the same as it had a half hour ago.

So why did it feel so different?

The carpet was the same. So were the tasteful art pieces on the walls and in a few carved-out niches along the corridor.

And yet…

He was different.

He'd walked Sloan down to his office with the intent to deceive. While it was a means to an important end, that reality had stuck a hard layer of guilt in his gut all the same.

Now, as he walked her to the front of the lobby, preparing to invite her to dinner, he realized something far more important had happened in the ensuing time in his office.

The guilt had faded in the face of the reality of their plan. Her expertise and her commitment to ferreting out a problem had helped him realize this really was the only way.

Yet something new had taken up root in his gut.

He was no longer worried about Colton Properties, or what his employees ultimately thought of his tactics to protect his business.

He was far more concerned he'd been deceiving himself.

Because no matter how he played out the ruse in his mind, Sloan Presley would be walking out that door for good once she solved the problems in his company.

And he was increasingly convinced he wasn't ever going to be the same man who'd welcomed her in.

Chapter Three

Sloan tapped a few keys and set up a small algorithm to run on one machine while she opened a browser window on another.

She'd done some research before taking the job—her standard background checks and basic vetting of her potential employer—but she hadn't done a real deep dive into the Colton family.

It was time to do that now.

Chase had been pretty forthcoming in his comments, so she hadn't walked out of his office thinking that he'd been holding back, but there were some things that would be easier to find on her own.

Even now, she could remember those layers of grief, anger and bewilderment that clouded his green gaze. They pulled at her, drawing on something she wouldn't have expected.

A not-so-subtle tug of emotion that she couldn't afford.

She was invested in this case, yes. But those emotions also left her with a concern that she was getting far too personally involved in the work.

The whole fake-dating ploy was a risk. One she'd believed herself able to handle, but now that she'd spent time in Chase Colton's company, she had to admit she might be a wee bit in over her head.

Could she handle it?

Again, *yes.*

But she'd prefer to feel no further tugs or feelings or *emotions.*

She was the investigator here, nothing more.

Which was why she was doing some digging on her own. Once she had those details, she could better frame her questions to Chase, avoiding asking about areas that were open-ended or left room for him to feel his way through the answers.

The man was still grieving his father, after all. More, he was grieving the loss of a life that would never be the same again.

In the moments when she wasn't actually thinking about the man, she'd focused on those changes. For reasons she couldn't explain, she sensed there was something in that distinction that mattered.

And if she could help Chase work through some of that grief—the portion that was wrapped around the aspects of his father's life he'd never known—she'd go a long way toward helping him through this time in his life.

Fanciful?

Yes, she admitted with a sigh.

She wasn't a person given to flights of fancy, so it was odd to realize how important this assignment had become to her.

And how quickly she'd become consumed by it.

But similar to the thoughts she'd had in his office earlier, something about this situation with the Colton family haunted her.

The idea of a mother leaving her children to go and have another family.

With her sister's husband, no less.

It truly boggled, that level of…well, selfishness.

Wasn't it?

Her children weren't at fault, but in so many ways she'd abdicated her responsibilities as a mother. Robert Colton had relinquished his duties, too.

Secret lives.

A secret family.

All wrapped up in a secret love.

Why do that?

If someone was truly in love with another, why not just leave your current circumstances and forge a new path?

Yes, it would be hard, but it would be a grief with purpose. And an endgame, of sorts.

Because these…well, these *lies* Chase and his siblings and cousins were dealing with now were far, far worse.

It was part of what always both amazed and comforted her about data. Data didn't lie. Numbers were numbers and they always added up.

But human emotions?

They were scattered and selfish for some. Profoundly felt and fathoms deep for others.

Waffles strolled into her home office, his tail switching. The little tuxedo cat had found his way to the doorstep of her apartment in Chicago about a year ago. After a quick internet consultation on how to handle a stray, she'd given him some water and can of tuna. The fish must have seemed a feast because he'd stayed, and after getting him checked out by a vet a few days later, Sloan had become the proud owner of a cat.

It had been a novel experience and she was pleased to see whatever had agitated his stomach this morning was long gone as he rubbed himself against her legs.

"You inadvertently added to my cover this morning,

young man." She scratched beneath the chin he'd lifted for her. "So I thank you for that, even as I'm very glad you're on the mend."

Waffles purred under her touch and seemed oblivious to her worry over his health, or her gratitude.

Such a simple response, Sloan mused as she lifted him onto her lap. No emotion necessary. No lies. Just a sort of simple existence, day to day.

For all their seeming evolution, humans found it far more challenging to live in the moment.

As she gently brushed long, full strokes over his back, she continued clicking around a search window for more information on the Colton family.

The same details on Colton Properties came up threaded through the results, but since she'd already been through those, she focused instead on the ones that detailed the family.

Owl Creek, Idaho, was a small town, about two hours away from Boise, but Robert Colton had had a vision for the place. A respite from the city and a place to vacation and get away. The area was rich with water sports in summer, the main lake in town wide, deep and full of options. In winter, they weren't far from ski resorts that offered cross-country skiing, snowmobiling and tubing down snow-covered slopes.

He'd obviously played on the same sorts of wide-open offerings that had made Jackson Hole in Wyoming and Bend in Oregon so appealing. And by all accounts, Robert had succeeded. Owl Creek had grown in reputation, with more and more visitors every year for the past two decades.

For a man with that sort of vision and focus, how hard would it be to add on not just the demands of one family, but two?

She clicked into an article that was more than a decade

old, coming across a picture of Robert and Chase, standing side by side in the very conference room she'd stumbled into that morning.

The resemblance between father and son was evident, even as Robert's body had softened with age. She gave herself a moment to study Chase, his broad smile and even broader frame suggesting a sort of comfortable competence and raw strength. What she saw, though, was something even more profound when it was matched with the ensuing interview beneath the photo.

Chase's smile was proud, but it was his words that really struck her. About all he and his father had planned and envisioned for the future of Colton Properties. It spoke of an excitement for the work and what lay ahead.

With the passage of time and the revelation of secrets, Sloan now knew the man who stood proudly beside his son, echoing his words in the article about their grand, ambitious future, was hiding secrets.

From his son.

From his family.

From everyone.

CHASE HANDED OVER his credit card as he ordered a Scotch on the rocks for himself and a tequila-and-soda for his cousin Max. They'd agreed to meet and Max's text that he'd pulled into the parking lot had ensured his drink would be ready when he sat down.

The bar was relatively new in Owl Creek, established the year before and quickly becoming a favorite of the young professionals in the area. As a real-estate man, Chase liked the town's newest entertainment offering. As a frustrated amateur detective, he liked the atmosphere even more for the low lighting and ability to have a private conversation.

Just what he needed for this meeting with Max.

His cousin walked in just as the bartender placed their drinks on the bar and Max gave him a small wave as he headed in from the front door.

Chase stood to give his cousin a quick hug and a hearty slap on the back.

"You're looking good, cuz."

Max smiled, that quick, flashing grin at odds with the lingering grief Chase knew the man carried, just like him. "What can I say? Life with Della agrees with me."

It certainly did.

Max's work hunting serial killers for the FBI had put him in contact with K-9 tracker Della Winslow the month before. Her skills were extraordinary, and it was her search-and-tracking work with her K-9, Charlie, that had led to the discovery of several dead bodies in the mountainous area not too far from Owl Creek.

The work had been dark and rather grisly, but Della had held up under the pressure. Even though the last body discovered had belonged to her cousin, Angela Baxter. Max had gone all-in on the case, determined to get answers, but ultimately decided his career hunting for depraved murderers had run its course.

Especially after he and Della realized they had feelings for each other.

Chase had always admired his cousin's dedication, but it was only now, when he saw a lightness in the man he hadn't seen for years, that he realized the real toll that work had taken on Max.

He was damn glad the man had decided to move on.

"Love and retirement from the Bureau look good on you."

"Everything's different. I can't believe just how different—" Max took a sip of his drink "—but I'm not questioning it."

"I appreciate you taking the time to talk to me."

"I wanted to hear how things were working out with SecuritKey and, well..." Max put down his glass, wiping a small bit of moisture from the lip. "We've all been through a lot these past few months. Your dad dying. Finding out he and my mom had a family. Meeting Nate and Sarah. It's..." Max trailed off, before seeming to regain his voice. "It's a lot."

Hadn't Chase said something similar to Sloan just earlier?

What he, his siblings and his cousins had all dealt with was more than Chase could have ever imagined, but he'd also gained enough perspective to realize that it couldn't have been any easier for Nate and Sarah. They might be viewing the situation from the opposite perspective, but it wasn't really any better, knowing their parents had kept such a huge secret from them, too.

"We both know what each other's going through, Chase. And if there's anything I've learned, especially after finding those bodies of the young women who will never get a chance to live their lives to the fullest, it's that we need to support each other."

"I keep thinking I'm going to wake up. That this is just some strange, extended dream and it'll all be over." Chase took a sip of his own drink. "But it's like, surprise! You're wide-awake, pal."

"It helps that Nate and Sarah are so great."

"Yeah, they are. And I want to give that a chance. A real chance. They're brother and sister to us all. And they're no more responsible for this weird situation than any of us are."

"No. You can lay that squarely at the feet of our parents."

Chase stared into his drink, seeking some semblance of wisdom from the amber liquid, even as he knew that was as futile as wishing his father had been a different man.

"You think it'll ever get easier?"

"Yeah, I do." Max nodded, his gaze thoughtful. "Finding

Della and talking to her about it all has helped. But more—" He broke off, that wide grin once again spreading across his face. "She's made all the difference, somehow. Even though I know I have to put in the emotional work and find a way through this, it's better." He shrugged. "Not easier, but somehow smoother that there's someone there with me. And I'm grateful for it. Damn grateful."

Unbidden, an image of Sloan from that morning in his office rose up in Chase's mind.

To be honest, I'd be disappointed if you weren't struggling a bit. I'm deeply sorry you're going through this, but you're human. You're entitled to a range of emotions and feelings that don't all line up like numbers on a balance sheet.

She'd been so honest and, even more, she'd been fair. To him. His emotions. And all that was swirling in his heart, his mind and his gut.

To a point, he'd recognized she was a bit embarrassed by it, but she'd risked the words, anyway. And with that risk, Chase realized, he'd taken her words to heart. He'd felt better that she'd acknowledged he didn't have to be some automaton, pushing his way through the situation without care or regard for the pain.

"I'm happy for you." Chase raised his glass, clinking it in a light toast with his cousin. "For you both."

Max took a sip of his drink, the smile clearing as he settled into the conversation. "Tell me what you think about Sloan Presley."

"The woman's sharp. Smart. And I think exactly what I need to do the digital-forensics work at Colton Properties."

"You worried there are more irregularities than you first thought?"

Max's FBI work and their close, lifelong relationship had made him the one person Chase had trusted to discuss what was going on at Colton Properties. It wasn't that he couldn't tell his siblings, but he didn't want to panic anyone. And with a family his size, he couldn't risk someone potentially saying something, even in passing.

So Max was the only one who knew he was concerned about the financials.

And once Chase had answers, he'd share all he'd learned and come clean with everyone.

"I think I want Sloan to scour everything top to bottom and tell me what she sees. I'm too close to it all. Which is why I know something's off but can't decipher exactly what."

"She's the best. Her company only takes jobs through referrals and still has a shocking amount of work, all the time. That's how good she is."

"Good is what I need."

Max's gaze was sharp, speculative and even as he asked, "How are you playing it for the office?"

"She's my unexpected and brand-new girlfriend."

Max's eyes widened as he let out a low whistle. "No kidding!"

"We hatched the plan as we worked through the details of what needs to be done. It's the only way we can get her in and out of the office with an easy reason for being there."

"You do realize the irony in it all?"

"Irony?" Chase wasn't sure where Max was going, but the man's pointed smile had him immediately curious.

"You're the great bachelor of Owl Creek. Surely you can see the joke in all this."

"I'm a divorced man. That hardly makes me a bachelor."

"You're wealthy, single and you never date a woman more than twice in a row. Trust me, people notice that." Max leaned over and patted Chase on the back before signaling their bartender for one more drink. "And you're the one who needs a fake girlfriend to get underneath the problems at your business."

CHASE WASN'T SURE he saw Max's humor with regard to his current situation. His cousin's words haunted him long after they'd wrapped up their second drink and their conversation.

He'd walked back to the office with the intention of getting a bit of work done, but after an hour of staring at his computer screen and intermittently checking sports scores online, he decided to call it a night.

As a man used to work and action, this strange, lingering malaise he hadn't been able to fully get rid of since his father's death had been endlessly confusing.

You're entitled to a range of emotions and feelings...

Again, Sloan's quiet and compassionate diagnosis was front and center in his mind.

He wasn't one who gave in to his softer feelings. Hadn't he even taken pride that he'd focused on work all the way through his separation and the months that came after as he and his ex-wife wrangled over the dissolution of their marriage?

Divorcing Leanne had been the worst time in his life. Or had been, until this situation with his father and the man's secret family. Chase hadn't gone into marriage expecting he'd end it two years later, but his wife hadn't been who he thought she was.

The woman he'd believed himself in love with had revealed herself to be a grasping, unfaithful partner, and after discovering her affair—what had been revealed to be one of many—he'd walked away.

Was that part of his problem with his father?

His bad marriage aside, his father's death and the revelation of his secret life would have been a horrible experience, regardless. But to add on his experience with Leanne?

Was he that poor a judge of character?

Did he see what he wanted to see instead of what was?

Was there anyone he could trust?

Those thoughts had swirled these past few months, stealthily creeping in at odd moments. He'd tried to ignore them, but the questions were there all the same.

More, the self-doubt had become crushing at times.

Add on the problems at Colton Properties and Chase had been forced to reconsider his ability to properly assess those around him.

It's why you've hired Sloan.

He mentally shook his head as he shut down his computer. It was why he'd hired SecuritKey.

He had to stop thinking of this job through the lens of the woman and start thinking of it through the work she did. He'd hired her for her skills.

Even if he found himself continually imagining the soft sweep of curls she'd brushed behind her ear, or those sharp, fathomless brown eyes.

Which was how he found himself ten minutes later heading across town to the apartment complex where she was renting a small one-bedroom.

He'd suggested the location himself, the reality of needing her close by in Owl Creek for the duration of the job ensuring she'd be too far away to stay at her own home in Chicago.

The apartment complex was only a few years old and had been another expansion in town directed by Colton Properties. The location boasted long-term rentals as well as a handful of furnished, short-term options for those who wanted a place to stay in Owl Creek longer than a hotel stay.

He'd pushed for the short-term options with the property

owner, helping the man round out his vision of what his investment could truly become.

As he turned into the complex's entrance, Chase was happy to see the place looked well-kept, and its parking lot was full.

"You might suck at reading people, Colton, but you've got damn good instincts for real estate," he said to himself.

Brimming with that subtle sense of satisfaction, he got out of his car and headed for the building that housed Sloan's apartment. Windows were open and he heard the strains of oldies music pumping into the air.

Instinctively, he knew the sound of Chuck Berry was coming from Sloan's place and at the same time, he recognized how the music fit her.

She was an old soul.

One with knowledge and understanding layered through her words and actions.

He walked up the exterior concrete steps to the second floor and knocked on her door. The music was louder now that he stood outside her apartment, and he knocked again. When the knocking still went unheeded, he waited for the last strains of Chuck's voice to wane before pounding on the door a third time.

Only to hear the rushing of feet before a bemused Sloan stood on the other side of the open door.

"Chase. Hi."

"Hey. Am I bothering you?"

"Sorry, no." She shook her head, before stepping back to gesture him in. "I was working and had the music turned up a little loud. Were you out here long?"

"Just a few rounds of knocking."

"I'm sorry."

Chuck Berry's rocking voice gave way to the familiar

strains of Ritchie Valens's guitar and she raced across the room to snap off a high-end portable stereo with built-in speakers.

The room quieted immediately and Chase could only smile. "I would have pegged you for Madonna. Maybe Janet Jackson or Pink."

"Oh, when the mood strikes I can definitely get into the groove. I was feeling the fifties tonight."

"Old-school."

"Definitely."

They both stood there. He knew it should have felt awkward, but instead it just felt…right.

Complete, somehow, to be here with her at the end of the day.

Since that only reinforced his earlier inward admissions that he needed to get his fanciful thoughts *off* Sloan Presley, Chase pointed to the couch. "Mind if I sit?"

"Sure. Can I get you anything?"

"No, I'm good. I met up with my cousin Max for a few drinks."

Sloan brightened at the reference to his cousin. "How is he?"

"He's good. He's left the FBI, you know."

"I'd heard rumblings from a mutual friend but wasn't sure if it was rumors or fact. That's a big change."

"A good one, I think." Chase thought about the happy man who'd sat opposite him in the bar. "Hunting serial killers is grisly work."

"It's terrible work. Necessary, but terrible." Sloan shuddered. "I think his calling was admirable, but it must be soul-sucking."

Chase had often thought the same, and even in the very short time Max had been away from it, he'd seen a difference in his cousin.

A welcome one that reduced the unceasing shadows he'd always seen in Max's eyes.

"I agree, which is what makes it great to see him so happy."

"That same friend who'd shared those rumblings was more descriptive about Max's last case. Those murders are awful."

Chase didn't know much more than what had been shared in the news—none of them seemed to—but the case had definitely captured local attention. Max, with Della and her K-9's help, had uncovered the bodies of seven dead women the prior month. An eighth victim had escaped and been placed in protective custody as she healed in the hospital, but a blackout had left her vulnerable to an attacker, who'd killed her.

Max had killed that man, but they hadn't been able to get any more details about the murders or why that woman had been targeted, either.

"The extensive loss of life has been a shock."

"Rumors say it's that strange Ever After Church." Sloan visibly shuddered. "Though *church* feels like a bad term for them."

"You know of them?"

"I did a bit of research after you emailed me, saying Max was our connection. I've spent my entire adult life looking into the weird, unexpected and flat-out off. Heck, I've made a career out of that work."

Sloan's comment hung there and Chase picked up on it. "Yeah?"

"Anything I've tried to dig up on them? It's all strange and oddly bucolic on the surface, yet feels deeply false at the same time."

"Max certainly thought so."

"I keep wondering why no one has followed the money because something's definitely not right there. Their nomadic lifestyle. Those bodies that were discovered. And then that poor woman in the hospital?" Sloan looked thoughtful as her cat jumped onto her lap, and she absently ran a hand down his back. "I know it's wrong to assign blame until actually proven guilty, but something isn't right with that group."

Chase considered Sloan's comments and once again recognized just how skilled the woman was. Her success at her work went far deeper than her computer skills, which were obviously expert.

But she had sharp instincts, too, and that couldn't be dismissed as anything other than a key part of her success.

Suddenly coming back to herself, she grinned over the top of her now-purring cat.

"Sorry. I got lost in my head there for a moment."

"I was just thinking it was an impressive skill." When her deep brown eyes warmed, Chase continued on. "You're observant and aware. Obviously, you know your way around computer code, but I think you've been successful because you apply considerable smarts over that."

"Oh." Her hand fumbled against the cat's fur before she lifted her gaze to his. "Why, thank you."

"You're welcome."

"I—" She broke off, then muttered, "What the hell?"

Intrigued, Chase avoided saying anything, giving her the room to continue.

"Most people find my curiosity annoying."

"You mean your intelligence," Chase corrected.

"I meant curiosity, but we can add on intelligence if you'd like."

"Let's add it."

She stilled for a moment, her hand settling on the cat's back, before she continued on. "I learned early that people don't like all the tech talk. They come to me when they want their computer fixed or are having some issue with a file, but no one loves the idea I can dig into databases and find information."

"Sounds like their problem."

"Maybe yes, maybe no. We live in a digital world and someone who can dissect all those ones and zeroes is threatening."

"To people burying something nefarious in those ones and zeroes, maybe." Chase shrugged. "I still say it's their problem. One of their own making, too."

"Yes, well, most men, well, really all men," she amended, her brow crunching into the cutest frown lines. "What I do is seen as aggressive, for some reason. And each time I've shared my business and my work with a man, he's gone running."

"Sounds like you've had some really crummy dates in the past."

"Are you being deliberately obtuse?"

"I'm processing what you're saying and discarding it as loads of BS that has been heaped on you."

"It's not a skill people appreciate."

"I appreciate your skills. In fact..." Chase shifted to the edge of the couch, leaning forward to look into her eyes.

"*In fact* what?"

The slightest catch in her breath warmed him clear through and Chase felt the air around them ignite.

"I appreciate them so much I've invited you into my home and my work to help me get to the bottom of my little professional problem."

"I'm here to help."

Chase sat back, suddenly realizing how effortlessly she drew him to her. "I appreciate it more than I can say."

It was so simple to sit here with her.

To breathe the same air and talk about the day. He'd

shared more of his life with her in less than twenty-four hours than he'd shared with most people of his acquaintance for the past year.

Even knowing there was nothing at the end of their time together other than a disappointing revelation about someone he presumably trusted, he couldn't seem to keep his mind on that fact.

Because he was more intrigued by Sloan Presley than he could have ever imagined.

Chapter Four

It had been close.

No, *they* had been close, Sloan amended to herself as she got into her car to drive over to Colton Properties, just as she'd corrected herself all morning.

They.

With their heads bent together in her living room, Chase's compelling green gaze had drawn her to him like a lodestone.

He'd been the quintessential gentleman, checking on her, asking how she was settling in and talking with her about his visit with his cousin.

She'd felt…connected.

And he'd complimented her with one of the nicest things anyone had ever said to her, she thought as she turned onto the main road that would take her into downtown Owl Creek.

While she was deeply appreciative of her own gifts as a human being—and valued what others brought to bear as well—her intelligence had often alienated people. Never intentionally, but the distance had been there all the same, especially when it came to dating and discussing her career with the men she was seeing.

It was never overtly mentioned, but any enthusiasm she

brought to discussing her work was typically met with polite smiles and blank stares. So she'd learned to push it down and suppress it, recognizing that what interested her and drove her wasn't get-to-know-you date conversation.

Yet with Chase, she not only didn't have to do that, but he also seemed to celebrate her professional accomplishments.

Not that they were dating.

Sloan shook off that thought.

Firmly.

They were *fake* dating and that was an entirely different matter.

Those confused yet utterly pleasing thoughts had rattled through Sloan's mind all morning, as she ran around the small reservoir in the center of her apartment complex.

They had vexed her as she'd come back and fed Waffles and made herself coffee and oatmeal.

And they'd haunted her as she'd showered and gotten ready, slipping into business attire for her trip to Colton Properties.

She was not a woman who got rattled, vexed *or* haunted, so it was all a novel experience.

"Just a little fanciful moment, that's all. And why not, with the change in time zones and living space and the job to be done?" she asked herself as she checked her reflection in the rear view mirror and used the moment as an abstract sort of pep talk. "Your body clock is upside down and this job is important to you. That's all it was."

Satisfied she'd finally explained it away, she grabbed her work bag, got out and locked her car, and headed for the building that housed Colton Properties.

In spite of the ruse they'd concocted to have their "meet cute," Sloan had legitimately been running late to the meeting because of Waffles's unceremonious delivery of his breakfast back to her. So she gave herself a few more moments this morning to catch her breath, all while taking in her surroundings.

Owl Creek really was beautiful. She'd never been to Idaho before this job and while she knew the weather would turn cold before long, September had a lot going for it. The morning breeze was fresh, and the sky was a vivid blue that made Sloan think of endless possibilities.

She'd been intrigued by this job. Although Colton Properties was smaller in scale and scope than the clients she usually took on, the business had real promise. And the change of pace from her usual workload was a plus. She'd recently worked a string of government contracts that, to borrow a description she'd used the night before, had been soul-sucking.

There had been several money-laundering jobs, drug trafficking and, most recently, a human-trafficking case that still managed to give her nightmares.

The opportunity to get out of Chicago for a few weeks and do some work that was decidedly less fraught with human suffering had been appealing when she'd gotten Chase's outreach email.

It had been humbling to realize that even with the more streamlined, business-focused work, there was still a fair amount of suffering. The Colton family was going through a real trial, and she was oddly glad she was here.

She might not be able to change Chase's personal situation for the better, but she could solve his business problem for him. And somewhere down deep she felt that the work mattered extra, somehow, because of it.

"There really is something to be said for all that clean mountain air."

She whirled at the voice, only to come face-to-face with Chase.

Had she conjured him up?

Quickly regrouping, Sloan fought for something to say, even as she could still feel his liquid gaze from the night before and those intense moments of closeness they'd shared.

"I haven't seen any mountains."

"Owl Creek is less mountainous than other parts of the state, but overall we can rock the fresh mountain air with the best of them. There are over three thousand mountains in Idaho, with the highest being Borah Peak at over twelve thousand feet."

"Wow." She considered what she'd read before coming. "The northern Rockies come through Idaho, yes?"

"Yep, on their northward climb to Canada. Which means we've got great ski weather in the winter and fantastic trails in the summer." Chase grinned, the look boyish and appealing in the bright morning sun. "And I sound like a walking advertisement for the tourist board."

"You sound like a man who knows where he lives and knows how to sell it."

He shrugged before gesturing her forward. "I'll take it."

They walked across the parking lot toward the building, and she scrambled for something to say. "I'm a little early but I wanted to get started."

Chase pulled the door open for her, his gaze appreciative. "I'd say you're right on time."

It was only a reference to her arrival, yet as she stared up at him before crossing the threshold, Sloan couldn't help feeling his words meant so much more.

Why did this all feel so right?

While that inward sense would radiate out to others and help keep their dating ruse intact, she knew well enough to realize these thoughts were dangerous.

This was a job.

There wasn't room for it to feel *right* or *wrong*—she just had to do the work she was being paid for.

With that sobering thought, she moved through the lobby and headed for the elevators that led to Chase's floor.

If he sensed her lack of equilibrium this morning, he didn't mention it, instead following her and holding the elevator doors as she stepped in. After the doors swooshed closed and they were ensconced in a small moment of privacy, he finally spoke.

"I can set you up in my office and give you the access you need into the systems. I think you should work off of my extra laptop so it looks like you're doing your own work, but you can access files through my log-in."

"You don't mind? That's still your personal workstation."

He shrugged but the ease that had carried him into the building had vanished.

"I don't have anything to hide. And I'm committed to finding the person who does."

"That will make it a bit easier for me to get in, especially initially. I can clone your access points and transfer over to my machine without IT being any wiser if you're okay with that, too?" Despite his complete lack of response to that offer, Sloan rushed on. "I can show you exactly what I've done and then show you how I'm removing it from my workstation when we close this job."

"I trust your work, Sloan. You've been clear about the skills you bring to this and I need your services. Do what you need to do."

And there it was again.

That endorsement of her and her work that held nothing back. No conditions and no excuses.

And maybe even better, that saw those parts of her as something to be trusted.

CHASE COULDN'T EXPLAIN it to himself, but something about Sloan Presley made him feel calm.

Centered.

And *interested*, despite all his better judgments.

Even as all that interest kept his senses heightened and his awareness of her became something he hadn't experienced in…well, ever.

He'd loved Leanne, that hadn't been a sham. They'd dated and when they'd connected quickly, he'd continued to press the relationship forward, carrying them along toward forever.

Had things been perfect?

No, but things had been good.

And he'd assumed that it would be enough to see them through forever.

It had crashed and burned in spectacular fashion. But whenever he thought back to their origins, Chase had always carried that clear personal admission that he'd progressed their relationship so quickly toward marriage because it had felt like it was time.

Like the big clock in his head that told him he was meant to grow up, be successful in business and start a family like his father, was ticking away.

Or counting down, more like.

So he'd found Leanne. She was an attractive companion, able to fit into any situation, be it social or business. She was full of sparkling conversation and pretty smiles, and he'd felt a deep sense of satisfaction knowing she'd fit the bill.

One that lived entirely in his head and was of his own making.

Whatever resentment he'd carried for her and her actions since the dissolution of his marriage, the one area he took full blame for was that unchanging truth: he'd searched for a wife that fit a set of criteria, not someone whom he loved simply for who she was.

It was part of why he'd sworn off marriage so completely.

He'd made his personal life a business transaction and he simply couldn't be trusted to chart a path forward with someone else. Colton Properties was too important to him, and, in the end, he'd accepted that about himself just as he'd accepted his role in the failure of their marriage.

Despite the scars he carried from his divorce, he had moved on. He didn't think about Leanne every day, or frankly, even most weeks. She'd even called him a few years back to tell him she was remarrying and that she was happy, and he'd been happy for her.

No lingering remorse or anger. Just acceptance.

So why had she occupied his thoughts so heavily these past few weeks?

Even as he asked himself the question, Chase knew the truth.

It was the woman he was currently ushering into his office.

Sloan.

He followed her through his office entryway before leaving the door open so anyone passing by or stopping in to discuss the day's business would see she was here with him.

With her bag stowed at the small meeting table he kept in his office, she crossed over to the individual coffee brewer on his sideboard. After selecting a coffee pod, she settled a mug in the serving tray and started the machine whirring before turning back toward him.

"You sure I'm not in the way?"

"Not in the least. Work through what you need in here and when the usual parade comes in this morning for meetings and updates, people will be sure to see you."

"It sounds like your day will be busy. I want to strike the right balance between starry-eyed new relationship and *not* looking like a leech sucking up time in your office."

She set a new cup down on the brewer for him before

hunting for the container of cream he kept in the small fridge built into the base of the sideboard.

Chase wasn't sure why, but something in that small domestic act pulled him up short. He'd have missed it if he hadn't looked up at just the right moment from logging in to his own computer, but he *had* looked up.

Had seen that simple gesture.

And realized he hadn't shared coffee with anyone in a long time.

"Chase?"

Her soft smile and expectant gaze pulled him out of his reverie.

"Oh. Yeah."

"Do you want cream or sugar?"

"I can fix it." He jumped up like a cat who'd been doused in water and crossed over to her. "You don't have to make my coffee."

She shrugged before stepping away from the machine with her mug. "Shouldn't I know how you like it?"

"Technically, we just met yesterday. You'd probably get a pass on how I drink my coffee."

"Fair." She appeared to consider for a moment, tapping the side of her mug. "We are going to have to figure out what conversations we would realistically have at what stage of things. To your point, coffee would be new, but would I know how many siblings you have? Or what's currently going on with your family?"

If the switch to business had something sour settling in his stomach, Chase ignored it as he lifted his mug and pasted on a smile. "Black with two sugars."

"Noted."

"But the situation with my family isn't a secret. You could just as easily hear it from me as anyone in this office."

His tone—the one he'd determined would sound as cheerful as possible—instead sounded like he'd been chewing nails with his coffee.

"I'm sorry. I keep bumbling over the same difficult ground." She moved closer and laid a hand on his forearm. "I do recognize this is a trying time."

"It's not your fault."

"No, but I could be a little more delicate. We're investigating your business. I need to leave your family situation off the table."

"It's hardly off the table, Sloan. Nor is it something that people are whispering about." He thought back to the conference-room discussion the day before. "People are talking about it with bullhorns in hand to amplify the message."

He saw the unmistakable sympathy in her eyes and something about that stuck in his gut.

Hard.

"I don't need you to tiptoe here. Do what you need to do. That's why I hired you."

Although he'd stand by every word he'd just spoken as truth, his tone was harsh. Unyielding. It bordered on obnoxious-bastard territory.

"Got it."

"Sloan, I—"

He was stopped by the arrival of Clint Roebuck and the lead of retail properties, Jamie Hunt. "Colton. Do you have a minute?"

Sloan glanced over at the two men, a beaming smile firmly in place. "You gentlemen discuss what you need to. I'm just going to get caught up on some email over there."

If the men were surprised to see her there, they hid it well, save for Clint's glance toward the small table where Sloan busied herself settling in, popping in earbuds before facing her computer.

"If now's a bad time, we can come back."

"Not at all." Chase pasted on a grin of his own, gesturing toward the coffee maker. "Help yourself and let's get down to what's going on. I'm betting you're here over the Lake Road property."

"It's a mess, Chase," Jamie began, waving off the coffee. "We've had a deal for some time, but the owner is balking now. Says he doesn't want a retail center marring the pristine lake environment."

Chase wanted to kick them both out and apologize to Sloan, but he had a part to play.

They both did.

And they'd all been working on the Lake Road deal for months now. It had been one of the last deals his father had initiated before his stroke.

Business as usual, Colton.

It's what he had to do.

More, what he had to focus on.

His thoughts had been full of fake dates, corporate espionage and all the damn problems that seemed to define his life right now.

Yet as he'd so eloquently told Sloan, that's why he'd *hired* her.

Chase Colton didn't do relationships. He'd learned that a long time ago.

But business deals?

Those he could see through in his sleep.

SLOAN HUNTED THROUGH FILES, downloaded what looked important and ultimately mapped herself a digital back door into Colton Properties. Chase had given her extraordinary access to his company and while she was grateful for his trust that she'd do her job, she had to admit the man had—literally—handed her the keys to his kingdom.

From files on property deals, to business expansion plans

and audit histories, there wasn't much she couldn't learn about the company. And even though she still smarted from their coffee conversation—she was hired help, after all—she couldn't deny her fascination all the same.

Do what you need to do. That's why I hired you.

Over and over, that specific part of their conversation had looped through her mind. And because those words had stuck, Sloan once again reminded herself of the plain truth.

She was here to do a job.

One she'd been hired for.

That didn't mean she was "hired help" in a derogatory way.

Yet even with the admonitions to herself, the discussion stuck.

Because nothing about this job had helped her maintain the professional distance she was known for.

Was it the fake-dating situation?

While she'd like to blame it on that—and the odd, swirling feelings for Chase she couldn't quite blunt or blot away—she knew it was something more.

Something about what the Colton family was going through pulled at her. It had flipped a switch she hadn't even realized she possessed.

And yeah…there was that incendiary chemistry, no matter how much she wanted to avoid it all with her inward commentary on how this was a job.

But it was also the family.

She knew who her parents were. Her extended family, too. And while she'd never dare to think that she was privy to every thought any of them ever had, she was quite confident that her father and mother were who they'd shown her to be. After a lifetime of knowing them, she knew the good and bad about them, their charms and their quirks.

But she also *knew* them.

How terrible must it be, then, to realize your parent wasn't just something other than you'd believed, but someone with a whole other life?

And a whole other family?

The very idea of it haunted her.

She was someone who worked in data. Things she could see or create, in and with code. It was part of why she was as good at her job as she was. Everything she did was about hunting for information.

But that information *existed.*

It wasn't about feelings or emotions. It was about finding the truth.

The knock on the door pulled her attention from her computer and Sloan quickly locked the screen.

"Hello?"

After the parade of people who'd trooped into Chase's office, she'd ended up moving to a small conference room off the front entrance. She figured she'd lasted long enough doing the "girlfriend show" and she needed some quiet, focused concentration to get through the setup of her digital back door.

"Yes, hello." She smiled, thinking about the dreamy, slightly unfocused look she'd practiced in the mirror.

"We're ordering in some food for lunch and Chase suggested I ask what you're hungry for."

"Oh, that was sweet of him." She pushed a bit more dreaminess into that smile, then added, "I'm fine with whatever he wants."

The words felt like syrup on her tongue but the woman clucked happily. "We're planning on pizza and a big salad." The woman stepped farther into the room. "I'm Althea, by the way. I'm the office manager."

"Oh, it's lovely to meet you. I'm Sloan."

They exchanged basic pleasantries for a few minutes,

but Sloan recognized two key facts beneath the chitchat. Chase might be the head of Colton Properties, but Althea ran the place.

And she was dying to get more information on the new woman in the boss's life.

Since this was the exact sort of opportunity Sloan was looking for, she leaned in.

Hard.

"I hope you don't mind my hanging out here. Chase said I could and then we could go straight to dinner from here later and, well—" She broke off, pleased to see the happy smile on Althea's face. "He's just such a wonderful man."

"Our Chase is wonderful. Can I tell you a secret?"

"Oh, you don't have to do that."

Althea waved a hand. "It's a secret in so much as the men around here pay little attention. But all the women here in the office have been hoping Chase will meet a great woman."

"We just met and—" Again, Sloan pasted on that loopy smile. "Do you think he likes me?"

"I've no doubt of it."

"Well then, I'll share a secret of my own. I like him, too. And it's just so fast, I'm not quite sure of myself, but I do know I like him. More than I could have imagined."

"Honey, when you know, you know. The night I met my Ben I was out with two girlfriends. I told them both that was the man I was going to marry."

Sloan's mom had often told a similar tale about her father, and while she'd thought it a sweet story, she'd never put all that much stock in it.

People didn't fall in love with a glance across a room or, even if their own response was strong enough to make them feel that way, there was no way of knowing with certainty the other person felt the same.

Since she worried she wasn't quite good enough as an actress to sell her agreement, she opted for an adjacent topic. "How long have you and Ben been married?"

"Thirty-three years next month." Althea beamed before she seemed to come back to herself. "I'd better get that pizza and salad ordered or we won't have it in time for lunch. I'll see you later."

"Do you need me to move somewhere else?"

"Not at all. I went ahead and booked the room for you in our conference-room system. It's yours for the rest of the day."

Althea turned to go but stopped just shy of the door. "There is something, if you don't mind my saying."

Sloan tilted the lid of her computer so that she could fully focus on Althea. "Of course."

"Be gentle with his heart. He pretends toughness but I've known him a long time. He feels a lot more than he lets on."

"I have no intention of hurting him."

Althea didn't say anything else, just nodded and left.

But it was long minutes later before Sloan lifted her computer screen back up and got back into her work flow.

Even longer for her to put those words out of her mind.

Chapter Five

The week sped by in a blur. Chase wasn't quite sure how it had happened, but he'd gotten used to Sloan's face. She didn't come into the office with him every day, but kept a good balance of popping in with a surprise lunch one day and then a big show of dragging him out to play hooky for the afternoon.

He'd spent the other day making his own show out of rushing out the door at the stroke of five to meet her for drinks and dinner.

And now, here they were on Friday afternoon, staring down a weekend.

He'd monopolized her time, between the work itself and their endless parade of dates to put on a show around town, and he recognized the woman deserved a break.

Even if he was surprisingly loath to spend the evening alone.

He'd gone out on a property tour a few towns over and had just cleared the front door of the office when he heard the commotion.

His sister, Ruby, and his brother Fletcher's new girlfriend, Kiki, were in the lobby, along with a puppy and what appeared to be half the office.

Sloan was there, too, on the floor with the pretty shepherd mix, her work bag abandoned near her feet.

"Hi." Chase said.

"Chase!" Ruby rushed for him first, the growing roundness of her belly pressing against him as she leaned in for a big hug. It still amazed him that his little sister was having a baby, but he was happy for her. Especially since she'd found forever with Sebastian Cross.

They'd all known each other since they were kids, with Sebastian and their brother Wade going into the marines together. Wade had stayed in the service until he was injured, but Sebastian had come back to Owl Creek after completing his tour of duty. They'd all recognized Sebastian was a changed man, but it was only once they got together that Ruby realized how much his time in the military had affected him.

Their work placing dogs with PTSD training to veterans was a passion project for both of them and Ruby donated her veterinarian services while Sebastian volunteered the training. But when something had ultimately sparked between them, Chase and his whole family had recognized just how perfect a match they were for each other.

He'd also never seen his sister so lit up inside.

"I'm always happy to see you," he murmured against his sister's cheek, "but what's going on here?"

"Kiki and I are training this little girl for service. We were downtown so thought we'd stop in. It's good for them to experience elevators as part of their training."

Chase almost pulled back when Ruby whispered heavily in his ear, "And you've been holding out on us about Sloan. She's great!"

Since there was no way they could continue this conversation in the middle of all those people while locked in a whisper war, Chase stepped away from his sister and turned to the team. “Looks like it’s time to get an early head start on our Friday. Once you’ve had your puppy time, feel free to get your weekend going a bit early. Thanks to everyone for a good week.”

The offer was enough to get people moving and after a few more polite smiles and oohs and aahs for the puppy, the crowd began to thin, leaving him, Ruby, Kiki and Sloan, who gently handled the puppy as she got to her feet.

“She’s adorable. Such a sweet girl,” she said, bending to give the gangly puppy one more pat on its soft brown head.

“Fancy’s coming along,” Kiki agreed, then turned to give Chase a hug. “Thanks for letting us intrude. We weren’t sure how she’d take to the elevator but she’s a champ.”

“I’m always happy to see you all. And let me introduce Sloan.”

“We met,” Ruby said quickly, her smile broad. “I’d heard some rumors you two were spotted out and about this week.”

Although he hated lying to his family about why Sloan was really in his life, he couldn’t deny his reaction was pure truth. “We’re having a good time.”

“Which means you can have an even better time this evening at my place. Kiki and I decided we needed a cookout tonight before it gets too cold to enjoy grilling.”

He glanced at Sloan, but she seemed okay with the plan he suspected had already been presented to her. “What prompted this informal gathering?”

Gathering intel on his love life, Chase had no doubt. Information that would be spreading around the family like wildfire the moment his sister could text out of his line of sight.

But Ruby stood there, innocence personified, and Kiki was quick to back her up. “She claims the baby’s hungry for a steak, so we figured that was as good a reason as any.

Plus, we haven't had much time with Nate and Sarah, and this is a casual way to all be together."

"Did you invite Mom?"

He liked Nate and Sarah and did want to get to know his half siblings, but discussion of them still gave him concerns for his mother, too.

For the first time since his arrival, he saw his sister's smile tighten, her green eyes, so like his own, clouding with those same concerns. "She already had plans tonight with her book club so isn't able to join us."

So he wasn't the only one looking out for Mom.

In fact, it was probably his mother's plans that had made it so natural to press for this evening's impromptu get-together.

With one last glance at Sloan, which she greeted with a happy nod, he said, "Then count us in. And let me know what we can bring."

"You've been working all day. Bring a few bottles of wine or a twelve-pack of beer and we'll be all set. We'll see you at seven."

As quickly as they'd rolled in, Ruby, Kiki and the now-sleepy Fancy rolled out and he was left in the lobby with Sloan. Althea was looking on from the small office that had a direct line of sight to the front area.

He avoided glancing that way, well aware they were the center of attention, and instead used the moment to his advantage, leaning in to press a soft kiss to her cheek.

"Hi."

"I probably would have said it, anyway, but the puppy inspired me." She smiled and Chase realized that warm visage packed enough punch to nearly make him forget his name. "Fancy meeting you here."

She kept her voice low, breathy almost, and Chase had

one of those abstract thoughts that had become more and more distinct over the past few days.

Why did this feel so real?

He knew it wasn't, but between having her here and now the dinner with his family, it was getting harder and harder to remember that.

When she only kept up that conspiratorial smile, he tilted his head in the vague direction of his office. "I need to get a few things and then we'll start our weekend, too."

"Sounds like a plan."

He heard a happy little sigh from the direction of Althea's office as they progressed down the hall and it wasn't until they were inside his office, with the door closed, that Chase turned with a quick apology.

"I'm so sorry for my sister. And my brother's girlfriend. Though, if I know Ruby, Kiki was innocent in plotting and planning this."

"It's fine."

"Yeah, but you didn't get a lot of choice there."

"Chase, really, it's fine. I'd like to meet your family, and to be honest, that steak Kiki mentioned sounds like a lovely end to the week. Especially with the merlot I have in my apartment that I will plan to bring along."

"You don't have to bring anything."

Her face fell at that statement, and he sensed he had overstepped, even though he couldn't fully figure out why.

"I can pick something up. You don't have to go to any trouble."

"It's not any trouble and I'd like to."

Although the subject of the wine seemed to have been figured out, he couldn't dismiss the feeling he'd mishandled the conversation. In fact, he'd felt that way a few times this week whenever he shifted into business.

The friction vanished almost as fast as it came, but it was

there all the same. That subtle sense that talking to her about the work she was doing was insulting, somehow.

Even as he considered that angle, Chase had to admit it wasn't exactly right. She sent him an update at the end of each day, and they spent time on each of their "dates" talking through what she'd learned or was working on.

So really, work wasn't the actual problem, was it?

He nearly asked when she tapped on the edge of her shoulder bag. "I do have a few things to share with you. If you'd like to pick me up a bit earlier than we need to get over to your sister's, I can fill you in."

"Yeah. Sure. That makes sense. Is it bad?"

"I want your thoughts. You may see something I don't."

She didn't answer the question and Chase figured it was the tip of the iceberg. His gut had told him something was wrong. Whatever digging Sloan had been doing must be reinforcing his concerns in some way.

With a heavy heart at the realization that someone he knew was at the center of it all, he just nodded.

"Alright. How about if I get to your place around six?"

"I'll see you then."

Before they could engage in any of the comfortable conversation they'd had before, Sloan was already headed for the door.

And as she left, he couldn't help but wonder if there was more truth in her words than he wanted to admit.

You may see something I don't.

He wasn't so sure about that. Especially because there was something standing right in front of him, and he hadn't seen it yet.

Worse, he had no clue what it even was.

"IT'S JUST A bottle of wine."

She'd muttered that to herself, or some version of it, including "get it together," "stop being a drama llama," and "get your head out of your butt" since she'd walked in the door.

Even Waffles had grown tired of her, his tail waving in the air as he'd headed for his favorite spot in the corner of the living room, where she'd set up a small feline entertainment center for him.

With the small sting of that kitty disdain still lingering, Sloan admitted to herself that it really was time to get her head out of her butt.

And really, *why* did she keep getting herself bent out of shape when Chase's comments suggested he had his own head on quite straight and was operating with the full knowledge they were working a job?

It didn't matter they'd had a great week together. Their dinners had been enjoyable, always professional, but human, too, full of easy conversation and shared thoughts.

It was the conversations that made her feel good.

Heard.

Understood.

But it still didn't mean there was any room for the emotions sparking all over the place on her side.

What did matter was that Chase had hired her to look into problems at the company.

And while she hadn't pinpointed the culprit yet, she'd dug deep enough to know there were problems.

Someone was very good at covering their tracks and at hiding the data, but the files were off.

Dates didn't match up.

There were small discrepancies that, once dug into and added up, led to an overarching larger issue in each month's financial close.

And a strange set of expenses she couldn't find fault with, yet couldn't connect to any major job, either.

Aware she wasn't going to figure it out standing there staring into space, she headed into the bedroom to freshen up. There wasn't time to bother with another shower, but she did want to look good for Chase's family. Where Kiki had been a bit more subtle, Ruby hadn't been able to hide her interest. Just like Althea earlier in the week, she seemed particularly happy that her brother was in a relationship.

It was interesting, Sloan mused as she added hot rollers to her hair and redid her eye makeup. That steady stream of everyone wanting to see Chase settle down. Although it wasn't talked about, there was that subtle hum in the air that suggested his first marriage loomed large in his life.

Which meant they were going to be hit with an awfully big bomb of disappointment once the case was over, and he wasn't "dating" Sloan any longer.

"A problem for another day," she muttered to herself as she walked back into the bedroom to get the slacks and thin blouse she'd already laid out.

Waffles looked up at her from where he groomed himself on the end of her bed and she sat down beside him, pulling him close. "You don't know how easy you've got it. Sleeping and eating and finding some warm spots in the sun. It's a pretty good life."

Waffles purred under her attention, and she rubbed her cheek against his soft head. "It's us humans who manage to make life far harder than it needs to be."

When he simply purred louder and pressed himself into her, Sloan figured it was worth taking a few minutes to snuggle her cat and resettle herself.

Maybe she was making this harder than it needed to be.

She was a professional and she'd taken this job with the intention of seeing it through, just like all the other work she'd ever done.

The ruse she and Chase had to concoct in order to get to

the end was a necessity. While she'd admit to losing her way for a bit, it was time to reset. Tonight's visit with his family would be good, in fact. She could prove to herself that she could handle this and mentally move on. Put these pesky sparks of attraction in a box—where they belonged—and focus on getting the work done.

Based on what she'd discovered, she figured she'd have a breakthrough in another few days of work. Then she could go back to Chicago and on to whatever came next.

And if that thought sent a small shot of sadness winging through her, then it was all the more reason she needed to buck up and face the truth.

A quick glance at her bedside clock let her know she'd dawdled longer than she had planned, and Sloan settled Waffles back onto the bed and rushed to finish dressing. She'd just stepped into her heels, adjusting the cuffs of her pants so they fell just so over the back of her shoes, when the doorbell rang.

She'd set up her computer on the small table in the kitchen and already pictured how she'd walk him through the information as she headed for the front door.

Straightforward.

Fact-based.

And life-cratering, she acknowledged as she reached for the door.

Later, she'd tell herself that advance preparation was a wise move. At the moment, however, the man who stood on the other side of the entryway practically took her breath away, all while managing to detonate a few brain cells along the way.

He was magnificent. His broad shoulders were perfection in a gray button-down shirt he'd left untucked over dark jeans. He'd obviously taken time for a shower, as his normally light brown hair was darker at the tips, where it curled.

But it was his eyes…

Those green eyes of his seemed darker. More focused and full of a personal history she wanted so desperately to explore. When Sloan finally realized she'd been staring into that captivating green a bit too long she waved him in. "Come on back. I have everything set up at the table."

He followed her through the small apartment, and in a matter of moments they were in her kitchen, which suddenly seemed a lot smaller with him standing inside of it.

"Can I get you anything to drink?"

"How about a soda? I'll wait and have something to drink at dinner."

"Sounds good. Why don't you sit down and read what I've got teed up and then I can answer any questions and walk you through it."

He did as she suggested, and Sloan busied herself pouring them both something cold. After placing his glass down next to him, she took a sip of hers when she sat down.

"You've been busy this week."

"You read it already?"

"It was a quick scan, but your executive summary was pretty straightforward." His gaze narrowed as it flicked back to the screen, then returned to her. "I've got someone in the company who's been skimming for quite a while. Especially since you've noted irregularities as far back as a decade ago."

"I'm sorry, Chase."

"Yeah. Me, too."

"So IT REALLY is true then."

Chase knew it was—Sloan had documented it all in black and white—but still, the gut punch of it all was shockingly real.

One more in a line of nasty surprises these past few months.

First his father's death.

Then the news of his half siblings and his father's secret life.

And now this.

Was anything in his life solid anymore?

"I'm sorry that it is. I don't know who yet, but I'm confident I can keep following the various threads and will get you the answers you need."

"Just like we planned."

He knew Sloan had found something. She'd told him as much before walking out of his office earlier.

And somehow, even with the knowledge the news wasn't good, the information that practically blinked at him off her screen was worse than he'd imagined.

A decade?

How could something so bad—something so nefarious—have gone on for so long?

"What questions do you have?"

"How was I so stupid, for starters. I've been groomed to lead this company for damn near twenty years and I've had no idea a snake's been inside the walls for more than a decade?" He slammed back from the table, the chair wobbling but somehow staying upright.

"But that's not your fault."

"Not my fault? It's fully my fault. I'm the leader of the company."

"That doesn't make you all-knowing. I can walk you through the data I've found, but whoever's doing this is good and they've had a lot of practice covering their tracks."

Since he was already standing, Chase turned on his heel and headed for the living room. The urge to pace was strong, and because of it, he found a spot near the window and stared out over the common area beyond.

Owl Creek was in that space beyond the limited view

from the window. His home. Where that thought would have given him peace in the past, all he could manage was a solid breath.

Inhale.

Exhale.

This he knew. Real estate. Land. Building. The urge to create something that would last long after he was gone.

He knew that work in his bones and he loved it.

But all the rest?

It was a stark reality to have spent more than three and a half decades on the planet and realize he still knew very little.

"Chase? Please talk to me."

He turned from the window, oddly grateful that she was there. He needed to get his head together and stop reacting each time he got news he didn't want.

"I'm sorry you're stuck with my reactions, whiny and immature as they are."

"Whiny?" Her mouth actually dropped a bit before she seemed to catch herself. "Is that actually how you see yourself?"

"Isn't it accurate?"

"Hardly. Chase, you've had to face more in a matter of months than most people experience in a lifetime. It's okay to have some messy feelings you can't fully reconcile. That would be true regardless, but you're trying to process it all."

"Or am I giving it all too much power?"

The question sort of hung there, like a live wire sparking in the midst of a storm.

"It does have power."

"Yes, but not over me. I can't let that happen."

"Then why are you fighting so hard against telling me how you feel? I'm a safe space. Even if I wasn't contractually unable to say anything, I won't. I've got the benefit of an outsider's eyes and, with the work I'm doing, digital ears. Lean into that."

It was an enticing thought. One he'd had more than once since embarking on this project with Sloan and SecuritKey.

Only now, standing here, Chase realized something. He'd let the fake-relationship aspects of the work dominate his thoughts, but now, at her words, he had to admit she had a point.

Talking to her wasn't fake.

Telling her how he felt about his business and his work and, hell, his life, wasn't made up.

She was that safe space she spoke of, but she was also a sounding board. And if he could get past the endlessly frustrating emotions that had dragged and pulled at him since the day his father had had his stroke, he realized Sloan was the one person he could speak to freely.

His siblings were all dealing with the matter in their own way. His cousins, too. And Nate and Sarah had an even bigger set of challenges to address, with the understanding that the very life created for them by their parents came at the expense of the rest of the Colton children, both Robert's and Jessie's.

What a mess it all was.

"Do you want to go tonight? If you don't, we can blame it on me and a sudden case of nerves to meet your family."

There it was again, that subtle sense of protection he'd felt from her from the start.

He was her full focus and it was…

Well, it was extraordinary.

"Thank you for that." He moved closer to her, taking her hands in his. "Truly, thank you. It's kind and thoughtful, and I appreciate it more than I can say. But I do want to go tonight. I think it'll be good to go and get away from this for a bit."

She glanced down at their joined hands before looking back up. "If that changes, just give me a signal."

Chase smiled at that, the first one since he'd read that dispassionate overview on her laptop. "You mean a couple signal."

"A what?"

"You know. That standard signal most couples have when one of them wants out of a situation. A story they both know to tell or a preplanned fib in the event of a quick getaway."

When she still looked stumped it made Chase wonder—more than he should have—about her past relationships. Had she never experienced that paired camaraderie that came with being coupled up with someone?

"So what is our story?"

"We'll fake an early start to the day and a long week. How about that?"

She nodded, her expression sweetly serious. "That makes sense. And it's not untrue, which makes it even better."

Chase squeezed her hands once more before letting them go. "Right. It's not a lie."

Even if every other thing that was going to come out of their mouths that evening was a lie. A big one he was keeping from his family.

He trusted them. Whatever he thought about the problems at Colton Properties, he didn't believe his sisters, his brothers or his cousins were involved. But with all that was going on in their lives—and the knowledge that Ruby had invited Nate and Sarah as well—Chase wasn't ready to give the real reasons Sloan was in town.

They'd hatched the dating scenario as a proper cover, and if there was one thing he'd learned from his various family members in law enforcement, you don't break cover.

Ever.

It was stunning, then, to realize a few minutes later as

they walked to the car to head to his sister's, that his father had taught him the same thing, albeit for entirely different reasons.

Robert Colton had spent a lifetime keeping his cover as a doting husband to Jenny and, as they now knew, as an equally doting husband to Jessie.

And he'd never broken cover.

Not even once.

Chapter Six

There were a shocking number of Coltons.

That was Sloan's constant thought as she roamed around the backyard at Ruby Colton's home, a large place she shared with her fiancé, Sebastian Cross.

The property the couple lived on, Crosswinds, was gorgeous. Rolling land, dotted areas of woods and even a stream burbling in the farther reaches of the place. It was so beautiful as to be picturesque.

The party's start at seven had given her enough time to still see the land in the light. She'd taken it all in, while Chase had navigated the long driveway into the vast property, and had loved every bit of it.

That easy, quiet time had also given her both the head space to think about all they'd discussed in her apartment, as well as be able to brace herself for the conversations to come that evening.

She knew how these things worked. She was the new "girlfriend," and everyone would want a few moments of her time to size her up. The same puppy she'd met earlier was one of the first to greet her and she'd dropped to a crouch, giving Fancy a big dose of affection. The introductions had followed on quickly from there.

She'd met three of Chase's five siblings, which meant she

now knew Ruby, Fletcher and Frannie. She'd also met Nate and Sarah, who both seemed as shell-shocked as she was.

It was only when Chase made a polite excuse to move Sloan on to more introductions that Nate winked at her. He offered a small, wry smile and whispered, "My sister and I thank you for taking a bit of the heat off of us tonight." Sloan got the sense Chase's half siblings might be settling in a bit, but were still nervous.

The fact that Jenny Colton was at her book club likely helped, but Sloan figured it was a bit of a relief not to be the center of attention tonight.

The grill was smoking away, the most divine scents rising into the air, as Sloan and Chase mingled through the crowd. She'd ultimately won the battle on the merlot and was drinking a glass as Chase nursed a beer, continuing with the introductions, clearly determined to have her meet each and every person there.

It got a bit tricky when they got to Max, but the man played off their meet-and-greet like a pro, no one any wiser that they already knew each other.

"This is my cousin Max and Della." Chase gestured to the large athletic man with twinkling blue eyes who stood with the woman who'd captured his heart, Della Winslow.

Della also worked at Crosswinds as one of the K-9 trainers and she had a dog by her side as well. Although older than Fancy, Sloan could tell by the large body and lithe grace that the dog was still young and very much in his prime. Della had introduced him as Charlie and Sloan found herself nearly as smitten with him as with Fancy when the black Lab had given her his paw.

Next to Della was another cousin, Greg. As she stood up from giving Charlie praise and his proper due in shaking his hand, Sloan could see the clear resemblance between him and Max as brothers. Where Max was a bit taller and leaner,

Greg had a solid, thicker build. When Chase had added on that Greg was co-lead at the Colton Ranch, Sloan could see how that sort of work had shaped the man's physique.

"Welcome to the melee, Sloan." Greg smiled as he shook her hand.

"Thank you." She smiled back, keeping her tone light. "Though I have to say, you all have a certain sort of orchestration to your crowd. Some cook. Some make drinks. Some keep the conversation lively. I'd definitely say it's more shindig than melee."

Greg's smile was broad, and she got the sense her comment had been met with a quiet sort of approval, even as Chase let out a distinct cough beside her. When she turned to see if he was okay, she saw nothing but a stoic calm.

She'd have questioned him if they were actually dating, but they still didn't really know each other. And since it was a party, she vowed to ignore his reaction for now and think on it later.

Chase had filled her in on the Colton Ranch on their drive over. Worked by his Uncle Buck for years, two of the man's four children, Greg and Malcolm, had followed their father into the business, while Max had chosen the FBI and Buck's only daughter, Lizzy, was a graphic artist.

Just like Chase's determination to do right by his siblings with Colton Properties, it struck her that this was a close-knit family whose lives were intertwined in their relationships as well as in their work.

"How did you and Chase meet?"

"At his office. I was late for a meeting and ended up rushing into not only the wrong office, but the wrong conference room, too."

"She actually barreled right into me." Chase put an arm around her shoulders, looking down at her with distinct notes of attraction, and her breath caught.

So much so that she had to think for a minute to recapture her train of thought.

"It was the first time in my life I found benefit in my clumsiness."

"Looks like Chase is the beneficiary." Greg was all smiles, but she didn't miss the distinct tightening of Chase's arm around her shoulders.

Before she could say another word, Della gestured toward the back porch. "Sloan, would you care to join me? Sarah looks a bit lonely over there."

Sarah had at least three other women fluttering around her, but Sloan recognized the lifeline and reached for it. Something strange had occurred between Chase and his cousin, and a bit of air would be welcome. She was oddly grateful no one asked what business she was in that had even brought her to Colton Properties, but that tension between the two men blotted out the relief.

"I'd love to."

The two of them headed off, Charlie trotting beside them and Della smiling as they went. It was only when they were fully out of earshot of the men that she spoke. "If they were two of the dogs I train, I'd tell you to watch out or you'd get marked."

"What?" Sloan nearly bobbled her wineglass at Della's bold remark.

"Oh, yeah, you heard me. That was definitely two men circling around each other. I figured we should get out of their way so they can do it properly."

Although she got the basic gist of Della's comments, Sloan struggled to understand why. While she had gotten the obvious notes of male appreciation from Greg, what did it actually matter? She and Chase weren't dating.

And it wasn't like Greg had been outwardly inappropriate. A little flirty, sure, but nothing that required the emotional equivalent of marking territory.

"What are they circling around?"

"You, my dear."

"But that's silly."

"No, that's men. And it's interesting, too, because the two of them normally get along very well." Della glanced over, her smile growing even bigger. "We've all been hoping Chase sees the light and finds someone. It looks like a little healthy competition might be just what he needs."

Sloan had never been a good dater. She'd dated from time to time, but her work and her focus on it usually scared off men before things progressed very far.

Which made the idea of being stuck in a tug-of-war between two men mind-boggling.

"I'm sure it's no big deal."

Della glanced back to where Chase, Max and Greg still stood in a conversation circle near the grill. "I wouldn't be so sure, but let's stay here a bit. I'm feeling the need for a bit of girl talk."

Since a bit of girl talk would give her a chance to get a broader sense of the Colton family, she was more than happy to oblige Della's whim.

And since it was also nice to just spend some time in the company of other women her age instead in front of her computer, well, she'd take that, too.

CHASE AND GREG were a year apart. They'd played together since they were in diapers and Chase considered the man one of his closest friends on the planet.

And right now, he'd happily punch his cousin in the face.

A fact, Chase knew, Greg was well aware of.

In fact, his cousin could have used a trowel he was laying it on so thick.

"Things sure are moving fast between you and Sloan. You met on Monday?" Greg's question was casual but there was as much interest stamped in his eyes as Chase had seen from every other family member tonight.

When you know, you know.

The words were actually on the tip of his tongue before he pulled them back.

It might have been an appropriate response, but that the thought felt as natural as breathing caught him up short.

"It's been a bit of a whirlwind but we're enjoying ourselves."

"And you're already bringing her to family dinners." Greg let out a low whistle. "Something's brewing, cuz. I'm looking forward to having a front-row seat."

"You're awfully interested in Sloan."

As comebacks went it was a lame one, but Chase couldn't shake off this frustration and annoyance with his cousin.

"She's a beautiful woman. Who wouldn't be interested?"

Max had given them room to circle each other but he used that moment to interject. "Greg, it looks like Sebastian could use a hand at the grill. Why don't you go help him?"

Greg gave him one final look before reaching over and giving Chase a hard slap on the shoulder. "I want you to be happy, Chase. Don't forget that."

He watched his cousin walk away and Max waited until his brother was across the yard before jumping in. "You're awfully touchy about Sloan."

"I'm trying to make sure Greg doesn't get *touchy.*" The comeback was harsh to his own ears and Chase tried to soften his attitude. "The woman is here to help me and instead has been subject to constant scrutiny, raised eyebrows and veiled questions and now an impromptu family party. It's a little overwhelming."

Max glanced in the direction of the women, all seated in

a circle talking and laughing on the back porch. "She looks like she can handle it."

Chase's gaze found Sloan immediately, and just as Max had said, she was talking and laughing and obviously fitting in. It warmed him to see her so comfortable with his family and whether it was fair or not, he couldn't help but remember the first few times he'd brought Leanne to family functions.

She'd settled in after a while, but those initial get-togethers had been tough. Facing his parents, his own five siblings, his uncle and his four cousins had been a lot for her.

But Sloan seemed unfazed by the same.

He took the moment to look at her—really look at her—without her noticing. The long dark hair she normally kept back in a tight updo was down, an ocean of pretty curls framing her face. She was beautiful, her light brown skin glowing under the soft yellow lights strung around the back porch. Her smile was warm, and as he watched her, she laughed at something Kiki said before bending down to pick up the tired puppy who'd curled up at her feet.

"She looks like she's been there forever," Max murmured, and Chase was already acknowledging the comment when he caught himself.

"Don't you start in, too. She's a guest and she's here on a job."

"Doesn't mean she can't look natural laughing and getting to know our family."

Recognizing he was in danger of overplaying his hand, Max smoothly changed the subject. "Has she found anything yet?"

"Unfortunately, yes. She's as good as you said, and it's only taken her a matter of days to uncover several irregularities."

Max's eyebrows slashed down over his light blue eyes. "Do you know who it is?"

With one last glance at Sloan, he shifted his full attention to his cousin. "Not yet, but it's only a matter of time."

"And then what?"

"Then I'll come clean with the family."

"Is your little charade with Sloan working?"

"Beautifully. The entire office is so caught up in my being besotted with her that they haven't noticed she's found some reason to be there several days this week."

"Be careful there. Someone who's been covering their tracks for this long will know to look for irregularities."

Chase considered that warning and thought back over the various interactions he'd had this past week at the office. Although, he couldn't think of a single person who asked questions more than usual or seemed to be acting out of the ordinary.

But really, what did he know?

This problem had festered for damn near ten years and he'd been oblivious.

"I know that look."

Max's stare was as tough as his words.

"What look?"

"The one where you carry the weight of the world on your shoulders, along with your belief that you must carry every member of this family, too."

"It's not like—"

"Oh, no?" Max challenged. "Let me see how close I can get. The problem you're dealing with at Colton Properties shouldn't even be happening. You should have known there was an issue. Not only should you have known, you should have rooted it out quite some time ago because you believe you should have some sort of omniscient superpower."

"I don't do that."

Max took a sip of his beer, the epitome of practiced cool. "How close did I hit the mark?"

"Damn it." Chase glanced down at his beer. "I should have known."

"I hate to break it to you, but that's why people get away with stuff far longer than they should. Because they do know how to cover their tracks. They know how to blend into society. Criminals doing bad things don't wear neon signs." Decidedly less calm, Max took another sip of his beer. "It'd be a hell of a lot easier if they did."

They were no longer talking about Colton Properties or someone committing fraudulent practices against the company. Max's experiences—taking down serial killers for the FBI—was proof that no matter how bad a situation seemed, there was always something worse to be found.

And his cousin had spent a lot of years running down and catching *worse* for a living.

At what cost?

"The job doesn't leave you, does it?"

Max smiled but there wasn't a trace of humor in it. "No, it doesn't. But I'm coming to understand that with the love of a good woman it's a lot easier to deal with."

Chase watched his cousin as the man's attention drifted back to the circle of women, his gaze unerringly settling on Della.

Although they weren't prone to diving into their feelings, Max had said something to him years ago, when Chase was going through his divorce with Leanne, that had always stuck in his mind…

"Hell," Max had begun as he shook his head, "people like to romanticize a significant other with a cause. It's all well and good until they see the toll it takes up close."

"Come on, Max," Chase had replied. "What's that supposed to mean?"

"It means people are quick to call you a hero, but they don't want to know you have the ability to delve into the mind of a killer. It's that old adage—no one actually wants to know how the sausage is made."

"You do a good, honorable and brave job."

"And I will be forever alone because of it," Max had replied, ending their conversation…

Chase had been lost in his own misery at that time, dealing with the end of his marriage. Add on the bottle of whiskey they'd shared that night in the kitchen at the Colton Ranch and he hadn't had the wherewithal to ask Max what he meant.

But he'd tried the next day. When Max had shut him down, Chase tried again on a few other occasions, only to get the same response.

Whatever had triggered Max's honesty, be it Chase's own pain or the liquor, Chase had never known.

But it had stuck.

He might not hunt killers for a living, but he did have ambition. A good job and a big family and responsibilities to both. He'd let Leanne behind the curtain into his world and she hadn't been interested in what happened when the fancy dinners and the courting stopped.

She hadn't wanted to live with the reality of a man who spent long hours at the office and demanded they also spend time with his family nearly every weekend. So when things had gone south, he'd recognized it for what it was.

And while he might not be hunting killers, Chase had realized then he was as ill-suited for a relationship as Max had been.

Because unlike his cousin, who eventually did walk away, Colton Properties was his life.

And a woman couldn't be expected to sign up for that.

JESSIE COLTON STARED dreamily at her swooping, swirling handwriting and wondered if she'd ever been happier.

Jessie Colton
Jessie Colton Acker
Jessie Acker

Oh, sure, she'd told herself she was happy with Buck all those years ago, but she'd learned soon enough it was simply a lie she'd told herself to mentally breeze past the fact that she'd really wanted to marry Buck's brother, Robert.

But her saintly sister, Jenny, had set her cap there and managed to land him first.

So she'd taken Buck and told everyone how happy she was and how perfect her life was being a rancher's wife.

Perfect?

Hardly.

Ranch life and four kids certainly hadn't agreed with her. She did love her children, but they were a lot of work, and they were always underfoot. And rowdy. Oh, goodness, had they been a handful. She'd had three boys in a row until she finally got her girl.

She might have stayed for Lizzy, but it was only after she was born that Robert had finally come to heel. He'd realized which sister he was truly in love with and they'd started a family of their own.

It had been such a happy time. She'd shed a few tears over leaving her kids, but life with Robert had been wonderful and they'd quickly started a family of their own.

It had truly been a blissful existence. For a few years, she had all she wanted.

Only to have Robert freak out about having two families before he finally ran off, leaving her with two young children. Sure, he sent money and kept them in a nice home, but he'd abandoned ship.

Left them and gone back to Jenny and their six kids.

And while it was still better than being stuck out in the middle of nowhere on a ranch, stuck was stuck.

She'd given up her life for those kids. And with Robert finally dead and their secret relationship out, she would have thought Nate and Sarah would have more regard for their mother.

More, that they'd be ready to take what was rightfully theirs.

Why should Robert's other six kids get all the family money and property and business? How was that fair?

Only, Nate and Sarah really didn't care.

She'd asked herself the same question over and over, but simply couldn't see it any other way. How was it possible they didn't care their father had essentially abandoned them?

And her?

Nate and Sarah both kept telling her they were happy with their lives, they didn't want any more of their father's money and that Robert had left them enough already, having set them up with his guilt money while he was still alive.

Couldn't they see they deserved more?

She'd struggled with that, trying so hard to work her way through her problems, finally turning to the Ever After Church for guidance. And still, she was no closer to understanding the children she'd begun to think of as ungrateful.

Thank goodness for Markus.

He'd been so wonderful and caring and patient, helping her process it all.

Jessie stared down at the name she'd looped over and over on the page.

Jessie Acker.

They would be married soon and that would be her name. She'd finally rid herself of the Colton moniker once and for all, moving on to something so much better.

Because Markus really was a wonderful man.

He loved her and he was preparing to make her his wife. Oh, they'd been careful, and he'd stressed to her that they couldn't go public with their relationship just yet. Too many single women in the Ever After Church had set their sights on him and he didn't want to ruffle feathers.

Great loves, after all, were a gift from God.

Hadn't he told her that, over and over?

That love needed to be nurtured and given room to grow in private, away from prying, spiteful eyes.

She'd agreed with him, and she did understand his point, even if it was getting a bit tiresome keeping their relationship all to herself.

But, oh, how she wanted to shout it to the world.

"Soon, darling." Markus would whisper those words against her temple each time she pressed him. Then he'd take her in his arms and kiss her, and she'd forget for a while that she wanted something more.

In the moment, all she needed was him.

She knew he felt it, too. Hadn't they confessed that to each other almost from the first?

All her life she'd been looking for a transcendent love. And now, she had it.

Markus had been so sweet. So vulnerable. He'd told her that he'd been seeking the same. That all his life he'd been willing to go where a higher power willed him to, all while giving up his own dreams of a family of his own.

He was doing good work, but, he'd confessed to her, it was lonely work.

But now, they had each other.

Jessie stared down at her looping signature once again. Soon, they wouldn't have to hide their great love.

Soon—so very soon—everyone would know.

CHASE CARRIED THE last set of folding chairs from a small shed about fifty yards off the back of the house, settling them into place along the big tables already covered with plates, napkins and serving spoons.

Ruby had put him to work, asking him to get a few extra chairs to supplement the ends of the tables so they weren't overcrowded on the picnic benches. He'd just set the last chair into place when he heard his name over his shoulder.

"Chase, I'm sorry. I could have given you a hand with that."

He turned to find Nate, the man's hands full of two fresh beers.

"Is one of those for me?"

His half brother smiled and extended one of the cold bottles. "You bet."

"Then consider yourself having helped."

They stood there in companionable silence for a few minutes, the *shindig*, as Sloan had called it, moving in full, orchestrated force around them.

And while they hadn't hit one-hundred-percent attendance this evening by his siblings or cousins, Chase figured any event that got more than eighty percent of his family out and together was a pretty solid hit rate.

Even as he was silently grateful his mother was one of the ones who'd stayed away.

He didn't need to protect her. Jenny Colton was doing just fine and had managed to develop a sort of equilibrium with the news of her husband and her sister's betrayal. She'd always focused on her children, and her nieces and nephews, and nothing was going to change that, she'd assured him just a few weeks ago.

And still…he couldn't help the overprotective streak he felt toward her.

Her feelings.

And the reality of the life she'd lived for almost four decades.

"Do you have a few minutes? I won't keep you long since we're all ready to dig into those steaks."

Chase recognized Nate's obvious sense of discomfort but gave his half brother props for pressing forward, anyway. "Sure."

Nate drifted a bit so they were still part of the party, but far enough away to have a private conversation. Chase's curiosity grew at what the younger man might want.

They hadn't spent much time together, as Nate and Sarah had only been introduced to them a few weeks ago. Even with their limited interactions, Chase had recognized them as good people.

Honest and caring and as churned up over this situation as the rest of them.

"I owe you an apology."

"For what?"

"This life." Nate gestured toward the grouping of family. "Your family. All you never knew about Sarah and I."

"That's not your fault. It's no one's fault but our parents'."

"I keep telling myself that. Sarah keeps trying to tell me, too. But the truth is, I knew."

"Knew what?"

"About you. About all of you."

"You what?"

Nate shook his head and the bitterness that thinned his lips and hardened his jaw was unmistakable. "We knew our parents weren't married. And because she'd been married to Buck, Mom was already a Colton and could easily give us the Colton name. As small children we didn't understand it, but Sarah and I both figured it out later."

If he was honest, Chase had wondered about that aspect. Whatever power his father had amassed over a lifetime, it never would have protected him on a charge of bigamy.

"How did you know about us?"

"Dad and Mom 'divorced'—" Nate added air quotes on the word *divorce* "—when I was about ten. He'd always traveled a lot. Or that was the excuse they told us for when he was here in Owl Creek. I'd always known something was a little off, but by then I was old enough to do some digging after he left. A few computer search queries and it was all too easy to find evidence of his other life."

Nate was a police officer in Boise. When they'd first learned of their half siblings, Max had done some digging of his own. He'd easily discovered Nate was a good cop, both by the cases he'd closed as well as the reputation several of Max's contacts shared. Tenacious. Focused. Willing to dig for the truth instead of accepting things at face value.

It was obviously a personality trait, because here he was, basically confessing he'd known about Robert Colton's secret life for close to two decades.

All while Chase had known nothing.

"I'm sorry. And more than that, I'm sorry I didn't talk to you about it from our very first meeting." Nate glanced down at the grass before his gaze lifted, that vivid blue direct and focused. "You deserved better than that. You all did."

Chase wanted to be angry. A very large part of him was angry, but oddly, it was an anger that sort of seethed with amorphous edges, swirling around yet having no place to land.

Would he have liked to have known this information sooner?

Of course.

Would another month have made a difference, seeing as how he'd spent a lifetime in the dark?

No, not really.

Am I giving it all too much power?

He'd asked Sloan that question earlier, in her apartment.

For all his confusion, anger and raw fury at his father's selfishness, Chase had genuinely begun to wonder about his own role in it all.

In what came next.

His father was dead. The image he'd crafted of the man was riddled with holes, all now visible in the light.

He could resent it and allow it to rule his actions, or he could find his way to some level of acceptance that every member of his family had the same disservice done to them as he had.

Which also meant he had a choice.

A very clear one, Chase knew, that he couldn't lay at Robert's feet.

He could turn on them, his newly discovered siblings most especially.

Or he could build something real and true in spite of his father's actions.

As he stood there beside his brother, his family laughing and shouting and enjoying one another across the expanse of lawn, Chase knew what he wanted.

Placing a hand on his younger brother's shoulder, he turned toward Nate. Their gazes met, and Chase saw clear traces of himself in the younger man.

The deep need to hold it together.

The feelings of responsibility.

And the determination to be strong, even when the world around them was cracking in half.

"We deserved better, Nate. We."

"Yeah, but I—"

"Not I, brother. *We.* This here—" He gestured toward their family. "That's us. All of us. And we all deserved better than what Robert and Jessie did."

"It's not that easy."

"Maybe it is. If we choose to make it that easy, we can have what they never dreamed of."

"What's that?"

"Family."

As that last word lingered between him and his youngest brother, Chase felt his first moment of peace since this all began.

He had a family. A rock-solid one.

And there was nothing he wouldn't do for each and every one of them.

Chapter Seven

A carefree bubble of laugher filled Sloan's chest as Fancy shot straight up from her position on her lap.

One minute the puppy was conked out, sleeping like the dead, and the next one, Sebastian had gotten close enough with a huge platter of steaks that the dog was launching herself off her thighs so she could follow the man like he was the pied piper.

"Training is a process," Kiki sighed as she watched her small charge racing around Sebastian's feet.

"She'll get there," Della assured her before standing. "But it's probably time to get her and Charlie settled in their crates."

As she and Kiki went off, and Ruby and Frannie headed into the kitchen to get the additional sides to go with the steaks, Sloan found herself alone with Sarah.

"Have you and Chase been dating long?"

Sarah's smile was sweet, and Sloan had observed how hard the woman had worked to fit in that evening. She'd been kind and a bit deferential, obviously still trying to figure her place in the Colton family.

"We met on Monday."

If Sarah thought less than a week of dating was fast, she didn't show it and instead only nodded. "It might be cliché, but it's surprisingly accurate. Life really does turn on a dime."

"With respect to romance, it's one of my mother's favorite sayings. She met my father and six weeks later was engaged."

"And things worked out?"

"They celebrated thirty-two years of marriage back in April, so things seem to be going okay."

Sarah laughed at that before something seemed to crumple in her face, tears welling in her eyes. "I'm sorry. I swore to myself I wasn't going to cry and then something triggers it. I—"

"It's okay." Sloan moved closer, angling her body so she and Sarah faced each other on the patio furniture. "I hope you don't mind my saying, but Chase told me about what you've all been living through. His father's death and then the discovery for all of you that you had siblings you didn't know about."

If it was possible, Sarah's visage twisted up even more. "That they didn't know about. We knew. Nate and I. It was all of them that didn't." Sarah swiped at tears, even as more spilled over her fingers. "Surprise!"

It was uncharted territory—Sloan figured on some level she was a handy listener, and on another she was safe since she was an outsider. But regardless of the reason, she was here and Sarah needed someone to lean on.

"You were children. How could you have known how to handle something like that?"

"They're my brothers and sisters."

"Who share parents with you. Parents who had a far greater responsibility to tell them the truth of their lives than you did."

"They're a family and we're just the interlopers who have turned it all upside down."

Whether it was her rapidly fading objectivity on this case, or just the sheer indignity over Robert and Jessie Colton's behavior she couldn't quite get past, Sloan wasn't sure.

But she refused to sit there and let Sarah take this all on herself.

"You're part of a family, no qualifier needed."

"I *was* part of a family."

"Please don't do that to yourself. It's not past tense." She reached for the woman's hand, putting hers over top of Sarah's. "I've watched you all tonight. There's genuine effort and care there. Between you and Nate and all your siblings, too. It's hard and no one's saying it's not, but you and your brother are welcome here."

"Everyone has made me feel welcome. Even Uncle Buck, who probably had the biggest right to feel otherwise, has been so kind to me. To Nate, too."

Although Buck was absent this evening, just like Chase's mother, Jenny, Chase had filled her in fully on his whole family. Buck was his father's brother and had been married to Jessie, the two of them bringing Greg, Malcolm, Max and Lizzy into the world before Jessie up and left when Lizzy was three.

How shattering would that have been?

For Buck, yes, but for his kids? To lose one's mother like that? A woman who was an essential aspect of a child's stability and foundation, to just vanish?

She may not have died, but Buck and Jessie's children lost her and they'd still all found a way to move forward.

To forge ahead.

Jessie might have gone on to a new family, but that also meant Sarah and Nate were now dealing with the reality of who their mother was. Any illusion they might have had about her character had to have taken a hard blow with the obvious proof she'd walked away from four children.

It was difficult and convoluted and a terrible example of what atrocities people could commit to those they claimed to love.

But it didn't have to define Sarah and Nate's future. It didn't have to define any of their futures, not if they didn't want it to.

"Your brothers and sisters want to get to know you."

"I keep telling myself that. And most of the time I can feel it. And then I stop and look around and all I can think is why? Why would they want to welcome us into their lives? The two people who are the living proof their parents perpetrated a lifetime of lies."

"You and Nate are dealing with the consequences of that choice as much as anyone else."

Sloan was under no delusions that a few well-meaning moments could erase what the woman was feeling, but she did take heart when Sarah brushed away the remaining tears and glanced toward the large picnic tables set up about ten yards off the back patio.

"I do think I'm hungry."

"Why don't we go get some dinner then? The steaks smell wonderful, and it looks like Frannie made enough potato salad to feed an army."

Sarah glanced around at the assembled people throughout the backyard. "We're sort of a small one when we're all together."

"Fair point."

Chase had crossed over to the porch and came up to the two of them, his smile broad even as Sloan saw a distinct gentleness in his green gaze.

There was a subtle haze of sadness, too.

"We're definitely an army. And our drill-sergeant sister, Ruby, will see to it that we all get into a line to fill our plates."

"I'd best get to it then." Sarah headed off and it left Sloan and Chase briefly alone on the patio.

Chase waited, watching until Sarah picked up a plate and began talking to Fletcher, who was already in line, before he spoke. "I overheard a bit of what you said to her. That was incredibly kind."

"It's true."

"It's still nice to hear." Chase looked around at the large group of people filling the yard, laughing and talking under the lights strung around the space. "And when we're here, together, it's easier to remember. It's when we scatter back to our lives it's a little harder."

"You've all dealt with a major trauma as a family. Everything about your life has been upended and changed. That takes time to process, and from this outsider's view, you're all handling it admirably."

Chase moved in, putting his arm around her and pulling her close. The move was casual and it wasn't especially romantic, but it was intimate. And as his well-muscled arm held her against him, Sloan felt her heart kick hard in her chest.

She placed a hand on his chest, looking up into his eyes.

Once again, that distinct sense of sadness was pervasive, even as he seemingly fought to keep his smile bright.

"Maybe even more important, Chase, you're all trying. I think that says all I need to know about this family."

CHASE STILL HADN'T figured out how Sloan had managed it, but in a matter of hours she'd charmed his entire family, become the adoring subject of two dogs and had somehow managed to make him even more enchanted with her than he already was.

And based on how hard he'd tried not to look at her with

anything but professional attention in their private moments, that was saying something.

But, wow, the woman was amazing. She had a quality, he'd quickly come to realize, that was the epitome of effortless grace.

Most of all, he acknowledged, she was *there*.

With him.

With his family, each of them fighting a battle to understand what had made them.

And all desperately trying to forge a new path forward.

He didn't need to be looking at her this way—needing her close—but heaven help him, he couldn't look away.

Even earlier, when he'd gladly have punched Greg, he'd understood his cousin's interest. Sloan was beautiful, yes, but that beauty went so much deeper than the surface.

A few hours had passed since he'd come upon her and his half sister on the patio, but even now he could hear her kind words running through his mind, and how she'd comforted Sarah.

What he hadn't expected was how comforting *he'd* personally found her sentiments. Especially with his own conversation with Nate still ringing in his ears.

He'd meant what he'd told his brother, even as the heavy weight of Nate's knowledge of their father's secret life pressed on him.

They *all* deserved better.

How much easier was it to accept that truth when he was with his family, talking, laughing and being together?

And how much easier was it with Sloan?

When he'd hired her, his only goal had been to uncover the rat at Colton Properties. Yet, now knowing they were close, that the answer to that puzzle would be solved soon, Chase found himself at odds about something else.

He wasn't ready for her to leave.

She made it all smoother somehow. Like what he was dealing with was something he could handle.

Like he had a partner.

It was the last thing he'd expected, and that depth of need scared him.

All while it lifted him up.

Up to now, he'd struggled with the concept of his father's secret life. His mind knew Nate and Sarah were as innocent of their family drama as his other siblings and his cousins.

But his heart had struggled with that reality, the betrayal a visceral blow.

Somehow, Sloan's presence—and her absolute lack of judgment or disdain—made it easier.

Better.

"I keep saying I can't eat another bite and then something even more wonderful comes out of that house." Sloan grinned beside him as Kiki and Frannie marched out of the house with desserts. "It's like a clown car of food. Every time you think there can't possibly be more, there is."

Her comment pulled him out of his wandering thoughts, and he caught sight of the platter in his sister's hands. "I can promise you that you do not want to miss Frannie's pound cake."

"Then, somehow, I'll persevere."

Although the table was crowded, with shouts, laughter and conversation flowing from one end of it to the other, Chase couldn't help but feel this moment was somehow just theirs.

A tender moment in an oasis of happy chaos.

One he was loath to let go, the seeming spell she managed to weave around him keeping them tethered.

He wanted to kiss her.

It would have been okay. More than okay, Chase admitted to himself, as he recalled any number of kisses shared by the couples around the table. Sebastian and Ruby, after hiding their feelings for each other for so long, made no effort to hide their affection now. The deep glances and lingering touches and the big, smacking kiss Sebastian had laid on Ruby as he'd finished up the steaks had made everyone smile.

Fletcher and Kiki, Frannie and Dante, and Max and Della were the same.

The Coltons weren't quite so single any longer and everyone was more than welcoming of the fact that Chase had brought a significant other to the party.

Which made it a special sort of torture to hold himself back.

"Your family is special." Sloan's voice was low, her observation meant only for him. "I'd initially expected this many people all in one place would be overwhelming. Especially when we drove up and I saw all those cars. But—"

She broke off, seeming to gather her words. "It's not that they aren't overwhelming, because there are certainly a lot of people. But there's a warmth there. And a sense of welcome. Like every person you meet is happy you're here. Just as you are. Just for yourself."

Wasn't that the core of it all?

Somehow, with that easy and rather lovely compliment, Sloan had gone to the heart of what he was so determined to puzzle through and make sense of.

His family was warm. And welcoming. And for all their size, there was a congenial camaraderie they all shared. Even Nate and Sarah had that quality and had shown it to full effect in a matter of visits.

Yet for all their generation knew how to care for one another and accept one another, it had all risen out of a cauldron of secrets each and every child of Robert or Jessie Colton had spent a lifetime oblivious to.

It was the seesaw of emotion he hadn't fully figured out how to manage.

He'd *worked* with his father. For years. And somehow, in all that time, he'd never known the man had a second life somewhere else?

How did a person live a life so completely separate that it was invisible to his loved ones?

That had gnawed at him for months now, and yet, when he sat here with Sloan, he was better able to accept it. More, he could settle himself in a way that he acknowledged it was his own father's choices, not anything self-directed.

So when her hand came over his, resting there in a show of support, it was incredibly easy for him to shift so that their palms touched. Almost of their own accord, their fingers linked together.

A solid bond as well as an outward sign to others.

He knew he shouldn't lean into that support. But here, with Sloan, surrounded by the family who did help him make sense of who he was in the world, Chase knew his first moments of peace since his father's death.

It was small and simple, and the outside world still awaited him.

But in that moment, it was enough.

SLOAN FELT HERSELF slipping back toward the passenger seat headrest and fought to keep her eyes open.

It would be so easy to close her eyes and revel in the warmth of an enjoyable evening and the company of a wonderful man.

Which were the exact reasons she needed to remain wide-awake.

She had to stay alert. Sharp. Focused.

More, she had to stop this lovely, drowsy feeling from taking her over.

Because it would be so easy to sink into those feelings of warmth and protection and *couple*dom she'd been trying to fight all evening.

She and Chase weren't a couple. It didn't matter they'd shared those moments of awareness when they not only felt like partners, but where it was also the two of them against the world.

Those flashes of awareness and attraction had happened in his office as well as on the dates they'd faked throughout the week. But tonight, with his family, it hadn't just felt right, it had felt real.

Deeply real.

Whatever she'd expected going into this job, never, not in a million years, would she have said she was at risk of losing her head or her heart over Chase Colton.

Yet here she was, imagining herself in his arms and tossing all personal *and* professional restraint to the wind.

"My family really liked you. My phone's been going off since we got in the car and I suspect it's a string of texts from my sisters telling me how awesome you are."

"They're pretty great, too." With those lingering thoughts of professionalism still running through her mind, Sloan added, "Glad to know we did such a good job of fooling them."

The temperature in the car changed immediately and Sloan was happy to see the turnoff for the street that ran in front of her apartment building. She was more than willing to own the fact that she'd tossed their professional relationship at him like a hand grenade, but really, what other choice did she have?

Sitting here, nestled all snug and warm in his car, was hardly the way she needed to behave with a client. Better to keep it business.

All business.

"We certainly did."

His voice was flat, a sure sign she'd hit the nerve she was aiming for. That her shot had ricocheted back and was currently doing a bit of damage inside her own chest was the logical outcome.

Just something she'd have to deal with.

It was also an important reminder that she needed to stay engaged in the work.

Chase said nothing more, and in moments was turning into her parking lot, navigating to the row of spaces in front of her building. He'd barely put the car in Park when she was unsnapping her seat belt and pushing out of the car in one burst of speed.

She needed to get away from him and all this misplaced emotion and just get inside.

Once she was inside, she'd be fine.

She could regroup with her computer and her files and her work and put all of this out of her head.

It was a good plan. A solid one, if only she had the ability to move more quickly.

But suddenly Chase was there, standing in front of her as she rounded the front of the car.

He was big, somehow seeming even bigger as he blocked the stretch of sidewalk she had to navigate to get to the stairs for her second-floor entrance. Yet for all his size, there wasn't anything threatening about him.

Instead, all she saw was about six feet two inches of hurt. Oh, he kept it leashed—coiled, really—but she saw it there all the same.

The man was in a vulnerable state, with the changes in his life upending everything he thought he knew.

And it was for all those reasons she had to get away. She couldn't let that vulnerability sneak beneath her own defenses. Nor could she let herself think that this temporary reprieve they were taking from their normal lives to play-act a relationship, as well as hunt down a criminal inside his company, was real.

Or maybe, more importantly, had a pathway to *becoming* real.

He'd created this facade specifically because he didn't want romantic entanglements in his life.

"Thank you for a lovely evening. I really did enjoy meeting your family."

"I can walk you to your door."

"It's just up there." She pointed toward the stairs. "I'm fine. Really."

He nodded, but she wasn't sure he'd heard her. Instead, he continued to look at her, full of that vulnerability and awareness that had shaken her to her core.

"You said something. Earlier."

She'd said a lot of things, so instead of responding, she just waited for him to continue.

"When I overheard you talking to Sarah. She told you that she felt like an interloper. And that why would I, or any of my siblings, really, want to have a relationship with someone whose very existence proved the lies we were told."

Whatever conversation she'd expected him to bring up, her discussion with Sarah wasn't it. Those moments she'd spent with his half sister had been a surprise, for all Sarah had been willing to discuss with a virtual stranger. But they'd also given her a better sense of what the entire family was dealing with.

Like a kaleidoscope, they all were crystals in the same lens. But shifting through each perspective painted a different story.

"She did say that."

"But it was what you said in return that meant something.

That she and Nate were dealing with the consequences of our parents' secret as much as anyone else."

"It's true. I think it's because I have the benefit of distance, but I can see the terrible disservice done to you. To all of you. I can't imagine the pain or the raw fury of it all. And it makes me angry for you."

She sighed but pressed on. "Despite the fact that it's not my place to feel that way."

"Not your place?"

An evening breeze whipped up, proof that the days might be warm, but the Idaho nights were rapidly cooling. She wrapped her arms around her waist and tried to convince him she was right.

"This is a job. One you're paying me to do." Sloan pointed once again in the direction of her apartment. "You're even putting me up and paying my expenses. It's very much a job."

"You're human. You've got eyes and ears, and you're entitled to build opinions based on what you see and hear."

"No, actually, I don't. In the confines of my work, I have to find answers. That's all I'm entitled to."

"That's BS."

"No, Chase, it's the truth. I have no right to an opinion on your circumstances. Whatever else this is, I have no illusions about that."

Wasn't that what she'd been trying to tell herself from the start?

That she didn't have a right to an opinion. About what Robert and Jessie did to their families. About how their children handled what came after that terrible revelation. Not even about how it affected each of them, collectively or individually.

But now, she'd crossed a line. Sure, she'd gone this evening at his request and under the ploy they were perpetrat-

Chapter Eight

Sloan.

Chase pressed his lips against hers, something so profoundly right welling up in his chest as her mouth opened beneath his.

He wanted her.

It no longer mattered how she got here or why she was here. Nor did it matter what secrets they were trying to unearth.

Right now, there was only one secret that mattered.

Discovering the woman in his arms.

Questions had haunted him for months now. About his life. His family. His very foundation.

All of it cracked and crumbled and faded to dust as he pulled her closer, taking the kiss deeper.

Sloan responded, her mouth opening beneath his. Her arms came around his waist and he pulled her even closer. The feel of her in his arms, pressed against his chest, was deeply satisfying after nearly a week of fighting how he felt.

She was everything he'd ever wanted in a partner. Responsive. Engaged. And deeply in the moment with him.

It was a soothing balm after so many months of questioning all he believed.

And it was an exciting push forward with a woman

who both challenged him and helped him see his way to the future.

And…

With a sudden tug of awareness, Chase pulled back.

What was he thinking?

Yes, he wanted her. He'd be lying to say otherwise. But there was so much unsettled in his life. So much to still figure out.

He'd spent the better part of a decade actively avoiding relationships and suddenly he was thinking differently.

Acting differently.

And forgetting that there was nothing to be gained from traveling down that relationship path other than pain.

Sloan stared up at him, the depths of her dark brown eyes nearly black in the light of the overheads that dotted the parking area.

"Chase, I—"

"I'm sorry. I shouldn't have done that."

He glanced down, realizing that he still had her pressed to his chest, and hastily moved back.

"*I* shouldn't have done that. You're my client and it was unprofessional of me and—"

He cut her off, laying a finger to her lips. It shocked him how much that small touch cost him, the desire to pull her back against him and continue their sensual exploration of one another raging through him like an inferno.

But he held himself back.

"You're not unprofessional and you don't need to apologize. It's been a busy week and it was an intense evening. Maybe we can chalk it up to a moment of indiscretion and leave it at that?"

She seemed to consider his words as he dropped his hand back to his side, before coming to a decision.

"I've lost my objectivity."

"Sloan, don't do this. You haven't lost anything."

She shook her head, her smile soft. "I have. And I'm not quite sure if that's good or bad or just a new experience. I've always kept a distance with my work, keeping the case firmly in place in my mind. And with you, with your family—"

She broke off once more, obviously searching for the words before pushing on.

"I care about you and your family. I care about what happens to you all. Your situation is unique, and I can't help but feel that you deserve better, Chase. And I feel the same for your siblings and your cousins, too. You all deserved better."

"I'm working on that part myself."

"I know. Which is the real reason I'm sorry. You need the proper distance to process what's happening. We set up this plan with a specific goal in mind. Allowing me to hide in plain sight."

Chase remembered their discussions as they'd set up her assignment at Colton Properties and had to admit to himself just how shortsighted he'd been.

It was the plan they'd hatched, yes. But it was also the whole situation, requiring him to spend time in close proximity to a woman he found fascinating.

He'd forgotten how lovely it was to enjoy an evening with someone, sharing conversation over dinner. Or sitting beside someone at a family event, laughing through stories and ordinary, everyday conversation.

Or even the simplicity of driving home with someone.

He'd spent so much of his adult life alone, keeping his "relationships" to nothing more than lone evenings, sharing a few hours of time and intimacy. It was only now, when he experienced that real intimacy of day-to-day life, that he acknowledged all he'd been missing.

Moreover, it was about all he'd shut himself off from.

He'd chosen his bachelor lifestyle for a reason. He wasn't cut out for marriage. He'd proved that to himself quite clearly with Leanne.

He didn't feel anything had changed—he still wasn't cut out for forever with anyone. But Sloan's arrival in his life had shown him just how much he'd been missing.

And it only sharpened the ache that had settled deep inside at the knowledge she'd soon be gone.

SATURDAY MORNING DAWNED dark and rainy, and Chase was surprised to realize how neatly it fit his mood.

He'd walked Sloan up to her apartment the night before—he'd do nothing less no matter how awkward those few moments after their kiss had become—and then hightailed it for home.

But the distance from her hadn't helped.

He'd fought against the lingering taste of her on his lips, yet no amount of inward admonishment *or* the glass of Scotch he'd had once he got home could erase it. And the sensation of cradling her in his arms, their bodies pressed together, seemed to have imprinted on his skin.

He could *feel* her.

When he'd dreamed of her, too, leaving him raw and achy at five in the morning, he'd realized sitting around the house by himself all weekend wasn't a smart idea. But for the first time in a long while, he had zero interest in going into the office and working off his frustration.

Which meant he needed to get out of the house and go *somewhere*.

After a quick shower and breakfast, he headed out, calming a bit as he drove through the entrance to the Colton Ranch.

The ranch had been like a second home growing up. Even

the simple act of driving up to the ranch house had given him a few moments of ease from his unsettled thoughts.

Greg stood out on the front porch, drinking his coffee beneath the overhang, and waved as Chase pulled up.

In a matter of moments, Chase was running up the front steps, trying to minimize his exposure to the rain.

"Good morning!" Greg smiled and Chase didn't miss the small shot of knowing in the man's brown eyes.

"Hey there."

They shook hands and at what must have been a longing stare at Greg's coffee mug, his cousin gestured him toward the house. "I need a refill and you look like you need a cup. We'll catch up inside."

"How'd you know I want to catch up?"

"Because it's barely nine o'clock and if you were okay, you'd be at home with Sloan instead of looking like a grizzly bear here with me."

Chase considered making an excuse, one nearly falling off his lips, when he stopped himself.

He was tired of the lies.

And he was tired of how his current situation had made him question what he could or couldn't say to his family.

Sloan was close to figuring out what was wrong at Colton Properties and maybe it was time he eased up a bit and talked to someone he trusted.

And despite his wholly inappropriate streak of possessive jealousy last night, Greg was one of his closest confidants.

"She's at home, exactly where she belongs."

Greg glanced over from where he'd pulled another mug from the cabinets. "Why does she belong there?"

"Because she's not my girlfriend."

Greg's eyes widened, the slight thunk of the mug on the counter his only response.

"She's an independent contractor I've hired to look into some problems at Colton Properties."

Greg recovered quickly, filling the fresh mug along with his second cup before speaking. "So you started dating and you broke up?"

"No, the dating's a fake-out to allow her to come and go at Colton Properties."

"You can't just give her a key?"

A small smile twitched at the edge of Greg's lips and for the first time Chase had to admit what had seemed like a solid idea when they'd hatched it did have elements of the absurd.

"This isn't funny. And if I let the office know she was there on a job, people would want to know what for."

His cousin gestured them toward the kitchen table, then took a seat. "I can see that. I might not have any interest in riding a desk all day, but I can see where someone coming into that environment would get asked questions." Greg took a sip of his coffee before something serious replaced the smile. "But why us? Why lie to the family?"

"There are a few more of us lately. I didn't—"

Chase stopped, unwilling to take the easy out.

"No, that's not fair. It's wrong to lay it at Nathan and Sarah's feet. I didn't want to tell the family because problems at Colton Properties are on me. And I'm embarrassed that I've got a potential financial problem and have been oblivious to it for who knows how long."

There.

It was out.

The real reason he wanted to hide Sloan's investigation.

"This isn't on you, Chase."

"How can you say that? It's entirely on me. I'm the head of CP and what happens there happens on my watch."

"People are capable of some pretty bad stuff. That doesn't rest on you."

Once again, there it was. It was that same push Max made last night. But how did he explain this?

Even if he could see his way to the point that he didn't own every action of the people around him, he was still the leader of the company. He'd made it his life, damn it, and shouldn't there be some benefit to that?

Some proof that all his time, effort and energy had created a company that was more than the sum of its parts?

Only he didn't say that.

He went with the easier truth. The one that demonstrated responsibility and accountability.

Not one more oblivious failure in what was shaping up to be a list of them.

"I'm the head of the company. If it doesn't rest on me, Greg, who does it rest on?"

Greg remained quiet, obviously thinking. For all his earlier teasing, the only thing that remained in the man's dark brown eyes was concern.

And the clear traces of stubbornness Chase recognized lived in his own eyes.

"I think you're confusing responsibility with deliberate action."

"Hardly."

"Hear me out. Then you can go back to being a stubborn ass. But seriously..." Greg paused. "Will you promise to listen for a minute?"

"Alright. I will."

"I've been thinking about it all a lot lately. We can thank our parents for that."

That same wry smile was there, but it was tinged with something decidedly more sober.

Grief.

"And I can't say I have it figured out, but I do think there's a space there."

"A space where?"

"Between responsibility and action. I might take responsibility for my own actions, but I can't own others'. And it's a tougher pill to swallow than it initially seems."

Chase wasn't entirely sure he understood where Greg was going but he knew the man sitting opposite him.

He was like a brother.

They'd spent their whole lives together and Chase knew Greg wasn't prone to fits of deep thoughts. He wasn't a callous man, or a superficial one, but his sense of himself was innately tied to the land he worked, each and every day. With that came a certain sort of centeredness that didn't depend on the opinions of others, *or* much worry or bother about what they thought.

So when the man spoke of those deep thoughts and the things he'd spent time working through in his mind, Chase recognized a kindred spirit.

He'd believed work—hard work—was the key to getting through it all. Hadn't he done the same to get through his marriage? And then to get through life postdivorce?

Work and effort and focus had seemed like the only answers he'd needed.

So how jarring to realize that doing those things—using work as the balm—was one more way of just running away.

And the things that hunted him always found a way to keep up.

"So what you're saying is I need to cut myself a break?"

"Yeah, you do. But more than that, you need to find a way to separate that innate sense of responsibility from feeling that you need to own every problem. They might rest heavy, but you didn't make the mess, Chase. You're just stuck cleaning it up."

They sat there quietly, drinking their coffee, Greg's words of wisdom filling the air between them.

Chase might not be fully ready to accept his circumstances, but perhaps he could see his way toward loosening the tight grip he had on that sense of responsibility as the oldest Colton. Maybe he could even relax a bit further and accept that for all the pain in their lives, they were forging a path to something new, too.

Something that included a new brother and a new sister, two completely awesome people in their own right.

And when the smile returned to his cousin's face, Chase realized they'd come to some sort of an unspoken agreement.

"Now we move to the most important part of our discussion. The beautiful woman you're parading around town as your girlfriend."

"Watch it, cuz."

"You see—that right there." Greg's smile only grew wider and far more mischievous. "That tells me she means something to you."

"Sloan's an amazing woman and an incredible professional. She's damn near solved my problem at Colton Properties and did it in less than a week."

Greg only smiled more broadly.

"What?" Chase pressed. "What are you trying to say through that stupid grin?"

"Your obsession with being the de facto head of the family and taking care of everyone. It's an admirable trait most of the time, even if you can't take us in your confidence and trust we can support you." Greg's smile faded, his tone laced with more heat and frustration than the man normally worked up in a year. "But right now? You're confusing responsibility with shortsighted idiocy."

"Gee, thanks." Chase fought the urge to get up and pace

the room, Greg's words settling over him like an ill-fitting jacket. "What am I being an idiot about?"

"You're talking like you're going to let that woman walk away without a fight."

"She's got two legs and a mind of her own. She can walk wherever she'd like." Even with each word of that statement being totally true, Chase felt heat creep up his neck at being read so easily.

"Yeah, nice try, but I'm not buying the crap you're peddling here."

"She's a contractor, doing a job for Colton Properties."

"Yeah, and she's amazing to boot. And you look at her like you can't stop looking at her."

Chase realized he hadn't taken his gaze off his coffee mug, so he looked up to face his cousin.

Because there it was.

The truth he couldn't run from *or* hide from his loved ones.

Sloan Presley was under his skin and had been from the moment she'd barreled into his office.

And it didn't seem to matter that he didn't want a relationship. Nor did it seem to matter she was only there in a professional sense.

"If you let a woman like that just walk away without even trying to get her to stay?" Greg shook his head. "That's major-league stupid and I've never taken you for that. Ever."

Chase hadn't taken himself for major-league stupid, either.

But lately his life had been bound and determined to convince him otherwise.

SLOAN HAD THOUGHT about calling Chase about a half-dozen times, but firmly tamped down on each wave. Calling led to talking, and talking could lead to seeing each other, and she needed distance.

Desperately.

Especially because that kiss they'd shared hadn't left her thoughts for longer than about eighty-three seconds at a time.

"Pathetic much, Presley?"

Sighing, she pushed back from the kitchen table and crossed to the fridge to root around for a midmorning snack. The rain hadn't let up and there was a gloomy feeling to the dark light seeping into the kitchen that made her think of something rich and decadent.

Which had then made her think of the leftover piece of Frannie's pound cake she'd stashed in the fridge last night.

Each time she'd been victorious against one of those urges to communicate, she'd forced herself instead to work through the irregularities she'd found in both the books as well as the record-keeping systems at Colton Properties.

This go-round she'd assuage it with some delicious butter and sugar.

With the cake and a fresh cup of coffee, she returned to her computer and figured it was worth trying a new tack on the hunt into Colton Properties. There were some particular irregularities, and she was curious if she could tie them by date to any specific happenings in town.

Sloan took another bite of cake, closing her eyes briefly in bliss at the perfect blend of sweet and buttery, before typing in the most recent date of the anomalies she'd uncovered from the prior month.

And she leaned in toward the screen at the page full of articles.

While each was written slightly differently, the headlines all said much of the same thing and she clicked into the one that was the most succinct.

Seven Women Found Dead in Wake County

How had she overlooked this?

It wasn't directly tied to the situation at Colton Properties, but it was pretty gruesome news.

Leaning forward, she read through the article and remembered she had gotten a few of these details before coming to Owl Creek, the biggest of which she'd forgotten. Max had worked this case. He hadn't spoken of it, but Chase had referenced it very briefly on their first call when he'd given her the information that his cousin had been the one to recommend her firm.

Goodness, how did a person live with doing that work?

She admired Max, his skills and his willingness to do the very hard work, but she couldn't imagine the toll it would take, day in and day out.

Her work brought her close to crimes, but she still had the safety of a computer screen and the distance of reading about something, not actually being there when a body was found or a killer's most depraved acts were discovered.

She scanned the article quickly, as was her habit, and read about the initial search-and-rescue and the discovery of the bodies over a period of days. But it was the link at the bottom of the article that caught her attention.

Law Enforcement Seeking Connection Between Serial Killer's Victims

"I guess I'm in now," she muttered to herself, following through to the linked article.

This one was full of speculation, she thought. There simply didn't appear to be any concrete facts for them to follow, but the enterprising reporter who'd written the story focused on the comparable ages of the women, their general similarity in appearance and the time period of their expected deaths.

"Just over two years." The shiver that skated down her spine was impossible to ignore. "What senseless deaths."

She was about to click on another link at the bottom of this article, leading her to the latest details, when her phone lit up with a text from Chase.

Come outside.

She smiled in spite of herself as three dots appeared on the screen, followed by another message.

It'll be worth it.

It was ridiculous to feel this shot of joy at the texts, but they did make her happy, the grisly articles quickly forgotten in favor of the man waiting outside.

And if that was a problem?

Well, she'd deal with it later.

Whatever had happened last night—and she'd tossed and turned endlessly trying to figure it out—was last night.

It was time to see what he had up his sleeve right now.

She slipped into a pair of sneakers she'd left by the couch and was almost to the door when an impish impulse hit her. Opening up the text string, she shot a quick text of her own.

Who is this?

The text went winging away as she opened her front door and she was just in time to see his reaction as she looked over the second-floor railing. His hair was tousled and his head was bent, but even from above she could see the way his mouth thinned into a straight line as he stared at his phone screen.

"Serves you right!" she hollered down, unable to fight the bubble of happiness that welled in her chest.

He glanced up then and Sloan had the wildest impulse to race down the stairs and into his arms.

"What serves me right?"

"Summoning a woman out into the rain!"

He smiled up at her before extending his arms. "Am I wet?"

Sometime between her last look out the window and now, the rain must have let up, even though it was still pretty gloomy.

"Come on down. I want to show you something."

She didn't skip, but Sloan figured she could have moved a bit more sedately down the concrete steps that led to the first floor. It was only as she got close that Chase reached out, snagging her hand and pulling her up close to him.

"There. Look."

She followed the extension of his hand as he pointed to something up over the roof of her building, a small gasp spilling from her throat as she took it all in.

"It's a double rainbow!"

"I had to show you."

"It's gorgeous."

She followed the distinct lines of the rainbow, each color coming to life in the sky in vivid relief. The second rainbow, a short distance from the first, had the expected fading, more pastel-hued in each color than the first rainbow, but equally beautiful.

And, in that moment, it was like a small piece of magic just for them to share.

"You really didn't know it was me texting?"

Sloan hadn't believed that bubble of happiness could grow

bigger, but at the anxious expression on his face, she realized that it had.

"I was teasing you. We've been texting for three weeks now."

"Right."

"Chase." She poked him in the chest before putting her palm against those firm lines. "It was a joke."

"Sure. Of course."

It was one of those small moments of vulnerability that simply melted her.

Did he realize how adorable he was?

And how hard he made it for her to keep her distance?

Here was a formidable businessman and yet he could still be stymied by a silly text.

It was…oddly sweet.

And one more chink in the armor she was desperately trying to protect herself with.

"I'm sorry."

The apology was out of place, especially seeing as he'd called her out here to see something so spectacular. "For what? The double rainbow is amazing."

"For last night. I was out of line, and I am sorry."

Sloan weighed her thoughts and realized there were two ways to play this. She could play dumb and pretend last night hadn't happened and that she hadn't actually spent most of the time since thinking about it, or she could push for what she wanted and stress her interest in having it happen again.

"You weren't out of line." She lifted up on her toes to press a kiss to his jaw. "And I don't need an apology." She shifted to kiss his chin. "But I really would appreciate it if you'd do it again."

This time, she pressed her lips to his.

For a fraction of a second, she thought she'd overstepped

and misread the cues, his lips firmly closed and his jaw still unmoving.

But then he opened his mouth, their lips suddenly locked in a delicious battle of wills.

And it was the moment his arms came around her, pulling her tight against his chest, that Sloan realized she'd won the battle.

Chapter Nine

Markus Acker stared at the text from his second-in-command, Winston Kraft, and felt a shot of pure satisfaction light him up from the center of his chest straight out to the very tips of his fingers.

Their latest scheme and tentative partnership with a new launderer had gone off without a hitch and their money was clean.

That quick hit of endorphins was short-lived since it hardly solved all their problems. Still, it was a step in the right direction.

He'd managed to grow his flock considerably in the past few years, and with their devotion came their money. He had to find ways to funnel it into the Ever After Church without all those dirty strings attached.

Speaking of attached…

He rolled his eyes as he thought of Jessie Colton. Easily manipulated, yes, but she had a certain streak of determination he was finding increasingly annoying. She wasn't nearly the subservient lamb he'd initially thought and her attitude of late had become downright demanding.

And, damn, the woman had quite a life story.

He'd believed he'd done a fairly decent job playing on her latent guilt. Since she'd left her four children to run off with her husband's brother and have two more in secret, it had been easy to subtly shame her, especially when she first came into his flock. But of late, he'd questioned just how effective he'd been.

His lamb had sprouted a few fangs.

The death of Robert Colton was tricky. She'd loved the man, well enough to leave her first marriage and her young children to take up with him. But Robert's subsequent leaving a decade later to go back full-time to his first family had left some wounds that most definitely hadn't scarred over.

No, Markus thought as he headed for the cabin they used in the woods outside the Ever After compound in Conners. That wound still had a lot of raw, seething pain in it.

Which still left him with a tool to manage her, but he did have to be careful. Overchanneling that anger in the wrong direction could backfire if she erupted like a loose cannon.

Up to now he'd focused on the two biological children she'd had with Robert.

Nathan and Sarah.

Both seemed rather oblivious to the benefits to be gained from their newfound family. But Markus innately knew that was the right button to push.

They were abandoned children.

Another family had received the majority of Robert's love and affection in life.

And now, most pressing of all, if they didn't act, those other children would receive Robert's wealth after his death.

Robert had set up Jessie and his secret children well and Markus already had designs on that money, but there was always a need for more. He wouldn't rest until Jessie had squeezed every last drop out of the rest of the family.

They'd already discussed their approach and how she needed to position her abandoned family to maximize their sympathy and, therefore, her children's inheritance.

Taking a deep breath, he prepared himself for the evening. At first, she'd amused him, but things had grown tiresome of late. Especially with the constant requests to marry. What had started as a murmur had moved to a fevered crescendo in the months since Robert had died and he hadn't fully settled on a dismissal that would work.

The jealousy from the rest of the flock had worked for a while, but he knew that excuse was wearing thin.

He rapped lightly before opening the door. Even with the fact that several women had been found dead in the area, Jessie was oblivious to any risk to herself.

She almost flouted it, truth be told. Walking around the compound and trying to meet him in the more deserted areas of the property as if nothing amiss had happened to other women out alone.

"Darling!"

Jessie flung herself at him and he braced for impact as he suddenly had his arms full of woman. Ensuring his next eye roll was a mental one only, he cooed back at her, "Darling, how I've missed you."

"It's been forever." She practically mewled the words against his chest and Markus held her in place there, his chin propped against the top of her head.

He'd just left her this morning, but he could play the besotted swain with the best of them. It was one of many in his bag of tricks.

"It's felt like ages, my darling."

She sighed against his chest before staring up at him. "It's agony. I can't wait until the day when we don't have to live in secret any longer. When the whole world will know I'm Mrs. Markus Acker."

"I wait with bated breath."

"Can we do it soon? I've been thinking, and really, my

love, there's nothing to be done for those selfish, silly leeches who will be jealous of me. Of our love."

It was further reinforcement that the jealousy-of-the-flock argument was losing its power.

He cycled through any number of responses, initially floundering before the perfect one filled his mind.

"I know, darling, and I feel the same. The women who will be jealous are going to be no matter what. But there is another issue. One that worries me even more."

Jessie's gaze narrowed, her clear irritation at being put off once more filling eyes that had grown far less adoring. "Now what?"

"It's Nathan and Sarah."

That gaze brightened right up. "Well, that's no problem. They won't be jealous."

"Of course not. They love you. I'm more concerned with pushing one more layer of upheaval into their lives. They're still grieving their father and meeting all those new brothers and sisters." He waved a hand. "I'd hate to give them any more emotional pain. I want them to celebrate our love right along with us and I fear that won't happen if we try to marry now."

He mentally applauded himself for the quick thinking and had to admit the point had merit. Even if he had been wildly interested in marrying their mother, her children were grieving the loss of their father and adjusting to a new family, all at once. A marriage at this time was hardly ideal.

He pressed a kiss to her forehead, keeping her close and practically willing her to his way of thinking. But as he pulled back, determined to keep his visage calm, his attitude easy and serene, he saw her start to wear down.

A sort of acceptance seemed to fill her eyes before she nodded.

"You're right, my darling. A little while longer. Nathan and Sarah have been through so much."

So very much, Markus thought as he pulled Jessie against him once more, his hands drifting down over her spine before settling low on her back.

He was still determined to use the way Jessie and Robert had brought their two youngest children into the world to his advantage.

Because there was no one serene enough or centered enough to overlook the slight of being excluded from an inheritance when the rest of their siblings got something.

He'd spent a lifetime reading human behavior.

And he'd bet his life he could work those two to his advantage.

I'D REALLY APPRECIATE it if you'd do it again.

Her own words ran over and over in her head as the kiss with Chase spun out and Sloan wondered how quickly she'd changed in so short a time.

When had she become so brazen?

And why did it seem so natural to kiss him beneath a rainbow-laden sky?

She should pull away.

There was no way she could get used to this. She was so close to uncovering the answers at Colton Properties. And once she did, she'd be gone.

But it was because of that very fact she stayed where she was.

She'd have to leave soon, and she needed to soak up every single moment of this. Wrapped up in Chase's arms, kissing him and exploring this magic between them.

Chase nuzzled her lips before gently lifting his head. "Does that mean you liked the double rainbow?"

"I like the man under the double rainbow. The beautiful sky was just a side benefit."

They stood there for several heartbeats, their gazes locked before Chase seemed to come to some decision.

"I can't say I'm sorry, but we shouldn't be doing this. Your work's impeccable and much as I hate the outcome, I know you'll have my problem fixed in a matter of days and be headed back to Chicago."

He was right.

Every single bit of it was fact. And yet…

Why did the thought of leaving make her sad?

Yes, she was attracted to Chase, but they'd only formally met less than a week ago. Even if she added the few weeks they'd spoken on the phone, Chase Colton had been part of her life for less than a month.

So why would completing a job and going home be something to be upset about?

"I will be."

"I—" Chase's hesitance was something of a surprise, especially when it was matched by him stepping back. "I can't thank you enough for all your help."

Those small embers that had sparked to life in the past, when he'd firmly put her in the professional box, were nowhere in evidence this time. Instead, she saw the cracks around the frayed edges of his control.

And with it, she laid a hand on his shoulder, willing him to understand that the challenges he faced now weren't permanent. They were earth-shattering, but they *would* pass.

"You and your family are going to get through this, you know." She held his gaze steady. "All of you. Together."

"There are some days I believe that. Like last night." His whole demeanor relaxed a bit, some of that tension that had lit him up as he'd stepped away fading. "When we're together I do believe we'll get through it."

"That's what you need to focus on, then. That there is a future for all of you and it's a good one. And it's built on a solid foundation."

"Oh, sure, rock-solid."

It was meant as a joke and she knew that. But as Chase said the words, she realized that there was something there worth digging underneath.

"There is, Chase. Think about it. Your mom and your Uncle Buck were there. Always there, for all of you."

As Sloan considered it, she realized there really was something there.

Something well worth celebrating.

"I haven't met either of them, but their presence was clearly felt last night at the barbecue. The way everyone spoke of them and whenever anyone shared a funny story, the names Jenny and Buck were at the center of it."

"They're good people. We've often joked quietly among all us kids that those two should have been the ones who got married."

"They built your foundation."

"I guess they did."

"They gave you the tools to get through this. The depth of your relationships with your siblings and your cousins. The understanding of the importance of family."

"It's a wonder how Nate and Sarah got that at all," Chase said on a sigh. "Especially seeing as who they got as parents."

"You'll see to it that they get the full benefit of being Coltons from here on out."

"You make it sound so simple."

"Maybe it is. Maybe for all the complications in all your lives, what your mom and what your Uncle Buck gave you is solid. Unshakable."

"I want to believe that, Sloan. You have no idea how badly I want to."

"Why can't you?"

"What if I'm wrong?"

HIS QUESTION SORT of lingered there between them. One more sign the man he believed himself to be had somehow vanished in the events of the past few months.

Those unassailable qualities about himself he'd have said were unbreakable had, in fact, broken.

"Maybe it isn't about being right or wrong, in this case."

Sloan's words had been spoken in a low, soft tone and Chase found himself caught up in that quiet, lilting quality.

Moreover, he was snared in the promise she offered.

"How can it be about anything else?"

"You have to find a way forward for yourself. Based on what I've observed, I believe your family will, too, but in the end it's their journey."

He'd bet on every one of his brothers and sisters and cousins in a heartbeat.

Why was he having such a hard time betting on himself?

Sloan glanced toward the fading rainbow before her gaze resettled on him. "Take me for a drive."

"Where?"

"Here. Around Owl Creek. A bit beyond if you'd like. I want to see what you do."

"You want to see real estate?"

"I want to see the home you love and the land you love. Show it to me." She spread a hand outward. "Whatever else has shaken your foundation, this is yours."

It was a unique sort of encouragement but as they exited her apartment complex grounds fifteen minutes later, Chase had to admit it was the perfect balm for all that had been bothering him.

Crisscrossing through Owl Creek, he pointed out various landmarks, silly things he'd done as a kid down at the town lake and even a piece of land on the edge of town that was his dream property.

"What's so important about it?" Sloan asked.

"I've believed for years we could sustain a resort here. A real one, that people plan trips around. We'd bring a significant amount of tourism along with a heck of a lot of industry and jobs."

"What's stopping you?"

"The land's the easy part on this one. Getting the right backers. Working with the right company. It's far more complex than a typical build and I haven't quite found the right promise to investors."

Chase pulled into a small gravel lot near the largest lake in Owl Creek. He put the car in Park and cut the engine, about to get out when Sloan put a hand on his arm. "You'll get there. I know you will."

"I'd always believed it."

"Then keep believing it."

Old habits died hard, and Chase knew more than a decade of choices couldn't be undone in a matter of days. But Sloan had changed something.

He didn't want a relationship. He'd been so firm on that count, quite sure heading down that path again would destroy him.

It was a mistake he had no interest in making again.

And even with all that *certainty*, Sloan had snuck through his defenses.

He kept fighting it but his reaction to Greg's interest in her had been a flag. The special combination of excitement and ease he always felt in her presence was another. And the fact that he wanted to share this dream with her was yet another.

In what felt like much too short a time, she'd come to matter.

And he wasn't quite sure what to do about it.

Which made the frown that subtly marred her lips a surprise he keyed in on immediately.

"What is it?"

"I have no way of making this sound better than I mean it, but I was sitting here looking at all this beauty and couldn't help but question those dead women discovered last month." A small shiver rippled through her shoulders. "It's terrible."

It had been horrific, and Chase knew the case had shaken a lot of people in Wake County. The brutality of it all and the sheer number of women who'd been killed had been staggering.

That another young woman had then been killed in the hospital, after seemingly escaping from captors, had only added to that underlying sense of unease folks had been feeling.

Although they'd spoken briefly about the Ever After Church before, Chase elaborated on what he knew.

"Max worked that case. It's where he met Della."

"I got the sense something dark had drawn them together based on a few things that had been said at the barbecue," Sloan said. "But I didn't feel last night was the right time to ask."

Chase caught her up quickly. He told Sloan how Della had been training her K-9, Charlie, in a new-to-him mountainous area, and while tracking, had found a dead body. Max had been called in as the FBI lead to work the case.

"Horrifically, they found seven bodies in total and then another woman who'd been badly hurt who died later. One of the seven was Della's cousin, Angela Baxter."

"That's awful."

"It really shook Della up, as you'd imagine. But she was committed to seeing it all through."

"Those articles I read? One reporter seems determined to link it to that local church we talked about."

It was Chase's turn to frown at that description. "Ever After?" When she only nodded, he added, "You hear things, working in real estate. They seem to move from place to place and have laid claim to a property a few towns over in Conners."

"Laid claim? Don't churches have actual structures? Buildings they use? A place they actually settle and develop?"

"My thoughts exactly. I've always been one to let people live their lives because you see a lot in real estate that's not really your business. Who wants to build a survival camp, or who's decided they need to carve out a ditch in the woods for a fallout shelter."

"People still do that?"

"They most certainly do." Chase shook his head. "But there's something about that church that isn't right. Max's mother has dabbled in that group and it's worried him."

"Jessie Colton's a part of that?"

"Appears so. My cousins all think it's a bad idea, but she's not exactly been a part of their lives and I don't think they know how to engage her on the topic." Chase shrugged, recognizing a deeper truth. "I don't think they know how to engage her on anything."

"What do Nate and Sarah think?"

"I'm not entirely sure but I don't get the sense they put too much stock in their mother's choices."

"One more choice in a long line of poor ones," Sloan murmured.

"What do you mean?"

"Leaving her children and her husband. Putting on a married facade with a new man who also happens to be her sister's husband. Now she's caught up in an *entity* that is under a cloud of suspicion. Those are some seriously questionable decisions."

Chase had never put much stock in the stories of his Aunt Jessie. Any woman who'd run off on her children—his cousins, who had become, through a lifetime together, some of his best friends—had never seemed worth his time or attention.

The fact that his cousins had gone out of their way to avoid speaking about her—a point his mother mimicked—had made Jessie a sort of ghost in his life. Someone who hovered on the periphery but wasn't really visible from day to day.

"It does make you wonder."

And now that Sloan had made the point, it actually had him wondering quite a bit. He had the details on the property in Conners the Ever After Church was purported to live on.

Maybe he'd do a bit of discreet digging.

It really had nothing to do with him, and yet…it had everything to do with him because it was about his family. Max, Greg, Malcolm and Lizzy were as close to him as his siblings.

He'd spent enough time wallowing in the things he hadn't considered or had the foresight to recognize, Chase realized.

But this he could look into.

This he could understand better.

If his Aunt Jessie really was making yet another poor decision in a long line of them, wasn't it important to understand that?

Because maybe if they did, they'd all take a big step forward in putting the past firmly behind them.

SLOAN WASN'T SURE what had prompted her suggestion to drive around Owl Creek but was glad for whatever impulse had struck. Their afternoon had been…restorative.

And it had given her yet another glimpse into the fascinating man Chase Colton was.

His love of this deeply beautiful part of Idaho was evident, as was his knowledge of real estate and the business of making a property a successful enterprise.

Even their discussion of the dead women had been laced with his knowledge and understanding of real estate, property management and the basic requirements to use the land.

And how odd to know that his Aunt Jessie—already suspect to Sloan's way of thinking—was part of that creepy group.

Although it was a distraction that she didn't really need to indulge, she knew herself well enough to know that she'd be doing a bit more digging later into the Ever After Church.

In the meantime, she was sharing an afternoon with a handsome, interesting man. It was time to start paying attention to that instead of the sad mystery that had spiked her curiosity.

"How long would something like that take?" she asked. "Building an entire resort?"

"Why don't we get out and we can walk along the shoreline? I promise not to be so boring you're tempted to jump in the lake to escape my incessant droning."

The wry humor combined with his captivating green gaze was all the encouragement she needed. Sloan scrambled out of the car, eager to hear all he wanted to share.

Although she was honest enough with herself to admit she was a bit besotted with Chase, a half hour later all she could see was the vision of his resort. It was coming to life in her imagination, rising from the land surrounding the lake.

"So really," he said. "It's not about just creating everything all at once. You could do it in phases."

"I'm not a real-estate expert, but I am a human being

who enjoys a vacation. What you're describing is incredible. From the spa to the outdoor activities to the hotel itself?" Sloan ticked off just a few of the images Chase had described for her.

She stopped, circling a full turn before coming back to where she started so that she could look up at him. "It's special, Chase. This place is special. Welcoming and bright and deeply restorative."

"I was thinking the same thing about you."

"Chase, I—"

He shook his head before holding up a hand. "Please. Let me say this."

The change in his demeanor was so swift, so immediate, she could only nod.

"I'm a bad bet when it comes to relationships."

"Chase, I'm sure that's not true."

"It actually is. And I've not only been content with that truth, but I've actively reveled in it." He laughed but the sound fell hollow before floating away on a light breeze. "It's why we've been so successful at the office with our little show we've been putting on."

Since she heard the brush-off coming, Sloan felt her spine stiffen, already bracing for it.

Which made his next words so earth-shattering.

"You're the first woman I've met since my divorce that has made me realize I've shut myself off from living."

"I…" She stopped, realizing a truth of her own. "I don't know what to say. But I do have a sense of what you're feeling."

"Oh?"

"I've put everything I am into building SecuritKey. And I don't regret it, in any way, but I've come to realize that I have used it as an excuse at times."

"Why?"

"Lack of successful relationships. A personality that's innately more comfortable behind a computer hunting for data than going out and engaging with others. Take your pick."

"You did well with my family last night."

"And that time made me realize that I've been hiding a bit. Perhaps more than a bit these last few years as my business has really taken off. It's easy to say there isn't time for a relationship, or that I'll work on it later when there's something else occupying my time. But I think I've been marking time instead."

It was a stark realization, but it was true all the same. It had been easier than she ever could have expected to use her job as the reason she wasn't in a relationship. Or, worse, why she'd slowly given up on trying, especially these past few years.

The number of dates she'd been on had dwindled. The number of second dates, after those few first dates she did have, had become nonexistent.

"What do you want to do about it?" he asked softly.

"I'm not sure. But I do know I've enjoyed the time this past week in your company."

She considered all that stood in their way, a few key details still glaringly obvious.

She lived in Chicago and he lived in Idaho.

She was here on a job only.

And most of all, despite his confession that he'd been running from relationships, he wasn't exactly seeking one out with her.

"I've enjoyed this time with you, too."

Chase reached out and brushed a wayward curl behind her ear. His hand lingered briefly against her jaw before he pulled away.

It wasn't much, Sloan admitted to herself. Not a declaration of interest or a request to see where things could go.

By either of them.

But it was a step forward.

An admission, really.

And despite her confused sadness at the reality that she was leaving as soon as she wrapped up the work for Colton Properties, she couldn't deny how sweet it felt to actually say the words.

It was even sweeter to hear them.

Chapter Ten

Sloan spent the rest of the weekend with work.

Yes, it was a bit of slinking back to her corner where she was most comfortable, but it was also the work she'd contracted to do. SecuritKey maintained its commitments, no matter how moony its owner was.

And she did manage to carve out a bit of time to herself. Time that wasn't spent obsessing over Chase Colton, thank you very much.

She'd driven around Owl Creek a bit more, retracing some of the roads they'd taken the day before while also finding a few more herself. And she'd taken a relaxing run around the lake she and Chase had visited.

She might not have been in the best frame of mind Monday morning as she opened a package of food for Waffles before making herself some scrambled eggs, but she wasn't in a bad place, either.

And, damn it, she was so close to figuring out the thief inside Colton Properties.

She'd dug hard the day before, forgetting to eat dinner until Waffles had squawked at her from his perch beside the makeshift desk she'd set up at the small kitchen table.

The irregularities in the books were subtle and very well done, but there was a pattern she'd nearly figured out.

It wasn't the same day every month, or the same week each quarter. Nor was it a specific amount, but more of a vague skim that never exceeded more than about two percent off a transaction. But she sensed there was something specific to the timing all the same.

She'd made a mental note to ask Chase if there was any specific payment schedule for his properties. Perhaps the way they collected on income or when they removed monies for tax assessments would give her a clue.

Regardless, she was close to the answer. And she'd effectively ruled out both the sales and marketing teams from any nefarious doings. Although that encompassed quite a few employees, she was hesitant to question those who were left.

Although few understood what she really did for a living or how she did it, Sloan had always been careful to rule people out, but avoid casting aspersions on those she hadn't yet eliminated. Proof was the only way to approach potential criminal activity and she was acutely aware she could ruin someone's life and reputation if she was wrong.

So she'd keep digging.

It was the only way.

She'd worked until about midnight before deeming herself suitably tired enough to sleep. Even then, she'd still tossed and turned a bit before finally drifting off.

Why hadn't he called?

Wasn't she glad he hadn't called? How else was she supposed to make a clean break when she went home to Chicago?

And why hadn't he kissed her, right there beside the lake?

I do know I've enjoyed the time this past week in your company.

Chase's comment had lodged in her thoughts, lighting up her senses with each and every restless turn in bed.

She enjoyed his company, too.

And Sloan instinctively knew they had moved into dangerous territory admitting that.

She didn't live here. And he didn't do relationships. It would be a really bad idea to form some sort of attachment under any circumstances, but especially when she was so close to cracking the culprit at Colton Properties.

She told herself all these things and had finally drifted off to sleep,

And then her eyes had popped open bright and early, and no amount of telling herself to go back to bed had worked. She finally got up, put in another hour and a half on the financial files and then cleaned up to head over to Chase's office.

It might have only been a week, but the Colton Properties offices never failed to inspire her, Sloan thought as she pulled into the parking lot. Chase's SUV was already there, and her heart gave a hard thump knowing she'd see him soon.

Frowning as she got out—really, was she a fourteen-year-old with a crush?—Sloan pulled her work bag from where she'd stowed it behind the driver's seat and put both the image and the anticipation of seeing Chase in his dress shirt and sharply pressed slacks firmly out of her mind.

And stared up at the building that housed Colton Properties.

For all the negative thoughts she'd had about Robert Colton and his actions to his families, both the one he publicly acknowledged and the one he didn't, she had to give the man credit for his vision. What had begun as the Colton hardware store when Robert first started his business had grown, expanded and flat-out evolved into what was now the family enterprise.

They'd managed to leave the original hardware-store layout as the first floor of the building, while adding to the place by going up. Colton Properties sat above, as modern and business-focused as the old store felt small-town and folksy in the very best sense of the words. The shelving and cash registers were still on the first floor, but the merchandise had long been removed. In its place were various stations full of photographs of properties in the surrounding areas, both for sale as well as those that had already been developed.

It was impressive, Sloan acknowledged as she headed for the elevators.

Vision was something she always respected.

And it was awe-inspiring to see how that vision had found a place in Robert's son, unwavering and true.

Althea was already standing in front of the elevator and Sloan smiled at the office manager as she moved up beside her. "Good morning."

"Oh." Althea shook her head, obviously startled by the greeting. But she quickly regrouped, even as she pressed a hand against her chest. "I'm sorry, dear, you scared me. I was wool-gathering about all I need to get done today."

"I'm confident you can do it all," Sloan said as she gestured the older woman into the open elevator. "You're certainly getting a good head start on your Monday."

"I could say the same for you," Althea said, and though there was a light tease in her words, Sloan didn't miss the clear signs she really was frazzled.

"I wanted to see if I could drag Chase out for a quick cup of coffee and maybe a little breakfast. Then I need to get some work of my own done."

"What is it you do again, dear?" Althea asked as she stepped off to the main floor of the business.

"I'm a consultant."

"Which is?"

The first question had seemed a bit off, the words strangely sharp even as Althea's tone held a flat quality. But Sloan quickly deciphered the real question underneath the continued probing as they walked into the open lobby of Colton Properties.

And in that moment she had a flash of those dates and stealthy withdrawals she'd reviewed, over and over, all weekend.

It hadn't been the dates in each month.

It had been the time stamp.

Each and every one had happened before eight a.m.

She glanced down at her watch before aiming a big wide smile, full of teeth, at Althea. "I take on clients who have need of digital-forensics services."

"What are those?" The light titter that skimmed beneath the question only reinforced the sudden shot of awareness and *certainty* flooding Sloan's veins.

"It's an ability to dig into digital files and understand that all elements are managed properly. Finances. Profit-and-loss statements."

"Why ever would anyone need that?"

"A variety of reasons, but it's the quickest way to suss out embezzlers."

Chase chose that moment to come into the outer office and Althea smiled at him, all cheerfulness and sunshine. "Chase, good morning! Your girlfriend and I rode up the elevator together."

Chase's smile was equally broad, his "good morning" winging back through the lobby area.

Sloan didn't know why she moved, but something about the entire tableau playing out in the lobby keyed her into one very important point.

Althea was about to run.

Without questioning it, Sloan moved into position between the older woman and the door.

And cleanly intercepted her when she made a run for it.

"GET OFF ME, you bitch!"

Chase stared at the scene unfolding before him and lost about three seconds simply trying to process what was happening.

And then he moved.

Sloan had captured Althea in a tight hold, locking the woman's arms at her side.

Although Althea had Sloan by a solid thirty pounds, Sloan had youth and strength on her side and kept a firm hold on the woman, refusing to let go of her quarry.

"What's going on?"

"This is your embezzler," Sloan grit out around the struggling woman.

Chase stepped forward, reaching for Althea by the shoulders in hopes of calming her down.

Or that's what he'd tell himself later when the woman freed an arm and decked him solidly in the left eye.

"What the hell!"

A lifetime spent with brothers and male cousins had taught him how to fight. And an equal amount of time with two wily sisters and a female cousin had taught him how to use finesse while still taking hold of a dangerous situation.

He'd never hit a woman, regardless of Althea's attack. But he had no compunction about placing a stronger hold around her arms to keep her in place.

He didn't have to hold her long when the hissing and spitting devolved into hard sobs as she curled into his chest.

"I'm sorry, Chase. I'm so sorry."

He glanced at Sloan over the woman's head. She only nodded, affirming what he'd quickly pieced together.

"Why, Althea?"

"Ben. It's my Ben."

As Sloan called the police, Chase escorted Althea into the conference room off the lobby, closing the door behind them. She continued to sob while Chase crossed to the small fridge beneath the side counter Althea always kept stacked full and pulled out a water.

He unscrewed the cap and handed over the water, then took a seat next to her. "Tell me what's going on."

Through fits and starts, and quite a few more tears, Althea told him of Ben's health problems and the increasing cost of his treatments and his medicines.

Chase didn't want to feel compassion, but he recognized the pain and couldn't quite help himself. He'd known Althea most of his life and he knew her family.

And he'd known Ben had "off days," as she'd mention from time to time, but he had no real understanding of just how bad things were.

His employees' personal situations were their business, but he could have helped. Could have found some way to help her manage this burden.

Or he believed he could have. But ten years? He'd been growing his influence but ten years ago his father was firmly involved in Colton Properties.

Would Robert Colton have been so understanding?

Would he have helped?

"Why didn't you come to me?"

"I—" She stared down at the hands folded in her lap. "You've had a lot going on."

"Not for ten years."

"Your father before you did." Althea hiccupped, then added in a low voice, "That's what made it so easy."

"Made it easy?"

"I knew, Chase. About your father's secret life. His other family. And I used his distraction and his willingness to keep piling responsibility and system access on me to my advantage. I figured if the great Robert Colton could keep two families, I could at least take a little bit to help care for my own family."

It wasn't logical, but as he sat there, staring at the woman he'd believed he knew, Chase had to admit he could see how it had happened.

Fifteen minutes later he'd made his statement to his brother Fletcher and his partner from the Owl Creek PD. Fletcher's partner left to take Althea down to the station, and Chase dropped his head in his hands.

"Ten years, Fletcher. Ten."

"It's a long damn time." His brother's green eyes, so like his own, were filled with a mix of compassion and anger.

A look, Chase suspected, he'd find in his own if he only had a mirror.

"Do you believe it? That Dad's secret life was why she did it? And it was those secrets that made it all so easy."

Fletcher nodded, tapping at the small notebook he'd written in while Althea had told her story. "I heard it. And for what it's worth, she's backpedaling an awful lot. She found an excuse she's comfortable with to make her own sins not seem so bad."

"Her husband is sick."

"And we'd have helped her. Somehow, we'd have found a way. But she stole from us instead. Don't forget that."

"I guess."

Fletcher moved closer, his hand settling on Chase's shoulder. "She made a choice, Chase. A bad one. Don't lose sight of that."

They said their goodbyes and Chase watched his brother leave. He was not at all surprised when Sloan showed up at the door, slipping in and closing it behind her.

"People must be wondering what's going on?"

"Yeah, they are. I told everyone to get settled in the big

conference room in about a half hour and you'd let them know you'd be out to talk to them."

"And tell them I've missed an embezzler for the past decade."

"And tell them you *caught* an embezzler who's covered her tracks—well—for the past decade."

Sloan's emphasis was in all the right places and still, Chase couldn't help but feel the spin.

"One more excuse. Just like Althea's."

"I'd call it the truth."

He heard the steel in her tone and saw it mirrored in the hard set of her features, her jaw fixed in place.

It should have been harsh, but instead…it was compelling.

And a reminder that he'd wanted answers and had gotten them.

This was never going to end in a good place. He'd called in Sloan and her expertise specifically because there *was* a problem with the books.

It was hardly the time to get angry at the messenger.

Which made the explosion that much worse.

"You can call it whatever the hell you want, it doesn't change the fact that a woman was just escorted out of here, broken by life."

He picked up Althea's half-full water bottle and hurled it at the far wall.

The move wasn't particularly satisfying, but the anger roiling through him softened a bit with the action.

In the desire to move and rant.

To somehow shed this rage that had filled him at the discovery of his father's secret life.

Yet Althea's excuses—one more dark mark in a column full of them—only made the thick miasma of it all heavier.

A weight that seemingly grew as each day passed.

Sloan didn't deserve any of it.

She'd helped, but in seeing her standing there, more than willing to shoulder the burden of her discovery, Chase knew a sense of shame.

And anger.

And a deep sort of fracture that separated the life he believed he had from the one he actually did.

It cratered through him.

And Chase wondered if he would ever be the same.

SLOAN WAS TEMPTED to just walk out.

Leave Chase to his anger and his need to process it, and head home.

She'd solved the case. It was time to pack up and head back to Chicago.

She nearly did all that, actually turning on her heel to head out the same way she'd come in, before something stopped her.

This wasn't directed at her. Oh, she was handy, but she wasn't the real target. And whatever she was seeing now had nothing to do with the raw, aching fury that was raging through him.

With calm, purposeful movements, she crossed to the sideboard and picked up a roll of paper towels, then went over and cleaned up the water. She'd sopped up the first seeping puddle when she felt a large hand on her back.

"You don't have to do that."

"It's fine. I can—" She didn't even finish her sentence when Chase was gently pulling her to her feet, taking the roll and the sopping handful from her. "It's my mess. I'll do it."

He tossed the wet handful in the garbage and already had a fresh length pulled off when Sloan laid a hand on his arm.

"Why don't we both do it and we'll get it done in no

time?" She couldn't resist adding a smile. "Your aim was solid, and you even cleaned that window there."

The tease had its desired effect and he let out a laugh when he saw the streams of water dripping down the window that overlooked Main Street. "Side benefit."

Chase handed her the paper-towel roll and within minutes they both had the room back to rights, the floor and the window dry once more. He resettled the considerably smaller towel roll back on the sideboard before turning to face her.

"I'm sorry."

His green gaze was bleak, but his voice was firm.

Solid.

And underneath it all, she could hear that Chase had regained some of his equilibrium.

"Apology accepted."

"Althea's been here for so long. She's part of the Colton Properties family."

Sloan didn't want to add to his pain, but she'd done enough work through the years to know that his thinking was a fallacy. Colton Properties, no matter how well-meaning, was a place to come to work. Althea's family was separate and always had been.

And when push came to shove, her focus and her bad decisions were in service to her own family.

Although she said nothing out loud, Chase must have seen her lack of agreement. "You don't think we could have done something different?"

"Harsh truth?"

"Give it to me," he said on a resigned sigh.

"I think this is your family business, but I think this is a job and a place to come to work for everyone else."

He nodded. "I suppose you're right."

She wanted to go to him—to touch him—but because she did, Sloan stayed right where she was.

"It's not a bad thing, Chase. In fact, if you can channel that properly, which I believe you have, you create a place where people want to come to work. Where they want to devote their lives."

"To steal from me."

"To build a career. To partner with you on your vision. To live a good life, with purpose and commitment every day. It doesn't have to be a family. A job can be a good thing. It can matter, just for itself."

Her own words felt a bit hollow as they echoed in her ears.

Hadn't she done the exact opposite?

She might have begun SecuritKey with purpose, but it had become something of an all-consuming mission, especially these past few years. She'd felt that all too starkly when she'd considered her dating life, but if she extended it even outside the realm of dating, she had made her job her life in all aspects.

Perhaps it was time to pull back on that a bit.

Whatever else this job was meant to be in her life—and meeting Chase Colton was obviously a part—maybe he wasn't the whole story.

And maybe this assignment had come at the perfect time to make her wake up and realize she needed to build a life that was more than work.

More than something to fill her days.

"I should get into the big conference room and update everyone on what's going on."

"Why don't I come with you? I can explain my role and why I've been here."

"You don't have to do that."

"I think I do. You said it to me from the first. That you didn't like foisting a ruse off on your employees and lying to them. I can explain what I did and what I've turned over to you."

"There've been way too many lies up to now."

"Yes, there have been. And because of it, let's tell them the truth. Push it all into the light and let everyone know how you're going to fix it."

MARKUS SAT WITH Winston Kraft in the luxurious trailer they used as an office and watched the numbers scrolling on the large computer monitor in front of them.

"We need her to come to heel. That Colton money will help solve some of these shortfalls." Winston pointed to three areas on the screen, all tied to recruitment and some payoffs they'd needed to do to manage the dead women.

Dead women who would have stayed buried if it weren't for those damn K-9 trackers.

He'd always hated dogs. They found more than they should and uncovered the stuff that needed to stay beneath the surface.

And wasn't it bad luck Jessie's son had been engaged in the case?

He'd guilted her about it and managed to buy himself a few extra weeks without her nagging him incessantly about marriage. How Max had turned to such dark life's work because she'd left him as a child.

He'd been subtle about it, Markus smiled to himself, but it had been an effective ploy. And the added benefit was how much he could then press her about her relationship with Nathan and Sarah and how much love and devotion she'd shown them.

Shouldn't they *want* to support her? Shouldn't they want more of their fair share of Robert Colton's money?

Despite manipulating her to the situation, it hadn't

changed the fact he'd had to pay out to keep a few county officials quiet.

It had been necessary dollars out the door, but they were operating in a deficit and would be fully in the red if Jessie didn't figure out a way to get her kids on board.

"How much time do we have?" Markus asked.

"Another month. Maybe two if we can squeeze a bit more out of the current patrons."

It wasn't much time. Markus considered how he'd approach some of his followers, who still hoarded some of their own money they thought he didn't know about.

He had a few tactics he could employ there. But the truth was, Jessie Colton's money would go a long way toward not just keeping them solvent, but putting them in a position to invest more. There was a trafficking ring in Boise he wanted a piece of and there were a few other big fish he'd had on the line he wanted to try and reel in.

They were skeptics, but prettying up his enterprise would go a long way toward getting those fish into his growing pond.

"She still at you to get married?" Winston asked as he shut down the program, tapping in the additional layers of passwords and encryption he insisted on.

"With damn near every breath."

"You know you may have to do it?"

Markus eyed his second-in-command. Winston had been with him for years now and the man was a slimy bastard, but effective and committed to the grift.

"I don't see you lining up to do it."

Winston flashed him a dark grin and batted his eyes. "I'm a married man myself. My sweet little wife is a good-natured follower and is eager to have children to increase our flock."

"How's that working out?"

Markus hit his friend with the dig on purpose. He knew it had been a serious bone of contention that Winston's young wife wasn't pregnant yet and he'd always found those well-placed barbs kept a person in line.

And ensured they realized Markus saw far more than his benevolent demeanor might suggest.

Winston's eyes had grown dark, and he pushed away from the computer. But when he spoke, he was his even-toned self. "In due time."

"Don't you have grandkids you could foist off on her?"

Winston didn't keep up with his first family. His estranged son, Rick, was unwilling to be a part of his father's life. Winston had always seemed okay with that, if not actually somewhat relieved not to have the baggage of his adult son nosing around in his business.

"Rick's not eager to have a family reunion, but I keep tabs on them."

Markus kept a few tabs of his own but held back from saying anything more.

It always paid to know the comings and goings of your flock.

Even when it was a lifelong friend.

Perhaps especially then, Markus thought.

It was a cold world and even the closest of friends could turn on you for the right incentive.

Which was why he'd always ensured he kept a stack of information at the ready.

Knowledge was power in every way. Sure, weapons and fear were endlessly effective tactics, but knowledge and the secrets most people held close to themselves were the foundation of a healthy enterprise.

The Ever After Church was the latest incarnation of that power, but it would be temporary, just like all that came before. Another year, maybe two, if they could keep reel-ing in the big fish, but that would be all. He and Winston would suck this part of Idaho dry before moving on, but they *would* move on.

It was inevitable.

Shaking off thoughts of what came next, Markus focused on the here and now, their budget spreadsheet vividly tattooed in his mind.

He needed to go talk to Jessie. It was time to amp up the pressure campaign for Robert Colton's money.

Every last cent he could get his hands on.

Chapter Eleven

Sloan watched Chase work the conference room, full of Colton Properties employees, from the initial speech he gave outlining what they'd uncovered about Althea's embezzling, to the real reason Sloan had come to Owl Creek, to then answering questions. He remained respectful of Althea's privacy, even in the midst of her destructive behavior, before directing everyone's attention to the future.

Even as he painted that vision, he was quick to answer each and every question, most of which dwelled on the past.

He was even quicker to take responsibility and outline how he and his family would absorb the costs of Althea's damages, going so far as to confirm everyone's bonus structures and salaries were safe.

It was hard work, that sort of dedicated leadership and willingness to helm the ship, but he did it well.

And when the last person had filed out of the conference room, Sloan's heart did a hard bump in her chest at the look of sheer exhaustion that painted his features.

And it wasn't even noon yet.

"That started the week off with a bang."

Chase reached for the center of the table and snagged a fresh bottle of water among several someone had thoughtfully put out earlier.

He swigged down almost half of it before looking back up at her, his smile wry. "Don't worry. I won't throw this one."

"I'm not worried about the water."

He glanced up after taking another large pull on the water. "Oh? What are you worried about?"

"You."

"Yeah, well I'll be fine."

"You will be. But right now, you're entitled to be angry and hurt and frustrated."

"Like I've been for the past four months?" Chase shook his head. "What's the point any longer? As difficult as today is, it's finally a step in the right direction. Finally a step forward, not wondering who's out to harm the business.

"I'm sad. But today's not the day to worry about me. I finally have some answers."

She didn't want to doubt him, but she knew how grief worked. Hadn't her mother always said that it comes in waves? No matter how well in hand you thought you had things, a rogue wave knocks the wind out of everyone.

And make no mistake about it, Chase Colton was grieving.

It was the second biggest point she kept returning to, over and over.

The first point she returned to was about herself.

Because she couldn't quite get past—or even begin to process—how naive she'd been in taking on this job.

She'd taken the work believing that it would be easier, somehow, to uncover secrets for a small, family-owned business.

Instead, she'd discovered that this betrayal took as large a human toll as a lot of the work she'd done for the FBI. The stakes were different, but pain was still pain and she hadn't really braced herself for that fact.

With the FBI, her work helped to uncover killers and brought them to justice.

With this work for Colton Properties, she'd uncovered yet more secrets that caused Chase pain.

"You do have answers." Sloan nodded, anxious to get out of there.

She'd changed lives today. Althea's was ruined. Chase's beliefs in an old friend had been shattered.

And she desperately needed to get away from the suddenly crushing weight of her work.

ONE MOMENT SHE was there and the next she was gone.

Wisped away like smoke was all Chase could think as Sloan made an excuse to leave and three other people walked into the conference room to talk to him.

Because even with a morning as wild as theirs, the work still had to go on.

He vowed to call Sloan later and then switched his focus to the evolving negotiation for a piece of property just outside of Conners. That was followed by a conference call he set up with his siblings, including Nate and Sarah, to fill them in on Althea's arrest. The call had gone well, but as they were wrapping up, Nate had asked if he was free to meet for coffee later that afternoon and Chase had agreed.

Chase used a visit to the property out toward Conners as the basis to set their meeting point and suggested Nate meet him at a small coffee shop he favored there. It cut a bit of time off his brother's drive over from Boise and gave Chase an opportunity to walk the property in question once more.

It also gave him a chance to replay all that had happened that morning during his time alone. Sloan's work had been impeccable—she'd laid out a clear trail and Althea's history of embezzlement was damn near impossible to dismiss.

His office manager's crimes were long, and he had every

expectation the Owl Creek PD would match what was taken from Colton Properties to deposits into Althea's accounts. Fletcher had recused himself from the case based on his personal proximity to the family business. But his partner would see this one through and help secure the evidence.

And Chase's siblings had all agreed that they would support Althea's husband's treatments for as long as he needed them.

None of it meant they weren't prosecuting Althea for the crime.

He hated it, deeply, but he wasn't excusing her behavior, either. Especially when so much of her rationale for her actions was that his father had done bad things, so she felt it was okay.

It wasn't okay.

Hadn't that been the root of their collective frustration and upset these past several months at the news of his father's misdeeds?

The man they'd all believed to be a strong, upstanding citizen and businessman hid terrible secrets.

"Those look like some pretty dark thoughts." Nate stepped up to the small table Chase had snagged when he walked into the bustling shop. "I hope it's not the coffee."

He glanced up at his half brother, dressed in a sport coat, pressed shirt and slacks. As a detective for the Boise PD, Nate no longer had to dress in uniform. But as Chase considered the younger man, he realized that uniforms came in all shapes and sizes.

This one said, *I'm in control and don't you forget it.*

Chase gestured to the cup he'd ordered and set on the other side of the table. "Nah, the coffee's great. Even my mood's not bad enough to spoil it."

"You sure about that?" Nate's smile was measured as he took his seat.

"It's been a hell of a day."

"I am sorry about that," Nate said, "I'm really not familiar with what you do, but I understand how important it is to you and I appreciate you including Sarah and I on the call earlier. A betrayal like that's hard to take."

"You're a part of this and you deserved to know like everyone else." Chase took a sip of his coffee, the bitter brew oddly soothing. It matched the unpleasant taste he hadn't been able to wash out of his mouth all day. "More than twenty years, Nate. She was with my father since he got big enough to need a real office manager and staff."

"And it allowed her to fly under the radar as a trusted employee."

"Every damn day for more than a decade she was stealing from us." He set down his coffee for fear his grip would crush the paper cup. "More secrets."

"You've had to deal with far too many of them. Which is why I wanted to meet with you. I wanted to make sure you heard this from me and know it for truth."

Although they'd only met recently, Chase had felt an affinity for Nate from the start. Smart. Strong. Upstanding. And a man who held a clear willingness to do right by others.

As Robert Colton's oldest son, Chase took his responsibilities to his family seriously. And as Robert's youngest son, Chase already knew Nate felt the exact same way.

"We don't want shares of the business, Chase."

"No, but you and Sarah are entitled to them. I've never questioned that, and I don't believe anyone else has, either."

Nate took a sip of his coffee, considering. "It's like we've both told you. Sarah and I don't need or want shares. Our mother doesn't believe us or agree with us, but I sure wish you would."

Although Chase knew precious little about his Aunt Jessie, Nate had mentioned the same early on. That Jessie had expressed heated, self-righteous fury that her children with Robert should be entitled to the same shares in Colton Properties as his six children with Jenny.

Chase didn't disagree they were entitled to something. But he recognized his brother and sister had their reasons.

What he hadn't expected was the steady layer of heat and vitriol Nate carried toward his mother.

"What's her reason for continuing to push it?"

"I'm increasingly thinking it's that damn Ever After group she's a part of."

It was Nate's turn to scowl and Chase knew it was for a number of reasons that didn't include the coffee.

"They call themselves a church," Chase said.

"Whatever else it is, *church* isn't the right word. The founder spews a lot of angelic, beatific bull. But he seems deeply engaged with the financials and little else."

"How so?"

"My mother's let it slip once he asked her about her inheritance as well as mine and Sarah's, then clammed up when I pressed her on it. It reinforces what I've heard rumor of. That the man has very little engagement with the souls of his flock, but a heck of a lot of it with their wallets."

"It has to be an expensive enterprise." Chase considered it, trying not to jump to an immediate assumption of guilt. "Don't they try to house their people, too? That takes money. Resources."

"More of what bothers me. Why can't people go home each week and live their lives? What's the point of having them all on the property like a commune?"

Chase had really only looked at it through the lens of the property needs. But adding Nate's description to the conversation he'd had the other day with Sloan, Chase had to admit things definitely sounded…off.

"Has your mom said anything else?"

"Nothing about that group she's a part of. She's been relentless with Sarah, though, pushing for her to take her inheritance. I think she's given up on me."

Not for the first time, Chase struggled against the dark feelings that swirled inside of him for his aunt. He'd spent years simply practicing disdain when it came to the subject of his mother's twin sister, but these past few months?

Jessie Colton was a problem. Beyond the betrayal of her family, she somehow had a way of getting herself into bad situations.

And now, to press her children over something they didn't want?

"I don't think I realized how bad it was."

It was Nate's turn to quiet down, and in the man's stoic features, Chase saw a match for himself.

"We'll get through it. I never put much stock in my mother's flighty ideas and neither does Sarah. In fact, my sister is the only reason I'm sticking close now. She shouldn't have to bear the heat all by herself."

"We're here for you. Both of you."

"I know and it makes all the difference."

Chase thought about his brother's words on the drive back into Owl Creek.

They *were* here for each other.

Not out of duty or requirement, but by choice. As a family.

And that mattered.

Wasn't that what Sloan had tried to impart to Sarah the other night at the barbecue? The Coltons were a family. No matter what their misguided parents had done to them, the children were rock-solid.

His conversation with Nate had gone a long way toward reinforcing those feelings and he'd be damned if he was going to stop now. Whatever it took to ensure Nate and Sarah knew they had a family and that they belonged was his only goal.

Which made the discussion about Jessie so troubling.

Shouldn't their mother be their biggest champion? A part of him believed that to be the case. That her focus on ensuring they get a piece of Robert Colton's estate was, at its core, a mother's desire for fairness.

But why keep pushing if her children said they were fine?

His father had provided for Nate and Sarah, both while he was still alive and in other property allocations he'd ensured would go to his children with Jessie. So really, her complaints that her kids were missing out were more tied to the settling of succession and the assets of Colton Properties instead of any real sense they'd been left out.

Was it this church she was a part of?

Sloan's disdain had been a match for Nate's. Even as an outsider, with minimal knowledge of the area, she'd keyed into how strange the Ever After Church was.

Furthermore, how their practices didn't seem to actually fit the mold of a church.

And now that Nate had shared Jessie's interest in the money, Chase had to wonder if he'd been too lax in his initial thinking.

Especially when Sloan's comments about his Aunt Jessie came winging back into his thoughts, like tumblers falling into a lock.

One more choice in a long line of poor ones.

Leaving her children... Putting on a married facade... Now she's caught up in an entity...

Those are some seriously questionable decisions.

Whether it was his discussion with Nate, or the morning's evidence that even people he thought he knew could make bad decisions, Chase wasn't too sure. But Sloan's comments from the other day had taken hold of his thoughts and he wasn't ready to let this go.

The vague thought he'd had the other day that he wanted to look into the Ever After Church had just gotten a lot clearer.

All he needed to do now was ask Sloan if she was interested in joining him.

WITH *PASTEL DE NATA* cooking in the oven, her mother's special recipe, Sloan tried to take solace in the comforting smells and *off* the still-roiling thoughts in her head.

Hadn't she grown up with this scent filling the kitchen? The rich custard tart her mom would sprinkle with cinnamon fresh out of the oven and then she'd eat it with a tall glass of milk. As she got older, her mother allowed her to make a latte to accompany the pastry.

It was only in the last few years that she'd gotten into the way her parents ate the treats—with a shot of espresso accompanying the dessert.

God, she missed her mom.

They normally spoke every day, but her parents had gone to Portugal for a month on a family visit. If she tried to call her now her mother would only worry.

The sweet treats would have to stand in for her soothing words and perfect hugs.

It had taken a good portion of the afternoon, but Sloan had finally calmed down a bit.

And had forced herself to honestly assess what had happened at Colton Properties.

She had done the job she was asked to do, but once she'd seen the impact of that work, she'd fled. Not only did it not make sense, but it also wasn't something she'd ever done before.

Which had only left her with more questions.

And the rapidly rising suspicion that she was far more attached to Chase Colton than she wanted to admit.

They had an attraction, one they'd both admitted to this past weekend. But her unhappiness at seeing him dealing with the outcome of her investigation?

It had cut shockingly deep.

The timer went off just as the doorbell rang. Chase was the only person she knew, so she figured it would be him. But she took the few extra moments to pull out the tarts before heading for the door to check.

And opened it to find Frannie and Ruby on the other side.

"Oh, hello."

Both women smiled at her, but it was Ruby who instantly moved forward, her attention already focused on the kitchen. "What is that divine smell?"

Frannie shrugged, but a smile twitched at the edges of her lips. "I'd like to say it's because she's pregnant, but Ruby likely would have done that, anyway."

"Well, come on in." Sloan waved Chase's other sister inside before turning for the kitchen. She'd just cleared the doorway when she let out a small cry at Ruby. "You'll burn yourself!"

Ruby stepped back, the hands wrapped around her pregnant belly quickly moved behind her back. "I'm not touching."

"You're going to burn your nose if you get any closer," Frannie admonished as she came into the already small kitchen and took a seat at the table. "Despite my big sister's manners, we didn't come here to eat."

"But we can once they cool!" Ruby quickly insisted.

Frannie shot her a dark look before continuing. "We spoke with Chase earlier and figured the lunkhead still hadn't come over to check on you."

"He's been at work."

The two women exchanged glances before Ruby gave a firm nod, then took a seat of her own. "Stupid lunkhead."

"Isn't that term a bit outdated?" Sloan asked before going to the fridge and pulling out a pitcher of iced tea. "It's decaffeinated," she added, directing her comment to Ruby, before crossing to get some glasses.

"Lunkhead was all our mother allowed when we were kids and it sort of stuck," Ruby said.

Since she was an only child and woefully ignorant of sibling politics, Sloan just nodded at the answer and went back to pouring iced tea.

"So what is that you just made?" Ruby asked.

"They're my mother's recipe," Sloan said as she set glasses on the table before each of Chase's sisters. "*Pastel de nata* are traditional Portuguese pastries."

"They smell amazing." Frannie shot a pointed look at her sister. "And I'm sure they'll be delicious once they cool."

"We can have one in a few more minutes. In the meantime, why are you upset at Chase?"

"We're upset at his *stupid* behavior," Ruby stressed.

Frannie shot her a dark look but didn't correct her sister, either. "We were just concerned. Chase called a family meeting after he'd finished speaking to his staff and we noticed you weren't on the video call."

Although she didn't have siblings, Sloan was absurdly touched at Ruby and Frannie's concern. She was surprised they'd even noticed she wasn't there.

"I figured out who was stealing from Colton Properties and it was time to leave. Chase had things well in hand."

The look that passed between the two sisters didn't give much, but it was enough to pique her curiosity. "You don't agree?"

"I think Chase has believed he has everything well in hand for a long time. And in business, he's great. In real life?" Ruby rolled her eyes. "He's spewed some ridiculous nonsense for years that he's not cut out for a relationship."

"I'm not sure I can say one way or the other, to be honest. We're not really dating."

"Yeah, he mentioned that, too, on the call." Frannie waved a hand, the gesture more dismissive than Sloan would have expected. "No one's buying it."

"I'm afraid it's true. We needed a plausible excuse so I could be inside the offices at unexpected times. That was the story we used."

The two women exchanged glances once again and Sloan held up a hand of her own. "I don't have any brothers and sisters, so forgive me if I'm missing what's underneath all this. But can you please just tell me what you think?"

Their loudly silent communication came to an abrupt halt as both women stared at her, guilty expressions lining their faces.

"We think you're perfect for him," Ruby said.

"And we love how the two of you are when you're together," Frannie added. "Watching each other when you think the other one doesn't know."

Sloan abruptly jumped up from the table, hoping the delicious sweet treat of the *pastels* would divert some of the attention off her rapidly heating face.

Because she did look at Chase when she thought he wasn't watching.

But to know he did, too?

She put the tarts on a plate and dusted them lightly with cinnamon before returning to the table. "The traditional way to eat these is with coffee. I can make some if you'd like but I don't have any decaf."

Both women brushed it off. "The iced tea is fine," Frannie quickly assured her. And since neither of them kept on with tales of their brother, Sloan took her first easy breath as she set down the serving dish on the table and then passed out small dessert plates.

It was only once everyone had taken a tart, Ruby already oohing and aahing around her first bite, that Sloan realized her mistake.

She'd just taken a bite of her tart, the creamy egg custard filling her taste buds with the comforting memories of home, when Ruby spoke.

"So tell us. What will it take to keep you here?"

Chapter Twelve

Chase pulled into a parking spot in front of Sloan's building and saw what looked like his sister's car a few spots away. He almost shook it off when something had him thinking better of it and he crossed over to the parking spot.

Only to look in and see Ruby's signature mess of doodads littering the cupholders.

His first thought was to ask why his sister was here, rapidly followed by a mental curse that his sister had decided to pay Sloan a visit.

"Why?" He moaned as he took the outer stairs up to Sloan's floor. "Why, why, why was I given a meddling younger sister?"

He nearly barreled through the door but stopped himself at the last minute and knocked.

Only to find a flustered Sloan answer on the other side.

She grabbed onto his arm and dragged him into the apartment without saying a word.

"Hi, Chase!" Ruby's voice filtered out of the kitchen, followed quickly by Frannie's slightly lower register.

"Hello, big brother!"

"Both of them?" he asked Sloan.

"Yep."

Since she didn't elaborate, he figured his sisters' arrival

was both unexpected and, at minimum, slightly harrowing as Ruby and Frannie could be when they decided to gang up.

Thank goodness, they hadn't brought Lizzy along, too.

Three Colton women all in one place, all on some mission of their own making, was the very definition of scary.

"You have to try these!" Ruby said with her mouth full all while gesturing to her currently empty plate.

"What are you doing here?" he asked, attempting his stern-older-brother tone. It hadn't worked on them when they were ten and six and he was sixteen, and it sure as hell wasn't working twenty years later, but he gave it the old college try all the same.

"They're delicious," Frannie added, completely ignoring his question.

"Well, what are you eating?" he finally asked.

"The most amazing Portuguese pastries." Ruby gestured vaguely. "Tell him, Sloan."

Sloan already had a fresh plate out of the cabinet and had set it, along with a napkin, at the only empty spot at the table.

"We're eating *pastel de nata*."

He'd never eaten what looked to be dessert tarts but the kitchen smelled incredible, so he did what any sane man would do when faced with his nosy younger sisters, a woman he had increasingly strong feelings for and a plate full of pastries.

He took one.

And nearly fell off his chair as the subtly sweet, rich taste hit his tongue.

He'd never considered himself a man led by his stomach, but in that moment, he could have gotten down on one knee and proposed to Sloan. Or to the dessert.

At the exquisite taste exploding on his tongue, he wasn't entirely sure any longer.

"You made these?"

"Well, yeah." Sloan nodded.

"Today?"

"They're still hot, aren't they?"

"Wow, these are amazing."

"I told you!" Ruby said enthusiastically. "And it's not even the baby making me hungry."

"The baby can't be the excuse for everything."

Ruby grinned at her sister. "It will be when I take one more *pastel de nata* for the road. Come on, let's go."

His sisters flew out as quickly as he assumed they'd flown in, even Ruby's increasing size not slowing her down in her quest to leave them alone.

And exactly four minutes after he'd sat down and tasted one of the best pastries of his life, his sisters had departed Sloan's home.

Sloan stood between the table and the doorway to the kitchen, a slightly dazed expression on her face. "It's really quiet once they're gone."

He mumbled his agreement around another pastry, and she pointed at him. "Don't eat them too fast. You'll get sick."

"It'll be worth it."

She shook her head at that. "I'm afraid Ruby won't think so in about fifteen minutes."

"Why were they here?" He heard himself and quickly continued, "Not that you can't entertain whomever you'd like. But it was something of a surprise to find them both at your home."

"They came to talk to me about their lunkhead brother."

He'd heard the term since they were kids and was well aware it was not a term of endearment. "What did they accuse me of now?"

"Not coming over here soon enough."

"And?"

"And nothing. That's all I got out of them before everyone dived on the tarts and told me that you and I seem to have a case of staring too hard and long at each other when no one is watching."

And there it was.

That remarkable truth serum she seemed able to wield with effortless grace.

Which meant it was only fair to give it right back to her.

"I *do* do that, but I didn't realize I was quite so obvious about it."

"Me, either." She let out a heavy sigh. "It's embarrassing. To be so transparent."

He stood then and crossed the small space to her. Without checking the impulse, he pulled her close and pressed a kiss against her forehead. "It may be transparent but it's not embarrassing. Never that."

The feel of her in his arms was like a soothing balm at the end of a very long day. Like the exquisite tarts, Chase savored the sensation.

He wanted her.

He could keep running from that fact, but it didn't make it any less true. Nor did it make the feelings any less intense, this ache deep inside he'd never felt before.

But what to do about it?

She was leaving in a matter of days, and he wasn't crass enough to ask her if she wanted to sleep with him as a going-away present.

Which meant he needed to keep his interest in check.

Yes, he wanted her. But he wanted her leaving Owl Creek with good memories.

And good thoughts of him.

"I'd also have told them that you weren't being a lunkhead for staying at work and doing your job, but we got distracted by the tarts. They'd finally cooled off enough so that Ruby could try them."

His sister had always been a champion sweet eater and he suspected that had only grown more pronounced with her pregnancy.

"I'm surprised she didn't try to eat one hot."

"Oh, she did, but Frannie stopped her."

Chase laughed at that, their antics as children still something that defined them as adults.

Which only brought him right back around to Nate and Sarah, and the laugh died in his throat.

His father and his aunt had taken that away from him. From all of them. A chance to grow up together. A chance to know one another.

Heck, in the case of himself, his full siblings and his cousins, even knowing Nate and Sarah existed.

"What's wrong?"

Chase stepped away, taking a seat at the table and reaching for the mostly full glass of iced tea where Frannie had been sitting. "I met up with Nate earlier. He wanted to make sure I was okay after what went down today."

"He's a good man and he wants to be a part of your family."

"So much so he's maintained his position that he wants nothing to do with the settlement around Colton Properties. Sarah, too."

"That's great, isn't it? The full transfer of the CEO role to you can happen now."

"Not if my Aunt Jessie has anything to do with it."

That subtle frown—the one that just slightly marred the edges of Sloan's mouth—struck like clockwork with the mention of his aunt.

He suspected she wasn't even fully aware she was doing

it, but each time he saw that thin veneer of disgust he was oddly heartened.

Here was a woman who had his back. His family's backs, too.

And there was something special in that.

Something that made him keep wishing there was a way things could be different.

Because Sloan Presley had made everything different.

SLOAN BUSIED HERSELF putting on a pot of coffee and then came back to the table. She had no doubt they'd nibble a few more of the *pastel de nata* and she'd rather have hers with coffee. She'd also ensure Chase got the full experience of the sweet tarts.

His arrival had been welcome—added on to his sisters' strange yet oddly wonderful visit—and it felt good to have him here.

When he was with her, she found it a lot harder to remember all the reasons she wanted to leave.

Or any of the reasons she'd fled Colton Properties earlier.

"Start from the beginning. What did Nate say about his mother?"

Chase caught her up on his coffee meeting in Conners and it struck her once again what strange circumstances Jessie Colton managed to find in her life.

An affinity for drama?

Or an inability to read other people because she was so steeped in her own selfish desires?

What could she possibly see in this so-called church that had popped up here in Idaho? And then to press her kids about their inheritance, seemingly to give it all to the organization?

"Nate doesn't seem to have a lot of regard for his mother?"

"No," Chase replied, taking another sip of Frannie's iced

tea. "I get the sense he's there more out of duty and a deep need to protect Sarah more than any real feelings for Jessie."

"That's sad."

"In every way. I think that's what I'm coming to realize more and more. The choices Jessie and my father made… they weren't just selfish, though that's a big part of it all. But they've created this legacy of anger and mistrust in all their children. Their actions have erased the good feelings and left nothing but duty, or this lingering sense of obligation to care for their memories."

"I am sorry for that. Maybe more than anything else since I've been here."

"What are you sorry about?"

"I've hated watching all of you suffer for the deeds of your parents. It's not my experience." Her gaze drifted to the tarts and Sloan recognized that truth on an entirely visceral level.

Here she was, comforted merely by making a dish of her mother's. Chase, meanwhile, was left to pick up the pieces of his father's secret life.

It didn't seem fair. And even the word *fair* felt like too small a description of what he was going through.

"Why did you leave earlier?"

His question broke through her musings, and she realized the answer was really quite simple. "Because it was time for me to go."

Chase nodded at that but didn't say anything more.

The last gurgle of the coffee maker echoed in the silence, indicating it was done brewing, and she jumped up to get them both mugs.

It was only as she came back to the table, steaming mugs in hand, that Sloan realized she owed him a better answer than that.

"That's only part of the truth. I was sad this morning

after you spoke with your employees." She stared down at her mug. "I was more than sad, actually. I hated that my work put you in that position."

"It's what I hired you to do. You fixed my problem."

"I ruined someone's life today."

"No, Althea ruined her life. She could have made other choices, but she didn't. Just like Jessie ruined hers. Just like my father ruined his." Chase reached for her hand, his fingers tracing the back of her knuckles.

"I'm done blaming myself or my siblings or my mother or uncle for things we didn't do and never saw coming. The people who chose a bad path. That's on them. There shouldn't be guilt because you shined a light on it. Brought it out of the darkness."

Chase stopped that warm, sweet tracing over the back of her hand and instead covered it fully with his. "Which is why I wanted to ask a favor of you. And you're under no obligation to say yes."

"What sort of favor?"

"I'd like you to look into Jessie and this church she's a part of. Something's not right there. You sensed it the other day with those articles about the dead women found in Wake County. And Nate's certain his mother is involved in something bad."

Sloan had never been able to resist a challenge, but this was a tall ask.

She knew digital forensics, but digging into the Ever After Church would likely require some hacking, too. Her coding and computer programming skills were strong, but she'd never had a real reason to go after private citizens.

Especially without the auspices of the government, who normally funded that sort of work with her.

"Do you think it's a good idea?"

"I think there's reason to look into these people and we

can do it without warrants or raising suspicion." He grinned, the look boyish and appealing.

So appealing Sloan felt the attraction pulling low in her belly, her interest in following him down this path both academic *and* wholly steeped in attraction.

"Well, *you* can do it. I'll watch and cheer you on since I'm lucky I know how to reboot my computer each time I have to do a software update."

"There are risks. The members of the Ever After Church are private citizens. The church is technically a protected organization."

"Nate doesn't even think they're a real church."

"A technicality if they're incorporated as one, but..." She trailed off and Chase's gaze never wavered.

"But what?"

"That might be the perfect place to start. It's all a bit suspect on my end but if they're not legally a church entity we might be able to make an argument later if push came to shove on the technicalities. Especially since you've got reason to believe your business is threatened based on what Nate shared with you."

They were very thin lines and Sloan recognized full well she was crossing them, but something inside of her recognized it was the right thing to do.

She felt it.

More than that, she *knew* it.

And it wasn't because of her attraction to Chase.

The Coltons deserved to know the truth.

Whatever else she'd uncovered over the past week, that lone thought whispered over and over in her mind, taking shape as she imagined how she could get in and out of the Ever After files without anyone knowing.

She had the skills to help them find answers and she wasn't going back to Chicago without trying to get them.

IT WAS SHOCKINGLY TEDIOUS, hard work to hack into computer files.

That thought had struck Chase hard around two that morning when he'd gone nearly bleary-eyed watching Sloan for the better part of six hours.

Even as he wanted to drop his head on the table in exhaustion, she kept on, her attention laser-focused on her laptop screen.

"Do we have any more coffee?" she asked before letting out a short, quick curse and tapping a few more keys.

"You've had enough coffee."

That was enough to get him a rather harsh side-eye when she glanced up from her screen. "I think I'm old enough to know when I want coffee."

"And I think you're a demon insomniac who's lulled me into thinking we're doing work when what you're really trying to do is suck my brains out my ears."

"You know that's technically impossible."

"Hardly." He made a show of slapping the side of his head and pretending something was falling out the other side.

It was enough to get a laugh out of her and pull her attention off that damn screen. Which meant he needed to act now and drag her away from the table.

"You've been at this long enough. Give it a rest and we can start in the morning."

"I'm close."

"You said that two hours ago."

"Which means I'm closer now than I was two hours ago."

The woman was relentless.

Had he ever seen anything more attractive?

She'd pulled her hair up hours ago and he was fascinated by the way small curls had broken out along her hairline. They made him want to reach out and wrap one around his finger, just to feel how soft they were.

Since he had no business touching her, especially since his *thoughts* of touching her had grown increasingly heated as each hour passed, he did what he was astoundingly good at. He pushed a serious overload of *obnoxious big brother* into his tone.

"Sloan, give it a rest. I didn't come over here to push you into indentured servitude to your laptop. We'll dig more tomorrow."

"I want to see where this takes me."

"See where it takes you tomorrow. It'll keep."

"I just—" She stopped, her eyes lighting up as her gaze remained totally focused on her laptop screen.

"What?"

"I'm in."

"In where?"

"The files at Ever After. It's locked down and hard to break through, but I'm in."

Chase leaned toward the screen, not sure what he was looking at but able to read details of member names, contributions and what looked to be attachments on each person.

Dossiers?

On church members?

"What is that?" He pointed toward the linked files. "Can you click on one of them?"

She tapped around, not clicking directly but looking like she was attempting to make a copy when the screen went black.

Another low curse tumbled from her lips. If the moment wasn't so serious, he might have laughed at her inventive string of words.

"Was it supposed to do that?"

"Not at all."

"Got it."

He stood, stretching his muscles and working the kinks

out of his neck while she futzed and fiddled with her keyboard. A few minutes later her screen came back to life, but her frustrated exhale suggested things still weren't right.

"I need to back out of this and run a full diagnostic on my machine."

"Why?"

"I think I hit a trap."

He turned at that, dropping his arms in mid-stretch. "Sloan, I'm sorry. I'm the one who pushed you to do this and—"

She shook her head. "I hate to break it to you, but this is hardly the first time I've had that happen. It means I'm close and we're on the right track."

Since she looked damn near giddy with the news, Chase wasn't sure what to do.

Was a high five appropriate in this instance?

And what level of delirium had he hit if this was what he was worried about?

"It's going to run for a while so let's leave it. I can pull out the couch for you. That way you don't have to drive home."

She seemed to catch herself, her own arms stilling in midair as she stretched, her dark brown eyes going wide. "I mean, if that's okay and you don't mind staying."

"I'd appreciate it."

Although he was dog-tired, Chase couldn't let the moment go, something mischievous sparking to life. "Unless, of course, you're worried you can't keep your hands off me, in which case I'll head home. It's not too far a drive."

She let out a hard snort at that. "In your dreams, buddy."

"What would you know of my dreams?" Pleased to see her flustered once more, Chase's grin only grew broader. "Or maybe I should ask about yours."

"I don't dream."

"Never?"

He moved closer, the exhaustion in her gaze fading as something sharper moved into its place.

Chase recognized it—*felt* it—because it matched what he knew she saw in his own eyes.

Barely banked need.

Heated desire.

And a confused, push-pull of emotion that kept seesawing between giving in to that desire and knowing that where it led might be disastrous for both of them.

So he stayed where he was. He didn't pull her into his arms or think about kissing her.

Instead, he reached out and traced a line down her forearm, her pretty, light brown skin so soft to the touch he nearly ached with the sweetness of it.

Of her.

And resigned himself to the fact that all the want and need in the world couldn't change the gravity of the situation.

She wasn't staying.

And he wasn't a forever sort of guy.

It had nearly driven him mad, like the ceaseless dripping of a faucet or an endless alarm he couldn't quite turn off as it raided his dreams, but he needed to accept the truth: he wanted what he could not have.

Was it cosmic payback for spending most of his adult life in the steadfast belief that love couldn't touch him? More, that it wasn't for him?

And why was the thought of love even crossing his mind?

Why had the idea of it steadily presented itself, over and over, rattling around his mind and taunting him as he spent more and more time with Sloan?

Love. Marriage. A family.

He'd decided long ago, well before his father's betrayal, that those things were for other people. He'd tried and ultimately been a failure at something most people found easily as they moved into adulthood.

His failure with Leanne had been bad enough. But now that he knew what horror lived in his own genes? How truly broken his father had to have been to live his double life?

It only reinforced all the reasons why there was no good end to this.

Because whatever else he wanted for Sloan, it was something good. She deserved it and he well knew he wasn't ever going to be the man to give it to her.

So he gently traced her skin once more, reveling in the feel of her and knowing it would have to keep him warm in his dreams for years to come.

Then he dropped his hand and backed out of the kitchen, leaving her to her computer and her notes and the untainted goodness he wanted for her.

And he didn't look at her, not even once, as he pulled out the sofa bed and settled himself for the night in her darkened living room.

Chapter Thirteen

Sloan wasn't overly experienced in love, but she'd had enough relationships to understand attraction, interest and desire.

She'd had varying levels of each in her past with the men she'd dated. There had been the one who'd attracted her yet bored her to tears. And another one who'd been fascinating to talk to but had been such a horrible kisser she didn't even contemplate having sex with him.

None of them had come close to what she was feeling.

And not one of them had been worth a damn in the practical-experience category. She didn't know how to deal with such an infuriating, sexy, irritating, mind-meltingly attractive man like Chase.

The real surprise was that despite having all six sexy feet of him a room away, she'd still slept like the dead.

Because while a half-nighter wasn't quite as exhausting as an all-nighter, she'd also struggled to sleep all weekend—again, damn you, Chase Colton. And all the digging into the Ever After Church had simply used up every bit of mental energy she possessed.

None of which seemed to matter as she was lying on her bed, staring up at the ceiling.

Now that she was awake, she'd become quite aware of

the fact that she had to walk back into the living room, and who knew how Chase slept.

Shirtless?

Pantsless?

Fully naked?

A warm glow suffused her as each image grew progressively hotter and she sat up, forcing the images from her thoughts.

He was a good, respectful man. He no doubt was still wearing what he'd worn yesterday. She was the one with the flights of fancy imagining him naked.

Which made the fully dressed, coffee-in-hand man who greeted her in her kitchen ten minutes later something of a surprise.

Especially since she'd only managed to throw on an old sweatshirt with her college logo emblazoned on it and brush her teeth.

"Good morning." Chase smiled over his mug. "I hope you don't mind I started coffee."

"Not at all."

As if to stress that very point, she crossed to the coffee maker. Instead of falling on the brew like a rabid dog, she offered him a refill first.

He extended his mug and, although he was a few feet from her, she couldn't deny how close he felt in her small kitchen. Brushing off the sudden attack of nerves, Sloan filled his mug and moved right on to filling hers, easing slightly when he settled himself against the sink.

"I fed the cat, too. I hope you don't mind."

She turned at that, mid-sip, and nearly bobbled her mug. "Um, that's okay."

Why would she mind?

She woke up to fresh coffee and a well-fed cat who was

even now licking his paws in the corner, seemingly uninterested in them even as he kept darting a curious eye toward the humans.

"Did you sleep okay?" Sloan finally asked, willing the caffeine to make her a semi-human, gracious hostess. "I haven't slept on it, but the couch looks pretty comfortable."

"It was fine."

"Good. Um, I'm glad to hear it."

Whatever lusty images had assailed her as she'd been lying in bed, Sloan realized a fully clothed, stubble-jawed Chase should have been in her mental list.

The man was lethal in the morning.

And this quiet little domestic scene between them was doing something to her. She'd never claim particularly well-ordered thoughts in the morning—she was way too much of a night owl for that. But she was definitely feeling out of sorts and knew he was to blame.

Or her hormones were.

Taking another sip, she decided she'd push that blame back on him.

She simply didn't share her morning coffee with a man who'd slept at her place. One more depressing fact that reinforced all she'd given up for her job these past few years.

No, Sloan mentally corrected herself. It was time to stop blaming the job.

She'd chosen to ignore that aspect of her life.

And now, here she was, twenty-nine years old and feeling like an immature teenager. It was rather overwhelming to have an attractive man in her kitchen at 7:00 a.m. who knew how to fend for himself *and* sort of care for her, all at the same time.

And…she was flustered.

That really was the only word for it.

"I realized we didn't talk about it much yesterday, but when I asked you to take on the digging into my Aunt Jessie and that group of hers, I'd be happy to extend your contract. I fully expect to pay you for your time."

Sloan couldn't quite say why—perhaps it was the flustered feelings—but something about Chase's offer to pay her waved in front of her like a red flag to a bull.

"How benevolent of you."

"It's hardly benevolent to ensure you're compensated for your work."

His eyebrows slashed over those glass-green eyes but his tone remained even. Measured.

And in that moment she had a sense of why he was so good at his job.

This wasn't a man who'd ever let an adversary across the negotiating table get the better of him.

"Yes, well, maybe I'm interested in solving the mystery of your aunt's weird group and don't want or need your money. I can take a few vacation days or, you know, work on whatever I want to."

"Sloan, why are you getting prickly about this?"

The question was fair.

If she wasn't in such a weird frame of mind it was entirely possible she'd have glossed over the entire conversation without giving it a second thought.

But she *was* in a weird frame of mind.

And suddenly his question seemed entirely *un*fair.

"For reasons that defy logic you kiss me or talk to me of private matters with your family and then in the blink of an eye you're talking about paying me and giving me work to do. What is it that you want? Am I your employee or your…friend?"

She nearly stumbled over the last word but caught herself at the last minute.

Because no matter how out of sorts she felt, it would have been mortifying to have said the world *girlfriend* by mistake.

CHASE KNEW THE signs of a fight.

He'd grown up with five siblings and four cousins who were close as siblings. Time spent together was as likely to be full of laughter as it was arguments and, as the oldest Colton, he'd learned early how to pick some and how to mitigate others.

And Sloan was spoiling for a fight.

The real question was, why?

When they'd finished up for the evening, she'd seemed fine. A little awkward as they'd decided he was going to sleep on her couch, but if he was honest with himself, he was a bit nervous, too.

And now this?

"What does paying you for your professional services have to do with our friendship?"

"I care about what happens to you and your family. And what your aunt did to all of you is wrong. I know it's not my place to judge but I can't get past that fact."

"Observing a lifetime of crappy behavior to others isn't judgment, so I appreciate that. More than I can say, actually. It doesn't change the fact that I'm taking up your time on a task you do as your profession."

He should have expected it, *especially* after his pedantic response, but the explosion still caught him off guard.

"I don't want a contract for this, Chase! I want to help you!" She slammed her mug down on the counter, the sound reverberating through the room. "I care about you. And for the past week I've watched you question yourself in every way."

The heat that carried her through the verbal explosion quieted as she reached for her mug once again, staring down at the ceramic as if surprised she hadn't broken it. "You need answers. And this is something I can give you before I leave to go home."

And there it was. That lingering reality that drove everything personal between them.

She would be going home.

Because she might be willing to do the work on her own time, but that time had an expiration on it.

"Do you honestly think this is going to make the situation better?"

Sloan's gaze lifted from her mug, direct and with a distinct fire burning in its depths.

"The way Jessie's own children don't agree with what she's doing and have actively taken your side over their mother's when it comes to matters of inheritance and the family business? I think it matters quite a bit. And I don't think you're going to have peace until you have some answers."

"While I don't disagree with you, that's not actually what I meant."

"Oh?"

The genuine confusion that stamped itself over her features was a match for all he struggled with inside.

"I meant the situation between us."

He went with instinct and a genuine need he was increasingly unable to ignore.

Moving in close, he took her mug, as surprised as her it wasn't in pieces on her counter. He set it down gently, followed by his own, then pulled her into his arms.

"We can't fight our way out of this, Sloan."

"It's damn inconvenient." Although her angry tone had vanished, she kept her arms firmly at her sides.

"It is."

"And it can't have a happy ending."

He lifted a hand and brushed a wayward curl that had slipped out of her ponytail back behind her ear. "Probably not."

"So what are we doing?"

"Giving in."

Chase bent his head, capturing her lips with his. She was so warm and welcoming, her mouth opening beneath his as her arms came around his neck.

The lingering taste of toothpaste and coffee flavored her tongue and Chase found himself utterly intoxicated. She was all warmth and welcome, and as he pulled her closer in his arms, he fought the very reality she spoke of.

How could this feel so right, even as he was so sure it would end? Soon.

The big part of him that had spent a decade protecting his heart knew it was a bad idea to keep giving in. But the part of him that wanted her so desperately—those emotions that grew bigger and bigger by the day—simply wanted to revel in her.

In what was between them.

So he took.

And gave.

And wildly, wonderfully, gave in.

MARKUS QUICKLY SCANNED his text messages before dropping his phone back into his pocket. He had about twenty minutes before the first members of his flock would arrive in the small clearing they used as a morning meeting area.

He'd been thinking about what esoteric words of wisdom he wanted to share today and had landed somewhere on the difficulties of managing to the practicalities of the world and avoiding greed, all as a mechanism to get his members to dig a bit deeper into their wallets.

He took several deep breaths of the fresh Idaho air, centering himself and testing a few of the tonalities he wanted to use.

Always soft and easy.

Never accusing. Never mad.

This was a welcoming place. *He* provided a welcome space. Like a father tutoring his young, the wisdom of the universe was channeled through him for their benefit.

He believed he'd settled on just the right cadence. He was mentally flipping through the order of his message for the morning guidance when Winston appeared at the edge of the clearing, stomping toward him in a way that suggested his hard-won inner peace was about to evaporate.

"Brother Kraft," Markus intoned when Winston stood before him.

"We've got a problem."

"No 'Brother Acker'?" Markus said quietly, even as steel threaded underneath his words.

"You know I hate that crap but—" Winston bowed, his hands at his side "—good morning, Brother Acker."

"Excellent. You know we can't risk one of the flock observing us in anything but prayerful solitude."

"Yeah, about that."

Winston was his right-hand man specifically because he handled problems, but Markus didn't miss the clear agitation that rode the man's features. "What?"

"Someone's nosing around the files. I picked up a flag this morning that the firewall I have in place was breached."

He paid Winston handsomely to avoid any mistakes like this. As news of an intrusion sunk in, all thoughts of calm, centered welcome vanished, a dark red haze of anger taking its place.

"Who?"

"I don't know, but I do know they're good. I wouldn't have even seen it if I hadn't been in myself checking the protections, which I do every morning. I noticed the breach, but it wasn't enough to trigger any automatic alarms."

"Find them."

"I need some time."

"Then take it," Markus growled. "And report back as soon as you have news."

"I'll miss morning reflections."

"Get out of here and get some answers."

Markus watched Winston walk off across the clearing, greeting members who'd begun the walk over to the field. He struggled to get his beatific visage back in place, even as he muttered to himself, that haze of red still edging his vision.

"And start praying if you don't find them."

THE KISS SPUN OUT, at times wildly erotic and at others deep, soft and precious.

It was an endless ride of emotion. Sloan wasn't sure how she'd gone from steaming mad to being kissed mindless in her kitchen, but she wasn't going to argue.

And wasn't quite sure she had the brain cells to argue, anyway.

So it was a bit of surprise, despite reveling in being in Chase's arms, that she was the one to pull back.

"I, um…" She trailed off, marshaling her thoughts. "I'm glad you're here."

"I'm glad I'm here, too."

"But I should probably check my computer and see if that program I ran overnight did its job."

His gaze consumed her, and Sloan was half convinced they'd fall right back into another kiss, but something obviously held him back when his focus moved to her computer and where it was still perched on her kitchen table.

"Let's take a look."

She should have been relieved.

Realistically, that was the only feeling she should be having. And yet…

Sloan could admit to a solid wash of disappointment that he'd agreed to go back to work that quickly.

And then took her seat to get down to business.

Nothing had changed between her and Chase.

This attraction had nowhere to go and she couldn't afford to forget that. Especially because she was increasingly worried that if she forgot that truth—if she really allowed herself to give in—she'd end up regretting the decision beyond measure.

Your life's in Chicago, Presley. Don't forget it.

Since her life *was* somewhere else very far away, she put her full focus on her computer programs and off the way her lips still tingled.

The way she could still feel the heat of his body, pressed to hers or the feel of his large palm, splayed across her lower back.

Every one of those delicious sense memories fled at the reality of what she stared at on screen.

"Oh, no."

"What?"

"No, no, no." She tapped several commands in rapid succession, each one producing the same feedback. "This can't be."

"Sloan. What is it?"

"I've been made."

"What?"

"My program? All that searching I did. The firewall on the other side knows there was a breach."

"You're talking about it like it's a human being."

She glanced up at him, suddenly aware there was another person standing in the kitchen with her.

"There is, Chase. A real live human sits on the other side of the machine I was trying to hack into. And he or she knows I was poking around."

His eyebrows slashed over those vivid green eyes, now dark with clouds. "Do they know it was you? Sloan Presley or SecuritKey?"

"I need to find out."

Everything faded from view once again as Sloan focused only on her screen and whatever information she could find to assess the damage. She spent the next several minutes tapping in commands and using various security programs she'd either purchased or designed herself.

It was nearly an hour later when she finally surfaced.

"What'd you find?"

Sloan blinked, bringing Chase back into focus. As she came back to her surroundings, she realized he'd fixed a fresh pot of coffee and placed a steaming mug beside her at the table, and had also found some way to freshen up because his hair was obviously wet from a shower.

"Um, sorry."

"For what?"

She forced a smile, even as a wave of embarrassment flooded her veins, her pulse pounding in response. "For disappearing on you."

"You look pretty here to me."

"I mean—"

He put a hand over hers. "You had work to do. Work I asked you to do, by the way. It would hardly be fair to then criticize you for it."

Whatever else she'd thought or wondered or learned since coming to Idaho, in that moment, Sloan knew—*knew*—that she'd been changed.

And it was all because of this man.

No one ever looked at her descent into computer land as anything other than an oddity and a quirk. Even her parents, who loved her and supported her in every way, tolerated that aspect of her personality with wry humor and gentle smiles.

But not Chase.

He accepted it.

All of it.

And didn't seem to even bat an eyelash, let alone want to tease her about it or stare at her in bemusement.

"Thank you for your support."

"What did you find?"

"Best I can tell, the Ever After Church monitored my intrusion into their files but hasn't traced it back to me."

"So that's good?"

"Yes, but it's still not great. They know someone's nosing around."

Chase tapped a finger on the table, obviously considering something, before he spoke.

"You were pretty close to something last night. Do you think you can get back in before they lock everything down or move it?"

"That's what I've been doing for the past hour."

"I thought you were checking the firewalls or something?"

It was her turn to smile before pointing to the screen. "I checked those first and then pulled down all the data I could."

"What'd you find?"

"The financials definitely look odd. A lot of deposits and multiple line items that seem to say the same thing yet don't add up."

"What's the same?"

"My guess is line one is where it's dirty and line two is after they've made it squeaky clean."

"Money laundering?"

"On an impressive scale."

"Let me guess," he added. "The squeaky lines are the only ones that add up."

"You bet."

Sloan moved the computer around so Chase could see what she'd managed to download after securing her laptop, files and any potential intrusion into her own systems.

"Look here." She tapped a few places on the screen. "They're even keeping a list of their big donors."

"Is my aunt on the list?"

"I haven't seen her name anywhere, but I've only scratched the surface."

Chase's attention was on the screen before his gaze narrowed. "Who's that? Winston Kraft?"

"His name comes up a few times. Best I can tell he's an employee of some sort."

"I know that name."

"You know someone affiliated with the church?"

"No, but I'm pretty sure that's the father of a friend of my cousin."

Not for the first time did Chase's extensive family and exhaustive network—in Owl Creek and well beyond—impress her. The Colton family seemed to know everyone.

And it wasn't hyperbole to say so.

"Do you think your friend's involved?"

"It's my cousin Greg's friend, Rick Kraft. I don't know him well, but met him and his wife a few times through the years over at the ranch. He's a good guy. Has two small kids. I can't see him being involved with something like this at all."

"We could call him. See if he knows anything or if he knows if your Aunt Jessie's involved in anything."

"A visit might be better." Chase stared at the screen once more before seeming to rethink his suggestion. "Is it worth trying to get a bit more information? Is that even possible?"

"My intention is to keep digging and get as much out of their systems as I can before they shut me down." She thought about the man Chase mentioned.

She trusted his instincts—and the friendship he'd mentioned between his cousin Greg and this man, Rick. But Sloan couldn't help but think it would be worth having a bit more information before they talked to the man's son.

"Tell you what. I'd like to keep going as far as I can and see what else I can find in the databases I have access to. Why don't I let you get back to work and I can update you later?"

Chase grinned at that. "Kicking me out?"

"Actually, giving you a chance to escape. Watching me tap away on the keyboard has to be about as interesting as watching paint dry."

"Lady, you have no idea what it's like to watch you work."

His eyes had grown dark and sultry with the compliment, and Sloan was trapped in that gaze, caught once more in that seductive quicksand that he seemed able to trap her in so effortlessly.

She nearly gave in—nearly threw caution to the wind and simply took.

But something in all that data on her computer screen held her back.

Something deeply wrong was going on with the Ever After group. And if she didn't act quickly, she was going to miss the opportunity to dive into their systems.

So she dragged her gaze from Chase's and focused on the task at hand.

And when he bid her goodbye a few minutes later and slipped out of her kitchen, she waited until he was gone before she turned to look at the empty doorway.

Chapter Fourteen

Chase attempted to use work to stop thinking about her.

He called meetings with his direct reports, read an environmental-impact study on a property they were developing and focused on getting through the emails he'd ignored over the past twenty-four hours since the discovery of Althea's crimes.

And still, Sloan filled his thoughts.

What had happened to him?

Work had always been his salvation in the past. When his marriage dissolved, he'd thrown himself into work.

The outcome?

He'd closed six major deals in the quarter following his separation. He brokered five more the next quarter, solidifying his position as heir apparent to the CEO of Colton Properties.

When his father had died and after all the devastating news that had come since?

He'd pushed through Robert Colton's agenda for the company, driving his team and the organization to greater heights.

So what was it about this one woman that had suddenly made him lose focus? Or, worse, *interest* in what he was doing?

"Chase?" Sonja Rodriguez stood in his doorway, her soft smile and earnest face a welcome change from his dour thoughts.

"Come on in."

As his marketing lead, he'd requested an update earlier on the new property they were highlighting at the edge of town. It was a tricky spot, the location a good one for the right buyer but close to the highway, with an odd spit of land that wouldn't ideally be developed with office space.

It would take the right client with the right vision for what they could put there.

Which made the spreadsheet Sonja slid across his desk a huge surprise.

"You've had fourteen interested buyers tour the property?" Chase looked up from the paper. "And three more who want to come back?"

"Yep."

Although he knew Sonja was worth her weight in gold with her impeccable marketing skills, the work on this was something of a professional miracle. "How?"

"We used a social strategy to build the property up slowly. A few ads highlighting the business district it was still part of, along with the other businesses you pass exiting Owl Creek. Then we did follow-ups, identifying the new housing development that was moving into its second phase of construction less than a mile away. And then…"

She left the words hang there for a moment, obviously enjoying his focus on the work.

"Yes?"

"We presented a simple yet precise vision for the space that succinctly outlined the steady stream of traffic predicted in the civil-engineering reports as well as the real and specific need for shopping, restaurants *and* a coffee house."

"Amazing."

"Never underestimate coffee addiction as a solid selling point." Sonja pointed toward the single-brew coffee maker on his sideboard. "Speaking of which, do you mind if I snag a cup?"

"Please, help yourself."

Chase scanned the sheet once more, specifically homing in on the vendors she'd highlighted.

"You do realize Sharon over at Hutch's diner might railroad you out of town for diverting her coffee business?"

It was only when Sonja turned from the sideboard, a cat-in-the-cream smile on her face, that Chase put two and two together with the name he'd read off the spreadsheet.

"It's Sharon's granddaughter who wants the space."

"You bet it is."

"You're a wonder."

Sonja took a seat opposite him, the self-satisfied smile fading, a look of motherly pride replacing it. "Susan's worked so hard in college, getting her hospitality degree at Idaho State. I think she has an even bigger vision of developing that property adjacent into a local attraction with an art focus as well as a children's activity center, but she wants to start with something she can build on."

"I'd be willing to hold it for her."

"The property?"

Chase considered it, realizing there was a significant benefit to the community, to keeping entrepreneurs in Owl Creek *and* to supporting his fellow business professionals.

Wasn't that part of his job?

Moreover, wasn't it why he'd stayed local, wanting to become a real member of the Owl Creek community instead of heading off to Boise or even farther afield after school?

"I think we can work out an arrangement. If she buys in where she is and is willing to give us a soft commitment of formal consideration in twenty-four months, I'll hold on it."

"Chase, that's amazing."

"Let's get Finance to run some quick numbers and we can have sales put together a formal offer." Now it was his turn to smile. "And I'd like you to work with them and present the deal."

"Chase!"

"More important, I will ensure you get a cut on the sales revenue once she says yes."

"I don't know what to say."

"I hope it's yes because it's your vision for the property and your unique way of positioning it that has put us here."

"Thank you."

"The thanks are all mine."

Sonja's happily shell-shocked expression never wavered, even as she shifted into mother hen-mode. "Where's Sloan today?"

"Working. She's helping me with a small project before heading back home."

"Home?" Sonja's eyes narrowed. "She's not local?"

He'd filled in the office on why he'd hired SecuritKey, but at Sonja's question recognized he'd given minimal details about the woman herself.

"She's based out of Chicago. My cousin recommended her and we're fortunate she was willing to take on the contract so far from home."

"How's she finding Owl Creek?"

"We've kept her chained to the project so I'm not sure she's seen much." A vision of the two of them standing at the edge of the lake on Saturday filled his mind's eye. "Though I did get a chance to show her a bit of town."

"No one shows off Owl Creek quite like you."

"I've spent my life driving this town from one end to the other. It's not hard to highlight the good parts."

Sonja studied him across the desk, and it should have made him uncomfortable.

Hell, if it had even been a few weeks before it likely would have.

But something had changed since he'd directed the project to uncover Althea's bad dealings. Since he'd fully taken the reins of Colton Properties.

Since Sloan had arrived.

And suddenly he realized that people had been looking at him his entire life. The oldest Colton son and heir, and the one who Robert entrusted with his life's work.

He'd seen himself that way and it was only in the past few weeks that he'd begun to realize that it was his own legacy to create, not simply a continuation of his father's.

"I'd say it's even rather easy when you're showing off the place you love to a special woman."

Sonja's look was direct—challenging, even—but he saw beneath it.

Saw the genuine care that she brought to everything she did.

"She has to go home, Sonja. In a matter of days."

The older woman shrugged, and despite her casual expression, the unmistakable mix of passion *and* compassion was evident in her dark brown gaze.

"Maybe she already is home."

WINSTON KRAFT STARED at his computer and forced himself to take slow, deep breaths.

He'd had a breach last night, of that he was sure. And despite going over everything, from lines of code, to his firewall protections, to the review of all his files, he couldn't find any other evidence someone had been there.

Yet he knew.

Markus might consider him paranoid, but his healthy sense of paranoia had kept them in business all these years.

And someone had breached his systems.

Who was after them?

And who had the skills to bypass his advanced security measures and encrypted files?

Those weren't ordinary skills. They took practice and knowledge and an impressive ability to maneuver through layers of security protocols, built like a web to avoid intrusions *and* to detect the intruders before they realized it was too late.

But why hadn't his trap sprung?

He'd worked long and hard on that sticky, digital web and expected it would work if ever needed.

Yet here he was, facing a breach from a very clever adversary.

Rubbing his eyes, Winston cycled through the events of the past few months, considering who might be looking their way. And quickly came up with more than a few ideas.

He'd told Markus over and over the dead girls were a problem. And despite how deeply they'd buried them, ensuring there was no way they could be linked to Ever After, those secrets had still come back to the surface.

Dumb luck that stupid reporter had been making a connection between the girls' "devout faith" and a local religious group.

It was infuriating, really.

But was the reporter really the problem?

Or maybe it was the feds? The dead girls had occupied much of local law enforcement's time as well as the federal team assigned to this backwater region, so it was a real possibility.

Yet even as he turned that one over and over in his mind, he had to admit it didn't quite fit, either.

No one from law enforcement had nosed around lately. And the four new members of the Ever After flock they'd acquired in the past few months had checked out clean.

So who was looking?

He and Markus had run this con repeatedly and this one had been working like a charm. They'd ironed out some of the kinks that had stymied them in the past and until their recent need to switch money launderers, things had been going well.

But now, they'd had a string of problems and Markus refused to see it. He was so focused on landing the big fish that was Jessie Colton that he refused to pick up stakes and get the hell out of here.

It made him antsy because he always trusted his instincts, Winston thought.

Always.

Initially, he'd been apprehensive to move back to an area so close to his son, Rick. Damn boy was a do-gooder through and through and had never appreciated his old man's entrepreneurial spirit. But Markus had convinced him the open yet relatively secluded space in Conners was perfect for them. Add on the area was ripe for some "spiritual instruction" for its wealthier denizens and they'd seen their coffers build.

Then a damn dog found the dead girls and it had all started to unravel.

Winston flipped through a few of his files, his son's smiling face filling the screen, his arm around his wife. Their son stood in front of him, looking like the very image of Rick when he'd been a kid, and the little girl was in his daughter-in-law's arms.

A shot of irritation filled him.

They were a good-looking family and they'd be a huge asset to him and Markus if they'd only get on board. But

Rick had sworn him off years ago, even before getting married, and refused contact.

Little did he know his dear old dad was a computer whiz and kept tabs, anyway.

He'd fallen off checking in on Rick of late, but it might be worth looking back in on his son.

He had no reason to think this breach had anything to do with Rick, but one could never be too sure. Especially when his own kid had made it readily apparent he thought his dad was the scum of the earth. Rick had never done anything to make Winston think he'd go to the cops, but he'd hedged his bets all the same.

It had been sheer dumb luck Jessie Colton was such a bad mother. The first time she'd visited, at Markus's invitation, Winston had nearly run out of the meeting room for fear of being recognized. His Rick had been best friends with her son, Greg, since they were kids.

If Jessie had stuck around Owl Creek, she might have known that, but she'd ditched her family the moment she got the chance. He'd even nosed around a bit when it was clear Jessie was becoming a more permanent fixture in their flock. The woman wasn't just uninvolved with her adult children in Owl Creek—she actively avoided talking about them.

It had served Markus well as he reeled her in, preying on that absence every chance he got.

Shaking off thoughts of Markus's new squeeze, Winston reviewed the files he had on his son. Rick's address and employment information had been easy to procure, so had his cell phone number. The rest had been harder. His grandson's preschool was solidly locked down, any information impossible to get at. He hadn't even bothered trying for hospital records after his granddaughter had been born.

But thanks to a social-media habit, he'd gotten a heck of

a lot more once his daughter-in-law, Wendy, had gone full-bore on her posting. Pics of the kids, family pics, even a shot of their SUV in the background of one photo had paid dividends and he'd collected it all.

He quickly flipped through those photos, considering his next steps. It might be worth hacking into his son's phone records, just to see what the kid was up to.

He could even drive past the house and see if anyone was out playing in the yard in these waning days of warmth.

The odds that his latest problems were tied to Rick were slim. But Winston had believed his computer systems were solid, too, and he'd obviously been wrong.

It was time to turn over every stone and check hard under every rock he could think of.

He was also going to put a trusted minion on Rick for a few days. See what his son was up to and what he'd been doing while Winston dug a bit more through his son's digital footprint.

And maybe it was time he started convincing Markus that the Ever After Church might have outlived its usefulness.

OVER COFFEE AND a few slices of toast, Sloan reviewed all her files and considered her and Chase's next move. He hadn't come back to her apartment the day before and a part of her was relieved.

She was...*confused* as to how she felt.

Not the attraction part. That was crystal-clear.

But what to do about it? *That* was an entirely different matter.

A big part of her wanted to throw caution to the wind, take the few precious moments they'd have together and go home to Chicago the better for it.

Yet even as that enticing vision pulled her in, the more practical part of her knew it was a fool's errand. She wasn't a love-'em-and-leave-'em type and giving in to her feelings for Chase had disaster written all over it.

Since she'd vacillated between those two options the entire time she'd been investigating the Ever After Church and its leaders, she knew she was in emotional danger.

So she'd taken the time to also get some needed distance from Chase, keeping their communication the day before to text only.

They'd agreed to meet today, go over all she'd discovered and then talk to Rick Kraft.

A big part of her was tempted to simply turn everything over to the feds she'd worked with in the past. But she was equally aware she'd dug into this information illegally and without the protection of a government-issued search warrant.

By choice.

And when Chase had seemed willing to talk to his cousin's friend, Rick, it felt like the right solution to continuing to pursue the inquiry alone.

They might not find a thing. She hoped they wouldn't.

Even as she worried she'd ruin the man's life in the process.

Because whatever else she thought they were sitting on, two things were abundantly clear. The Ever After Church was more of a cult than any sort of real church.

And Winston Kraft was their digital mastermind.

How could they break that to the man's son?

Oh, sorry, I come bearing bad news?

Do you know what's been lurking in your family tree?

Talk to your dear old dad lately?

Any way she'd spun it in her mind, nothing felt right. Nor could she erase the subtle sense of dread that even though she and Chase might need to talk to Kraft and share all they'd found, they also risked hurting the man beyond measure.

Nothing in her line of work was worse than a lose-lose situation, but that's where they found themselves.

She'd also done a bit of hunting on the "church's" leader, uncomfortable with what she'd found there as well. Markus Acker was Kraft's apparent partner, but the details were fuzzy and had a quality that made her think whatever information was out there about him online had been tampered with.

It wasn't impossible to do, but it did take skill. Based on the weird dead ends she kept running into as she tried to look into the man, her experience suggested there was something deliberate in the way Acker's image had been crafted in the digital world.

One more sign things were not right with this Ever After group.

She'd just finished cleaning up her breakfast dishes when she heard the knock on her front door. Fighting back the sudden excitement that leaped in her chest at the reality that Chase had arrived, she moderated her walk to the door to avoid appearing too eager.

And opened it to find both Chase and his cousin Greg on the other side.

"Oh, hello."

Greg's smile was broad and slightly mischievous as he leaned in to press a kiss against her cheek. "Nice to see you again, Sloan."

Suddenly bemused at the thunderous expression that filled Chase's face, Sloan put on her brightest smile. "Welcome to my home."

Both men filed in, and Waffles shot out of the bedroom, making a beeline for Chase to weave around his legs.

"You've got a friend there." Greg pointed to the small feline form currently rubbing fur all over Chase's dress slacks.

"What can I say, he's got good taste."

Greg snorted but avoided saying anything further as Sloan gestured them both toward the kitchen.

"I went to talk to Greg first," Chase began. "I filled him in on wanting to talk to Rick and share some of our concerns about his father, Winston."

"Chase said you've found some incriminating stuff," Greg added as the two men gathered around her as she took a seat in front of her computer. "About Rick's dad. Possibly about my mom, too?"

Sloan recognized the emotional land mines in the question and stepped carefully. "My focus has been on the Ever After Church. I haven't found much about your mother beyond the fact that she appears to be a member."

"That's hardly a surprise."

Although they hadn't shared much more than those few minutes of conversation at the barbecue last Friday evening, it was impossible to miss the man's pain, Sloan thought.

And the very real proof that no matter how far into adulthood Jessie Colton's children got, they'd always carry the realities of abandonment inside.

Something about that thought both broke her and solidified all the reasons she was doing this.

The flouting of privacy rules.

Even putting her heart at risk for Chase.

The Colton family deserved some sense of closure, as well as answers. And she had the professional skills to help them.

All of which she'd wrap around herself like a cloak to hide the deeper feelings that swirled inside her.

Although the kitchen wasn't large, something about having both Colton men in the room and hovering behind her suddenly made it feel quite small.

And made her realize just how big both of them were. Chase might have that attractive, broad-shouldered swimmer's build, but Greg had the tight, strapping build of a man who spent his life working outdoors and that had a distinct appeal, too.

Her feelings might be increasingly directed toward Chase, but since she still had breath in her body, she could admit his cousin cut an attractive figure. All the Colton men did.

One more aspect of Owl Creek to miss when she went home.

"Rick never did have a good relationship with his dad," Greg stated. "It was difficult when they were young, his father in and out of his life a lot. And then as he got older, he saw through the old man's veneer of big smiles and flashy talk."

"What does that mean?" Sloan asked, curious as it matched her opinions even though all she'd done was sift through a large digital footprint.

"Winston Kraft is always after his next mark, trying to run whatever his latest big con is. He's a huckster." Greg frowned, his expression narrowing with a thin layer of barely banked fury. "Or he was. Rick doesn't talk about it much, but I get the sense that things have turned darker."

"Darker how?" Chase asked. "A flashy salesman is one thing, but what you're suggesting sounds far worse."

"It's just a sense I get. Rick and I are good friends, but something about his dad's always been off-limits. So I listen on the rare occasions Rick brings him up and leave it alone the rest of the time."

Greg's discomfort at the conversation was clear, but there was something else there, just hovering beneath his words, that Sloan couldn't ignore. "Do you think Rick's afraid of his father?"

"He'd likely want to punch me if I said that to him, but yeah, I think so. Maybe he never was before, but now that he's got a wife and kids? I think he sees his father's life and choices in a whole new light."

"One that puts his family at risk?" Chase probed.

"Exactly."

It would be so easy to dismiss Greg's light-hearted humor and cocky smile as vapid and uncaring, but in that moment, Sloan saw just how much the man cared. About his friend and the things that had shaped Rick's life. "Are you okay if we go talk to him?"

"I am. I don't know how happy he'll be about it, but he should know about your suspicions. More—" Greg shook his head "—he deserves to know."

"I appreciate it," Chase said, putting a hand on his cousin's shoulder. "I really think we need to understand this group and what they're up to."

The joviality Greg had walked in with had vanished, replaced with a grim man carrying a heavy weight. "And how my mother's involved."

Neither she nor Chase said anything as Greg pulled his phone from his pocket. "Let me go give Rick a call. Let him know you're heading his way."

Sloan waited until Greg was in the living room, engaged in conversation with his friend, before speaking. "I wish there was an easier way."

"I do, too. One that didn't involve destroying families. Or at least adding a painful reminder into an otherwise ordinary day."

"It's not just Rick Kraft," Sloan said. "Your cousins are facing a hard road here, too."

"I know." Chase dropped his head before looking back

up at her, a bleakness in his eyes she hadn't seen since they'd started working together. "I know we need to see this through, but it's really hard to feel we're making the right decision."

Since his comment so closely mirrored her earlier thoughts, she could only agree. "I know."

"And then I remind myself that the elder generation functioned with secrets and lies, and we need to get every last one of them out in the open."

"Do you think this Ever After group is going to harm your family?"

Although she should have questioned that before, it was the first time Sloan actually felt a genuine shot of fear.

Was the Colton family at risk?

Was Chase?

"I don't know what to think, but it's not a big leap to see the awareness and press my father's death has received and make a connection with my aunt. She hasn't exhibited the most rational decision making. Now she's a part of that group?" The question seemingly hung there as Chase obviously weighed his words. "I think it's entirely possible she's at risk simply by being a member."

"And the family?"

"If we're not in danger, by extension we're at least at risk."

"Of what?"

"Having a very large target on every Colton back."

Chapter Fifteen

Rick Kraft and his wife, Wendy, sat opposite Chase and Sloan at their kitchen table, a visible sense of nervousness arcing between them. They held hands on top of the scarred oak, an obvious unit as Sloan laid out for them all she'd learned in her digging into the Ever After Church.

"I am sorry to have to share this with you," Sloan added after walking through each piece of data she'd uncovered. "But we feel you should know and, if you're willing to talk to us, wanted to see if you can shed any light on the church."

"First and foremost, don't call it a church. Ever." Rick's tone was low, but it quivered with a barely leashed fury that Chase could practically feel beneath his skin.

Wendy's hand tightened over her husband's, clear support and strength in their hold. "Churches aren't meant to manipulate their people."

"The Ever After group does that?" Chase asked.

"All that and more," Rick said. "My father has been hooked up with Markus Acker for years. They're men of death. To suggest what they do is a church intimates something holy and I can assure you God has no play in any of it."

"Have you been in contact with your father?"

Sloan was compassionate and while he knew she was as determined as he was to get answers, Chase was again impressed by her deep well of kindness as she spoke with the couple.

Yes, she wanted those answers.

But even more, she obviously wanted to provide as much kindness and support as she could to Rick and Wendy.

It was one more facet of her that both impressed and humbled him, all at the same time. She put others first and she did it so naturally—so intuitively—that it was a part of her.

Although he was obviously shaken by the need for the conversation, Rick had agreed and had answered every question they'd posed to him. He didn't shirk away from giving a response, even with such a direct question.

"I avoid my father at all costs and have for more than a decade now. He and I never saw eye to eye on anything, and if it were a simple matter of differences, I could find a way past it."

"But it isn't?" Chase asked, aware now more than ever before in his life how challenging and potentially tenuous father-and-son relationships could be.

And at the same time, he recognized a strange sort of grace as well.

For the past months, his memories of his father had all become clouded and warped by the realities of Robert Colton's decisions around his family and his secret life. Yet as awful as it had been, he'd never seen his father as a monster.

A misguided man, yes.

But one he feared? No.

"I don't want my father anywhere near my life and I most especially don't want him anywhere near my family."

"We have two children," Wendy added. "Justin is four and Jane is fourteen months."

"How sweet," Sloan murmured. "Do you have photos?"

It was the right question and Wendy's obvious pride in

her children was evident as she pulled up a photo on her cell phone.

The firm line of Rick's mouth never softened but Chase could clearly see the pride in his gaze as he stared down at his children.

"Nothing is more important than them. Then Wendy." Rick shifted, wrapping an arm around his wife's shoulders. "And I'd like nothing more than to see you put an end to this once and for all. My father and his crony, Markus Acker, have been getting away with this for years. Creating these fake church groups, bilking people for money and doing far worse. They've always been able to outrun the law and I have nothing I can definitely pin on them, but I can promise you they're guilty."

"Thank you for agreeing to talk to us. We're committed to seeing this through," Sloan assured the man.

"Greg was clear on that point, and I know that now. It's why I agreed to talk to you."

"We're going to uncover what they're doing. I'm not letting this go," Chase said.

And as the words left his mouth, Chase not only recognized them for truth, but also as something even deeper.

He knew them for the vow they were.

"Rick's scared, just like Greg said."

Sloan spoke as they drove away from the Kraft's home, their conversation with the couple filling her thoughts. She'd recognized Greg's frustration for his friend that morning, but even she hadn't fully prepared herself for the deep anger and terrible fear that Rick Kraft obviously carried about his father.

It sat on his shoulders, as clearly as a physical weight.

"What's clear is that this has changed for him. At some point it shifted from anger and disgust with his father's choices to genuine worry for his family," she added, thinking through all the man had shared with them.

"It must be a terrible weight."

"The person who should care for you the most is seen as your greatest threat? It's nearly impossible to fathom."

She'd seen difficult things throughout her career. The work she took on—and the ways she used her talents—had ensured she was regularly exposed to some of the worst sorts of humans.

But this?

A man who preyed on people, weaponizing their faith? And doing it in a way that scared his own son?

"Are you okay?" Chase asked as they drove the increasingly familiar streets through Owl Creek.

"I wish I could say yes, but no, I'm not. I keep thinking I can't be surprised by the choices people make, yet once again, I'm shocked at the darkness that lives inside of some."

"Rick's father is bad news."

"Everything about that Ever After group is bad news. I can't help but think your aunt is in danger."

Sloan recognized it was quite a departure from her negative thoughts up to now about Chase's Aunt Jessie. But after all Rick had shared, she had to believe that the woman was in trouble. Jessie Colton might not know it, but how could she possibly be a part of that group and not be at risk?

Especially if she'd come to their attention because of her relationship with Chase's father and the wealth and power the man had wielded in life?

In fact…

"Chase? When Nate spoke to you about his mother, he also brought up that she wanted him to press for his inheritance. That he should be determined to take more. Do you think she's getting pressured by these Ever After people?"

"You mean she's being manipulated rather than being a direct part of it all?"

"It would play, wouldn't it?" Sloan turned the idea over in her mind. "She's been a conniver, but she's also been a product of her misguided thinking her entire life. Leaving her husband and children for her own sister's husband? That's..." Sloan trailed off, looking for the right word. "Well, it's small in so many ways."

"Small?"

"Yeah. She doesn't have the best interests of others at all. Not her children. Not her husband. Not her sister. But more than that, she also didn't go looking very far with her choices. If she were that unhappy with her life, wouldn't she have gone farther afield? More, wouldn't she have sought out a life that she could live without the secrets and having to remain hidden away? She and Robert weren't even able to marry, despite the deception of looking like they were a couple."

Sloan wasn't entirely sure where she was going with this theory, but something about it rang true.

Jessie Colton had jumped at whatever was in front of her. It was destructive, but it also didn't scream a sense of thinking things through with any degree of cunning or calculation.

Rather, it appeared as if she was simply being dragged along by whatever impulse was directly ahead of her.

"So if we play out your way of thinking, she's being manipulated by Winston Kraft?"

"Winston or the guy he works with, Markus Acker. She's easily fascinated by a bright and shiny promise placed in her path."

"Her children certainly don't seem to have been enough to keep her priorities straight."

"No, they weren't." Sloan thought again about what she'd

managed to dig up on the Ever After Church and its leader, Acker. Everything rang patently false about the group, their leader most of all.

"I think that might give me a new line to tug."

"On what?"

"Rick's information was helpful, but his father, for all his power and influence, is functioning in the role of support staff. Keeping the computer. Cleaning up any messes. I think I need to dig deeper into the leader. Markus Acker."

"I thought you had details about him in your files?"

"I did and a lot of impressions about him that seemed off, somehow. Like a sanitized, polished version of him was all I could find online."

"You think it's fake?"

"I think it could be. And with some of the information Rick gave us, I'm going to do some more digging to see if I'm right."

"WE HAVE A very important job for you, Brother Jasper."

Markus kept his tone level and easy, pushing the lightest touch of urgency under his words as he sat in the clearing. His crossed legs and prayerful position belied the anger at their current situation roiling deep inside.

He was gratified to see that urgency was working when Jasper shifted his position, nearly squirming to get closer, his pale blue eyes lighting up with the fervor of the believer.

"Of course, Leader Acker. How can I help?"

Jasper was one of his true believers. He wasn't wealthy, but he was useful. Markus was well aware he needed both types of followers to make Ever After the success it was.

A point that had been proven in spades when Jasper had helped with the disposal of a few of those dead girls.

"It seems Brother Kraft's son has been speaking ill of our work."

"Ungrateful boy." Jasper practically spat the words.

"Ungrateful *betrayer*," Markus said with emphasis.

Winston's son had always been a bone of contention between him and Winston, the man's willingness to sit back and leave the boy to his own devices concerning. Sure, Rick and his little family kept to themselves, but it was a problem to have such a threat out roaming free.

And now that threat was visiting with Jessie's family.

There was no way it was a coincidence.

Winston had managed to tap into his son's door camera earlier that afternoon and found the proof standing on the other side of the porch.

"How can I help you, Leader?"

"I believe Winston's ungrateful son has been spying on us. Talking about us. And telling others that our peaceful life is fake."

"But it's not!" Jasper's agitation spilled over as the man leaped to his feet. "We're a peaceful sort. We do our work quietly and away from prying eyes. It's only the betrayers that must be silenced! Like those girls."

"You know how to work quickly and quietly. I need you to confirm Rick's actions and assess if the threat to our peaceful life grows too great."

"I will, Leader. I can do that."

Markus slowly got to his feet, the motion meant to convey serenity to his obedient follower. He'd learned long ago that ability to project a certain untroubled tranquility often did far more good for advancing his goals than any other tactic he possessed.

People liked calm.

They liked order.

And they responded to someone who competently wielded both.

He came to his full height, looking deep into Jasper's eyes. "I'm so grateful I can count on you, Brother Jasper."

"Of course, Leader. Ever After must be protected from that rabble."

"I know you're right." Jasper had nearly turned away, happy to head off to his task, before Markus added one final admonition. "I'm sorry to say his wife is a problem, too. I believe she's contributed to the darkness in Brother Kraft's son."

"I'll keep watch, Leader," Jasper promised, that fervency in his eyes like a form of desire. "I'll see that they can't do us any harm."

CHASE PACED SLOAN'S small living room, updating Greg on their visit the day before with Rick and Wendy. He'd meant to get to his cousin sooner but after their visit he'd had to race back to Colton Properties for an emergency meeting to make an offer on a property they were at risk of losing. Sloan had headed back here to her place to tug more lines of information they'd received from Rick.

Beyond a few text messages and missed phone calls between him and his cousin, a full day had passed until he'd been able to provide updates.

"I know this is hard for Rick and Wendy. I appreciate your willingness to talk to him on this. He wasn't happy to see Sloan and I, but he was a real help."

"He knows what a problem his father is. He—" Greg broke off, his sigh traveling through the phone line. "It was one of the things that bonded us young. His dad. My mom. Rick was the one friend who understood what that betrayal was like."

"I'm sorry, Greg. More than I can say."

"For what?"

"For never realizing just how bad it was. For not realizing how deep the hurt was. It's only now, after knowing what my own father did, that I realize how much I never said. Or understood."

That truth flowed out, a product of years observing his cousins. He'd always known Greg, Max, Malcolm and Lizzy had struggled with their mother's abandonment. But he'd never had the words before.

It was only as Sloan walked into the room, setting a small tray on the coffee table full of cheese and crackers, that he finally understood why he could say them now.

Sloan.

She'd come into his life for a difficult purpose. But she'd found a way to help him through all the things he'd never had the words for.

His cousins' pain of abandonment.

His own frustration and loss after his marriage dissolved.

And then the deep, cavernous pain of betrayal at his father's actions.

Sloan had seen it all and she'd had the compassion to help *him* see that they might be facets of his life, but they didn't have to define him.

"We were kids, Chase. You didn't have to say anything. You were there for me. For my brothers and my sister. So was your mom and so were *your* brothers and sisters. We got through."

A level of certainty filled Greg's voice that humbled Chase.

Here was a man who'd faced a lifetime of challenges—and was still facing them—from the actions of a parent. Despite it all, he didn't blame others or lash out.

"I'm still there for you. I hope you know that."

"Right back at ya, cuz. Now. Get off the phone with me and get back to that lovely woman who's dumb enough to spend time with you."

"I'll be sure to tell Sloan you said that."

Whatever seriousness had laced their conversation had vanished, Greg's normal level of mischief and good humor firmly in place. "See that you do."

Sloan glanced up from where she settled the snack, a broad smile on her face. "Tell me what?"

"Greg says hello, in his own inimitable way."

It was a facet of his cousin's personality, one Chase was finally coming to understand had been forged in the fires of his mother's abandonment.

Smile. Laugh. Joke.

Wonderful traits in their own right, but also weapons that could defend, deflect and protect one's emotions.

He hadn't really understood it before now, but hadn't he done the same when it came to relationships?

Avoiding anything serious—on the surface—looked like a carefree lifestyle. But it was only now, when faced with someone who had truly begun to matter to him, that Chase realized all he'd done was hide behind his own emotions all these years.

Because Sloan had come to matter.

No matter how much they both had tried to disregard that fact, it had become increasingly impossible to avoid.

Or ignore.

"Sloan." He reached for her hand, oddly pleased when she not only took what he offered, but also gave his hand a light squeeze. "I'm glad you're here."

"I'm glad I'm here, too."

"I mean really here. In this moment. In Owl Creek." He stared up at her, his heart racing. "With me."

She moved closer, her free hand settling on his shoulder. "I'm glad I'm here, too."

"It's inevitable, isn't it?" He murmured the words as he

stared up at her, gratified when he saw the same acceptance in her eyes.

"I think it is." She nodded.

"What should we do about it?"

She stood there, staring down at him for several long moments as she seemingly came to some decision.

"I don't know if this is a good idea."

He wanted her, of that he was certain. But he couldn't deny the reality of their situation. Or the risks that no amount of want could get them to the other side of this attraction. "Me, either."

"But increasingly, I've come to realize it's the only idea."

Before he could respond, she bent her head and pressed her lips to his, a world of want and need and sheer desire in the play of her mouth over his.

Chase placed his hands on her hips, pulling her close until she tumbled into his lap.

And as she fitted into his arms, cradled against his body, he asked the question they'd been leading to from that very first moment in his office.

"Let me stay with you."

Her gaze never left his, those fathomless depths of the deepest brown pulling him in.

"Yes."

YES.

Such a simple word.

Such an easy agreement.

And yet, for all the simplicity, Sloan thought, there was power in the acceptance of all that was still to come.

Their kiss on the couch had spun out, delicate and urgent all at once. And it was only now, as she held his hand and led him to her bedroom, that Sloan recognized everything up to now had been leading them here.

The attraction between them was undeniable.

But the need to be together physically had become an ache she could no longer ignore.

More, she no longer wanted to ignore it.

She was a woman in full possession of her faculties and her will.

And every bit of both wanted Chase Colton.

The back of her legs brushed the side of the bed, both stopping point and decision point.

Continue to go further on this journey?

Yes.

It pounded through her in lockstep with her heartbeat as Sloan reached for the hem of Chase's dress shirt, dragging it from where it was tucked neatly into his black slacks. The man was well-dressed, sharp and natty, and all she could think of was messing him up.

Of getting beneath that refined look to the man who was flesh, blood and beating heart.

The man she loved.

That awareness hit hard and fast and Sloan stilled her movements to stare up at him, drinking in the moment even as it scared her beyond herself.

Love?

Was she really there?

Or was she confusing the overwhelming need to give in to passion with feelings that had her dreamily thinking of forever?

There was no way to really know. But dissecting her feelings in the dimming light outside her bedroom window seemed rife with the potential to miss the moment.

She'd think on it later. Then, she could turn it over in her mind to her heart's content.

But right now, she'd take.

With renewed focus, she finished undoing the row of buttons that ran over his chest, stripping the thin material of his shirt over those impressively broad shoulders. His T-shirt quickly followed and as she ran her hands over the wide planes of his chest, she reveled in the feel of him. The light dusting of hair beneath her palms. The wide, flat nipples that were sensitive to her hands, his green eyes darkening at her touch. And the thick bands of muscle over his stomach, solid and firm beneath her seeking fingers.

He was impressive. So hot and so responsive to the lightest touch.

But it was the thick length of him as she slipped her hand beneath the waistband of his slacks that drew her in. Beckoned her toward all that was still to come.

And that had her quivering in anticipation when he growled against her mouth before pulling her fully against him.

SHE WAS KILLING HIM.

Slowly. Determinedly. Exquisitely.

And he'd never been more ready to give in and simply accept his fate.

Sloan was a marvel, his own personal miracle. And as he mimicked her earlier motions, slipping her now-open blouse from her slim shoulders, Chase took a hard breath.

She was beautiful.

High, rounded breasts spilled over the lacy edges of her bra, while that small rib cage tapered down into a flat stomach and the secrets that still lay beneath her jeans.

Secrets he was determined to uncover, one achingly slow moment at a time.

With her blouse removed, he shifted his attention to her bra, unhooking the delicate material and taking in his fill as it followed her blouse to the floor. With firm hands, he cupped her breasts, his thumbs playing over her erect nipples, her skin so soft he wondered if he'd ever touched anything so perfect in his life.

He'd wanted before.

Needed before.

But never had he been so overwhelmed by a woman so as to forget everything but the pure magic of the moment. And she was so responsive—so achingly beautiful as her eyelids dropped with her pleasure—that Chase gave himself the joy of simply watching her take the pure power of what was between them in physical form.

A need that pushed them harder, faster and more greedily toward a finish line that waited in the distance.

A finish line they'd cross together.

With that temptation awaiting them both, Chase laid her down on the bed, his gaze never leaving hers, as he took the final steps of removing his slacks, then reaching for her to pull her jeans and panties down the slim lines of her legs.

And then, it was just the two of them, naked bodies pressed together as he stretched out beside her on the bed.

Her pretty brown skin practically glowed in the soft, end-of-day light that filtered through the window as he traced his fingertips over her flesh. She followed suit with gentle traces of her own, from the surprisingly sensitive skin on the inner curve of his elbow, to the achingly hard length of him she returned to with fervent strokes.

They shared it all, there in the dying light of day. As the lazy discovery turned more urgent—as the need for her that had overwhelmed him from the start grew so intense he could think of nothing else—he positioned himself over her.

She'd already sheathed him in the protection he'd retrieved from his wallet and as her thighs opened for him, Chase touched that endless sweetness, her slick folds waiting and ready for him.

She reached down to guide him into her, her body drawing him in, closer.

Deeper.

And in the most erotic moment of his life, they began to move. The rhythm was fast, hard, exquisite. Pleasure built in his body, the magnificent force building behind his eyes even as he desperately fought to keep his gaze level with hers.

More, as he wanted to watch her the moment she was as consumed as he.

The moment her world exploded in starlight.

He didn't have to wait long, and when she cried out in pleasure, he let himself go.

That final race to the finish.

The final driving beat of body into body.

The beauty of—finally—falling over the edge into the soul that waited for his.

Chapter Sixteen

She shouldn't feel this decadent.

This wanton.

This wrapped up in Chase.

But that's where she was and had stayed for nearly twenty-four hours.

It had been a sharing unlike anything she'd ever known. An erotic, sexual feast that at times was so intense she'd never imagined she could feel like this, and at others so warm and intimate and funny she couldn't find her breath.

How could two people experience such a range of emotions?

And how had she lived so long without it?

Sloan had done her level best to keep herself in check, avoiding those types of mental wanderings in favor of taking the pure joy of the hours spent with him. But despite all her efforts, those thoughts kept creeping in.

She had to give this up.

In a very short time, she'd be heading home.

And while he'd been attentive and so thorough, there were moments she'd wanted to cry at his aching tenderness, Sloan admitted the truth, if only to herself.

He hadn't told her he loved her. Or that he wanted her

to stay. Or that this meant more to him than these special hours together.

And it was that truth that she tried to focus on as she watched him walk back into the bedroom, the plate of cheese and crackers in his hands.

"Is that from last night?"

"I'd hardly be a gentleman if I poisoned you on rancid cheese." Chase bent over and pressed a kiss to her lips before setting down the plate. "This is fresh from the fridge."

"I'm starving."

"I figured this would hold us over and we could think about going out for dinner." His gaze drifted down over her nakedness as he settled in beside her. "Or maybe we order in dinner."

She reveled in that warm appreciation. "Maybe we will."

It had been like this since the day before. That intense awareness of each other and an inability to remain apart. As if they were both trying to absorb all they could in this brief interlude together.

Sloan reached for a cracker, settled a piece of cheese on top and nibbled a small bite. "We haven't talked much about the Krafts. Do you think it's worth pulling your family in and talking about the discussion we had with them?"

Chase swallowed around a bite of his own before responding. "It's worth filling everyone in on what we've discovered so far, but we don't have a lot to go on. Rick and his wife's fear is real, and I don't want to underestimate that. We can put my family on alert as well, but there's nothing specific we can call on other than keep a careful watch if my Aunt Jessie reaches out."

"It's interesting she's only pressed Nate and Sarah so far. Not her other children."

"I suspect she knows her antics won't be welcome."

"Perhaps." Sloan shrugged and finished the small square of cheese, something tugging at the back of her thoughts.

That conversation they'd had, about Jessie's actions being small and a product of whatever decision was right in front of her, struck Sloan once again.

It was instinct, nothing more. She didn't know the woman, nor did she have a sense of how Jessie Colton would behave in the real world. The sum total of Sloan's impressions was tied to past behavior and the few things her family had said about her.

And yet…

"Those look like some very serious thoughts." Chase pressed a gentle kiss to her cheek. "Want to share them?"

Sloan surfaced from her musings, only to glance down to see her half-nibbled cracker still between thumb and forefinger. "Sorry. Habit."

"Not at all. Walk me through it. What are you thinking?"

"Jessie's been pressuring Nate and Sarah. And from Nate's feedback to you, he and his sister aren't budging."

"Not at all, based on my read of him."

"Then how long will it be before she goes after her other children?"

"Go after them how?"

"A pressure campaign to get them on board. To either use them to influence Nate and Sarah or to pull them into her narrative that her children deserve a share of the Colton money."

"Everyone's doing okay in life. My father was the wealthier brother in terms of income, but my Uncle Buck has done fine with the ranch. More than fine," Chase added. "The money isn't what drives us."

"But your aunt doesn't know that."

"I can see something's there, something that you're working through, but I'm not following the same thought process as you. My cousins are grown adults. Max is former FBI, even. They can handle themselves if their mother comes back calling on them."

"Yes, but does this Ever After group know that? What resources do they have? Or worse," Sloan said, thinking of those dead girls dumped in hand-dug graves. "What if that church has set their sights beyond Jessie."

"To my family?"

"Exactly. What if the Colton family is the endgame here?"

IT WAS A sobering thought, going from a day of nonstop sensual pleasure to talk of his family's lives at risk.

But Chase was rapidly catching up.

He'd like nothing more than to stay right here, keeping the world at bay with Sloan, warm and responsive in his arms. Only the real world had intruded, and he knew they needed to follow her concerns.

"Looks like it's time for another Friday-evening family meeting."

Sloan was already out of bed, heading for the en suite bathroom to shower. Chase watched her beautiful body as it was backlit from the light of the bathroom doorway.

Even more, he now knew that body matched the beautiful heart that beat in her chest.

He'd seen that from the first, her compassion and care such obvious traits. But now, after spending these hours with her, he recognized how deeply it ran in all she did. She was a warm, generous lover, but it was an extension of the warm, generous person that she was. And even now, her mind was rapidly processing, wanting to ensure his family was okay.

Her thoughts were always focused on others.

Hadn't Max said that in their very first conversation, when his cousin had recommended Sloan for the job?

How foolish he'd been, Chase realized, not to recognize

the real risk to his heart it would be to bring in someone so competent and so deeply caring as she translated difficult work into help and support for others.

But he'd been so foolish and so deluded. He'd thought his life would continue the way it always had, indefinitely in limbo, always able to keep his heart protected.

In reality, he'd only been protected because there'd been no one worth falling for. No one who mattered so much. No one who'd truly put his heart at risk.

Until Sloan.

The sound of the shower had him imagining joining her, even as he knew there was work to be done and a family meeting to plan, when his phone went off on the bedside table. He saw Greg's name painting the face of the screen and connected to the call.

"Chase."

That flat use of his name and the odd urgency that transmitted through the phone lines in a heartbeat captured him immediately.

"What is it?"

"It's Rick and Wendy. They were in a car accident about an hour ago. Both were pronounced dead at the scene."

"Walk me through it."

Despite his whirling thoughts and the sheer impossibility that the healthy, vibrant people he and Sloan had spoken to a few days before were now dead, he forced himself to concentrate.

To *listen* to the words Greg spoke.

To accept that no matter how much this looked like an accident on the surface, there was no possible way it was.

This was all part of the swirling, writhing evil that the Ever After Church was capable of. And he and Sloan had brought the wolf directly to Rick Kraft's door.

IT WAS WORSE than he'd imagined, Chase thought two hours later as he sat in the kitchen at the Colton Ranch.

Rick and Wendy were dead, and Greg had headed off with Wendy's best friend, Briony Adams, to pick up the couple's children. They'd been sheltered at a day-care facility that had been watching the children through the madness of trying to sort through the accident, but Briony and Greg had both been designated as caregivers in case of emergency.

And this qualified in the worst of ways.

"You okay?" Max sat down next to him, fresh mugs of coffee in hand. Chase wasn't all that interested in drinking anything, but it was something to do in the endless roiling of his thoughts. A strange sort of anchor as his hands wrapped around the heat of the mug and his senses took in the heavy, rich scent of the coffee.

"I did this."

"What's that supposed to mean?" Max's demand was quick, the narrowing of his eyebrows into slashes over his light blue eyes even quicker.

"I asked Sloan to dig into the Ever After Church. Into Winston Kraft. There's not a chance in hell that accident was really accidental."

"We don't know that."

"Oh, no?" Chase glanced up from where he stared into the depths of his coffee, anger at himself eating a path from throat to gut. "Can you honestly sit there and tell me you think this is just a massive coincidence?"

"Until proven otherwise, we have to keep all reasonable options open. People do have car accidents. It's sad and horrible and ruins lives, but it happens."

Chase wanted to believe that. In every way, he wanted to believe that it was simple coincidence that he and Sloan had met with the couple, and two days later they'd lost their lives.

But something deep inside refused to accept it.

Because something equally deep recognized something far bigger was at play. It was the same sense he'd had that there were issues at Colton Properties.

Something was *off.*

And Rick and Wendy Kraft had paid the price. Their young children would pay an even higher one for the rest of their lives.

"Since I can see you don't believe me, walk me through it." Max held up a hand. "Not the guilt-ridden version where you have to hold the responsibility for the whole world, but the one that your gut's telling you."

"Two people are dead, Max. This isn't me playing overbearing big brother."

"No, but if you are correct, you're taking responsibility for the actions of a killer, which isn't right or accurate. *If,* and it's still an *if,* Rick and Wendy were murdered, then that responsibility sits with the person who did it."

Chase wasn't so sure about that—they'd never have been in danger if not for his poking around—but he saw Max's point all the same.

And a killer on the loose was a danger to them all.

"At my request, Sloan's been digging around the Ever After Church."

"Speaking as a former representative of the US government and a law-enforcement professional, surely you understand why that's a problem?"

"Yes."

Max's gaze was direct. "Do you?"

"Max, come on. These people are corrupt in every way. And—" He stopped, well aware he was treading into very dangerous personal territory. "Your mother's involved with them. We needed to know what we're dealing with. Sloan had the skills to find the answers we needed."

"What the hell, Chase?" Max practically spit out the

words. "You do realize this is a massive violation of privacy and could backfire on you both? She could damage her incredibly stellar reputation."

One more point of guilt to add to all the others.

And while Sloan might have been a willing accomplice, this was all his doing.

"I'm the one who pushed for this, Max. I want answers."

"I want them, too, but we're not going above the law to get them."

"And if this church is doing some dangerous things?" Chase knew he had responsibility here, but he couldn't quite rid himself of the importance of that point. "Things even the government hasn't been able to find?"

"That's a low blow."

"Not a low blow. It's the reality of the situation. They've shielded themselves so much that they were nearly able to bury the story about those dead girls. If you hadn't been on the case, I believe they *would* have buried it. They've got skills and some clout, and we need to fight fire with fire."

"A handy excuse until you get burned."

"Rick and Wendy sure did."

And there it was again. That steady drumbeat he couldn't see past. It suggested his insistence on the truth and on cracking open the details on the Ever After group was tainted with danger.

"Walk me through what Sloan has found. Step by step."

"You do understand she did this for me?"

"Yeah, I get it." Max shook his head before crossing to a small drawer near the fridge and pulling out a pad of paper and a pen. He sat back down and flicked the ballpoint. "Tell me what you've found."

JASPER THOMAS MILES.

Sloan tapped a few more keys, hunting through her databases to see if anything popped on the man. It was a long shot, but she'd been digging for hours and still wasn't sure if she had anything or if she was going in big, tired circles.

But if this person, Jasper Miles, had anything to do with the Krafts' deaths, she was determined to find it.

He'd popped up when she'd followed a trail from the Krafts' accident report Chase's brother, Fletcher, had been kind enough to share. The driver on scene, a Mike Arnold, was responsible for the car that hit Rick and Wendy. He'd been taken into custody for driving under the influence and everything about the situation had seemed run-of-the-mill. A real and tragic accident that had resulted in loss of life.

But something about the timing of the accident and the fact that she and Chase had just seen the couple had her digging further.

Because no matter what, she couldn't shake the feeling it was made to *look* like an accident, even as it was deliberate, intentional action.

She'd hunted through Arnold's social media and uncovered two interesting things. A social post where he'd checked into a local bar and tagged a friend who was meeting him there, one Jasper Miles.

When she'd clicked into Jasper's account, she'd seen several photos of him out in the wide-open air that looked like this part of the country. He had also posted spiritual quotes about the "ever after way" and "building a life to last ever after, even past his last breath."

Odd phrasing? Yes.

Actually incriminating? It was hard to say.

But it bothered her, especially the use of the words *ever after* in his language.

So she continued to dig. And was finally rewarded late in the day with a clear and obvious hit.

Jasper Miles spent two years in prison more than a decade ago for a violent incident. He was ultimately released on good behavior after finding his faith in prison and went on to preach to his fellow inmates.

One of whom was Mike Arnold.

Parole-board testimony for both men made the connection along with the matched timelines of their incarceration. Sloan recognized there was way too big a relationship to simply brush this off.

Or call it a coincidence.

She texted Chase with the news, only to get a text message come winging back.

Max said send over the details and he and I will go visit Mike Arnold in jail.

She quickly wrote up the details and emailed both men, texting back once it was done.

Call me or come over after you're done. Too much coincidence here. Just sent you and Max all the details.

As work went, she was satisfied with what she'd found. There was a connection there—a clear and evident one—and she'd peeled back layers of the onion that was the complex and convoluted actions of the Ever After Church.

What she couldn't quite peel back or wish away was the strange way she felt, texting with Chase as if nothing was out of the ordinary.

As if they hadn't had sex and slept together for nearly twenty-four glorious hours before the news of Rick and Wendy's death reached them.

Where had that intimacy gone?

He hadn't even sent an assurance back that he'd come over after visiting Arnold in jail.

It was one more sign she needed to hold tight to her common sense and even tighter to her heart.

She'd gone into this with her eyes open and still had managed to fall in love, anyway.

Maybe it was time to acknowledge that was a fantasy. One steeped in mutual attraction, but not destined for anything more than the time she was slated to spend in Owl Creek.

CHASE WATCHED MAX navigate his way through Owl Creek, the past several hours still lodged in his chest like a deal gone sour.

He'd worked through specifics with Max all while Sloan had hammered away at potential suspects. Based on the information she'd managed to uncover in a short period of time, they should all feel *very* good.

They had a lead, and he didn't need to be a law-enforcement professional to understand it was a strong, solid one.

But even with that encouraging news and the very real possibility they would have answers about Rick and Wendy Kraft's death in no time, he felt strangely empty.

He wanted to solve this and figure out what was roiling underneath the surface here in his home and with his family.

And he wanted Sloan to stay.

He might want that most of all.

"Do you think this guy's actually going to talk to us?" Chase asked Max, willing away the sense of malaise and frustration.

He'd talk to Sloan about staying later. Sure, he had a reputation for being averse to relationships, but things had changed and it was time to approach this head-on.

He'd talk to her and see what she wanted.

And he'd put himself on the line. All the way, no half measures. Not like with Leanne, when he told her he wanted to marry her and move onto the next stage of their lives simply because some magical list of check boxes had been ticked in his mind.

He'd focus on what Sloan wanted as much as his own needs and desires. On what it would really look like if they tried to have a relationship, even if it was long distance at first.

His life was in Owl Creek and that wasn't all that easy to untangle. But he'd already found himself imagining how he could juggle a life in Idaho along with one in Chicago, managing his personal life and his professional life across two places.

For Sloan. And for the relationship he believed they could have together.

They'd work it out because he wasn't making the same mistake this time. He was committed to talking through how he felt.

But in the meantime, he had a bigger problem staring him in the face.

"We've put you in a really difficult position, Max. I'm sorry."

"Less difficult since I'm out of the FBI, but yeah, you really need to leave this sort of work to professionals." Max side-eyed him before continuing. "Not the professionals we hire for jobs, either. Sloan should have left this alone."

"We both should have."

"While it pains me to say this, because you're both outside the law, your nosing around has opened a few avenues law enforcement can't quite as easily breach."

"So you're okay with it."

"I'm making the best of it."

Max couldn't quite hide the smile and Chase figured he'd passed some invisible hurdle. He wasn't off the hook, but his cousin was determined to help them.

"While you're doing that, could you ask Sloan to stay off her computer?"

"I think we both came to that conclusion on our own."

"Yeah, well call her and stress the same. We'll visit Mike Arnold in jail and can come straight to her place to fill her in."

Chase was just ready to do that as Max turned into the entrance for the prison. Flashing lights filled the parking lot and an ambulance was parked near the front door of the facility.

"What's this all about?" Max hit the speaker on his phone, giving voice instructions into his device to call one of his contacts in local law enforcement as Chase scanned the lot for any clues to what was going on.

"Owl Creek PD. Will speaking."

"Will. It's Max Colton."

The two men exchanged quick pleasantries, then Max said, "I'm over at the prison hoping my former FBI status gives me a bit of an okay to talk to a suspect. There's a lot going on over here."

"A lot," Will agreed. "I'm manning things here at the station, but the chief sent over a few squads. EMS is on high alert as well."

"For what?"

"An inmate died. He was brought in earlier and was found unconscious about fifteen minutes ago."

"Did his name happen to be Mike Arnold?"

Will hummed as he checked his information, the sound of computer keys tapping in the background, before his grim voice filled the SUV.

"Michael Arnold. EMS confirmed death ten minutes ago."

Max said his thanks before pulling into a space and turning around. It was only as he was headed back out of the lot, the prison filling the rearview mirror, that he finally spoke.

"What was that I said earlier?" Before Chase could even ask, Max added, "About some accidents just being accidents?"

"Yeah?"

"No way in hell this is an accident."

Chapter Seventeen

"You did well, Brother Jasper." Markus's voice remained soft and calming as he spoke the words.

This was a delicate time and any misstep in his handling of Jasper could lead to a problem.

They'd nearly had a situation with the girls a few months before, but Jasper had come around. He'd calmed at Markus's gentle words and the reassurance that he'd had to do the deed. That the killing and burial of several of the women had been necessary.

More, as Markus had told Jasper, he'd had to protect the flock, assisting the leader with the difficult work of culling the bad seeds who'd infiltrated them.

It was the same technique he'd use now, but he needed to work up to the approach. Jasper *was* a true believer, but he'd struggled when the girls were discovered. It had taken several personal sessions to calm him down and Markus had even begun to wonder if the man had outlived his usefulness.

Winston didn't seem to think so, but Markus wasn't so sure.

Nor was he convinced the events with Winston's son couldn't have been avoided with a bit of planning instead of rash action. The problem had been handled. But the death of a young couple with two adorable children was not going to go unnoticed.

Which made Winston's arrival in the small cabin they used as an office a few minutes later an opportunity to regroup.

"Brother Jasper…" Winston bent his head. "Hello."

Jasper nodded. "It is done, Brother."

Done?

Markus watched the exchange between the two men, increasingly connecting what they were talking about. He'd understood that Jasper had acted, but had believed it the man's inability to control his more violent impulses.

But to discover it was at Winston's direction? "What is done?"

"My son was poking into our work. He met with one of Jessie's family after my computer was hacked. He was a problem."

Markus struggled to keep himself in line. Although he'd been more than willing to show Winston his temper over the years, it was a display he avoided in front of his followers except in extreme circumstances.

People talked and they remembered when a person administered harsh words.

So he fought to keep himself in control, his words careful. "He's kept his distance from us for all these years. Surely you overreacted with this course of action?"

"I don't think so." Winston's gaze was challenging to read, as if the reality of his son's death was finally sinking in. What Markus didn't miss was the subtle sense of satisfaction that broke through. "And it was Brother Jasper's quick thinking that ensured we didn't have a bad situation on our hands."

"Computer hackers." Jasper shook his head. "It's devilish, invading others' privacy with those devices."

Markus nodded, adding his reflections to Jasper's, even as he kept a steady eye on Winston.

His right hand had acted alone, and it left him with a bothersome problem. Should he address it? Or take heart that the man stepped in and solved a situation before it became a problem.

If he was convinced that was all, perhaps he could have settled himself, but this was a bit much to take in.

The man had seen to it that his own son was killed.

He hadn't plotted or planned, but he'd taken swift action the moment he'd felt threatened. The two of them had worked well together for a long time, but this would take some reflection and review.

"Brother Jasper, you've earned a quiet night in private quarters. Why don't you go lie down in the Ever Rest hut and I'll see to it that a nourishing and restorative steak dinner is brought to you."

Jasper's smile was eager as he took in Markus's direction, and he was gone shortly after, on his way to the small, richly furnished hut they kept for special rewards. Markus waited until the man was fully out of hearing range before he turned on Winston.

"What the hell? Your son! Are you insane?"

"It needed to be done."

"Needed to be? Do you hear yourself? Do you have any idea what a mess you're going to bring down on us with this? Your do-gooder boy has a reputation and friends in connected places."

"Which is why he was dealt with. It's a Colton nosing around in our business, Markus. One more freaking Colton."

"That's who hacked you?"

"A woman Robert's son hired, who has the skills, is the one who did it. I nearly overlooked it. But I found a small signature she likely doesn't realize she left and it was enough for me to circle back and find her. She's been digging in places she has no right to."

"Why?"

"I haven't figured that out yet. Did Jessie talk to them? Say something that might make them start wondering why she wants Robert's money so bad?"

"Jessie hasn't left the property in days."

"No calls then?"

"Nothing. I've gently asked if she's spoken to her children, and she's maintained that they're ungrateful and she needs to regroup before she tries to deal with them again."

"The Coltons are a problem."

"They're the big fish we need before we pull up stakes here."

Winston's mulish expression suggested he didn't agree, but he held back.

"I want the Colton money and then we poof. We have our normal exit plan in place. It'll be a simple matter of quickly executing it once Jessie gets the money."

"And if they find us first?"

"Clearly, you're quite adept at quick thinking and getting rid of threats, *Brother* Winston. I have every confidence you'll handle any nuisances from Colton quarters, too."

"MIKE ARNOLD IS DEAD?" Greg sat at the table at the Colton Ranch as he ran his fingers through his hair. "The guy who got into the accident with Rick and Wendy?"

He'd asked a series of similar questions, about what they knew, who the guy was and how it came to be that he could have died so quickly after the accident, especially since he'd walked away unscathed.

"I keep pressing my contacts at the Owl Creek PD, but they don't have a lot of details yet." Max sat next to his brother, an encouraging voice in the midst of the chaos that seemed to have descended in the middle of their lives. "The situation's still developing."

"But you think it's all related to the group Mom's involved with?" Greg asked. "The one Rick's dad is a part of?"

"It all seems to stem from the same."

"There are two children at Briony's house right now who've lost their parents. Increasingly, it's looking like they were murdered. By their grandfather?"

"That's the connection we don't have," Chase interjected, happy to have something to contribute. "All Sloan found is the strange link in social-media posts between Mike Arnold and a man she believes is part of the Ever After Church. It doesn't mean Rick's father was responsible."

"But he's the link. He has to be."

While Chase had long stopped believing in coincidences when it came to this situation. A man had his son killed? One he'd left alone for the man's entire adulthood?

It seemed…extreme.

Yet the more they uncovered, the more it seemed the Ever After group operated at the very edge of extreme.

"There has to be enough evidence to take Winston Kraft into custody," Greg said.

"I've asked." Max's jaw set in a hard line, a match for his brother. "There's not a single thing linking Winston Kraft to Rick and Wendy's deaths."

"But he did it."

"Not according to the law."

Chase watched as Max tried to explain it, step by step, even as it was clear Greg was having none of it.

And how could Chase blame him?

Everything about this situation suggested the Ever After Church—and by extension one of its heads, Winston Kraft—was involved.

But the person who'd actually killed Rick and Wendy was now dead and unable to reveal secrets, no matter how badly they wanted them.

"So who killed Mike Arnold?"

They'd circled around it earlier. But it suddenly dawned on Chase that uncovering that piece might get them what they needed.

"Owl Creek PD's digging in but nothing's popping on the prison cameras. One minute Mike Arnold is alive and well in his cell, and the next an alert's going out and the ambulance is getting called."

"He didn't just die, Max," Chase argued. "Something happened."

"Which is why I keep telling you to give the police the time to do their work."

It felt so useless to argue and so endlessly depressing to just sit there.

Helpless.

Which shifted his attention to even darker, more dismal places.

"How are the children?" Chase asked.

"Briony's very good with them, but Justin is really confused and keeps asking for his mom and dad. Jane's too small to fully understand, but she gets upset each time her brother gets upset. It's heartbreaking."

One more sin to place at his feet, Chase thought. Guilt, anger and utter sadness for the Kraft family became a noxious brew in his blood.

But he knew the truth. Max could argue all he wanted about the person responsible for Rick and Wendy's deaths, but Chase had been an unwitting accomplice.

He'd pushed this course of action, desperate for answers.

And got several he never could have imagined.

SLOAN PULLED ITEM after item out of her closet, folding each piece of clothing into a neat pile on the bed. The room still held Chase's scent, a lingering reminder of what they'd shared.

She didn't have much, just what had fit in her suitcase, and the exercise didn't take overly long to complete.

But it was done.

It was time she left Owl Creek.

She'd known this was coming from the first day of her arrival, a return ticket—albeit open-ended—in her possession.

This was a job and while she'd fought to remember that specific point, she'd still managed to lose her head, anyway.

A small glint of metal reflected off the bed and she realized it was one of her many GPS tags. She'd learned after losing one of her electronics to put the tags with her equipment, and even her luggage, to ensure she could find them should they go missing.

The flash of a message floated over her cell-phone screen, alerting her to the tag's proximity and still-active status, and she turned to slip it back into her luggage when a small form slipped into the room. She dropped it into her pocket, then bent down and picked up the cat instead.

The rest of the packing could wait.

"I've made a mess of this, Waffles."

The cat's only reaction was a small meow and Sloan rubbed her cheek against his head.

She'd spent the better part of the afternoon thinking about her next move. But now, as she looked over the bed, her sense of action faded, her spirits plummeting.

Why hadn't she protected herself? She was a smart woman. She ran a successful business. Would it have been that hard to resist the abundant charms of Chase Colton?

"If he'd simply been charming, yeah, it would have." She murmured the words against the cat's soft fur, realizing it for the truth. "But he is so much more than that. He's…everything."

If this had only been about simple attraction, it would have been so much easier. Either ignore it for the duration of the job or give in, but the outcome would have been a still-whole heart and a readiness to go home at the end of the job.

Instead, she'd fallen for the man, hook, line, sinker, heart and soul.

"What other dumb clichés can I come up with?" she muttered to Waffles as the heavy knock came from the front of the apartment.

After gently setting the cat back on the bed, she headed for the front door. It was probably Chase, which meant it was time to tell him that she was leaving.

She had the door open, words nearly spilling out of her mouth to that effect, when she realized it was a man standing on the other side of her door in maintenance clothing.

"Oh, I'm sorry. Can I help you?"

"Yes, ma'am. I'm here to fix things."

The man had a sweet if dull look about him, his salt-and-pepper hair wisping out over his ears from beneath his navy blue cap, a small tool belt slung about his hips.

"Fix what?"

"You."

The swift strike against her shoulder was the first clue she was in trouble. He'd been prepared for her response and his arms were surprisingly strong as they wrapped around her.

Despite her struggles, she was no match for his hold or the obviously practiced movement that had a cloth going over her face.

Sloan fought to hang on.

Fought to hold her breath.

But the natural, desperate need to take in air took over and as she breathed deep, she felt her world go black.

CHASE WAS STILL thinking about Rick Kraft's small children an hour later as he paid the delivery service for several large pizzas.

How were they going to get by?

Greg had suggested he and Briony had some sort of guardian status but what did that really mean? Rick's estranged relationship with his father meant there wasn't support in the form of grandparents and Greg had confirmed Rick's mother was long gone. Wendy's parents were both dead as well.

One more layer of circumstance that felt so sad.

And terribly, horrifically bleak.

Pushing away the sadness and vowing to talk to Greg later about what he might need and how he could help, Chase set the pizzas on the kitchen counter. Then he checked his phone. He'd texted Sloan a while ago, expecting she'd beat the pizza over to the ranch, but hadn't heard back yet.

Greg stepped into the kitchen as he was wrapping up a phone call. Della had arrived a short while before, her arm now wrapped around Max's waist.

"Thanks for this." Max gestured toward the boxes.

"We all need some food. Go ahead and dig in."

"We're not waiting for Sloan?" Della asked.

"I haven't heard back from my text yet." Even as he said it, something about the total lack of response bothered him and Chase hit the screen on his phone, reaffirming nothing had come in. "Let me go call her."

Two minutes later, with nothing but her voice mail to show for it, Chase stared at Della, Max and Greg. "I'm not sure where she is."

Greg didn't hesitate. "Let's go over there."

"She—"

Chase stopped, the swirl of fear only spiking harder in

his chest. "She'll think we're out of our minds if we show up, guns blazing."

"So?" Max said, already reaching for his keys on the counter.

He'd worry later if it was an overreaction to the stress of the past few days.

In that moment, all Chase wanted was to see Sloan and hold her in his arms.

"Let's go."

THE DESPERATE NEED for water was all Sloan could think of as she awakened on a hard exhale.

Where was she?

That thought struck hard, with another swiftly following.

What had happened to her?

She struggled to a sitting position, her hands bound in front of her. She leaned to her side and used them as leverage to move onto her knees before struggling to stand, trying to figure out where she was.

Her stomach turned over violently and she stood still for a moment, the quick movements to stand so soon after coming awake nearly causing her body to revolt. With deep breaths, she gave herself a moment, even as her mind raced with the implications.

Who was that man at her door?

The Ever After Church.

Although she had no proof, she'd bet anything that man was affiliated with the church, even as she struggled to figure out who he might be. He wasn't one of the leaders—of that, she was certain. Something tugged at the back of her mind, fighting for her attention through the nausea, and she stilled once more, trying to remember.

The kindly face. The gray hair. The hat.

What was it about the hat?

A shaft of light streamed in through the window, the late-afternoon sun a vivid yellowish red as it illuminated the room.

Was she still in Owl Creek?

Since it had been about four when she'd headed into her bedroom to pack, she estimated she couldn't have been out that long, especially if it was still light out.

But…

"Hello."

She glanced toward the door, her pulse spiking at the intrusion.

What did he want with her? Because attacking her and drugging her in her home wasn't the act of someone who simply wanted to chat.

Which meant she needed to get as much information as she could as fast as she could, all while figuring a way out of this. Chase had no way of knowing where she was, and nor did anyone else, for that matter.

She was going to need to get through this on her own.

"Did you sleep okay?"

Sloan considered how to play this, especially since the man clutched his hat in his hands, twisting it back and forth.

"What?"

"Did you sleep okay or did I use too much?"

The pounding in her head suggested that *yes, he'd used too much*. But she heard the vague concern in his tone and decided to try and use it to her advantage.

She had precious little to fight with, so she was going to need to use her wits as much as any physical advantages she could find.

"I'm okay."

"You're a little thing. It's never easy to judge."

Under other circumstances, she'd have thought a statement like that was designed to be a compliment, but all she got from him was an overwhelming sense of fact.

And a sort of resigned purpose in what he was doing.

"Why did you do that at all?"

"You've been bad."

"I've been what?"

"You've got those fancy computers and are using 'em to spy on people."

Had he walked through her home? Worse, did he know her, somehow?

Speaking softly, she tried to delicately step her way through this one.

"I'm visiting Owl Creek for work. I needed my computer with me to do my job."

"What do you do?"

"I run a consulting business."

He eyed her suspiciously, his easy tone fading on a sneer. "Fancy words for computer hacker."

"Everyone uses computers."

"To do bad things! How'd you think I got back in touch with good ol' Mikey?"

"Mike Arnold." The name came out on a hard exhale as the puzzle pieces she was struggling to work through snapped firmly into place. "Which means you're Jasper. Jasper Miles."

Sloan suddenly realized that she'd overstepped at the use of his name.

Especially when he moved toward her, something scary and oddly fervent building in his eyes, a gun appearing in his hand.

Chapter Eighteen

Chase stepped on the second-floor landing in front of Sloan's apartment. The panic that had spiked off and on during the quick drive over from the ranch was now going nuclear.

The door to her apartment was open and Waffles raced around the entryway, obviously agitated.

He bent down to pick up the small cat, cradling him close and trying to soothe him as Max and Greg followed him inside.

"She's gone," Max said after a quick search of the apartment.

"Taken." Chase spit out the word. "She was taken right here."

He held tight to the cat, the animal a sudden lodestone as the absolute pain of responsibility hammered his body with hard, punishing blows.

He'd done this.

He'd pulled her into this mess and put her in danger.

Just like Rick and Wendy, Sloan was going to pay far too high a price for his damned insistence on looking into the Ever After Church and his aunt's involvement.

"Chase!"

Max's tone was insistent as he stood across the room.

"We're going to find her. But first, I need you to help me look through her things. We need to find something."

Chase had never felt so helpless in all his life.

Not the day he knew his marriage was over. Not the day his father had his stroke. Not even the day he'd discovered his father's betrayal and lies.

Nothing compared to the abject pain of knowing he'd done this to her.

"I found a cell phone!" Greg hollered as he headed back out of the bedroom.

"She doesn't even have her phone?" Chase didn't know her password, but he extended a hand for the phone as Greg walked over.

"This might work to our advantage," Max said, moving closer. "Anyone who would have taken her would likely have ditched the phone."

"It won't do any good if we can't hold it up with her and use facial recognition to open it," Greg muttered.

"She doesn't use it," Chase said, one of their date-night conversations coming back to him.

"Why not?"

"She gave a host of reasons that seemed scary at the time, but she said that she only uses a passcode."

"Any chance you know what it is?" Max asked.

"No." Chase nearly tossed the phone, but something lit the face before he could heave it away.

Curious, he brought it close, his gaze narrowing in on the alert that flashed on the screen.

"What is it?" Max asked.

"I think—" Chase stilled, hardly daring to hope this was as good a sign as he thought it might be.

"Let me see." Max took the phone, his movements gentle as he tilted the device in his hand. "Damn, that woman is amazing."

The comment was part reverence, part awe, and Greg pressed for details. "We all think that. What's this about?"

"She's got a GPS tracker somewhere on her person," Max said.

Chase held the cat close, the small animal now calm. He took heart from that calmness and desperately fought to believe the cat's faith in his arrival meant he had faith he'd see his owner again, too.

He took his first easy breath as his gaze remained on the phone screen. "Which means we can find her."

"HOW'D YOU KNOW who I was?" Jasper practically quivered where he stood, far too close for comfort in front of her. "Those damn devil devices again?"

"I only looked at your social-media pages."

"What?"

If the situation wasn't so dire, she might have laughed at his confusion. As it was, his abstract inability to link his social feed with how he was found wasn't information she was going to share. Instead, she pressed the very small advantage she had at his confusion.

"All your posts about faith and peace. They really spoke to me."

"My faith keeps me going."

"A testament to your leader, I'm sure. The Ever After Church is doing very good work."

His eyes flashed once again, that fervent madness filling his irises, and Sloan's stomach sunk.

Damn, she'd overplayed her hand.

A point that didn't play out, as he nodded, his smile wide. "People don't understand that. They don't know all the good that our leader does. But the church is a haven. A home."

"A place of safety."

"Yes."

"Then why are we here? Why didn't you bring me there?"

"I can't allow you to soil my home."

"I—"

That deep, fervent conviction was back, only this time the menace was being telegraphed loud and clear.

"The evils of technology have you in their grip. You don't believe in us. You won't believe in us."

"You don't know that."

"Oh, yes, I do. Because if you did believe, you'd never have gone to talk to that traitor Rick Kraft."

Pure, undiluted fear beat through her body.

Whatever she'd hoped or believed, conversation was not going to get her out of this. Conciliatory remarks or interested chatter weren't the keys to her escape.

The only way out of here, Sloan knew with absolute certainty, was through Jasper and his gun.

Which was why she didn't give herself another moment to think. Whatever determination Jasper had to take her wasn't going to be assuaged by her outsmarting him.

Without another word, she charged.

Head low.

Shoulders braced.

Everything she had focused on ramming into him and dislodging the gun in his hand.

THE GPS DEVICE on Sloan continued to beat, their homing beacon as Max flew through the streets of Owl Creek toward the edge of town.

Although he had no way of getting into her device, the GPS pinged alert, appearing on Sloan's phone screen with each mile they got closer. They used a mix of the technology itself and Chase's knowledge of Owl Creek to assess where she was.

It was only as they got closer to the lake at the edge of town that Chase knew the spot.

"The old caretaker's cabin. Down along the lake."

"The one that's been up for demo for a few years?" Greg asked.

"One and the same." Chase considered the small hut. While he'd believed it an eyesore for some time, the city had control over the place and hadn't seen fit to approve its demolition yet.

He was going to kiss someone at the next town-council meeting if that lack of foresight was what saved Sloan.

Max slowed as he pulled into the graveled parking lot that abutted the lake. They saw an old truck at the end of the parking lot.

The phone flashed once more, and Chase knew they were close. "She's here."

Max and Greg both had guns, retrieved from the glove box. Chase had briefly considered asking for one of them, but knew he was a businessman, not a gunslinger. Max was well-trained and Greg carried around the ranch to ensure he was safe from dangerous wildlife.

He rode a desk all day.

Right now, Sloan needed protection and he wasn't sure he could remain steady enough, anyway.

But he was the first one out of the car, moving gently over the gravel to avoid making noise.

He needed to get to her. It was his only focus.

His only goal.

But as a gunshot filled the air, he didn't wait, or give a care for quiet.

He took off hell-for-leather for the old cabin.

SLOAN STRUGGLED AGAINST the solid weight that seemed to hold her in place, nearly pushing her back, even as she pressed and drove herself into the solid mass of flesh over and over again.

Through.

She had to get through Jasper in order to get away from him.

The heavy sound of a gunshot echoed above her head, the noise so loud she nearly fell to her feet from the sheer power of it, but still, she held her ground.

Her hands were still bound, but she kicked and pushed and even used her teeth at one point to keep fighting.

To get away.

And then, there was no obstacle.

No push of flesh.

Instead, there was another loud shot as all the counterforce against her simply vanished, her foe falling to the floor.

Sloan glanced around, her gaze wild as she sought out the new threat, panic spiking once more as she took in three large forms. A scream welled just as her understanding broke through the fear and adrenaline.

Chase.

He was there.

And he'd brought reinforcements, in Max and Greg. Max was already moving toward Jasper, kicking the man's gun out of the way while Greg stood at the door, his own gun firmly in hand.

But it was Chase who came to her.

Who pulled her tight against him.

Who spoke to her through the angry ringing in her ears that seemed to fill up her head.

He was here.

And she was safe.

It was her last thought as she broke into a sob against his chest.

CHASE HELD SLOAN tight against his chest and let her cry it out. Hard, unrelenting shakes ripped through her body, and he held on, helping her through it, crooning mindless words to see her through.

To see himself through.

His own adrenaline rush was still sky-high, coursing through him in wild spikes of energy, but he held it at bay.

He'd break down later.

When he thought of how close he'd come to losing her…

And how ridiculous he'd been for all these years in pushing away the possibility of love.

He'd recognized it the moment they'd met, that first time he'd held her in his arms. And for so much of the time since he'd run from it, convinced his head knew better. Convinced he'd had his shot and ruined it.

But now, as the woman he loved huddled against him, gathering herself as the storm of emotion burned itself out, he knew just how foolish he'd been.

And how deeply grateful fate had given him a second chance.

Her eyes were red-rimmed as she stared up at him. "You came."

"I'd have hunted for you to the ends of the earth, but I have to thank you for making it a heck of a lot easier on me."

"Easy?" Confusion filled her features, then something dawned bright and clear in her eyes. "The tracker."

"You're a technology wiz, woman. It's amazing."

"I was going to put it in my suitcase and Waffles came in."

"He loves you, by the way. And he was beside himself you'd been taken."

She smiled then, and Chase knew there'd be more than enough time to tell her what had happened. How they'd come to her apartment. How Greg had found her phone and how he'd found the cat, agitated beyond measure until he knew there were people there to go after his mistress.

Later, Chase thought. There'd be time enough for it all later.

Right now, there was only time for one thing. And as he stared down at her, he felt the power of each and every word.

More, he leaned into that power and reveled at all he'd found.

"I love you, Sloan."

He saw the spark of happiness fill her eyes, even as her face remained set in wary lines. "I thought you weren't cut out for love. Isn't that why we cooked up a fake relationship in the first place?"

"Turns out I'm a dumb businessman with a fear complex over putting myself on the line. And I guess a fake relationship was just what I needed to take the pressure off."

"And now?"

"I only want what's real, Sloan. With you. Forever."

The smile that lit her eyes filled her face, transforming her before his eyes. Her smile was warm. Welcoming. And wide open to that forever he spoke of.

"I love you, Chase Colton. Make it real. With me."

"I'd like nothing more. Every day for the rest of my life."

And as he bent his head, pressing his lips to hers, Chase knew he was the luckiest of men.

He'd believed himself incapable of loving again.

How wonderful to be so utterly, absolutely, mind-bindingly wrong.

* * * * *